Ocean of Sin and Starlight

A DARK ROMANTASY

KARINA HALLE

Cover Design: Hang Le

Editing: Laura Helseth

Proofreading: The Fiction Fix + One Love Editing

Interior art of Larimar and Priest by: Kaylerin Arts

Playlist

"Grace" – (+++) Crosses

"Mermaids" - Hans Zimmer

"Goodnight, God Bless, I Love U, Delete" – (+++) Crosses

"Last Rites" – (+++) Crosses

"Holier" – (+++) Crosses

"Thholyghst" – (+++) Crosses

"Bitches Brew" – (+++) Crosses

"Cross" – (+++) Crosses

"Death Bell" – (+++) Crosses

"The Line Begins to Blur" – NIN

"Discipline" – NIN

"Right Where it Belongs" – NIN

"The Hand That Feeds" – NIN

"Various Methods of Escape" – NIN

"Find My Way" - NIN

"God Given" – NIN

"Capital G" – NIN

"Sanctified" – NIN

"Sin" – NIN

"Heresy" – NIN
"La Mer" – NIN
"Help Me I Am in Hell" – NIN
"The Albatross" – Taylor Swift
"Guilty as Sin?" – Taylor Swift
"Judas" – Banks
"Ocean Eyes" – Billie Eilish
"Hostage" – Billie Eilish
"No Time to Die" – Billie Eilish
"Should Be Higher" – Depeche Mode
"Heaven" – Depeche Mode
"Before We Drown" – Depeche Mode
"The Sinner in Me" – Depeche Mode
"Mercy in You" – Depeche Mode
"In Chains" – Depeche Mode
"Halo" – Depeche Mode
"Last Cup of Sorrow" – FNM
"Ashes to Ashes" – FNM
"King for a Day" – FNM
"The Tradition" – Halsey
"Bells in Santa Fe" – Halsey
"Devil in Me" – Halsey
"Way down We Go" – Kaleo
"Hallowed Ground" – How to Destroy Angels
"A Drowning" – How to Destroy Angels
"Going to Heaven" – The Kills
"Kingdom Come" – The Kills
"God Games" – The Kills
"Still Don't Know My Name" – Labrinth
"Babel" – Massive Attack
"Angel" – Massive Attack
"Nocturne" – Mark Lanegan
"Spell" – Nick Cave and the Bad Seeds
"Messiah Ward" – Nick Cave and the Bad Seeds

"Lovely Creature" – Nick Cave and the Bad Seeds
"Do You Love Me?" – Nick Cave and the Bad Seeds
"I Let Love In" – Nick Cave and the Bad Seeds
"Loverman" – Nick Cave and the Bad Seeds
"The Vampyre of Time and Memory" – QOTSA
"I Appear Missing" – QOTSA
"Someone's in the Wolf" – QOTSA
"Un-Reborn Again" – QOTSA
"Fortress" – QOTSA
"Villains of Circumstance" – QOTSA
"God Hates a Coward" – Tomahawk
"Somebody's Sins" – Tricky
"Nothing Matters" – Tricky (feat. Nneka)
"Atlantic" – Sleep Token
"High Water" – Sleep Token
"The Night Does Not Belong to God" – Sleep Token
"Dark Signs" – Sleep Token
"Gods" – Sleep Token
"The Summoning" – Sleep Token
"Aqua Regia" – Sleep Token
"Take Me to Church" – Hozier
"Son of Nyx" – Hozier
"Foreigner's God" – Hozier
"First Light" – Hozier

(Come find me on Spotify!)

To those readers who like their men feral, their women wild, and their fantasy dark

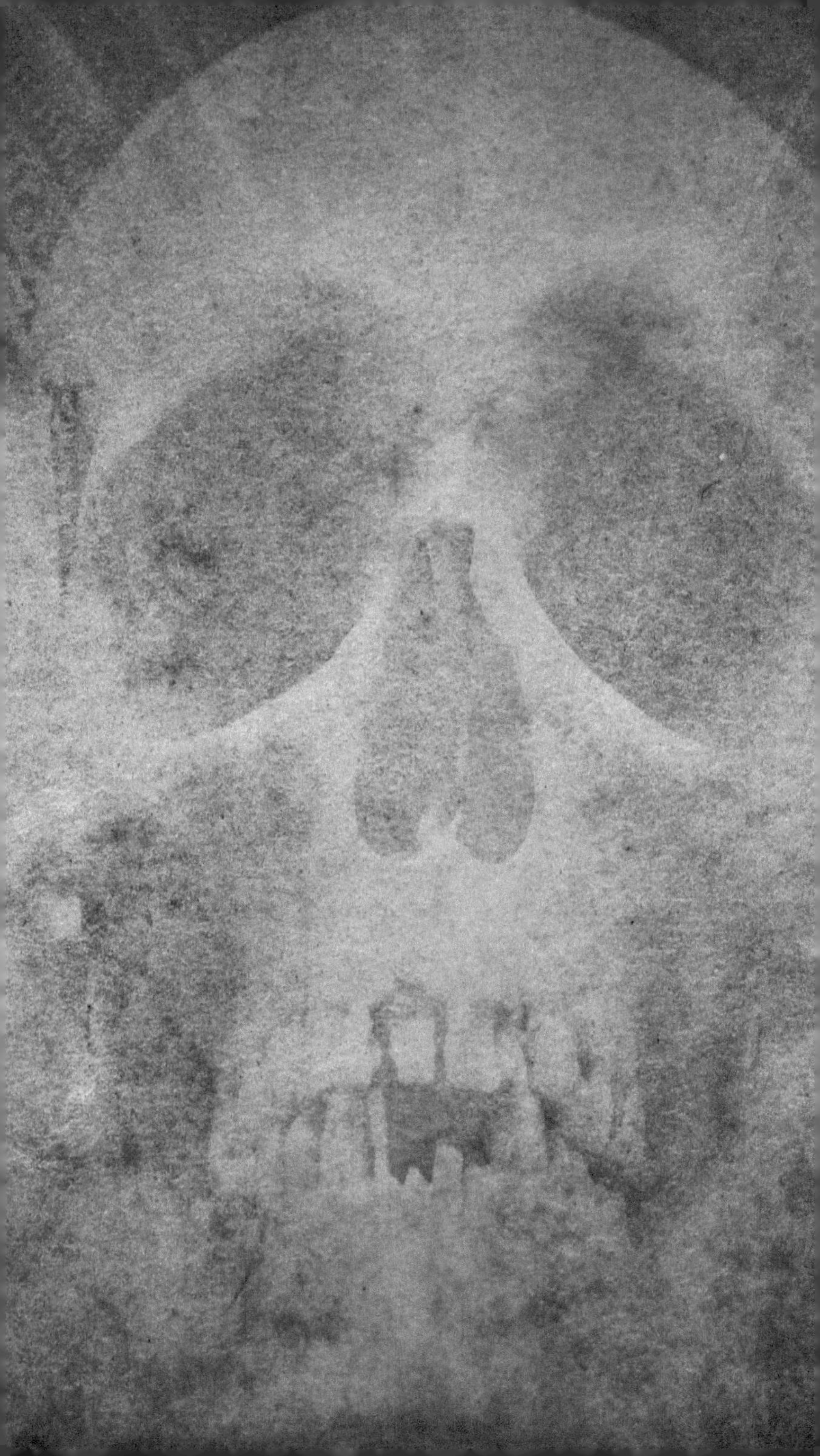

Author's Note

This book is a standalone, but it is also a spinoff of *A Ship of Bones and Teeth*. If you read this book without reading ASOBAT, you won't be lost. HOWEVER, if you were planning on reading *A Ship of Bones and Teeth*, then I suggest you read that first, then come back to this book, as *Ocean of Sin and Starlight* will have many spoilers for that book (and you want to go into ASOBAT blind!). And just so you know, *A Ship of Bones and Teeth* is a retelling of The Little Mermaid. This book is not a retelling of anything. It is about vampires, witches, pirates, and mermaids, though.

(Speaking of vampires, it is vaguely related to my books *Black Sunshine/The Blood is Love* and *Blood Orange/Black Rose*. You may want to check those books out prior as well for more context, but you don't *need* to).

Read on for the important content warning.

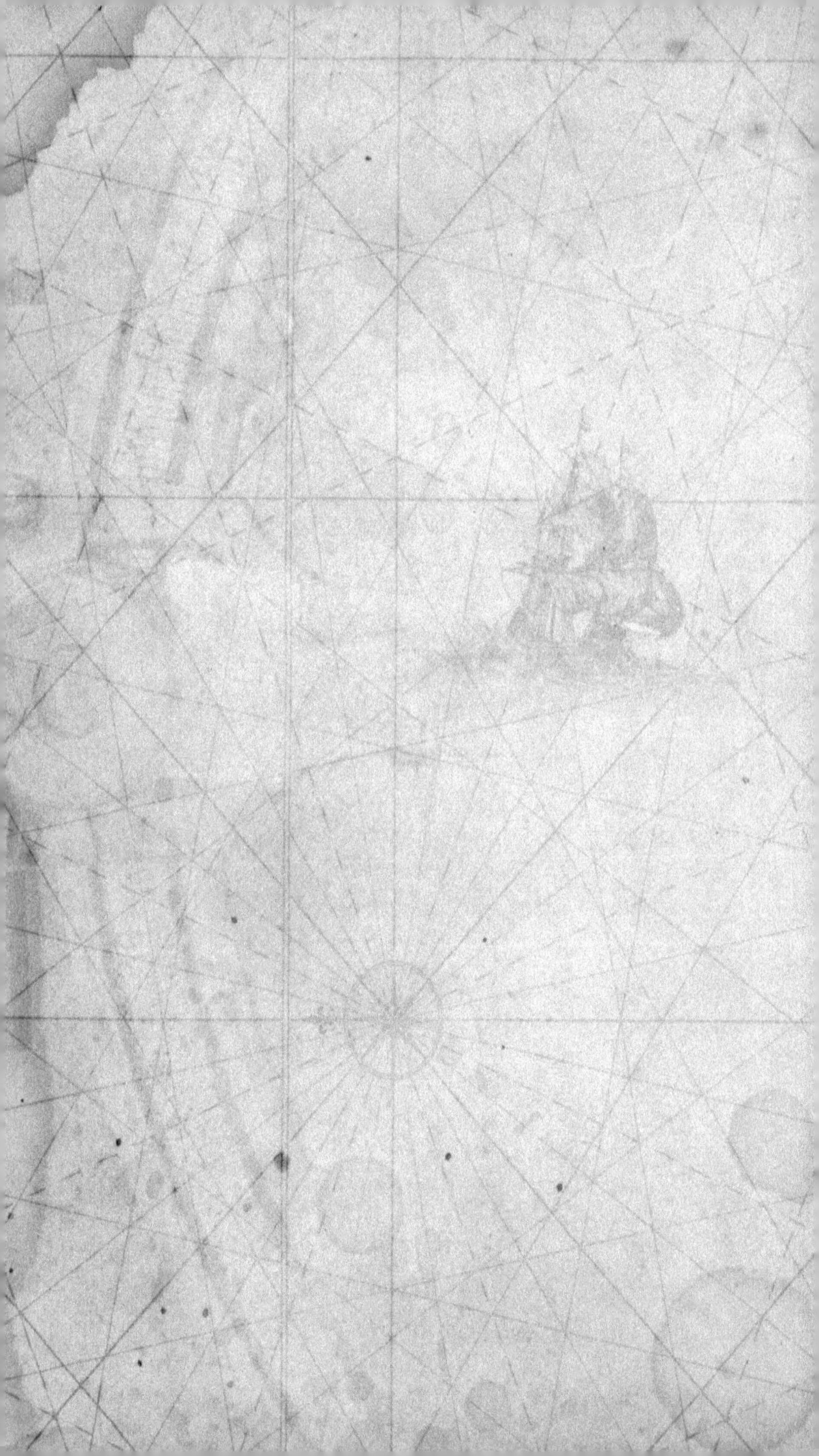

Content Warning

Rated R for Blasphemy, Dub-Con, Rape & Torture

Ocean of Sin and Starlight is in the dark-fantasy genre—which means it is a fantasy (or romantasy) that contains frightening or disturbing themes.

Does that mean this can be considered a dark romance?

Not exactly.

In my opinion, dark romance has many shades of gray, and I like to dabble in all of them. But I won't call this a dark romance, because then dark romance readers will go into it thinking it's going to hit certain levels of depravity and, IMO, I don't think it does. So, **if YOU are a dark romance reader, this is me saying it's not a dark romance** because I do not want to lead you astray. In other words, you can't say you were disappointed it wasn't dark enough, because I am telling you right now...it's probably not dark enough for you.

BUT, and here is a big but (heh), **if you are *not* a dark romance reader, then some scenes in here may be offensive, shocking, or make you uncomfortable**. Aside from violence, gore, harsh language (speaking of language, I took liberties with their speech so it didn't sound as stilted as it did back in the 1700s. That wouldn't be enjoyable to read), blasphemy on all counts, and explicit sex scenes (including on-page rape, not involving the MCs), there are scenes that are dub-con, especially when it comes to abuse of power dynamics and coercion. The heroine is also held captive for a period of time and has been essentially kidnapped and tortured. Did I mention crucified? Literally?

There are also some BDSM elements, such as bondage in chains, lots of biting and blood play, cum play, anal sex, butt stuff, breath play, insertion of foreign objects... Did I mention blood play?

Last but not least, our antihero is a man of the cloth. I'm not saying he's a good priest, given his bloodsucking and murderous and super-horny nature, but there are some religious elements turned into scenes of a graphic nature, including sexual, that will offend you and be considered blasphemous/disrespectful to those who are devoutly Christian. Hell, even those who aren't religious might feel offended. My goal isn't to purposely offend anyone, but I am just doing what the characters tell me to do.

SO PLEASE, if you are sensitive to scenes of that nature, or anything I listed above, this is not the book for you. I am providing this content warning so that you can stay safe and make the right choice for yourself! Don't read stuff that will make you mad. It's not worth it!

If you decide to read on, I hope you enjoy the bloody ride.

Part One

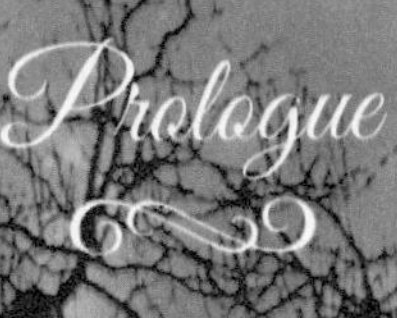

Prologue

THE MONSTER

The creature had been subdued by heavy rusted chains and tied up for weeks by the time the doctor found him. The villagers had said it had killed several of their own, while it had taken a dozen of them to finally restrain him.

The doctor wanted to reward them for their bravery but there wasn't a soul in sight at this point, just deep grooves in the dried mud where the villager's heels must have dug in, savage marks around the trunk of the nearby oak, the bark having been shaved clean off by the chains, and the splashes of blood here and there, adding color to the scene.

There was only the doctor and the creature in the middle of this yellow flower speckled field, on this warm summer morning, the dew already evaporated.

Of course, the creature was indeed a man. The doctor took a tentative step toward him, peering down at the tormented-looking figure. He was curled up in the fetal position, eyes closed, matted hair around his face, his naked body caked in mud, but despite his fragile state, he was tall and broad-shouldered, built like an ox. He had the sleek muscles that so many other creatures had, but there was a roughness to him, as if the muscles had been earned doing hard labor and not given to him naturally.

There's nothing natural about this, the doctor thought, pushing his long red hair behind his ears and adjusting his hat against the sun that was slowly becoming stronger with the day. *There's nothing natural about these monsters.*

It made him sad to learn about instances like this, these monsters who were created to be mad men, but this was the nature of his work lately. He had grown fascinated by these abominations, that were so like him in many ways, and yet so different. He wanted to study them up close and personal. He wanted to prove that their humanity could be uncovered.

But it was a long road ahead for both of them. The doctor could barely be described as a man sometimes, and the beast even less so.

The doctor sighed and crouched down beside the creature, noting how little it breathed. The poor monster could not die, but it no doubt wished it could. Even if it had been chained to this tree for centuries, without a single drop of food, it still would not die.

And barring his head being torn off, the doctor wouldn't die either. So he didn't have much fear when he reached over and gently brushed back the creature's hair off its face.

It was a strong face, and a handsome one. If the creature wasn't so large and brawny, if that chin wasn't so strong, he could be called beautiful, a delicate kind of grace in long black lashes, a straight nose, full lips. Most of the doctor's kind had their own kind of magnetism that was supernatural, but he could tell the creature, back when it was a man and before it had transformed, had been blessed by God.

Blessed before he became cursed.

But if the brotherhood at the monastery couldn't help the creature find God—or something that resembles one—and become a man, then at the very least the doctor would do all he could to help.

After all, the more these monsters roamed the earth, the more that the doctor and his ilk would be at risk, and their secrets discovered by a world that was never ready to understand them.

"Can you hear me?" the doctor asked in a low voice. "My name is Abraham, but you may call me Abe."

The creature stirred but didn't open its eyes. Its mouth parted just a little.

The few creatures that Abe had come into contact with didn't speak English, or Spanish, or any language. Many of them were in an even earlier state of depravity, their bodies covered in matted fur or leathery wings. Some even had tails.

But this creature was past that stage, though it didn't make him any less dangerous. It was still a monster, and yet it had potential to become a man again.

The creature suddenly snapped his jaws at Abe, trying to get a bite of him, but only got air before it fell back down to the ground, all strength gone.

"Now, now," Abe said to him. "Anger is necessary for survival sometimes, but I will teach you to control your anger. I will teach you how to put that monster aside for now. I will get your soul back, as long as you're willing to work for it. Are you willing to work for it, Man from Aragon?"

This was always the test. Give the man a choice, and the man might come forward. If the man made the choice, and not the beast, if the light broke through the shadows, then the creature had a chance to be saved.

The soul could be redeemed.

And this time the creature made a low hissing noise at Abe's request.

He took it as a yes.

Chapter One

PRIEST

Two Centuries Later

"You have enough blood to last you a month," Abe announces as he steps into my cabin. The wind howls like a rabid wolf through the crack as he shuts the door.

I press my fingers onto the papers to prevent them from flying away and look up from my desk. The candles flicker out, plunging my cottage into darkness, but I can see the doctor clearly.

"A month," I repeat, panic making my mouth taste sour. Four weeks of absolution until I have to sin again.

Until I have to kill again.

I hope my voice doesn't betray the despair inside me, twisting into acidic knots, but Abe's expression softens, and I know he can smell my fear.

"You knew I had to leave," he says gently as he slowly

crosses the room. "I can only keep you company and do your...*dirty work* for so long."

The dirty work. That is my term for my appetite. Abe uses more innocuous words: our instincts. Our hunger. Our drive. As a doctor, he looks at our affliction as merely that: something that had befallen us, like a disease, to be dealt with matter-of-factly. But Abe isn't like me, not exactly. He was born with an appetite for blood. I wasn't. I was born human. I had a family, a future.

I had a soul...until I didn't.

"There are others," Abe says as he stands by my desk, his fingers tracing the gold-foiled script stamped on the Holy Bible. "The last correspondence from the monastery said it resembles an epidemic. More of your kind have been created in a surge of violence. Some of them were witches, such as yourself."

"By him? By Kaleid?" I whisper. Saying his name causes my heart to race, even after all this time.

The doctor stares at me for a moment, as if weighing the truth, then nods once. "I fear it may be worse than I originally thought, and my expertise is needed. They can't be allowed to roam. They must be rehabilitated. They must be saved. You know there is a word for us now? The humans are catching on. They call us *Vampyres*."

"Vampyres," I repeat. The word seems fitting.

"There are people at the monastery..." I begin, but I trail off because there is no one like the doctor. I knew he wouldn't be down here with me at the bottom of the world forever, but when he stepped off the ship eight months ago, I had hoped he would stay at least a couple of years.

Yet I know there is nothing for him here, nothing but me, and I'm not good company. My job is to become the voice for God in this cold, barren, windswept region, to provide both faith and guidance for the settlers who have been stationed here in Nombre de Jesus by command of the Governor of Chile. The people are here to prevent English privateers and pirates from taking over the Strait of Magellan, and I am here to provide salvation.

This place is supposed to be my salvation too.

But I haven't found it yet.

"When will you be back?" I ask.

"I don't know," he says, sighing again. The doctor is my oldest friend—my only friend. Abe was the one who saved me from staying a monster forever. Through his faith in me and in the rigid teachings of the monastery, the beast I became has been tucked away in the deep, black recesses of my former soul. Abe keeps me fed, keeps me pure, keeps my demons at bay.

But though I am his reason for being here, I am not his purpose in life. He has devoted his study of science and medicine to the very things science can't explain, that medicine can't control and magic can't save. Through his help, the teachings of the Lord, and the discipline of the doctrine, I have turned myself back into a man. Perhaps a shell of a man, but enough that people no longer have to fear me.

And there are others like me who need his help.

So, I know he must go.

Still, it sits inside me like a spreading stain, the sense of terror and futility of what I'll do—what I'll become—when I'm on my own again.

"Eight months wasn't enough," I manage to say, my voice thick. I want to tell him more. I want to beg him not to leave me, to choose me instead of his life's work, to let the monsters roam freely in the world so long as he can keep me sane and in his company.

Alas, even after all this time, I have my pride.

"I will be back," Abe says, putting his hand on my shoulder and giving it a squeeze. "I don't know how long it will be, but what's a few years when you're immortal? You'll have visitors in the meantime."

He removes his hand, and I glance up at him. "Who?"

"Men such as ourselves," he says, looking around the sparsely decorated cottage as if he'll see something new instead of paintings of mountains and crosses on the walls.

"Men like you? Vampyres? Or monsters like me?"

He gives me a chastising look. "You're not a monster, my priest. You are Father Aragon. You were born a man. I wasn't."

"That man died when my family died," I say bitterly. "I was turned. You've always known of your true nature, always been in control."

"That may be, but we both drink blood to survive, and we do so discerningly, do we not? That makes us the same in my eyes. But yes, men like myself, blood-drinkers who call themselves the Brethren of the Blood. They're pirates who sail the high seas on their ship, the *Nightwind*, nicknamed by mortal men as the Ship of the Undead. They've made quite a name for themselves in all parts of the world, looting merchant ships and ports, hunting Syrens for their blood. It's partly the reason they'll be by here one day."

I nod. "The colony." There have been rumors that a colony of Syrens live below the icebergs and barren cliffs of Roche Island. The sea between, the Mar de Drake, is treacherous, so the rumors have been mostly unfounded, said to be started by shipwrecked crew hallucinating from hunger. But I know that such creatures are real—I found one washed up on the beach once, just flayed skin, dried scales, and brittle bones. An abomination worse than me—half-human, half-fish.

I also know that even a drop of their blood sustains us drinkers for a very long time. I had heard that rumor, too, and didn't know it was true until I bit the shriveled neck of the corpse. I couldn't tell if it was a male or female, and it tasted like pure salt and death. And yet the dried, powdery blood of the creature was enough to satisfy me, as if I had just drunk from a living human.

"Yes, the colony," Abe says. "Either way, these Brethren will be coming through the strait. I can't say when. Could be two years. Could be ten years. But they're pirates at heart, and the Chilean government will sound the alarm once they enter Spanish waters. There will be an attack on both sides. You will be presented with a choice: stay and fight for Spain, even as a man of God, or join the Brethren."

I frown. "Ten years? But surely I'll see you before then."

"I hope so," he says with a bow of his head, clasping his hands at his waist. "With any luck, I'll be on the ship with them. But if not, I'm sure I will find you. The world isn't so big when you have all the time in it."

I stare at him, slow to blink. He might be leaving for that long? I expected two or three years at the most.

"I don't like this," I whisper. I grasp the cross of the rosary around my wrist, squeezing it hard enough that the gold draws blood, like I have done so many times before. My skin will heal itself in a minute.

"You don't have to like it, Aragon," Abe says gravely. "You just have to accept it. And I have to accept that even though you are a dear friend of mine, I am needed elsewhere by others who need me more. It's taken time, but you have been rehabilitated. You have been saved. My work here is done."

He turns and starts walking toward the door, and I watch him go, his red hair bright even in the darkness, with the confident walk of a man who has accepted who he is, sins and all.

I get to my feet suddenly, overwhelmed by a clawing sense of desperation. "You're my moral compass, Abe," I cry out. "I'll lose my control if I don't have you."

He gives me a sympathetic smile, a doctor's smile. Then, he nods at the portrait of Jesus on the wall. "He is your moral compass. You've been a priest for over a century now. It should be God guiding you, not me."

"You don't even believe in God."

"And neither do you," he says.

Then he nods and opens the door, swallowed up by the frigid winds and endless night.

When I was human, I was able to sleep at the drop of a hat. My wife would always tell me she was jealous of my ability. Whether it was when the children were screaming, as children are wont to do, or when the farm cats were fighting and the donkeys were braying, nothing could wake me up. The minute my head hit the pillow, even with a leak in the thatch roof that succumbed to the rain, I was dreaming.

I told her I could always concoct her a sleeping potion, something she couldn't do for herself. Our witchcraft rarely worked on ourselves, but it would for others. But she was stubborn and decided to tough it out.

Then, after a *Vampyre* killed me and forced me back to life as a monster, I was never visited by the sweet spell of sleep again. I spent a hundred years without a dream, a hundred years without any escape, and I was forced to reckon with the vile creature I had become.

It was only in the monastery that sleep would come in fits and starts.

Sleep that brought on nightmares, ones that continue to this day.

I pray to the God I try so hard to believe in and ask for release from the terrors, to be visited by that dulcet slumber, but still, he only grants me what I fear.

So I don't sleep most nights.

Tonight especially.

It's been a week since Abe left. The stores of blood he keeps in casks at the back of the church, casks that, if anyone was to stumble upon, they would assume is the wine of the sacramental union, are starting to run low. I have only enough to last a few more weeks before I must find my own sustenance.

Before I must kill for the first time in eight months.

The weight of it bears down on me, like a vise pressing down from the heavens themselves.

Who will I choose? One of the natives in the area who keep to themselves, naturally suspicious of the settlers and me? Or one of the villagers who comes to my church every week, ones I have gotten to know? There are only a couple hundred here, scattered throughout the settlements of Nombre de Jesus and Primera Angostura, along with the stationed military personnel. Or will I have to venture further to the larger town of Ciudad del Rey Don Felipe, as Abe had done, disappearing for a night or two until I find a victim?

And when I choose them, what will I become? Abe says it's not our fault we need human blood to thrive, that we were either born or created that way. He says it's no different than slaughtering a cow, that we shouldn't feel shame for something driven and decided by our biology. But the act of murder, of violence against another human, lets the monster come out, enough to remind me how damn good it felt to succumb to such a primal being, to become, to exist, to live without morals or guilt.

It's the monster inside me who is glad that Abe left so that I might return to that beast once more, and because of that, I am afraid.

And I don't dare sleep.

Instead, I step out into the dark night. For once, the winds have died down, giving the landscape the feeling of a long exhale, as if it can finally find peace. My cottage is surrounded by tussock grass and stunted brush and pine, a clergy house located behind the chapel, built close to the water's edge. Tonight, the waves lap gently on the rocky shore, and my sensitive vision can pick out the craggy peaks of the mountains across the strait.

It is strangely calm while I am a storm inside.

Under the light of the waning moon, I walk past the chapel and pause by the small graveyard where so many people have been buried. This settlement has seen its fair share of hardships, none related to my appetite. I feel like I am starving half the time, but they are starving too. Most of the settlers are from Andalucía, close to where I grew up. They are used to a Mediterranean climate, of sweet fruit and dry summers and soft, warm breezes. They are not built to withstand the hostility here at the end of the world.

For a moment, a terrible thought crosses my mind. I think of the dried blood of the Syren and wonder if I were to dig up the bodies of anyone who perished recently, would I find some sort of substance in the dead blood of a decaying human corpse?

But before I can even feel guilty over such a vile thought, a scream rings out, clear across the bay.

My head snaps up from the graves, and I look over to see a small speck of light moving back and forth on the dark water, and then a boat being rocked, waves splashing. My ears pick up a growl and snapping sounds, then more screams, like someone is being torn apart.

"Help!" someone from the boat yells. "Help! We are drowning! Lord help us!"

I can move fast when I need to, faster than any creature can. I run to where the rowboat is tied to shore and quickly push it into the water. There is no one around to see me in the darkness, see me moving at unnatural, inhuman speeds, and I'm in the boat in seconds, rowing fast across the calm water.

I reach the sinking boat and see a scene of horror.

There are three men. Two are alive and terrified while the other is dead, sliced down the middle with his entrails pulled out. There is evidence of a fourth person, the bloodied stump of a leg in the corner.

The smell of all the blood makes my mouth water, my vision growing sharp, and I feel my teeth turning into fangs.

I make the sign of the cross and pray I can keep the monster at bay. I need to save these men.

"Father Aragon!" one of them cries out. "Please, help him."

The villagers here know I can heal others thanks to the help of God. They don't suspect my witchcraft. But even I can't heal a man whose heart and liver are missing.

I shake my head, swallowing hard. "What happened here?"

The two men look at each other. Alonso and Jose Carlos, I believe their names are. Honest fishermen.

"What happened?" I repeat, wanting to get away from the blood and gore as quickly as I can.

"You won't believe us," Jose Carlos says, voice trembling, eyes wide. "But we were fishing for the toothfish. Then, she appeared in the water. We thought it was a drowning woman, needing help. Caught on our line, maybe. But we were wrong." He pauses. "It was a Syren."

Chapter Two

PRIEST

News of the attack on the fishermen spread before the sun rose over the strait. By noon, military troops stationed in Primera Angostura arrived to join the ones here, puzzling over the incident and arming the cannons. They talked to the surviving fisherman to get their accounts, examined what was left of the bodies, and then came to talk to me.

By then, I was in the chapel, tidying with a broom. In the mornings, I like to give myself busywork, a lasting habit from my days at the monastery. Idle work cures idle minds, and idle minds are apt to sin. As a result, the chapel, and my cottage, are always as neat as a pin. At any rate, it gives me something to do.

I never liked the military. There were a few soldiers who came to my church in need of penance for the people they had killed under the order of their country, and I listened to their burdens as I listened to everyone's, but in general, I find them to be more hypocritical than most believers. They are supposed to protect the people, but where were they when a band of bloodsuckers rode across Spain? Where were they when my village was under siege? They were nowhere to be found—cowards, the lot of them.

The soldiers stationed here don't seem to like me much either. I know I have a certain way about me—all my kind do. To make matters worse, because I was a witch before I was turned into a blood-drinker, I think they can sense that too. Either way, they don't see my *otherness* as being holy as the other villagers do—they see it as a threat they don't quite understand.

Sometimes, I dream about killing all of them, of letting them see they were right to fear me.

"Father Aragon." The tallest soldier strides forward, bowing his head slightly in a show of mock respect. His eyes are dark and cold. "The men say you saved them last night. We would like to hear your account of what happened."

"Of course," I say, resting the broom against the pew and then straightening out the front of the black robe I wear in the church. I look into the soldier's eyes, perhaps a little too deeply, because he goes quite still. I can hear his heart slowing, his breaths becoming shallow and long, his pupils dilating into black pools. I can often compel people this way, placing them under mild control, but Abe does it better than I. The more power I exert over someone, the more likely I am to lose control of myself, so I try not to do it too often.

But this morning, I want the soldiers to hear exactly what I'm going to say.

"I heard the screams from across the water," I tell them, keeping my gaze focused on the main soldier. "I got my skiff and rowed toward them as fast as I could. Thank the Lord they had a lamp lit, or I would have never found them in the dark."

"The men said this happened in the middle of the night," one of the other soldiers says brusquely. "Were their screams so loud that they woke you up?"

I don't glance at him. "I wasn't asleep. I was here in the chapel, praying."

The head soldier slowly nods. Even if he wanted to break away from my eyes, he can't. He's enraptured and bespelled. "What did you see when you came across their boat?"

"Exactly what you've seen. One man ripped down the middle, and all that's left of the other was his leg."

"And what did the men tell you that happened?"

I manage a small smile, as if we're sharing a joke. "They said they saw a woman in the water. She had tricked them into thinking she was drowning. They said it was a Syren who suddenly pulled their friend under and ripped him apart before she leapt out of the water and onto the boat, attacking the other one. Apparently, she ate his heart and liver before the men fought her off with the oars and stabbed her in the back with their knife. Only then did she let go and sink below the surface."

"And you believe that?"

Another placating smile. "Of course I don't. I am a man of faith, a man of God. God would never create such an abdominal creature. There is no such thing as a Syren or a mermaid or a monstrous woman in the sea."

The other soldier grunts. "Then what do you think really happened?"

"I think the men had a bit too much to drink while they were fishing, and they attracted some other sea creature. We know that sharks swim the strait. I believe the other two men must have fallen overboard from their love of the drink; you know how fond they are of that sinful libation here. They were attacked and killed, and the other two tried to save what they could."

The soldiers all fall silent, and I finally look away, gazing at the rest of them. They seem suspicious of me, even though what I just told them is the most logical explanation.

"May I ask what *you* think happened?" I ask them.

The soldier I was compelling blinks slowly and then gives his head a shake. He frowns at me. "I think it must have happened as you said. It is simply not possible for a woman to tear off a man's leg like that."

"And there are no such things as Syrens," I remind him.

He nods. "And there are no such things as Syrens."

Then, he clears his throat and gives me another nod, this one more courteous. He motions for his men to leave the chapel, and they quickly do so, as if this place suddenly terrifies them.

I watch them go and smile, the first genuine one I've had since Abe left.

They want to believe in monsters because monsters are real, and some part of them knows it. But logic always wins.

For me, the less they believe, the better.

Because that Syren does exist.

She did attack those men and eat them.

And she's somewhere out there in the waters right now, injured, perhaps slowly bleeding to death.

That blood is going to waste.

That blood could sustain me forever if I act now.

Tonight, I'm going fishing.

Last night's attack happened around one or two in the morning, so I bide my time until then, thinking that might be the Syren's hunting hours. I clean the church, rewrite the sermon for this Sunday so that it focuses on calming people's fears of the unknown. Under the moon that slices in through the window, I pray the rosary as only a heathen would, each bead not directed at God but at myself. It's a chant I repeat over and over again, reminding myself to stay in control.

And yet, I feel that control slipping the more the night ticks by.

I'm starting to welcome it.

My pulse is quickening, blood rushing to my cock until my pants are tight. I find myself wondering if the Syren is as beautiful as they say, getting harder and harder at the thought of finding her, feasting upon her...defiling her.

The thought causes a jolt to run through me like burning lightning, and I grip the rosary tighter as I squirm in my chair.

"Salvation," I whisper to myself, my voice blending in with the wind outside the windows. "Salvation."

It has been centuries since I've been with someone, man or woman. Sometimes, with Abe, it had come close, but he knew better than anyone that celibacy and keeping my vows was paramount to staying human. We are sexual creatures by nature, and because of my monstrous beginnings, my appetites are savage, depraved, and uncontrollable. Blood and sex are my two weaknesses, and because I have to consume blood to survive, it means I can't give in to the other, or I'll lose myself entirely.

But tonight, as my body pulses with the energy I'd been denying myself for ages, I think of the Syren I hadn't yet seen. She would have blonde or red or black hair. Her tail would shimmer like frost under the moon. Her breasts would be full, pale nipples pink and hard in the cold air, begging to be touched, to be bitten.

I think about dragging her out of the water, heavy and wet. She will cry for help, and I will smother her mouth with my hand. I will punish her for her sins and hope that, somehow, it will absolve me of my own.

I think about biting her neck, my fangs piercing the artery before the blood rushes into my mouth. I think about how the blood will taste—more heavenly than God could ever grant me—and how hot it will feel, the sounds as it splashes all over her chest, my throat making greedy noises as I swallow it all down.

If the powdery blood of a dead Syren can give me life for a day, then the pulsing blood of a live one will make immortality that much sweeter.

Before I know what I'm doing, I'm bringing my cock out of my trousers, stroking it hard. A few vicious yanks, and I'm coming with a choked gasp, white ropes spurting out across the black cloth of my thighs.

"God," I swear, gritting my teeth as my head goes back. Immediately, a sense of peace envelops me like a warm haze as I feel the world drift away. I know it's temporary—it always is. I know that when the feeling goes, my hunger will come back tenfold. The hunger for blood, the hunger for sex. It's a damned and sinful slope to be on.

But right now, I close my eyes and fall into a dulcet, dreamless slumber that rests my tired bones and soothes my wayward soul.

I don't know how long I am out for, and when I wake up, it's like a cannon has gone off. I sit straight up in my chair, my heart pounding, my half-hard cock still out of my pants. I eye the dried cum with disdain. It would look better sprayed across a round, pale bottom than leaving a stain on my holy clothes.

There's no point in taking them off and washing them in the basin. It will come off in the ocean.

I get to my feet, tuck my cock back in, and stride out of the cottage into the night. A man would bring some sort of weapon to fight off such a savage beast, but I'm a savage beast myself, and there is no beating me. There's no killing me, either. As lethal as this Syren is, they aren't immortal, and whatever way she'll try and injure me, I'll heal before her eyes.

The wind is steady, bringing in the sharp, bitter cold of the glacial, southern seas, but it's never been uncomfortable for me. Instead, it's bracing, giving me virility, causing a vicious stab of hunger to my gut.

I glance around, my preternatural senses trying to listen for anyone nearby. The cannons that guard the entrance to the strait are a mile away and out of sight, as are the stationed soldiers, and there are no fishermen this evening. I don't think anyone will dare fish after nightfall ever again.

I also listen to the sound of the water—not just the waves crashing against the stony shore, but the splashes out across the strait. Some are whitecaps, one is a seal poking up for air followed by a sharp huff, and one is a floundering sound. Could be a dolphin, a fish, even the shark I blamed for the attack.

Either way, there's something over there.

I walk across the shore and through the crashing surf until I'm swimming past the break. I could have taken the boat, but that would only attract unwanted attention to myself. This way, I can move quickly and undetected.

Under the moonlight, the snowcapped and craggy mountains on the other side of the strait appear like a row of jagged teeth. I swim as fast and as quietly as possible, spending most of the time underwater, where I don't need to breathe. Even in the darkness, my eyes can see clearly through the murky depths.

I smell her before I see her.

The scent of woman, heightened and combined with something primal. A young woman. I smell sex and energy.

I smell an animal.

I open my mouth and take a delicate taste of the ocean.

There's salt, and then there's blood.

Her blood.

My Syren is bleeding.

I pretend she's bleeding for me and let it flow through me, the lust, the hunger, the need for this creature I haven't even met.

Salvation, I think. That's what she tastes like. Just the faintest hint of what's to come.

Then, out of the dark, I see the faint outline of her body. Blonde hair moves around her head like seaweed, glowing silver in the moonlight. Her breasts are full, pale, and exposed, her torso curving down to a soft, round belly that fades into a long, thick tail of shimmering pink scales.

She's the most stunning creature I've ever seen, shining in this watery darkness like a beacon, a North Star, a light that will lead me somewhere.

Except I already know she's going to lead me straight to Hell.

And I'm going to go willingly.

Chapter Three

Salvation, I think again as I stare at the Syren. *Or is it damnation?*

I watch as she hovers in the current, her body so sinfully soft and curved that I have a hard time imagining her as a vicious creature. She's too beautiful for that, too delicate.

I want to see her monstrous side in action. So far, she has not spotted me. She's just hovering in the water a few feet below the surface, and though I can't see her back fully, I spy faint splotches of blood coloring the water from where the fisherman must have stabbed her.

It takes all my resolve not to make a move for her. I could be at her in seconds flat, tearing her apart.

Instead, I shoot up to the surface, breaking through. I gulp in the cold night air, staring up at the moon as I wait for her to attack.

I hear her approach, a snarling sound from the depths beneath me, and brace myself.

She grabs my ankles first, sharp claws digging in through my flesh and tendon and bone, surprisingly strong. If I was a normal man, she would have broken my bones like splintered twigs.

I could fight back right away and stay above the water, but I let her pull me under.

Until she has pulled me right down to her level.

She spins me around, silver-blonde hair swirling around us.

I am staring at two large, hooded eyes that glow like violet flames, pupils a diamond of coal at the middle. Her brows frame them like archways. Her nose is short and pert, her face the shape of a heart, with small, full lips above a dainty chin. For a moment, I trick myself into thinking I'm staring at a beautiful woman until those lips part, and she bares her teeth at me. Her smile is razor sharp, like looking into the mouth of a shark.

A shark that thinks it's about to devour its prey whole.

But I don't want to lose my nose, even if it will eventually heal, and I don't feel like experiencing pain—the gouges she dug into my ankles still throb.

I duck out of the way just as she lunges for me, teeth bared, letting out a roar that travels through the water like a wave.

I bite her before she has a chance to bite me.

My fangs pierce her neck, her skin surprisingly tough, and she lets out a scream. I put my hand at the back of her head, making a tight fist in her hair, the other hand squeezing down her back until I find the knife wound.

I press my fingers inside it, *hard*.

Her back arches, buckling in my grasp, her cries of agony filling the water, but at least I've gotten her to stop fighting. The pain has stunned her.

I start drinking, pulling the blood into my mouth.

The moment it hits my tongue in a burst of salt and vitality, I feel the beast inside me rattling its chains. If I let go, it will rip this Syren to shreds, and while it will feel good in the moment to succumb to the very thing I've fought so hard against, to lose all the humanity I've earned, I know it would be the foolish thing to do.

I could devour her, and she would keep me going for a long time.

But not forever.

Yet if I brought her ashore, kept her as a prisoner, as a pet, I could slowly drain her of her blood. I could take as much as I could without killing her, put it in the casks with the rest of my supply as a backup in case I accidentally do kill her, and then, every few days, take more from her. It wouldn't have to be much, just enough to sustain me.

I know what Abe would say, that it's immoral and inhumane.

But the more I drink from this Syren, the more I realize that's something I'll never be able to escape, no matter how often I pray to a God who doesn't hear me, no matter how the world sees me as a man of faith.

I *am* immoral.

I *am* inhumane.

I'm not even human anymore.

Yet I need to drink human blood to survive. And if it's a Syren's blood, that's even better. Isn't it kinder to keep one savage creature, such as this fish-woman, as my food source than it is to slaughter people every week? I'd be doing the world a favor, saving the lives she would have killed, as well as the ones I would have killed.

I'm doing God a favor.

She really will be my salvation, I think.

With that thought, I manage to tear my teeth from her neck before I lose all control. Blood flows freely in the water, and she's losing consciousness, her eyes fluttering closed as she becomes limp in my arms. Hopefully, I haven't already killed her.

I want to keep her alive forever.

I want to keep her. Forever.

I turn around in the water, one arm hooked under hers, and start swimming toward the shore. It doesn't take long before I feel the stones under my feet, and I stagger out of the water, holding the Syren in my arms. Here, in the bitterly cold wind that ushers in a thick, rolling fog, she looks utterly vulnerable and out of her element. If I ignore her tail, she could be a damsel I just rescued.

But I am not here to rescue her.

I'm here to make her bleed.

I don't waste any time taking her directly to the chapel. My cottage is small, with thin walls and too many windows, and while the church itself is always open to everyone, the back room is locked and has no windows.

I kick open the heavy main doors, hoping that some wayward soul hasn't come inside to pray while I've been gone. The church is empty, quiet, like it's been holding its breath and waiting for me.

I stride down the aisle, leaving a trail of water and blood behind us, and head straight to the back door of the chapel. I don't dare glance at the altar or the paintings of saints on the walls, disapproval apparent on their faces. They'll realize I need to do this; they'll understand that I'm saving their flock by taking out another wolf.

The back room smells like muddled herbs, wood, aging linens, and old blood. The casks are in a row along the far wall, and there's a small desk and chair with stacks of extra Bibles. I keep everything else organized in woven bins, half of which have gone moldy in this climate, no matter how dry the room seems to be.

Then, there is the heavy, life-sized cross leaning against the wall. When Abe first brought me here, the government was in the middle of upgrading their church and had taken down this worn cross above the altar, one that had been made from a giant oak in Salamanca, and put up a smaller, more ornate silver one. It was supposed to signify a more dignified future for the village, perhaps a more dignified God.

I always found it to be a bit insulting. God wasn't found in the riches; no, he was found in the simple things, like worn, rough wood from the homeland. An expensive, lavish cross didn't mean this village was any closer to heaven than with an old wooden one.

But none of that matters now. I have a cross at my disposal, and God would want me to use it.

I carefully place the Syren on the floor. She's completely still, eyes closed, and I stare at her for a moment to see if she's breathing. She has gills on her neck, three lines that attempt to flutter open, then stop, sticking together.

Perhaps she will die, and my plan will be thwarted, but either way, I need to get more blood out of her now while I can.

Though I can see well in the dark, I need light to do this properly. I light a few candles around the room, and then I go to the cross and yank out the long spikes that have been drilled in the arms for morbid reverence. I grab some rope that's stacked in the corner, and with a grunt, I pull the Syren up off the ground and place her back against the cross, quickly wrapping the rope around one arm, then the other, until she's suspended.

She slumps forward, her long, wet blonde hair hanging in her face, dripping on the floor. The weight of her upper body pulls on her arms until they dislocate with a pop, so I let her tail rest against the ground to give her some support. I know enough that it's not the nails that killed those who were crucified. No, it was suffocation from the pressure on the lungs. I am unsure how much a Syren can take, but a human on a cross would die in less than twenty-four hours.

I don't even know if she's still breathing.

I stand close to her, grasping the spikes in my hands. The seawater drips off her in a steady cadence, but other than that, she doesn't move. My gaze lingers on her breasts, a temptation I have to ignore, even though my cock is already throbbing wildly at the slightest provocation.

Then, I see it. The slightest inhale. Her chest rises and falls, her nostrils flaring slightly. She's breathing through her nose and into her lungs. The Syren can both breathe underwater and above.

Satisfied that she's still alive, I grab two silver chalices, placing them beneath her wrists. I then grab an empty cask and position one of the spikes right below her wrist. With a swift motion, I drive the butt of the cask against the top of the spike, driving it right through her arm and into the wood. Blood spills from the wound, pouring into the chalice below as splashes of red dot the floor.

She lifts her head up and stares at me in horror.

Right before she screams.

Chapter Four

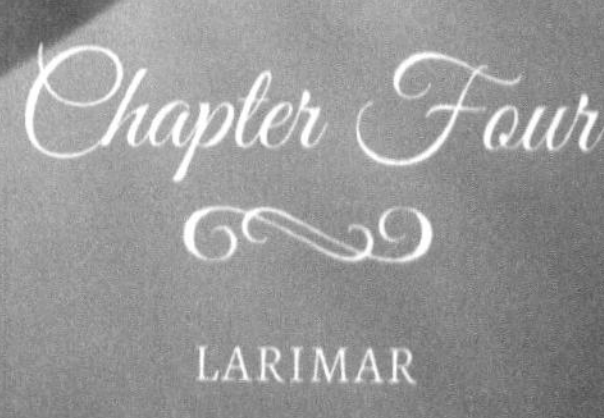

LARIMAR

Pain explodes from my wrist, shattering inside me, pulling me out of the comfort of darkness until I'm thrust back into the world.

A horrible, dry world.

My eyes open, a high screech ripping from my raw throat, my lungs burning as they struggle to be used, to find oxygen in the air. It feels like I have stones set on top of them, and I'm gasping, wondering why I have been brought back from the dead and into such agony.

There is a man right in front of me, the strange, other-worldly scent of him filling my nose. He winces at the scream coming from my mouth, and somewhere, I hear glass shattering from the power of my voice.

But the man doesn't stop what he's doing. I see a long, sharp spike in his hand, and he quickly places it against my other wrist before slamming it in through my arm with a round wooden object. He moves so fast my eyes can barely track his movements; he's just a blur, a smudge in the air.

The pain hits me even faster.

I scream again, thrashing against the spikes that have me

nailed against a plank of wood. It causes my flesh to tear, blood flying everywhere. The man tightens the ropes around my arms, ensuring I can't do any more damage to myself, and the pressure on my lungs lifts a little. My tail below smacks wildly against the ground until I'm able to keep myself supported.

Then, the man takes the end of the rope and slams it into my mouth, as if he wants to keep me from screaming.

As if that will help.

Fool.

I stare right into his eyes and bite down on the rope, my teeth slicing through it with just a few snaps of my jaw until it falls, frayed and free.

His brows rise, and he looks impressed more than anything.

This is the first moment I really take a look at him.

Because he's not like most men, is he?

When I saw him in the ocean, I thought perhaps he was another fisherman, one who had come to investigate what I did to the others. One who wanted revenge.

And I welcomed it. Because of my injury, I knew that eating another's heart and liver would go a long way to fuel me until I healed.

It seemed too good to be true, and it was.

I had grabbed his ankles hard enough to snap the bones, and yet, they didn't break. I hauled him down from the surface and went in for my attack.

But when I got a look at his face, I realized this was no ordinary fisherman.

He was handsome in a beautiful way that most humans aren't, with a strong jaw and nose, bright blue eyes framed by long black lashes, coupled with a brushy dark beard and long, black hair. His aura was unlike any human I'd ever had the pleasure of devouring.

But it was his eyes that struck me as the most unusual, that made me think he perhaps wasn't human at all.

They held no fear in them whatsoever.

Instead, they danced with excitement.

With violence.

Before I could act, he opened his mouth, showing off a pair of sharp fangs, and simultaneously found the knife wound in my back, digging his fingers in until I screamed in agony.

The last thing I felt was his teeth on my neck, a hit of pleasure until I blacked out from the pain.

Now, the man stands in front of me, those same cruel blue eyes staring at me with a mix of respect and malevolence.

What are you? I want to ask. *What do you want with me?*

I decide to scream again since it bothers him so much.

The corner of his mouth quirks up in a cold, calculating smirk. With regular humans, a Syren's scream can immobilize them, but with this man, it does nothing.

Suddenly, he moves away from me in a blur, and in that moment, I manage to take in where I am. I'm in a windowless room with white walls, the only light coming from candles placed here and there. Despite the pain and confusion, I feel proud of myself for recognizing what these things are. My friendship with Jorge, the boatbuilder's son, wasn't for naught.

The man comes back to my side, a heavy rattling sounding as he adjusts a chain in his hand, like the one a ship would anchor with but thinner.

Before I can figure out what he's about to do, he snaps the chain taut between his hands and then shoves it at my face, pressing it between my lips.

I let out a growl, tasting rust, the metal cold, hurting my teeth. He quickly pulls the chain back until my head hits the wood behind me, then wraps the chain around until I'm held in place.

He says something to me in a deep, rough voice that makes tiny bumps appear on my flesh, but I can't understand what he's saying.

"Or do you speak Spanish?" he says, staring right into my eyes until I start to feel a little dizzy, though perhaps that's the loss of blood pouring from my wrists and into silver cups below. Then, he shakes his head. "Of course you can't understand what I'm saying."

But I do understand what he's saying, at least I do now. He's speaking a human language Jorge managed to teach me during those nights I'd meet him at the shipyard, when I learned everything I could about humans and their world in the chance that it could somehow lead me to my sister.

Not that I can inform the man of this when I'm gagged with a chain, and not that I want to be having conversations with this monster.

He steps back and looks me over, as if he's admiring what he's done to me. Like he's created art out of my pain.

His blue eyes meet mine, the color of the cold ocean pierced by sunlight, and I hope he can read all the animosity in my own gaze. This is not the first time I've been held captive, but it is the first time it has been on land. While I can survive out of water for long periods of time, I will eventually dry out and die if I don't get wet. I don't think this man knows that, and I'm not sure he'd care.

The man nods thoughtfully, as if understanding this, and then he gestures to my wrists. The blood has slowed down to a trickle, collecting in the silver cups, and he stoops down to pick one up.

He holds out the cup in front of me, my own blood a pool of dark red, like the wine Jorge used to steal from his father.

I growl at him, my teeth gnashing at the chains until they hurt.

He keeps those eyes focused on mine and then slowly lifts the cup to his mouth.

He stares right at me as he takes a sip.

He's drinking my damn blood.

I stare at him in utter horror. Even Syrens don't drink blood; we eat the organs of creatures so we can sustain ourselves. Humans aren't particularly nourishing—they don't have as much fat as seals do—but they are especially tasty.

But blood-drinking is utterly depraved.

What the hell kind of man is this?

No, not man. Creature.

Monster.

He swallows the blood down, his thick throat bobbing, until he's drained the whole glass. A trickle runs from the corner of his mouth, dripping onto his bare chest. He's made of power, muscle, and strength, every inch of him taut and hard, giving me the impression that he could rip me apart with his bare hands if he wanted to. He doesn't need claws—or his fangs—for that.

He wipes his bloody mouth with the back of his hand and then takes the cup to a table on the other side of the room. With his back to me, he looks through his desk drawers, and I hold my breath, wondering what he's going to do this time, what other ways he plans on torturing me.

When he turns around, he's got something in his hands giving off smoke, a sweetly herbaceous scent. It looks like a bundle of dried leaves tied up with twine, the ends smoldering with bright embers.

"This will hurt," he says, and I brace myself.

He reaches over and removes the spike from my wrist in one fluid motion, the pain making my eyes roll back in my head. Then, he presses the burning bundle to my wound.

I scream against the chain, watching as he holds it against my bleeding flesh, chanting in a language I don't understand.

And then, the unthinkable happens.

I feel a prickling around the burn, and then the pain starts to fade until it's barely noticeable.

He takes the herbs away, and I stare in complete awe as the bloody wound at my wrist begins to heal itself, the flesh growing over it as if the injury is being erased before my very eyes.

"I don't want you to bleed to death," he says quietly. "I need you alive."

How fucking noble.

He goes over to the other wrist and does the same. This time, I try to stay composed. I don't want him to revel in my suffering.

Finally, he steps in close to me, so close that I can see tiny flecks of silver and green in his eyes. It's hypnotizing, the way they pull me under those dark long lashes, and the scent of him, similar to the stuff he's burning but with something sweet, only adds to the headiness.

"I can fix your back as well," he says, his voice low, and he stares at my mouth as he reaches back behind me. My breasts brush against his warm chest, my nipples hardening despite the fear and hatred I feel for him, and my breath hitches. His gaze drops even lower now, the corner of his full mouth quirking up as he watches how my body responds to him, how it betrays me.

Then, he finds the wound at my back and presses the herbs on it until I feel that heal too.

"There," he says with a satisfied nod as he looks me over. "Like no harm ever came to you. I'll collect more blood in a few days, give you time to heal and recuperate. You'll get used to the cycle, and the magic should make things easier."

Magic? My eyes widen, and he notices.

"Yes, magic," he says. "You seem to know this word? Do you know of us witches? Do you have blood-drinkers? Or is all this new to you? Perhaps you are used to being the only monster around."

I am not a monster, I want to scream at him. *I am doing what I must, what I am made to do. Is that what this is all about? Is this punishment for what I did to those men?*

"It should be a pity that you can't understand me," he says as he stoops down to pick up the other chalice. I expect him to drink my blood like he did with the other one, but he doesn't. "But I am used to talking to someone who doesn't understand me and never talks back." He glances up at the ceiling, and my gaze follows, expecting something or someone to be there.

"I wonder," he says, looking back at me, the coldness in his eyes softening slightly, "do you have God under the sea? Do you Syrens worship sharks? Other Syrens? Man itself? Do you ever wrestle with how God could create a horrid creature such as yourself, how they could ever let something like this happen to one of their precious living souls? Have you ever spared a thought for who created you?" He gives me a caustic smile. "What a blessing that would be, to never have to believe in anything."

Then, he starts to walk toward the door.

He opens it, cautiously looking outside before he turns back to look at me.

"I will be back after daybreak," he says. "I know you don't understand what that means. I just want you to know that I will be back, for better...or for worse."

Then, he exits the room, shutting the door behind him. There is a loud click and rattling of the handle, then nothing.

There is relief in the silence of this room, with only the crackle of the candles surrounding me. My body aches from the position it's strapped in, my tail starting to dry out a little as I press myself up to get the pressure off my shoulders and chest.

He will be back, for better or for worse, he says.

I know what he means for the worse.

More bloodletting, or some other form of torture.

And there probably isn't anything for the better.

But he is magic. He called himself a witch. A blood-drinking witch.

I've spent eleven years looking for Edonia, the sea witch who tricked my sister into giving up her fins for legs, hoping that, if I found her, she could either tell me where Maren was or give me legs so I could cross the world to find her. My search brought me to Jorge, then across the Pacific, then back to my kingdom of Limonos until the last of our Syrens left. Then, I traveled down here, to the frigid southern oceans, forever searching, unwilling to give up.

And now, I've been captured and tortured by this blood-drinking witch who seems to have malevolent plans for me.

But I have plans too.

If he can give me legs, the same way Edonia did for Maren, then I am prepared to give this monster exactly what he wants.

No matter what it costs me.

Chapter Five

PRIEST

I took a risk leaving the Syren crucified on the cross. Though I had locked the door behind me so she was as secure as possible, both roped and chained, there was always a chance something could go wrong.

But I couldn't be in there a minute longer. With her blood coursing through my veins, making it harder to control my impulses, I had to separate myself from her. There was a moment there, when I used my magic to heal the wound on her back, that I felt her nipples brush against my bare chest, and I thought my cock would explode. I was hit with the urge to run my lips over her breasts, to bite and feast, to let my hands roam southward. I have no idea what a Syren's anatomy was like, but I wanted to find out.

I was a monster, I knew, but I didn't want to be of that kind. Wicked men were like that, those who preyed on women, who defiled them. Perhaps all men have some sort of beast inside them, driving them to do such things, but that was the last bastion of humanity I had to hold on to.

God, help me hang on.

Now, in the quiet of my cottage, with only the occasional

howling gust of wind outside to keep me company, I need to formulate a plan. I need to be able to think clearly without that Syren occupying my thoughts, not to mention my desires.

Tomorrow is Sunday. People will be here for the funeral of the two fishermen, and then they'll be in church. I have to ensure she is subdued and quiet. If she happens to fall from the cross or get out of the chains, then she's no longer a secret. Then, she becomes a spectacle.

Maybe I can put some sort of spell on her, perhaps one that takes away her voice without the use of chains. I'll see what I can muster. My magic was stronger before I had been turned into a blood-drinker, back when I was merely a human witch. I had to bury my magic entirely in the monastery, for such power is an indulgent act already, and I was more likely to lose control of myself.

Now, I use it on occasion—to heal people under the guise of God, to compel people when I need extra persuasion, to spy on people if needed. I've always had the gift of being able to enter the mind of any animal, so as long as that animal is in my sight, and I can control them to an extent, seeing through their eyes. For a moment, it crosses my mind that if the Syren was more animal than human, perhaps I could do that to her. I could at least try.

Dawn breaks the cloudy sky by the time I feel more in control and composed, and I head back to the chapel.

The Syren is right where I left her, a vision in holiness.

Her head is slumped to the side, the chains taut around her mouth, blonde hair hanging around her face like an angel. Her breasts remain full and perfect, her arms held back by the ropes with no sign of her impalement. There is no light in the room, the candles having all burned out, and yet it seems like she's shining.

Just for me.

I stop and close the door, quietly locking it behind me with the skeleton key that I slip into my trousers.

She hasn't moved at all, and I feel a pang of fear that perhaps she's dead. But then her chest rises, just a little, taking in a quiet breath.

I walk toward her and stop to get a closer look, wanting her to raise her head and meet my eyes. I want to see that fire in them I saw last night, that devilish beast within her.

Perhaps our beasts could both come out and play.

But I shake that thought from my mind and focus on her crucifixion, on the cross. It reminds me to stay pure, to stay in control, to do what must be done and *only* what must be done.

"Hello," I say, standing in front of her. My voice sounds hollow in the room, and I feel a bit silly for saying something so bland, given the situation.

But she doesn't stir. I don't expect her to understand Spanish, but she doesn't even flinch.

I reach out and grab the hair at the top of her head, pulling her head back so I can see her clearly. Her brows come together faintly, and she lets out a soft moan against the chains. But she doesn't open her eyes, and when I let go of her hair, her head slumps forward again.

I glance down at her tail. Up close, it looks like the scales are flaking off, as if it's starting to shrink and dehydrate. Does she have to be in water to survive?

I quickly leave the room, locking it behind me, then step out of the chapel with a bucket I use to fill the stoup. Roosters crow with the rising sun, and I hurry to the sacramental well, where the holy water is drawn from behind the chapel, filling up the bucket before heading back into the church.

Once I'm locked in the back room again, I stand a few feet back from the Syren and then heave the contents of the bucket at her. The water splashes over her like a slap, and she lifts her head with a muffled gasp.

Relieved, I put the bucket down and go over to her. I reach out and brush her wet hair off her angelic face.

Those angry violet eyes stare back at me, her nostrils flaring.

I can't help but smile.

"I was worried you were close to death," I say to her. I know she doesn't understand, but it still feels good to talk. "I don't know much about keeping a Syren alive, but perhaps you need water, just as I need blood."

She frowns, delicate brows knitting together, and lets out a low growl. To see the fight in her return brings me a perverse sort of joy.

A drop of water rolls down over her nose to her lips, sinking behind the metal chain, and I see her pink tongue dart out to lick it, a sight that makes my cock twitch. I do my best to ignore it.

"I suppose you might want something to drink," I muse, stepping back and looking around the room. I'll have to go back out again later for more water, and I'm not about to offer her blood, especially not her own, so I go to the cask I know has wine and open it. The chalice I drank from last night is empty, so I pour wine into it and bring it over to her.

"I'm going to assume you've never had wine before," I say as her eyes focus on the chalice, fear and curiosity mixing in shades of a bruise. "I can't promise it will taste good to you. Frankly, the wines they give us for the church are not of the highest quality, and I don't know if it will be enough to quench your thirst. But Jesus turned water into wine, and I can only hope I can turn this wine into water."

I step closer to her and reach out with one hand for the back of the cross, finding where I had latched the chains together. Once again, her breasts are against my chest, though because of my black shirt, I don't feel them as I did last night.

"I'm going to undo the chain so you can drink freely," I murmur, staring down into her eyes. "You can try and bite me, but rest assured, you cannot hurt me. You can scream, but I will either put this chain back in your mouth or take away your voice. It's up to you."

Her nostrils flare as she stares up at me, but she eventually relents, a tired sigh rumbling through her.

I undo the chain and pull it away from her mouth, quickly stepping back with it. Her mouth widens and stretches, and she winces, obviously sore. The chains have left rusty red grooves at the corners of her mouth, reminding me of blood.

"Behave," I warn her, coming closer again with the chalice. "You bite me, and I will bite you right back. I won't turn the other cheek."

She stares at me intently and swallows, licking her dry lips, wriggling the tension from her jaw.

Then, she nods. She may not speak my language, but she understands me.

Acquiescence.

"Very well," I say, lifting the chalice to her lips. "Drink while you can."

She sniffs the chalice, most likely checking that it's not her own blood, then takes a tepid sip, her full upper lip softly clasping the edge. I tip the cup forward so the wine pours into her mouth slowly, careful not to spill, and watch as she swallows it down. Her face contorts for a moment, perhaps shocked at the taste of wine, and then her eyes flutter closed. She looks angelic again, young.

Suddenly, I'm hit with two conflicting desires—the desire to protect this creature from any harm and the desire to do harm to her. To feed from her, to defile her, to know what those lips would feel like if they were pressed against mine or, heaven forbid, wrapped around my dick.

But then, she gulps the rest of the wine down in a frenzy, the red liquid spilling everywhere, and her razor teeth chomp into the edge of the metal chalice, biting it.

I quickly rip the chalice away from her.

"I told you to behave," I scold her. "To disobey a priest is blasphemy."

"I won't behave," she snarls at me.

I stare at her, mouth agape. "You speak Spanish?" I ask, blinking at her. How is that possible?

"I speak enough," she says in a beguiling accent.

Then, she spits on my face.

I wipe it away and grin at her. "Well, this has certainly made your little predicament a lot more interesting. For me, that is. I'm so used to talking to a God who doesn't answer back, it might be nice to talk to someone who does."

She growls in response and spits on me again.

This time, I wipe it away, glancing at it between my fingers, tinged with wine. I give a small shake of my head and rub her spit along my tongue, swallowing it. Even her saliva tastes divine.

"If you think spitting on me is a deterrent, you are sadly mistaken," I tell her, tipping over the empty chalice. "I drink your spit like wine. Speaking of wine, I could give you more, but it all depends on your temperament. So far, I'm not sure you're taking any of this seriously."

"Damn you, whore," she sneers.

I burst out laughing, my own laughter foreign to my ears.

The Syren can curse, albeit creatively. She grows more interesting by the minute.

"I like you, you know," I tell her, still chuckling. "That's not a good thing in the long run. But yes, I like you very much. Tell me, Syren, where did you learn to speak my language?"

"It is none of your business. Let me go."

I raise my brow, running my fingertip over the rim of the cup. "Let you go where? To do what? You know, had you been a human who had murdered those men like you did, you would already be dead. That's how we deal with things in this world. You kill them, we kill you. It's safer for the world for a savage creature like yourself to be put in the ground, turned into fish food."

"Put me back in the water or..." She trails off, licking the wine off her lips. I'd like to lick it off for her.

"Or what?" I ask idly.

"I'll scream," she threatens. "You know what a Syren's scream can do."

"Actually, I didn't. Not until I met you. I confess. I know nothing about you or your kind. The only thing I know, the only thing I *need* to know, is that your blood sustains me for very long periods of time. That's the only reason why you're here. That's all I want from you."

Her eyes darken. "I don't believe you. You are here to punish me."

"Well, I suppose there *is* a little punishment involved. God is the judge, but perhaps I am the jury and the executioner." I lean in closer to her, daring to brush away a strand of wet blonde hair that's fallen across her eye. "I will treat you fairly, but you must understand that if you were to scream, if you were to escape, you would find no safety in my world. These men would either chop off your tail or sell you to a museum. Can you imagine a real Syren for the world to see? Do you want to spend the rest of your life in an aquarium, having people crowd around you, tapping on the glass?"

She jerks her head out of the way, growling like a rabid dog.

"I am your only ally here," I inform her, my voice low. "And through me is the only way you'll reach any kind of salvation. Perhaps I do want to keep you here as punishment. Perhaps I just want to make sure I get the most out of you that I can. You are going to bleed for me, little fish, until you have nothing left to give. Then, and only then, will I even think about letting you go."

"You're a monster," she says, baring her teeth at me.

I drop my hand from her face. "You have no idea."

I lean in closer, inhaling her scent. I've been so entranced by the sweet smell and decadent taste of her blood I've barely registered what her natural aroma is. Like her blood, it's sweet and rich, but there's something fresh and bracing about it. It brings memories to the front of my mind, ones I thought I'd forgotten. She smells like the time I traveled to a village on the Mediterranean, back in Spain, back when I was human. I had my son with me, and we had traveled through olive and lemon and almond groves until I glimpsed the sea for the first time. The woman at the inn gave us a slice of cake with honeyed lemon rinds...

The memory catches me off guard, disorients me. This creature smells like the last time I remember being happy and whole and—

With a snap of her head, she leans forward and bites my hand, which I had rested on her shoulder. Pain explodes as her teeth sink in and savagely tear at my fat and sinew, tearing my ligaments to shreds.

I holler and rip my hand out of her jaws, but her bite is tight, and she keeps part of my hand in her mouth, the bloody mess hanging from her teeth.

I look down at my ravaged and bleeding hand. I'm lucky she didn't take a finger. Tissue and muscle can repair and regrow, but bones rarely can.

She grins at me, a gruesome sight.

To think, this creature made me feel something for a moment.

I let out a roar, and my other hand shoots out, wrapping around her neck. She manages to swallow part of my hand before I squeeze her throat tight until I feel her vertebrae close to snapping.

"What did I just tell you?" I hiss at her. "You bite me, and I'm going to bite you right back."

I yank her head to the side, exposing the skin of her neck, and sink my teeth into her jugular. She yelps, jaws snapping, but I'm stronger and keep her locked in place while I take my fill of her blood. I wasn't planning on feeding from her so soon again—if my plan is to work, I have to be strategic when I take blood, give her time to replenish—but I refuse to let her win this little game she's playing.

In time, she'll learn that her freedom is an illusion.

And if the monster inside me escapes, he will always win.

Chapter Six

LARIMAR

For a moment, I think I'm elsewhere.

The ocean.

I'm in the cold, bottomless depths, that stretch of blue that goes on and on forever. There is nothing here that can hurt me. No one I've lost. No pain, no sorrow, no grief. Just blissful nothingness in which to float forever.

But then, reality sets in.

The pain sets in.

A sharp stabbing in my neck.

The sensation of having my soul, the very essence of myself, ripped out of me while, at the same time, I am filled.

Filled with something I didn't know I needed, didn't realize I craved. It strikes hot and quick, like liquid lightning that sinks into my very core, causing an insatiable hunger like I've never known.

This man is sucking the blood from my neck, feasting on me, swallowing me down his throat, and there's almost something pleasurable in the pain, enough that I let out a low moan.

The man stops.

Goes still.

Unhooks his fangs from my neck.

He pulls back and stares at me. His bright cerulean eyes are the color of the ocean in that blank void I was afloat in. Perhaps I had been floating in his eyes that whole time. They take me in, his pupils contracting and widening again, like a black sun in a blue sky.

But there is a change from the way they were before. Earlier, his eyes glinted with cruelty, combined with something like piousness, a smugness that rattled me. He clearly enjoys having power and will do everything he can to hold on to it. He also seems to think he has some Christian god on his side. I know enough about that god from Jorge to know he's never on anyone's side.

Now, there is a flash of shame on his face, or something close to it.

Does this cruel bloodsucker have the capacity to feel remorse?

I think about screaming. I could probably get one loud screech, my Syren song, in before he either bites me again or slams the chain into my mouth. Didn't he say something about taking my voice away? Isn't that what Edonia did to Maren?

But he mentioned how the humans would treat me if they discovered me, and I know he's right. I've seen how cruel they can be, the way those pirates hauled my older sister, Asherah, right out of the water while we were on the search for Maren while Jorge kept me hidden from his brothers.

"I shouldn't have done that," he says quietly as he stoops to pick up a bucket. "You need to heal and replenish your blood before I take more again."

He pauses, seeming to think. "Then again, I did just watch you eat a part of my hand." He lifts the one I bit, which is still bloody and missing a chunk of flesh. "Perhaps I should eat a piece of you to keep it even."

I swallow hard.

"I could start with your nose," he says. "It seems so sweet and delicate, too much for such a vicious animal. Or perhaps I'll take a bite out of those plump lips of yours. Or chew on these decadent tits."

In any other circumstance, I would feel disgusted, and yet I can feel heat flare on my cheeks. "You have a filthy mouth for a holy man."

He seems surprised by my comment. "I suppose only a filthy creature like yourself could bring it out of me."

I glare at him. "You say I need to heal. I'll heal faster if you keep me wet."

His black brows rise. "How wet are we talking here?"

I frown. I am not sure we are discussing the same thing.

"I need to be in water, or I will dry out and die," I tell him, my patience tried. "If you wish to hold me captive, then you'll need to put water on me constantly, especially my tail."

In other words, I need him to get me down from this wooden structure and put me in a bathtub or a pond if he won't set me free in the ocean.

"How constantly?" he asks.

I nod at the bucket. "You best be filling that up soon. I'll dry out again in a few hours. I have to be hydrated from the inside as well. I can go weeks without eating, but I need water. However, I am fine with the wine you have given me. Though I must say, I've had better," I add.

He frowns, turning the bucket over in his hands. "How have you had wine?"

"That's none of your concern," I tell him, enjoying the flicker of annoyance in his eyes. He wants to know more about me, that's clear as ice. It's the one advantage I have, and I plan on using it.

I go on. "Of course, if keeping me wet seems to be getting in the way of your plans to keep me alive so you can drink my blood, I have a solution for you."

He folds his arms across his chest, and I can't help but admire the way his muscles bunch. Pity he's such a malicious brute. "And what might that be?"

"You said you have magic. Use that magic on me. Turn me into a human. Give me legs."

He blinks at me for a moment and then chuckles, giving his head a shake. "Give you legs? Just like that? I'm not sure you know how magic works."

"I know very well how it works," I tell him with a raise of my chin. "We do have sea witches. You think I haven't seen what they can do?"

You think I haven't been searching for a sea witch for the last eleven years so she can do to me what she did to my sister?

"Sea witches," he says with a slow nod. "So, what have you seen them do?"

I don't want to tell him about Maren. I feel like giving him personal information might be like giving him a weapon.

"I know a Syren who wanted legs instead of a tail," I say carefully. "She wanted to become a human, to walk and live on land. The sea witch was able to do that for her."

He frowns. "And you saw this happen with your own eyes?"

I shake my head. "No. But it happened all the same."

A look of disbelief comes over him. He starts to pace slowly in front of me, hands behind his back. "Tell me, then... What is your name, anyway? Or should I just call you little fish?"

I press my lips together. I'm not about to tell him my name, and being called a fish isn't an insult where I'm from.

"Little fish it is," he says, and though his face is ever so serious, I catch a look of delight in his eyes. "So tell me: why should I use my magic to give you legs? What would I get out of that? If I were to make you a human, surely you would lose all the special properties in your blood, the very thing I crave."

"How do you know that would happen?" I ask him. "All you need to give me are legs. I can keep my gills. I can keep my ability to breathe underwater. I can keep my long life. You don't need to change my blood."

He studies me for a moment. "Why do you want legs?"

"Would it not be easier for you to manage me? You can't keep me in this room forever. Eventually, someone will discover me. You said so yourself: my screams would bring attention. Therefore, that means there is an audience to be had. If I had legs, you could pass me off as perhaps some woman who has been shipwrecked."

"Yes," he says slowly. "I could do that, though I would need to figure out a way to keep you from escaping, from talking to the villagers. You wouldn't be any freer than you are now. So I want you to answer the question: why do you want legs? What is in it for you?"

"I suppose I get to experience something new before I die," I tell him. It's the partial truth.

"Speaking of death, you don't seem to fear it," he says, taking a tentative step forward, his gaze searching my face. I can't tell if he's afraid to come closer because of me...or because of himself.

"I fear death," I admit quietly. If I didn't confess it, I have no doubt he would try and make me fear it in torturous ways.

"But you haven't once tried to beg for your life. At least, not really."

"Perhaps this is me begging." Perhaps I've been through worse before and lived to tell the tale. You don't get to roam the seas alone as a female Syren without running into trouble.

"No," he says dismissively. "I know what begging looks like. I know it very well. You aren't afraid of me, at least not as much as you should be. Tell me, where were you before you showed up in these harbors? Does your kind not live in colonies? Why were you alone?"

"Who says I was alone?" I ask, my voice growing hard.

"You were alone," he says after a moment. "I can tell when someone is running away from something—or running to something. It's my calling to take those in, no matter which direction they're running."

I can't help but curl my lip at him. Again with this pious talk. He should know it doesn't have any weight with me. "You have a strange calling, kidnapping Syrens and bringing them into your church to torture them in secret."

He gives me a sharp look, black brows knitting together. "I am not torturing you."

I nearly laugh. This man is terribly delusional.

"Oh, so I suppose tying me to a plank and putting holes in my wrists isn't torture? Biting me and drinking my blood isn't torture? Gagging me with a chain isn't torture?"

The sharpness in his eyes doesn't dissipate. "It isn't a plank."

Now I laugh, the sound acidic. "My sincerest apologies for not knowing your terminology."

"It's a cross," he says, though his voice is softer now. "A crucifix. To symbolize the death of Jesus, who died for our sins."

"Then he died for *your* sins, not mine," I tell him snidely. "So what are you trying to do? Make an example of me?"

"I'm trying to remind myself not to get carried away," he says, his gaze searching the cross I'm tied to.

"Is that so? And what does getting carried away look like?"

He doesn't answer at first; he just rubs his lips together in thought. "I need reminders to keep myself in line. I fought so very long and hard to become the human I am today. I can't afford to slip up and throw it all away just because I...because I lost control. I need a reminder of who I need to keep being."

"And who is that?"

His eyes darken. "A man looking for salvation. A man who might deserve it."

I snort. "If you think you're going to find salvation, you best look harder. I may not know a lot about your religion, but I'm sure this isn't how you find it."

"I'm not torturing you," he says again. "I'm not trying to cause you pain. I am doing this because I need you to survive. You have no idea what it's like to be a creature like me."

"I think I might."

He shakes his head. "No. You are from a world where your monstrous side can freely exist. I live in a world where it cannot. This world doesn't know what I truly am, doesn't know my kind even exists. Not yet, anyway. And if they ever do, we'll be the ones put in a cage in an exhibition to suffer for all eternity."

"Is that supposed to make me feel sorry for you?"

"No," he says quietly, his gaze flitting over my features. "I don't want your pity. None of us do. It is the way God made us. Well, the way he made everyone else." He pauses. "God didn't make me."

"Who made you, then? Why are you so special?"

He doesn't say anything to that. "I suppose I better go get another bucket of water before the day gets away from me."

"If you gave me legs, you wouldn't have to worry about that," I quickly tell him.

He gives me a bitter smile. "No. My worries would only grow."

And then, he's gone.

Chapter Seven

PRIEST

Dearest Abe,

It's nearly been a month since you've gone. Knowing you, you're probably thinking of me at this moment, keeping track of how much time I have until I run out of supplies. You're probably worrying about me, about my psyche, how I will deal with being alone, how I will deal with having to kill again.

If only you'd known what was about to be thrown my way.

Would you have still left me to my own devices?

Would you still have picked those poor souls over my own?

It is hard to say.

And by the time you read this letter, I'm

not sure if you'll be regretting your choice or not.

A few days ago, local fishermen were attacked by a Syren. I heard their cries and swam out across the strait to help. I saw the remains of two, or at least what was left of them—it was gruesome, no doubt ripped apart by this creature. The fact that we now had a dangerous Syren swimming in our waters, no longer out by the icebergs, was a problem for this village, but it also provided a solution for me.

The next evening, I went into the waters and captured the Syren.

Now, she is in the back of the church, tied to the cross. I crucified her in the hopes that it will remind me of what I have fought for, what you have helped me become. I know you don't believe in God, Doctor. I know you use God to inspire discipline and constraint and devotion in your monsters. You took God and used him to make us human, and it worked.

Right now, I need that discipline more than ever.

The things I want to do to this creature are unspeakable.

I thought the lust inside me had been buried for centuries. In the monastery, it didn't even exist. Here, at the bottom of the world, I didn't dare let it out to play. Not with you, not with anyone. And yet, now that this creature is in my presence, I fear it. I fear it as much as I fear the desire to devour her whole, drink all her blood until she's a shriveled corpse.

I sound like a heathen, a madman. I fear I am turning into both those things, and I am powerless to stop the transformation. The longer this Syren is in my hands, the more I think she won't survive.

That I might not survive.

I know what you would say—that it's best to kill her and be done with it. Don't prolong her torture any longer, that such sins are beneath me. You would say I shouldn't prolong the risk of me snapping and becoming that dreadful thing you once discovered chained to a tree in the motherland. Do whatever you can to not regress.

But think of the people I'll save by keeping her. Instead of killing several times a week, I can feed from her indefinitely. I will save humans, and isn't that all I've wanted to do? Isn't that the heart of my absolution? To make up for all those lives I took, not out of survival, but because killing felt good to the murderer inside me?

Aragon, you would say, you must not feel guilty for what you are made to do. To drink the blood of humans is divine. To torture a sea creature, no matter how much they might deserve it, is beneath us. We must always pick the route that leads to salvation, no matter what logic tells us.

I don't know what I'm going to do. You are clearly on my mind and in my ear, even though you are probably in the middle of the Atlantic by now, getting further and further away from me. I know what you want me to do, but...

Perhaps I am just too curious to do it.

I haven't felt this alive in centuries, Abe.

The excitement, the lust, the dark desires... She is becoming my obsession, my reason for being, and I've only just begun.

Your oldest friend,

The Priest

I lay my fountain pen down and peer at the crinkled paper, waiting for the ink to dry. Outside, an owl hoots before its cry is swallowed by the wind. In a few hours, the sun will be up, and I will have to hold a funeral for the fishermen, followed by mass. I should be brushing up the eulogy —though I didn't know the men well, the village will expect me to act like I did, to say all the right things, to help them make sense of such a tragedy. There has been enough tragedy in these parts, thanks to famine and disease, but this was of another nature.

To my dismay, my thoughts keep drifting to the Syren.

My little fish who won't give me her name.

Perhaps she doesn't have one, or at least not one that translates.

But I feel she does. She just doesn't want me to know, for she thinks it will give me more power.

She's right.

If she wants me to do magic for her, I'll have to know her name to make it work. Something of that magnitude requires it.

Not that I'm considering it.

To do a spell of that enormity requires serious consideration. There are physical sacrifices to be made. The timing has to be right. I can heal those who are hurt, but my talents have been on the humbler side. The idea that I could manipulate her tail to become legs, that I could give her human anatomy, is beyond my scope.

And even if I *was* able to perform it successfully, I would make my whole situation more difficult. A Syren is easily contained. A woman is not. I would have to have additional security measures in place for her. She would still need to be constrained, though perhaps not to a cross. I would have to make the back room into a jail of sorts. She wouldn't be able to yell or call attention to herself. She wouldn't dare let herself be known as she is right now, but if she can pass for an ordinary woman, there's no doubt she'll seek safety and sanctuary in the arms of others.

You should be her sanctuary, I chide myself, folding up the paper.

I know I should be, but I can't be. I'm already picturing

her as a woman, and I'm having a hard time coming to terms with what I'll have to do to keep her here.

It's easier to be a monster when you're dealing with one.

The minute she becomes human, it will only show how much humanity I lack.

But all these thoughts don't help when she is waiting.

I melt wax over the candle flame and pour a neat circle over the letter, sealing it with a press from the clergy ring. Then, I place it on the shelf beside my door to remind me to bring it into town later to send off on the next ship. There's always a chance someone can read it, but the fear of God is strong here. To break the seal is to break a holy man's trust.

Besides, who would believe them?

This time, I take a bucket I have in the cottage, since I'll need the church one for mass, and step out into the frigid wind. It's still dark out, though there's a rim of gray on the east horizon. This will be the fifth time I've made the journey to the well to keep the Syren damp, and I'm already growing tired of it. Perhaps she was lying when she said she needed to keep wet—maybe she's making me do this as some sort of petty revenge.

It's April. It won't be long until the snow falls here in the Southern Hemisphere, and those winds from the unknown seas to the south will make the villages inhospitable. The water in the well will freeze, and people often take refuge in the church when their houses fall due to inclement weather. Taking care of a Syren will be harder than it already is.

Do what the doctor would have you do, I think to myself. *Drain her of her blood, store it, then kill her. Or throw her back in the sea for the sharks if you can't stomach that.*

After I get the water, I head into the church and the back room.

Each time I've unlocked the door and stepped in, the Syren has been waiting for me with hate in her violet eyes. This time, however, she's slumped over, her hair in her face, still damp from the last time I poured water on her.

I clear my throat, noisily locking the door behind me to see if I can wake her. When she still doesn't stir, I feel a flutter of panic in my chest.

I stride over to her and consider throwing the bucket of water on her like I did last time, but somehow, that feels harsh.

I set the bucket down at the base of her tail, noting how much drier it seems. The pinkish-orange color has faded away to a white gray, and each scale is raised and peeling back, drying out before my eyes.

I know I'm taking a chance getting close to her—my hand has only started to repair itself from where she bit off a chunk the other day—but I put my fingers under her chin and lift it up.

"Little fish," I whisper to her.

Her mouth parts slightly, and she lets out a ragged gasp, her lips as dry as her tail. Black eyelashes flutter for a moment, but her eyes don't open.

"You need some water," I tell her, wishing the feeling of concern I have for her well-being wasn't so prominent.

I pick up the bucket and tilt her head back again, pouring some of it into her mouth. It spills over her lips, but she manages to swallow some of it down.

"What do you need?" I ask her. "Food? Was the side of my hand not enough to sustain you?"

She doesn't answer, not even with a pithy remark, and her head slumps against my fingers.

I let her go, trying to think. I go to my desk and grab a spare pair of white bands I wear tied under my collar during mass then bring it back to the bucket. I kneel and soak the cloth in the water before I start pressing it over the fins of her tail. The texture is strange under the cloth, smooth yet rigid, and I carefully make sure each inch is well moistened before I move on to the rest of her tail.

It's a curious feeling, touching a creature like her with such patience and care. It's the first time I've been able to really observe her from up close. Though she may be a monster, she still seems like she belongs in this world, even if it's not her own. Her scales remind me of the trout I would catch in the mountain lakes, while her upper body...

I close my eyes for a moment, pausing with the wet cloth pressed against the side of her tail. I want her to remind me of my wife, of the woman I loved before I lost her. But time has erased so much of that life from me. I remember her, I remember my children, can recall the memories and feelings, but I can't see them anymore. They are nebulous, blank faces. I know what it was like to caress my wife's body, to spill my seed inside her, to lose myself to the throes of passion, but I can't say what color her eyes or hair were or what her skin tasted like.

I don't even remember her name.

But I do remember how she died.

"What are you doing?"

I glance up to see a pair of purple eyes shining down at me.

I clear my throat and take a step back. Why do I feel as if I've been caught doing something I need to feel shame for?

"I was sponging your tail," I tell her. "I thought it might help it soak in better than just tossing a bucket of water on you."

She nods, licking her lips. "Were you going to do the rest of my body?"

My eyes immediately go to her breasts, her nipples contracting into hard, pink pebbles. Though she's always been topless, I go out of my way not to dwell on her nudity, lest I lose my mind.

But now, she's making me look. She even juts out her chest

a little, as if she wants my attention, wants my hands on her with my holy cloth, making her wet. For a moment, I imagine throwing out all constraints, all inhibitions, and having my way with her. I imagine leaving little bites along the full swell of her belly, along her fleshy sides, leaving just the tiniest trails of blood, which I would delicately lap up with my tongue like a feline. I would make her moan that same deep, breathless sound that she expelled when I was drinking her blood.

Then, I would search for her most intimate spot, perhaps a slit hidden along the front length of her tail, pull out my already rigid cock, and thrust inside her until I heard her screams.

"Yes," I hear her whisper, so faint that I might have imagined it.

But it's enough to pull me back in control.

I swallow thickly and avert my eyes from her chest. "I would say my job here is done."

Before I can change my mind, I take the bucket and throw the rest of the water in her face. She cries out, sputtering as the water cascades over her head, and then I pour what's left in the bucket over my own.

I need to slap some sense into myself just as much as she needs it.

"I must conduct a funeral and a sermon," I tell her, wiping the water off my brow. "You'll have to survive while I'm gone. I can get you something to eat if you tell me what that is."

She glares at me, rivulets running down her face. "A human heart. Yours, preferably."

I can't help but give her a tepid smile. "You'll never have my heart, little fish."

Besides, I'm not even human.

The funeral service and the sermon that followed were just what I needed to get myself back on track. Being so wrapped up with the Syren, I'd forgotten what it was like to really perform my role. It's not just about my relationship—or lack thereof—with God; it's about my relationship with the villagers. They look to me for guidance, especially in times of stress and fear. Death may be no stranger to these parts, but gruesome accidents, like the ones that had befallen their neighbors, are few and far between.

Yes, there is the occasional skirmish with the native population who live on the outskirts of the settlements, and every now and then, there is a situation of abuse and brutality between a husband and his wife, or two drunks at the ale house, but for the most part, violence isn't common here, unless it came on the deck of a pirate ship.

These people needed to hear God's words of wisdom, to feel hope and make sense of the world around them. I needed to remember why I am stuck in this outpost. It's not just because I deserve isolation—it's because I have something to offer.

But even though I felt recharged by the time the worshippers left the church, I can't say my mind was completely focused on my flock, for I kept thinking about the wolf I had behind closed doors. While I gave my sermon about living with sin and finding the courage to rise above it with grace, I was wallowing in the muck and the mire by holding that creature captive for my own gains. Though I kept telling myself I needed to do this for my own sake, it didn't stop the urges and shameful thoughts from sinking in.

It didn't stop the truth.

I acted like a man of God when, in truth, I was a man of the Devil.

I was no man at all.

What I really wanted from the Syren wasn't her blood, and it wasn't my survival.

It was *her*.

Just her.

She's been my captive for less than a week, I don't even know her name, and I can't imagine ever letting her go.

If you're going to have an obsession, make sure it's the right one. Abe's words ring in my head. He meant for the monastery and religion to become my obsession because if I was fixated on that, then I wouldn't have time to think about the beast I was trying to escape. And it worked.

But the last thing he'd want is for my obsession to turn to something physical.

At that thought, my skin prickles anxiously. I quickly walk down the aisle and shut the doors to the cold wind, hoping everyone is done with God for the day. I know I am.

My gaze sweeps over the church, making sure everything is in its orderly place, and then I unlock the back room and step inside.

She's where I left her, strapped to the cross. Her eyes are closed, and she looks listless, her tail even paler than earlier.

Pitiful, I can't help but think. *The longer I keep her here, the less of a vibrant, ferocious predator she is.*

I know I'll have to refill the bucket from the well and wet her down again, but first, I need to take off my cassock robes so I don't get them wet. Things take forever to dry out here.

"Father Aragon," the Syren says in a low voice as I place my robes on the chair. The sound of my name snaps my gaze to hers.

I frown, about to ask how she knew my name when she adds, "I have especially good hearing."

Figures that her senses are better than most. If she's like me in that way, she also has a superior sense of taste, sight, and smell.

"Do you actually believe what you're telling those people?" she asks. Her voice is rough, and she licks her parched lips.

"I tell them what they want to hear," I say, walking toward her while adjusting the collar of the black shirt I wear under the robes. "What they *need* to hear. It's not easy to be a settler in these parts. All these people and those who came before them moved from a land much more hospitable than this one. They need God to give them faith, to remind them that everything they're doing is for a reason."

"Is that so? What is the reason?"

I tilt my head as I look at her. Despite how sallow she looks, those eyes of her spark with antagonism. "For their country."

"And what country is that? Is that a kingdom?"

"Yes, the kingdom of Spain."

"Is that where you are from?"

I pause. "Yes. And what kingdom are you from?"

I don't expect her to answer me, so it's surprising when she says, "Limonos, but it doesn't exist anymore."

Interesting. "What happened to it?"

She just stares at me for a moment and then raises her chin. "You deflected my question."

"Just as you're deflecting mine?"

"I asked you first. Do you believe in what you were telling those people? Do you believe in this God you say speaks through you? *Does* he speak through you? Do you hear him?"

Her questions give me much to ponder. I walk toward her, stopping a foot away. "I recite the words I have learned," I admit. "I know what the Bible says, and I know what people expect to hear. God doesn't speak through me. I don't hear him. I don't even think he exists half the time."

"You question his existence, and yet you are a priest? Even I know that is preposterous."

I squint at her in wonder. "How did you learn so much?"

"Why are you pretending to be God's messenger?" she asks instead.

"Because I must," I tell her.

"Why? Is it something you are forced to do in this world?"

"For some, yes," I say carefully.

"For you?"

I sigh and run my hand through my hair. "For me as well. I don't have to do this; I need to do this. It's the structure of religion and God that keeps me on the path I need to be on. It keeps me from…"

Her eyes flash curiously. "From what?"

"I've told you before: it keeps me from becoming a monster, something worse than how I stand before you now. I know you think I'm cruel and immoral, but you really have no idea the lengths I have gone to make sure I hurt as few people in this world as possible." I wait a beat. "I realize that's something you may never understand."

She frowns. "If you're trying to guilt me, it won't work. I don't feel guilt. I kill men not only because they taste good but because they deserve it. I have seen what men to do creatures, to women, to Syrens. One less man is doing this world a favor."

"Then you should realize I am worse than the worst men you've ever heard about or come across. I was turned into a beast by the Devil himself. If there's anything you should be ridding the world of, it's me."

She grins at me with sharp teeth. "Then step a little closer."

I stare at her for a moment, trying to find some sort of plan in all this chaos.

Then, I reach down for her tail, and I pluck out one of the dried scales.

She winces as I slip the scale into my pocket.

"What was that for?" she says, grinding her jaw.

"For the spell," I tell her, and her eyes widen. "For my magic. You said you wanted legs, did you not?"

She nods warily.

"It might take some time—a night or two, a ritual, a new moon. I might need more from you. More scales, your hair, perhaps your blood. And I'll need to figure out what you'll give me in return. This is a bargain, not something done for your benefit."

"You're getting my blood in return," she says.

"I would be getting that from you no matter what I did," I inform her. "You benefit here more than I do. I will have to think of something that will make this worth my while, or perhaps you can think of something yourself. What could you offer me that I would accept?"

I'm pretty sure I wouldn't take anything less than her soul.

"Oh," I add, "I will also need to know your name."

Chapter Eight

LARIMAR

I stare at the priest.

He needs to know my name.

I suppose it's only fair since I know his.

"It's Larimar," I tell him.

His eyes flash appreciatively. "Larimar. That's unusual. What does it mean?"

"It means *soul of the sea* in Limonos," I tell him, feeling a surge of pride. My mother said the name came to her in a dream right before I was born. "What does Aragon mean?"

"Nothing as poetic as yours. It's an area in Spain, where I'm from."

"You were named after where you were born?"

Darkness comes over his gaze. "Not exactly. I was given the name because that's where they found me. I was born with a different name, but...I don't remember it anymore."

"Where who found you?" I ask, intrigued.

"It's not important," he says with a tired sigh.

I shouldn't want to know more about him, but I do.

"Then I shall call you Priest," I tell him. "Father Aragon is a mouthful, even if you are a father."

"I'm not a father," he says quickly before he swallows, the sound audible. "I'm not a father to anyone, not anymore." He looks pained, and then the look passes. "It's just a term of the church, a measure of respect given to a spiritual leader."

"And you are none of those things to me," I tell him. "Not a spiritual leader and not a man of respect. But a priest, that is simple enough."

"Very well," he says. "Priest it is. Now, if you'll excuse me, *Larimar*, I'll go fetch you more water."

He takes the bucket and leaves the room, locking it behind him.

It's only then that I exhale.

He's going to try to give me legs. He's going to try and make me human, or at least able to pass for one. I know it will all come down to his magic and if the spell is successful, and I shouldn't get my hopes up, but I can't help myself.

For the last eleven years, all I wanted was to follow in my sister's literal footsteps. All I wanted was to be able to walk amongst humans and find her. I knew searching the seas was futile, dangerous. I had told Asherah as much. She learned the hard way when those pirates pulled her up from the depths. I learned it when I stumbled upon Syrens I shouldn't have.

And yet, even after losing both my sisters, I didn't give up. I knew that this drive, this obsession with finding Maren, would eventually put me on the right path. I would get where I needed to go.

Maren traded in her fins for legs so she could become human. Some said she even married a prince from some far-off land. I knew she wouldn't be found in the ocean, but until I had legs, that's the only place I could look.

I also know that if Priest is successful in my transformation, I'll have other problems I'll need to deal with. If I even make it out of here alive, it's the question of finding Maren in this big, dry, foreign world. It can't be easy, but nothing about this can be.

So now, I have to figure out what I'm supposed to offer him in exchange for this. He doesn't know my plans. He doesn't know about Maren. I have to give him exactly what he wants and then some, then wait for the right moment to escape.

That's all I have. A moment. I'm a fighter. I've survived this long, and I know that if I play my cards right, I can find my freedom at the first opportunity.

Syrens are sexual beings by nature. I know of our reputation when it comes to the world and will of men. We are known to seduce and destroy. It's how we charm so many men into the water, how we kill so well.

This priest isn't like most men, that much I know. He talks about being a blood-drinker and a monster, and clearly, he is both.

But I see desire in him.

That's what I'm good at.

Seeing desire and exploiting it.

He doesn't want to give in to it because it scares him. That's why, whenever our encounters sway towards something intimate, he panics. I see it in his eyes, torn apart between his lust and his need for control. It's as if he can hurt me all he wants, but the moment he actually *craves* me, that's when he thinks it's a step too far.

It's his weak spot and exactly what I need to manipulate to my advantage.

Seduce, destroy, escape.

Unfortunately for me, the priest takes his time to work on his magic. It's hard to know what day it is here when there is no glimpse of the outside world. Minutes, hours, days? A good internal clock is necessary when you're living in the deepest depths of the ocean, where sun and light can't penetrate, but here, everything blends together. I only know time is ticking away by how dry my tail is getting and how parched I feel from the inside out, like no amount of water could ever quench me.

Priest comes and goes, ever so serious, always with that permanent line between his dark brows that arch over his eyes. Sometimes, he just throws a bucket of water at me, brimming with some simmering anger. Other times, he takes his time, soaking each inch of my tail with a wet cloth.

When he works this way, I can't help but hold my breath and watch him. His touch is so methodical, thoughtful, even tender. I feel as if I'm getting a glimpse of his humanity, of the man beneath the monster. It's in these moments that I want to ask him questions about who he was before. He had said he had another name he doesn't remember, a previous life when he was a mortal man. I want to know more about him.

But I've learned that asking him questions works the same way as him asking me questions. It makes him clam up, so I keep my mouth shut and let him touch me. When I feel like putting part of my plan into action, I sink against his hands, or I might moan a little, as if I'm getting some perversion out of it.

He always stops after that, but I want to make sure I have that power over him.

I want him scared of me, feeling desire and lust for me.

Because, eventually, he will have to snap.

I know enough about holy men to know that they take vows, and I will do all I can to make him shred his vows to pieces.

It's my only means of escape.

"Larimar?" I hear his rich voice ask in the darkness.

I raise my head and open my eyes to see the faint outline of his figure in the black. I didn't even hear him come in.

He puts a jar down on the table and starts lighting candles, the flickering glow illuminating his face. Darkness pools beneath his heavy brows and slashes under his high cheekbones, making him look more dangerous and otherworldly than usual. His black clothes only add to the effect of a man comprised of shadows.

A man of the night.

It's always night here.

He picks up the spikes that had been in the cross and comes over to me, sliding them into his pockets.

"In the event that something goes wrong tonight," he says solemnly, "I'll need to take as much blood as I can."

I gulp. "Are you planning on something going wrong?"

He gives his head a small shake, but the hesitation in his eyes doesn't inspire confidence. "Magic can be tricky. Sometimes, it uses you as much as you use it." He pauses. "There's a chance you could die in the process. Do you still want me to do this?"

My brows rise. "A chance I could die?" I repeat.

"I told you," he says patiently, "I haven't done a spell of this magnitude before. Certainly not since I turned. I can't offer you any guarantees. Do you still want to proceed?"

I want him to talk about what turning means, but I suppose I'll have to save that for after the spell.

If I survive.

I stare into the swirling ocean blue of his eyes, but I can't see my future there. I know he doesn't want me to die; if I do, he also loses. But in the end, my life isn't much to him. He'll consume my blood until I have none to give and move on.

I nod. I've come this far. I can't give up now. I owe it to my sisters.

"Then have you thought about what you will offer me for my services?" he asks, turning his back to me as he goes to the jar on the table and picks it up.

"I figured whatever I thought of, you would have a better idea."

"You're probably right about that," he says, peering at the jar in his hands. The bottom quarter is filled with some clear liquid, and there are some things floating in it, most likely my scales and strands of hair he unceremoniously plucked from my head the other day, along with some green herbs. Then, he picks up the two silver chalices he used to collect and drink my blood on the first night, placing them on the floor directly under my wrists.

I know where this is going.

"Can you not just bite me?" I ask, trying to keep the fear from my voice.

The corner of his mouth lifts. "Oh, I will. Don't worry."

He sets the jar under one arm as he places a spike against my left wrist and pulls out a rusty hammer from his pocket, the kind I used to see at Jorge's shipyard.

I don't even have time to brace myself.

He pounds the spike directly into my wrist with an explosion of pain that brings acid up my throat, causing me to scream in pure agony. Gray fuzz forms at the corners of my vision, and I feel myself starting to slip away.

"I thought you would be used to pain by now," he comments quietly as the blood pours from my wrist into the chalice. "Perhaps you're becoming more human by the second."

He crosses in front of me and does the same to the other wrist.

This time, I bite down on my tongue until it bleeds. I'm reminded of Maren, how the sea witch cut out her tongue. Maybe it's part of the bargain.

The blood spills from my wrists, and he places the jar underneath, letting a few drops splash into the contents. Satisfied, he takes the jar away and holds it out in front of me.

"I need you to drink this," he says simply.

"Fuck you." I scowl through the pain, unable to keep from whimpering. The sound of my blood hitting the chalices echoes.

He stares at me thoughtfully, and I'm tempted to spit on him again, but he would only like that, especially with the taste of blood in my mouth.

"Before you drink it," he says, his voice measured, "I need you to agree to the terms of the bargain. I will do my best to grant you legs. In the process, I will do what I can to keep your Syren blood intact. This might mean you'll have your teeth and your claws and your gills. It might not. It is a risk I am willing to take, but you must give me something more than just your blood."

"What?" I ask through gritted teeth. I feel as if I'm growing weaker by the second.

"You must promise to belong to me forever, body and soul."

I blink at him, the pain fading for a moment while I try to understand his meaning.

"Body and soul?"

His eyes darken. "You will always be mine, Larimar. You will always be bound to me."

That's all I have to do? I can tell him I will always be his, and he'll just give me what I want? "Alright," I say warily.

He gives me a cruel little smile and takes a step forward, still holding out the jar. "I'm no fool, little fish. You may think you can tell me what I want to hear, but this spell will bind you to it. No matter where you go, I will find you. I will take you back, take what's mine. I know you mean to escape any way you can, but even if you're successful one day, I will stop at nothing to hunt you down. This magic will ensure I find you, no matter how long it takes. And believe me, you won't want me to find you."

I don't say anything to that, just continue to breathe through the pain, which is slowly abating. Why does he want me so much? Is it just because of my magic blood? Or does he actually want me? My body? My company?

"In addition," he goes on in a clipped voice, "this spell will remain entirely at my bidding. If I ever need to turn you back into a Syren, tail and all, all I need to do is immerse you in the ocean. The salt water will reverse the magic. I can take it all away as easily as I can give it." He waits a beat, long lashes flicking as his eyes scan my features. "Well? Do you accept this bargain?"

"Do I have a choice?"

His eyes dance at that. "Don't sell yourself short, little fish. You know you always have a choice, even if it feels like you don't."

I exhale as heavily as I can. Even though I've gotten used to being tied to the cross with my tail supporting me from the bottom, it's still challenging to get a proper breath into my lungs.

Though I suppose I won't have to worry about my tail much longer. I only hope my feet touch the ground.

Feet. At the thought of having feet, my heart starts to race. I'd be lying if I said that seeking out Maren was my only reason for wanting legs. The truth is, I want to know what it's like to live in this world. Maren was fascinated with the land of humans from a young age, but I kept my curiosity to myself. I pretended it held no interest to me, though, secretly, I wished I could be something other than a Syren.

And now, under the worst circumstances possible, my wish is about to come true.

"I accept," I tell him.

"Good girl," he says, his face impassive as he brings the rim of the jar to my lips. "Now, drink up."

I open my mouth, and he pours the vile concoction inside.

"*Caudam capio et tibi pedes dabo*," he chants in a low voice, in a language I don't understand. Chills run through my body as he continues. "*Vocem capio et servitutem tibi trado*."

But as I start swallowing it down, he grabs the top of my hair, making a fist, and then sinks his teeth into my jugular.

I try to scream, but I choke on the liquid, forcing me to swallow the rest.

Priest keeps sucking, drawing my blood into his mouth in greedy gulps, and that dizzying sensation from earlier is back. I'm bleeding from both my wrists, and he's feeding from my neck—I'm losing too much blood at once.

"Priest!" I try to yell, but I can't. The word only comes out as a whisper. I try to scream instead, that horrible sound that only Syrens can produce to stun their prey, but though I feel my throat vibrate with the effort, only a harsh whisper emerges.

What have you done to me?

But then I feel a tightness around my body, squeezing me all over like a rope but from the inside out, and I realize that it's only just beginning.

A loud crack suddenly fills the room, a burst of bright light, and it's as if lightning has burst through and struck me right in my core.

I scream and scream, more ragged whispers, and it feels like my tail is being split in two, burned down the middle and split apart. I can feel my bones break, my muscles sever, before fusing back together. My scales quiver and then sink into my body like a million needles. My blood feels like it's boiling inside my veins.

At some point, Priest lets go of my hair, unhooks his fangs, and steps back. I writhe on the cross, crying out, moaning, trying to escape the pain of my lower body, and then...

I hear Priest suck in his breath.

I manage to open my eyes, too afraid to see what's happened to me.

He meets my gaze.

I expect to see violence and excitement in them.

Instead, there's lust.

His pupils are dark pools of desire.

I glance down at my body and gasp.

My tail is gone. Below the waist, I have a pair of legs—pale, like the rest of my body, hairless, knees, ankles, feet, toes. They all burn like they're on fire, but at least the pain is smoldering.

"It worked," Priest says thickly, his gaze between my legs, right at my new womanhood. This is what is driving the lust in him, a woman bare in front of him.

I use this to my advantage.

I'm standing on my tiptoes—toes!—with just enough leverage to keep the pressure off my shoulders and arms, but I decide the pain is worth the gamble. I slowly lift both legs, stretching them out. My shoulders pull forward, and my lungs are squeezed from the pressure, but I watch Priest's eyes as I open my new thighs for him, as I show off my most sinful parts.

He's practically licking his lips.

"Touch me," I whisper to him.

He blinks and takes a step back, finally meeting my eyes. "Pardon?"

"I want to know if I can feel. I want to know what my skin feels like. Touch me."

I reach out with one leg, pointing my toes at him teasingly, rubbing them up the hard muscle of his thigh, up, up, up. Despite his black clothing, I can already see that he's hard.

He swallows, and I see him trying to think, trying to use logic.

"Grab my foot," I tell him, giving him a starting point.

He slowly reaches down and takes my foot in his hand just before I can rub against his erection pushing against the front of his trousers. His fingers are strong and hard, his palm surprisingly warm. I didn't realize how good it felt to have your feet held. Our tails are so tough and scaley we don't feel much of anything.

Carefully, he grabs my calf with his other hand and gives it a soft squeeze, supporting it and alleviating some of the pressure on my shoulders. Then, while his eyes are locked to mine, he raises my foot up to his mouth, my knee bending.

My breath hitches, wondering what he's about to do.

He presses my largest toe against his lips.

Please don't tell me he's about to eat my toes before I have a chance to enjoy them.

But when he opens his mouth, he gently sucks my toe. His teeth don't make an appearance.

My eyes flutter closed, head back against the wood, because I've never felt anything like this before. Is this normal for humans? Toe-sucking? Or is it because every part of me is brand new?

"Does that feel good?" he murmurs as he pulls my toe out of his mouth, caressing it with his tongue as he keeps staring at me intently.

I nod, letting out a breathless moan. It does feel good, especially as I start imagining what that tongue might feel like on other parts of me. Still, I am exaggerating, because I know the more aroused I seem, the more he's going to want to explore the rest of me.

And the more I can exploit his weaknesses.

His gaze drops to my mouth, then to my breasts, my nipples hardening from the graze of his tongue, then to my belly and the shadows between my thighs. His nostrils flare, and I realize he's sniffing me. A muscle feathers on his jaw, his pupils expanding until his eyes seem black.

He starts running his tongue over the top of my foot now, his hands working their way down my calf, the surprisingly sensitive spot under my knee, down my thighs.

Then he lowers my leg back down, seeming to hesitate, but I take the opportunity to wrap my legs around his waist. It's keeping me supported and him enclosed.

A trap.

His gaze falls between my legs, and he inhales sharply again.

"Please," I whisper to him. "Touch me there. I need to know if I can feel."

He frowns, but it's a look of utter helplessness.

I bite my lip, but I'm really biting back my smile.

I might be the one nailed to a cross, but I'm finally in control.

Chapter Nine

PRIEST

Larimar's words ring in my head.

Touch me.

Touch me there.

And there is no mistaking what she means.

Her supple, surprisingly strong legs are wrapped around my waist, her heels touching at the small of my back, and directly in front of my hardened cock is her cunt. Small, wet, so perfectly pink.

I think I might burst into flames. Damnation is coming for me in one fell swoop.

Part of me is sounding the alarm, telling me to get out of there. The spell worked, and she's a human. I gave her what she wanted; she doesn't deserve anything else.

But I *want* to touch her.

I think I might die if I don't.

Not for her, but for *me.*

Because I barely remember what it was like to explore a woman's body.

Because it's been centuries since I took my vows.

Because I want, crave, need to feel her from the inside. I want to touch, suck, taste this ripe new cunt.

Aragon, you're becoming an animal, the tiny voice in my head says. *Tread carefully, or you might stay an animal.*

But why should I deny myself what I truly am?

Oh, I am truly bargaining with myself now.

"Please," she says again on another ragged, whispered moan. With the spell, I took away her ability to scream or raise her voice, so she'll always be stuck whispering, but these breathless sounds are like a lightning bolt to my cock.

Fuck it.

With a grunt, I run my hand down the downy softness of her inner thigh, so pale, so perfect, until my fingertips brush against her bare cunt, warm and smooth as velvet.

Christ, I swear, though he can't help me now.

No one can.

She sucks in her breath and stares at me in such a way that I feel like I'm falling down a rabbit hole. And I thought bloodsuckers were the only ones who could compel. Then again, she is a Syren. It's what they're known for.

And in this moment, I don't care.

I slide my hand up until my fingers meet her where she's hot and wet, so damn wet, and I fear my cock might break through my trousers.

She groans, her head rolling back, her mouth open, and I feel like a starving man at a banquet, ravenous and wild and unsure where to start. I want to lick the blood that still trickles from the puncture wounds I left in her neck. I want to kiss that hot, wet mouth. I want to take my cock out and thrust it inside her until the breath is knocked out of her lungs, another way of nailing her to this cross.

Your vows, I remind myself. *Remember your vows, Father.*

I grunt in frustration and then drive two fingers inside her instead.

She gasps, staring at me with wide eyes as I start pumping my hand, letting her coat me. My thumb slides to her clit, swollen already with need, and I can't help but moan myself, the feeling of her satiny smooth, slick skin enough to make me lose my mind.

"Can you feel this?" I murmur, leaning in to lick up the side of her neck, tasting her sweat and blood.

"Yes," she cries out softly. "Don't stop, please."

The word *please* sets me off. The soft begging. My God, all I want is for her to beg me for the rest of my life.

"You want me to make you come?" I ask, my voice ragged and raw as I suck at the soft skin beneath her ear as I continue to work my fingers in and out of her, adding another, feeling her drip down my hand. "Do you want to know what that feels like with this new cunt of yours?"

She lets out a whimpering noise, and I slide my thumb harder around her clit.

God, she's perfect.

She's so perfect.

"Oh!" She gasps, and I can feel her body tighten like a knot, smell her desire reach the threshold.

Then, her legs tighten around me, her breath caught in her throat, and she goes off like cannon fire. Her eyes roll back in her head, chest brushing against mine, back arched as if a woman possessed. She squeezes my fingers as she comes, bucking against my hand like a wild horse, her torso clenching with each gyration.

I don't think I've ever seen something so heavenly before.

She's an angel.

She's a devil.

She'll be my downfall.

While her breathy moans fill the air, I lean in and suck at her neck, lapping up the trickles of blood I left earlier. To my delight, the fresh blood that comes out of her tastes the same as before, creating an electrical storm inside my ribs.

She hasn't lost her power; she still has the blood of a Syren.

I pull back, licking my lips, and brush her hair off her shoulder. There are faint lines from where her gills used to be, three pinkish scars.

She's human now, and she can still give me everything I need.

For now.

For eternity.

Bound by magic, bound by blood.

I straighten up, removing my fingers from between her legs. While she looks at me with dazed, sated eyes, I slide my fingers over my tongue, making sure she can see how much I enjoy every inch of her. She's delectable inside and out, and my cock throbs angrily, begging to finally come, but now that she's panting, her legs growing limp against me, I have a moment to think, to gain clarity.

She wants me to lose focus. If I fuck her, not only am I throwing away my vows, but I'm one step closer to losing control of both the monster *and* the man. I have to hold on to something.

"How do I taste?" she whispers, her gaze focused on my mouth.

I raise my brow at her boldness. Then again, I shouldn't be so surprised. She may have a human cunt, but she's still a Syren underneath.

"Like the seas," I tell her, sucking the rest of her off my fingers. "Like uncharted waters."

And I'm the first to discover them.

The sound of blood sprinkling into the chalice draws my eye. Her blood from the cross has slowed, but the cups are full, and I can't afford to let her bleed anymore.

I unhook her legs from around me and go to my desk, my

cock aching as I grab the sage bundle. I light it briefly on a flame before blowing it out. I proceed to yank the spikes out of her bloodied wrists, one at a time, the pain causing her voice to catch in her throat, and I quickly press the burning herbs against the open wounds. I murmur my spell over and over until the wounds begin to heal.

She looks to me with big eyes. "Might you let me down too?"

I see what's happening. She thinks because I made her come, I'm about to get sweet on her.

I smirk. "I already gave you ecstasy with my fingers. Don't get greedy, little fish."

Then, I turn and walk to the door, leaving her naked on the cross.

I don't plan to be gone for long. I know she can stand on her toes to support herself, but soon, she'll be too exhausted. She has to know that she is at my mercy, that I am not at hers, and yet I don't want to go out of my way to be cruel.

Not unless she deserves it.

So, I steal into the night and head north. It's cold, the smell of frost in the air, and the wind is just a whisper. I hear sounds in the bush, animals scurrying away as I run through the stunted forest. I move fast, a blur to the naked eye, heading toward the town of Ciudad del Rey Don Felipe. The general and his wife live there, and she wears fine gowns that look as if they would fit Larimar.

Tonight, I am a thief.

The town is quiet, with only a few babbling voices coming from a pub at the end of the muddy road. I've done a house call at the general's when his aging mother was on her deathbed, so I know my way around the house.

I climb the side of it and look through the window. The general and his wife are asleep in bed, and though their house is still tiny in comparison to one they would have had in Spain, I know she has a dressing room for her gowns.

Truth is, I'm not stealing clothes so Larimar can feel more comfortable. It's so *I* can be more comfortable. Her breasts were always on display, but now that I'll see that pink cunt of hers every time I come into the back room, I fear I won't be able to function. If I end up letting her down from the cross, that will make matters even worse.

I climb through the window of the next room over and find her wardrobe. I do my best to take what a woman would wear: linen shifts for sleeping and under clothes, whalebone stays, a petticoat, three stomachers with matching gowns, plus a pair of stockings and boots. I grab a woolen cape with a hood, hanging it off the top of my head before I head back down the window and into the darkness again.

If anyone sees me running through the town and back into the woods with a pile of women's garments in my hands, it must be quite the sight.

When I get back to the church, only a few hours have passed, but Larimar looks as petulant as when I left her, though there is a strange smugness in her eyes. Not that I stare at her eyes for long—it's hard to keep them focused when she's so terribly, beautifully nude.

I place the pile of clothes on the table and walk toward her, stopping when I realize the cause of that haughty look.

She's knocked over both chalices, her blood spilled in either direction.

Serves me right for not removing them right away.

"I suppose you're proud of yourself," I comment, swiping up a cup from the floor. If I were any more of an animal, I'd get on my hands and knees and lick the blood up, but I'm not about to supplicate myself in front of her like that.

I grumble to myself and go to the other chalice when she suddenly kicks me in the face, my teeth clanking together.

"Fuck!" I holler, holding my jaw. That actually hurt. If I was human, that would leave a bruise.

I glare at her, willing the anger inside me to rise so I can lash out at her.

Yet I can't help but be impressed, perhaps a little turned on. Doesn't help that she's still so incredibly naked.

"Do you feel better now?" I ask her mildly, wriggling my jaw. She has quite the kick.

"A little," she says. "I was waiting to see your face when you saw I spilled all your blood, and I wasn't disappointed."

"Careful," I warn, putting the chalices away. "The more you spill, the more I'll have to take." Thankfully, I got my fill anyway, and now that I know she still has Syren blood, I don't have to stockpile.

"How come I can barely talk?" she asks as I start rifling through her stolen clothes.

"Because I took away your ability to yell or scream," I explain. Women have always worn so many layers it's hard to know where to start.

She lets out a small cry of despair, and I pick up one of the gowns, this one a dusky blue gray, and move over to her, holding it up to her shoulders to see if it will, in fact, fit.

"You took away my voice?" she whispers.

"The strength of it," I tell her. The gown does make her eyes seem punchier and more vibrant. "I'm not about to let you holler for help now that you can pass for human. Better than the chain in your mouth, wouldn't you agree?"

She makes a disgruntled noise. "What are the clothes for?"

I give her a steady look. "For you to wear, quite obviously."

"Why?"

"For modesty."

She snorts. "I've been naked this whole time. Why start now?"

I clear my throat and head back to the table to gather the rest of the items that go with it. "Things are different now. You were an animal. Now, you are a human."

"And you just had your fingers inside me," she points out.

My cock twitches, and I growl lightly in response.

A moment passes.

"Are you ashamed of my body?" she asks, quieter now.

I glance at her over my shoulder, puzzled. "Why would you say that?"

Her expression turns vulnerable, her eyes soft, lips practically pouting. It's like a stab to the chest.

"I don't know," she says, looking down at her legs. "I don't know if mine is normal or not. It seems normal, but...you brought those clothes to cover me up, like you don't want to look at me."

God help me.

I stride over to her and put my hand at her face, making her look at me. Her cheeks seem so small and warm against my palm.

"I am a man of the cloth," I say, lowering my voice now that my face is so close to hers. "I know I'm not a particularly good one, but I am trying my best. I might do things that seem blasphemous, and maybe they are, but I'm not about to throw away my vows for you. Your body, this beautiful, perfect body, is a distraction. It's a road to Hell, straighter than any other I've been on."

"But you..." She trails off.

"Yes. I am a blood-drinker. I do bad things, things that would make your skin crawl. I am a man, and I'll never be rid of my monster. But I'm trying to leave my past behind me, and

I still need to drink blood to survive. I do what I can to make peace with that. But this...you..."

"Touch me again," she whispers, batting her long lashes. "If I am beautiful, then touch me again."

I shake my head. If I touch her again where she wants to be touched, I'm going to end up fucking her on this cross, plain and simple.

"I'm taking you down, and then I'm getting you dressed," I tell her, reaching for the ropes. "That's the most I can do."

"But you've already broken your vows by making me orgasm, haven't you?" she asks.

I give her a wry smile. "Not quite. The devil is in the details."

I suddenly pull the rope loose from around the wood, and she cries out, half of her slumping forward. I quickly reach under her free arm to prop her up before I undo the other rope until both arms are free.

She lets out a deep moan, and I know that if I hadn't taken away her voice, she would be screaming.

She collapses right into my arms, and I wrap them around her, holding her firmly but not tight enough to cause her more pain. I can smell her hair, that sugared lemon and saltwater scent doing something foolish to my heart, and the fact that I'm actually holding her—naked—is dizzying.

"Your shoulders are dislocated," I tell her. "They will take time to heal."

I attempt to pull her forward away from the cross, but she stumbles to her knees, whimpering in agony. "It will take you time to learn how to walk too," I say, bending down to scoop her up in my arms. I'm reminded of a few weeks ago, when I first brought her out of the ocean and carried her into the church. It feels like so much has changed since then, and yet I can't forget why she's here in the first place.

She's my sustenance.

She's my *meal*.

And if I was back in that ocean with her, I have no doubt I would be hers.

I place her in the chair by the desk, positioning her so she's upright. Her arms hang helplessly at her sides; she won't be able to use them for some time.

"Normally, I would suggest bathing before getting dressed," I tell her. "Cleanliness is godliness, after all. But I've given you so many baths already, I think you'll be fine."

She doesn't say anything to that, just sits there looking miserable.

I grab one of the linen shifts. "One of these is to wear at night when you go to sleep, the other underneath your gown." I lift her limp arms and manage to get the shift on her, pulling it down over her breasts. The fabric is thin enough that I can still see the faint outline of her nipples as they poke through.

I grunt at the sight and then quickly grab her stays to cover her up further.

"Why are you giving me more clothes?" she asks, a pitiful sound to her voice as she tries to twist away from me. "Isn't this enough? It's not as if I'm ever leaving this room."

I pause, considering that. I'm so used to never sleeping that it didn't cross my mind that she might be tired, so getting all these layers on her might not be necessary.

I put the stays back with the rest of the garments and lean against the desk, studying her. "Perhaps one day, you'll be allowed to go out into the world with me at your side. Perhaps one day, you won't want to leave here."

Her gaze hardens. "I would die before I would ever want that."

My smile is bitter in return. "I know you would." I straighten up. "I should make you a bed. I think if I pull out two of the back pews and—"

"The floor is fine," she says sharply. "Just go. I'd like to be alone."

I consider that for a moment. "Alright," I say, grabbing the gowns and petticoats and tossing them onto the floor beside her. "That can be your bed, then, since you don't wish to wear them."

She rolls her eyes. "You're acting like a child, upset that I'm not appreciating your gesture."

"I told you, the clothes are for my benefit, not yours," I tell her. Then I reach down and grab her by the waist, hauling her straight out of the chair and placing her roughly on the pile. "There."

I stare down at her, looking so helpless in that shift, with her lifeless arms and untrained legs, but I'm learning not to take anything at face value when it comes to her. I have no doubt she is in pain, that she really is powerless for the time being, but she's still an opportunist through and through.

I can't take any chances.

I grab the ropes off the cross and stride back over to her.

"What are you doing?" she whispers, panic in her voice.

I grab her ankles and quickly tie them together, then grab her arms and pull them behind her back, forcing her on her stomach on the mound of clothes.

"You still have Syren blood," I tell her, securing the rope around her wrists. "That might mean you still have a Syren's strength. I can't afford to lose you at this stage of the game."

I get up and peer down at her. Her shift has lifted, exposing part of her full, round bottom. It takes all my conviction not to bend over and sink my teeth into it.

"If the pain gets to be too much, feel free to have some of the wine. Enjoy your time alone," I add, though I wince at the sound of my voice. In all my long, storied life, I have never heard such petulance in it.

I really am acting like a child.
Which means she really is getting under my skin.

Chapter Ten

LARIMAR

Pain pulls me out of a dreamless sleep, from darkness into dying candlelight. Every part of my body hurts; my arms are numb when they aren't on fire, and my legs ache from the inside out. Even my cunt is sore from where Priest worked his fingers hard. Not that it hurt at the time—at the time, I only felt a greedy sort of bliss—but I suppose I'm getting used to having a whole new anatomy.

It doesn't help that I've been dumped in an unceremonious pile on top of these garments, my ankles and wrists bound together. He said I could drink wine if I wanted to dull the pain, but getting to the casks won't be an easy feat.

Then again, what else do I have to do?

With a groan, I slowly sit up, the room spinning slightly. My arms were useless even before he tied them behind my back, but I'll have to do what I can. I lean back on my rear, not used to having such a soft, natural cushion either—tails never had a lot of fat in them. I start moving my legs in unison so it's pulling me forward across the floor. Priest may have thought he was immobilizing me by tying my legs together, but this is how my body worked until recently.

I move toward the casks, pretending I still have a tail, then use my feet to push one off the stack. It bounces onto the floor, but the wood doesn't break. I use my toes to turn it on its side and then remove the cork just as I had seen Priest do.

Red liquid spills out onto the wooden floor, and I sniff the air, making sure it is wine and not my own blood—or anyone else's blood. Then, I lie down beside it, the wine splashing over my face as I place my lips over the spout.

I suck the cask dry. Perhaps wine tastes better when you're a human.

It certainly feels better. It's not long until I pass out, back into that dreamless sleep again. I know I should be making plans now that I have a human body, now that I have a chance of survival in this world once I escape.

But my thoughts soon fade to nothing.

"Larimar?"

I hear a faraway voice.

"Larimar?" the voice says again, louder now.

I feel a tapping at the side of my face.

I can only smile. This must be a dream. A man has come to save me.

"You're drunk," the voice says. "Come on."

The tapping gets hard.

I feel a twinge of pain from a slap, but it's not enough to... *Ow!*

Something pierces the skin on my neck.

My eyes fly open, and all I see is long, thick black hair as Priest buries his fangs into me. I attempt to scream, but instead, it's that horrible feeling of having the scream die inside you. Nothing comes out but raw, ragged gasps.

Priest lifts his head and looks at me through his dark lashes, amusement dancing in his eyes, a trail of blood trickling from the corner of his mouth.

What a beautiful, evil creature he is.

"I'm just getting you back for spilling my blood," he says in a low voice. "Or should I say, your blood." He reaches up and brushes a strand of hair off my face. I can't help but flinch at the gesture. "Plus, I can see that you got into the wine. I brought you some food to help with that."

I blink as he grabs my shoulders and pulls me up until I'm sitting with my legs tucked to the side. It's only then that I notice he's holding a wooden plate with a few slices of bread on it smeared with something shiny and yellow. He puts it down and starts to untie my hands.

"Promise you'll behave, and you can have something to eat."

I nod eagerly as he undoes the rope. My wrists ache from having been restrained for so long.

"Here," he says, handing the plate to me. "It will make you feel better. You shouldn't drink wine on an empty stomach."

"My stomach isn't empty," I manage to say as I take the plate from him, my hands shaking, the muscles weak. "The last thing I ate was your hand."

A ghost of a smile comes across his lips. It's rare to see him smile—then again, there's never been much to smile about— but when he does, even if it's just a hint of it, it lights up his whole face, as if, in that moment, he's no longer a man of shadows.

You shouldn't want him to smile at you, I tell myself and bring my gaze down to the bread. *It just means he wants to eat you.*

"Have you had human food before?" he asks, and to my

surprise, he sits down across from me on the floor. "Have you had bread?"

I nod. "Jorge would sometimes bring me scraps from his dinner, though I often shared it with his dog."

"So, tell me: who was this Jorge?" he asks. He's trying to sound casual, but there's a strain in his voice.

Is it possible he's jealous? Should I lie?

Maybe a little.

"Jorge was someone I befriended," I say cautiously. "A human. He worked for his father's shipyard in a place called Acapulco. He said it belonged to New Spain. Does this place belong to New Spain too?" I gesture to the room with the plate.

Priest nods. "We are in Chile, but it is part of the same empire. It's funny; you've never once asked where you are."

"Maybe it's never been important until now."

Maybe I never had hope of escaping until now.

"So, this Jorge, he taught you how to speak?"

I nod. "He did. We met every evening after his dinner. He and his family lived on one of the large ships. We would meet at the end of one of the docks, out of sight, stayed up most of the night together for a year, at the very least. He taught me everything he could about humanity and human nature."

He clenches his jaw slightly. Ah, he does seem jealous.

"Did this Jorge end up being your first..."

"Love?" I ask before I grin. "No. Jorge was ten years old. The only reason I was talking to him was because I..."

I trail off and nibble on the hard crust of the bread. I don't feel like talking about Maren right now. If I do, he'll know why I wanted legs.

"You..."

I shake my head. "I was curious. That's all." I motion to the plate. "What's the yellow smear?" I ask, peering at it.

"Butter," he explains. "There's a lady in the village who

always brings me bread on Fridays, and she puts salt and dried kelp in the butter. I thought you might appreciate that."

Interesting that he brought me something I might appreciate.

"That's rather kind of her to bring you that."

"People are often kind to the village priest," he says. "They think they do it out of the goodness of their own hearts, but it's so they can win favor with God. In the end, I get gifts."

I pick up the piece of bread and bite the edge of it, chewing thoughtfully for a moment. The butter is good—it tastes like the sea—but Jorge's bread was better.

"Can you eat this? Or can you only have blood?"

"I can eat food. There are some things in this village I still consider appetizing, but it doesn't sustain me the way blood does."

"And none of the villagers know the truth about you?" I ask.

He gives his head a small shake. "I think some of the soldiers suspect since they aren't as devout. The villagers, they know I'm different, that I'm not like them deep down, but they pass it off as me being a messenger for the divine. They can excuse it, make sense of it, because God is involved."

"But how do you manage? What...who did you...*consume* before I came along?"

Something like shame washes over his features, and he looks away, his eyes going to the cross. "I wasn't always alone here. I had a friend, Abe. My oldest friend. He saved me from myself, brought me here so I could learn to be human outside of the monastery, so I could hide from those sinful parts of myself. He was my moral compass, and he killed others so I wouldn't have to. He never had to worry about losing control."

"When did he leave?"

"Over a month ago," he says in a quiet voice. He sighs

softly. "He would be quite disappointed in me if he knew what I was doing."

"And what are you doing?"

He glances at me out of the corner of his eye. "Keeping a woman as livestock."

I swallow uneasily. That is what I am, isn't it? First, he saw me as an animal, a creature, and now, even with legs, his view of me hasn't changed.

"What would Abe tell you to do?" I ask, trying to appeal to this moral compass Priest has lost sight of. *Would he tell you to let me go?* I think hopefully.

"Abe would tell me to kill you," he says plainly. "Alas, he isn't one for sentiment. He's a doctor. He would tell me to kill you and be done with it, then continue to hunt in the villages or in the native settlements for my prey, just as he would do for me."

Alright. Perhaps Priest needs a new compass.

"And my blood allows you not to hunt."

His mouth twists. "Your blood gives me more vitality than I thought possible. Beyond that, I can go for weeks without another drop. By keeping you, by feeding from you every now and then, you're saving a lot of that humanity you learned about. Jorge would be proud."

"Don't bring his name into this, trying to justify what you're doing."

He shrugs. "Fine. But I *can* justify it. And if you cared about human life at all, you would appreciate it."

"Well, I don't care about human life," I tell him. "If you've forgotten already, I eat humans."

"You did," he points out. "Would you have eaten Jorge?"

I jerk my chin back at the question. "Of course not."

"Then there are some humans you care about, aren't there?"

I ignore that. Jorge was the exception.

"So how many of your kind are there in the world?" I ask, switching the subject. "Are you all priests and doctors? Are you all trying to battle some monster inside?"

He gives me a measured look. "There are monsters inside everyone, Larimar. The only difference is we're the only ones who know how to deal with them." He pauses. "But no, most of us aren't priests. Only the ones at the monastery. But we were a different...breed."

"What does that mean?"

His sun-bright blue eyes stare at me for a moment, and I feel unsteady, like the room has started to spin. It's hard to tell if it's the wine or if he's trying to do some sort of magic on me.

But then the sensation stops, and he looks away, letting out a long exhale, running his slender fingers over the shiny fabric of the dresses we're sitting on.

"They say there is a name for us now," he says in a low voice. "Vampyres. We've always called ourselves bloodsuckers, blood-drinkers. The fact that there is a name for us is troubling. It means the humans are starting to catch on."

"I'm sure they've noticed people going missing, drained of blood with teeth marks in their neck," I comment.

"We know to be careful," he says quickly. "Or, should I say, most of us do. When I say I'm part of a different breed, I'm part of the ones who aren't careful. You see, there are two ways Vampyres are created. The first and most common is that you are born to Vampyre parents. If you're a female, you turn into a Vampyre at the age of twenty-one. If you're a male, you turn at thirty-five. But you are born knowing what you are, and you are raised accordingly. You know how to hunt, you know how to blend in with humans. These are the ones who walk amongst everyone else."

He pauses for a moment, eyes seeming lost. "Then there are...the beasts. The monsters. The ones who were born human and turned into a Vampyre by another bloodsucker.

They are killed and brought back to life by drinking the blood of the Vampyre who slaughtered them. When this happens... you are born a creature of Hell. You have no mind, no conscience. You are pure power and bloodlust, and you don't even look human anymore. It's these creatures who kill indiscriminately, without mercy. They are hard to control, even harder to kill, and they become the subject of every frightening bedtime story told to children."

Priest looks at me, his eyes taking on a red sheen I hadn't seen before, his mouth opening into a gruesome, fanged smile. "Want to guess which one I am?"

Fear runs down my spine like an icy finger. For the first time, I actually fear him. For the first time, I realize his monster isn't a figure of speech.

"But you're..." I whisper.

"A priest," he says matter-of-factly, the redness disappearing from his eyes. "The monastery was started by Abe and a few other Vampyres to take care of creatures like us. He figured it wasn't our fault that we were turned. All Vampyres know the consequences, but not all Vampyres are good. Some only want chaos. I was turned by one called Kaleid, who led his band of bloodsuckers across the middle of Spain to create an army of killers. I suppose he succeeded. He just happened to pick a witch when he did it."

My eyes have been wide the whole time I've been listening to him, thoroughly engaged. We have our own problems in the underwater world, and there are Syrens who are cruel and dangerous to others, but all of this seems utterly fantastical.

"So learning about God kept you in line, kept you human?" I ask.

He nods. "Yes. In the beginning, it was hard to understand. All I knew was hatred and rage. But I suppose the Good Book has some good use. It got through to me. I started believing it. Combined with the discipline that was a part of our lives, we slowly came around. Eventually—and we are talking centuries here—I realized it was all made up, just stories to keep people in line. But the rigid routine, the vows, the structure? That kept me in control. That brought me to here and now, how I'm able to talk to you without wanting to rip your head off."

I swallow uneasily at that. "So you stopped believing in God…"

"No," he says, biting his lip for a moment. "No, I believe in something. Maybe it's God. Maybe it's something else, *someone* else. But all these rules, this guilt? That's all man-made."

"But you're peddling it," I point out. "You're spreading these rules and the guilt to the people here, and you don't even believe in it. You're spreading lies."

He lifts his shoulder in a shrug. "In time, they will come to their own conclusions. Maybe on their deathbed."

I think about that for a moment. We have our own beliefs in Limonos, but none so complicated as this. Then again, my head feels foggy from all the wine I've consumed.

"Earlier, you said it's Friday. How long was I out for?" I ask him.

"Twenty-four hours," he says.

My eyes widen. "You left me tied here for a whole day?"

"You said you wanted to be alone," he says mildly. "Besides, now that I don't have to wet your tail every couple of hours, I don't need to tend to you as much."

"I see," I say, suddenly not hungry. I put the plate down. "So I'm just supposed to spend my days in here like this, with you only dropping by when you feel like it to throw me some bread?"

He stares at me, his expression curious, like he's trying to figure out a puzzle.

"What is it exactly that you expect from me?" he asks.

My mind spins, fueled by alcohol.

I can't forget my plan.

Seduce, destroy, escape.

I'm still a Syren, no matter what.

"What about company?" I ask him, making my voice softer. "Don't you care at all about how alone I'll feel in this cold, dark room? Don't you know what loneliness is?"

He flinches like he's been slapped. "Of course I do. Loneliness is all I've known. I'm marooned at the bottom of the fucking world."

"Then you don't have to be so cruel to me," I tell him, twisting in my seat until I'm on my knees in front of him. "You don't have to torture me."

"Cruel?" His throat bobs as he swallows thickly, his gaze on my chest. "I will keep you clothed, bathed, fed. What more could you ask for?"

"A warm body," I tell him. "A little company for these dark nights."

"You're my prisoner. You're...a pet."

"Even pets deserve some kindness, don't they?"

"Not if you're planning on slaughtering them one day."

He says that as a way to scare me off, and it does scare me because I hear the bitter truth in his voice. But even so, I lean toward him, enough that I lose my balance and pitch toward him.

He reaches out and grabs me by the shoulders, holding me back.

I stare up at him, pouring every ounce of seduction into my eyes, hoping they'll have some effect on him.

I know he wants me, desires me; there's no question there.

I just need to loosen the rope that has him bound too, the one he doesn't know he's tangled in.

"You wanted to take away my voice," I whisper, watching as his pupils become black holes. "So kiss me until

I can't speak." My gaze drops to his lips. "Kiss me before I—"

"Christ," he says through a growl, his eyes flashing wildly.

But instead of kissing me, he reaches out and grabs me by the throat.

And squeezes me until I can't breathe.

Chapter Eleven

PRIEST

One of the most crucial teachings in the monastery was the mastery of one's emotions. While I was a beast, my emotions controlled every aspect of my savage life. Granted, my emotions weren't very complex—they were simplified to only anger and desire, but they were the ones steering the ship, so to speak.

Every day, we would wake at four in the morning, in the dark and with the birdsong. The monastery was located on top of a jagged rock that had broken away from the mountain pass long ago. We were completely isolated, with few visitors daring to traverse the ladders to reach us.

Despite this, my job every morning was to haul up the ladders and clean the rungs. We were told that when we did welcome people, they couldn't dirty their feet—it would be unholy—so each rung had to be wiped clean before the day began.

The problem was that the rock was also home to a nesting colony of wallcreepers that used the ladders as a perch as they pecked at insects on the rock. Where they perched, they would shit. As soon as I cleaned the ladder, I would lower it, and the birds would fly back to use it as their own little latrine.

Again and again.

One could see how this was a lesson in patience and anger management. In time, the seemingly pointless and bothersome work taught me how to store my rage away. I became even-keeled, methodical in my thoughts, and learned how to put distance between me and my emotions, to be an observer and not a participant.

I no longer let anger rule me.

I no longer let desire rule me.

Until tonight.

Until Larimar batted her damn lashes and stared up at me with those seductive lilac eyes, asking for me to treat her kindly, if I knew what loneliness was, as if I hadn't spent most of my life in its clutches.

So fucking lonely.

Then, she told me to kiss her until she couldn't speak, and all I wanted to do was exactly that. To stop her from saying those words that were starting to sink into my heart like bile. To feel her lips and her tongue and taste her so deeply that she'd become part of my veins.

But desire didn't win out—not at first.

Instead, it was anger, a fanged, hairy shadow that shot out of me as I grabbed her throat.

I hold it now, my fingers squeezing her soft skin tightly, and I'm watching the light start to leave her beautiful eyes. In this moment, I know I'm willing to *kill* her to not feel anything for her.

This terrifies me.

She terrifies me.

I let her go.

She gasps, her hands going to her throat to soothe the bruises I left behind.

I think to those early mornings on the mountain.

I think of birdsong until the anger dissipates.

Anger quickly replaced with desire.

And for desire, there is no cure.

I want her.

I need her.

I reach out again and grab her face, holding it roughly in one hand while my other hand goes to her hair, making a tight fist. I want to see if her tongue tastes like sugared, salted lemons.

She lets out a cry, her mouth falling open, petulant and pink and wet.

Blood thrums in my groin as lust takes hold.

And I lean into it. Lean into *her*.

I kiss her.

I kiss her *hard*.

This is punishment.

For her for being a little brat.

For me for not kissing her earlier.

Christ, I want to kiss her until we both choke on it.

When was the last time I felt a woman's lips? I can't remember, but my body knows exactly what it wants. It wants her tongue fucking my mouth, slick and soft. It wants her greedy little moans.

She gives me both, offering them up on a silver platter.

I grunt into her mouth, her tongue teasing, licking me as I'm licking her. It slides beside mine—slick and smooth, tasting of the sea and herbs—and the heat in my trousers grows until it becomes unbearable, a fire that will consume the both of us if I let it go on too long.

Let us burn.

My mouth opens wider, wanting to devour her whole, and she matches me, gasping in a way that has a lightning storm forming in my chest. I twist my fingers into her silky hair, bite her lips, fuck her tongue like a starving man.

She pulls back, just enough to catch her breath, and my fist in her hair grows tighter, as if it will help me stay in control.

But I'm losing hold.

"Take me," she whispers, her voice raw, roughed up with need.

I try to swallow and can't.

It's too much. There's something clawing up my chest, into my throat.

The monster thrives on this.

I want to give the monster everything.

I want him to feed.

"Forget your vows," she rasps, leaning in to take my bottom lip between her teeth. She tugs on it hard, my eyes rolling back in my head. "Forget your vows and take me. Please."

This beautiful creature of mine.

Begging for me.

Bound to me.

Therefore, I must keep her.

I must keep her alive.

Anger is a firestorm in my chest, but it all seems to go to my cock, and I let out a frustrated roar.

I shove her back to the floor and reach down for her. My shaking hands almost go for the bottom of her shift, but there's a moment of divine intervention, and I grab the fabric of her neckline instead.

I growl as I rip her shift open down the middle, exposing those full tits of hers. I'd been staring at them for weeks now, and suddenly, after being covered up for a day, it's like I'm seeing them with new eyes, seeing something I shouldn't.

Forbidden fruit to eat.

I lean over and spit on her chest, once, twice, and then move over so I'm straddling her. She stares up at me with wild, questioning eyes, her blonde hair spilling around her like a halo. I want nothing more than to shoot my seed all over that beautiful face, to revel in the depravity of it all, and from the wanton way she's biting her lip, I think she might want the same.

My sea goddess wants to be taken, but I'd be a fool to give her what she wants, so I'll take her as selfishly as I can.

Like I'm running out of time, I bring my cock out of the flap of my trousers, heavy, solid, and hot in my hands, my movements frantic.

Her eyes go even bigger at the sight of it—longing mixed with a dash of fear. I can't help but feel satisfied at her reaction; it has been a long time since anyone has looked at me like that.

I move up so I'm just below her chest, my rigid cock hitting the skin between her breasts with a heavy smack, making the spit fly. This will be hard to do without her help, but she's a quick learner. She reaches up, setting her hands on either side of her breasts, pushing them in so they engulf my dick.

"Yes," I hiss, planting my hands on either side of her head as I begin shamelessly rutting myself between her tits like a fucking animal. I know I must look utterly depraved, full of dirty sins I want to unleash on her, like a man so driven by the primal need to come that I have to take it any way I can.

I'm desperate now, reduced to a savage creature as I pump and thrust on pure wild instinct. When the friction becomes too much, I spit on my palm and stroke over my cock, making sure to capture the weeping precum at the tip before spreading it down my stiff length.

"I want to see it," she whispers, her head rising to catch my earlobe between her teeth. "I want to see you come."

A feverish growl rumbles through me, and I pump my hips harder, the tip of my cock hitting the bottom of her chin, making me wince. It's messy, animalistic, and about to get messier.

Wildfire spreads down my spine, gathering at the base with a sharp stab of sinful need, and I'm unable to hold back. I erupt, watching as long, thick ropes of cum stream over her chest and neck, face and hair. I keep coming, pumping fast and hard, and Larimar opens her mouth so some of my release slips through her lips and onto her tongue.

Finally, I'm empty, my cock spent and twitching, though I know I could go again in a second. Except I wouldn't fuck her tits again. Maybe her mouth. Or maybe I would throw my vows to the wind and wedge into that pretty little cunt of hers, just like she wants. Maybe I'll find salvation there.

Maybe I'll find hell.

For now, though, I am dizzy and somewhat sated, the fruitless anger dissipating and that sweet haze of peace washing over me. I get to my feet carefully and loom over her. I want to sear this image of her into my brain: lying below me, my ejaculate sprayed over her, her eyes dancing with coy excitement as she stares up at me.

Filthy, filthy priest, I think.

I tuck my cock back into my trousers and then grab one of my robes before kneeling beside Larimar and dabbing it across the mess I left. It's the least I can do. Besides, the stains will remind me of her while I'm delivering my sermon.

She sits up and looks at her shift. "This didn't last very long."

"Thankfully, I brought you a spare," I say, pulling up the shift on her shoulders, just so her breasts are barely covered.

"May I ask where you got these clothes from? Do you keep women's garments on hand, perhaps locked in a trunk some- where, just in case you find a Syren?"

I give her a wry smile as I sit down on the chair. "I stole them."

She looks surprised. "From who?"

"The general's wife. They live in another town, about a full day's ride from here."

Her lip pouts slightly as she frowns, thinking. Now that I know what her lips feel like, what her mouth tastes like, I can't help but want to kiss her again.

But that would be a mistake. If I kissed her, I would become ensnared by her feminine wiles. Only now is that haze starting to lift, hard clarity settling back into my bones. I need to put distance between us again. I need to stop thinking with my dick.

"When did you do all this?" she asks.

"Last night."

"But when?"

"When I left you on the cross."

"But a full day's ride..."

"You know I can move fast. Being a blood-drinker isn't just about drinking blood to survive. You know how strong I am. All my senses are heightened, and I'm fast too."

"Anything else I should know?" she asks with a small smile.

"I'm immortal."

She seems surprised by that admission, her mouth forming an O, and for one lewd second, I dream about grabbing her head and shoving my dick past her lips.

Lord, protect me from my thoughts.

"You mean you can't die?" she finally says.

I shrug. "Well, it's not that I can't. I can, but it takes a specific kind of effort. Otherwise, I will live until the end of time. How long do you Syrens live?"

"Three hundred years, give or take," she says.

"That's still a long time."

"I suppose, though it's hard to know now that I'm in this body," she says, gesturing to herself, and I try not to stare at the body in question.

"You still have Syren blood. You have your gills, though thankfully, not your teeth."

"No," she says in an odd voice, looking away as she curls her fingers into her palm. "Or my claws."

"I'm sure you'll still live a very long time."

She looks up at me sharply. "A long time in your care," she says, the bitterness clear in her tone.

I nod, giving her a placating smile. "Yes."

One day, she'll get used to it. She might even like it.

"Kind of funny, isn't it?" she says slowly. "To be a priest when there's no chance of you being called to the afterlife to meet your maker."

"That might still happen. I could be terribly unlucky. There are only three ways to kill a blood-drinker."

"What are they?" she asks with glinting eyes.

I chuckle. "I wouldn't dare give you that information, not when you want me dead."

"I don't want you dead..." She trails off. "But I would kill you if I had to."

I shrug, taking no offense. How can I, when I claimed I would slaughter her one day?

She studies me, her gaze sliding over my features, pausing at my mouth, my nose, my brow, as if she'll find some answers there. "You had said you were a father once."

I visibly bristle, shoulders stiffening.

"Did you have a family?" she goes on, her voice gentle now. "Children? A wife?"

A dull pain forms beneath my chest, the kind I usually run from. But her eyes are looking at me more closely now, and I feel trapped, with nowhere to go.

"I had a wife, a son, and a daughter," I manage to say. I

shouldn't have even said that, but it's as if I was compelled to, as if I want to tell this little fish everything.

Distance, I remind myself. *Put distance between you in every way.*

"What happened to them? Were they turned too?"

I glance down at my hands. These same hands that pray to God are the same hands that belong to a beast.

I can only shake my head. "No." My voice comes out in a hush. "It was only me." I close my eyes, and I can see it now: the moments I try so hard to bury alongside my demons. It comes slowly, like a dream descending through the fog, one I know will quickly turn into a nightmare.

I take in a deep, shaking breath.

And, against my better judgment, I tell Larimar my beginning.

And my end.

"I was in the village, at my shop as a blacksmith, about to finish my work for the day," I say to her. "My shop was at the end of a cobblestone street, and it was quiet that early evening. The sun was still in the sky, summer twilight a few hours away. There were early crickets and the smell of sunbaked wheat from the surrounding fields, and suddenly, the crickets stopped.

"Darkness descended, and I remember looking at the sun shining beyond the oak, but the air had a shadowiness to it that I couldn't explain, and suddenly, I was chilled down to the bone. The magic I could always feel in my veins was starting to buzz like hornets.

"They came out of the forest, a band of them on foot, and I remember wondering why I hadn't heard them. How could this group of men have come so fast through that thicket without making a sound?

"But as they came closer, I understood. The magic in my veins had been warning me. They were not men.

"The one at the front, dark hair, wide jaw, was smiling like a fool. I saw the fangs. Then, I saw the sword. It plunged straight into my heart, killing me on the spot.

"My last memories of a man, of a pure human being, were of me on the ground. The one who stabbed me took the sword from my chest and told me his name was Kaleid, that he was the Son of Skarde, and I was going to join his army of monsters. Then he took his sword and sliced open his wrist. I was dying as he put his wrist to my mouth. I remember tasting his blood, and that was it."

I glance over to see her leaning toward me, worrying her lip between her teeth. "That was it?" she whispers.

I nod. "Everything after that was just...shadows. Anger. Hunger..."

"What happened to your family?" she asks in a small voice.

I give my head a shake. I can't admit it, even to her, even though, somehow, I know she would understand.

Clearing my throat, I get to my feet. "I better go back to my house," I tell her. "Another villager might stop by with more bread."

She blinks at me. "You're leaving me again?"

I'm about to tell her yes and walk away, but I remember her hands are undone. Despite what I just confided in her, the intimacy between us isn't real. She is still my prisoner, my captive, my pet, and she will do all she can to escape.

Even kill me if she has to, I think. I'm even more glad I didn't tell her how.

I pick up the rope and stand over her, and she flinches, backing up as if trying to get away.

"I'm sorry," I say, reaching for her arms. She tries to yank them out of my grasp, but my hands are large, my grip strong.

"No, you're not," she cries out softly, still fighting me.

"I *am* sorry," I snap, quickly wrapping the rope around one wrist before pushing her over on her stomach and tying her hands behind her back. "I wish I wasn't this way, but I am. I've done far worse than what I'm doing to you. Perhaps you should try to be a little grateful."

"Grateful?" she yells through her ruined voice. "Grateful that you keep me here to use for whatever you want?"

I flip her back over and lean over her, grabbing her chin between my fingers. "Don't act like you're not trying to use me too."

"Use you for what?"

"A stepping stone for what you really want."

"And what's that?"

I press my lips together in a grunt. That's the problem: I don't know what she really wants, but it's something.

And it's sure as hell not me.

"I'll be back tomorrow," I tell her, letting go of her face and straightening back up. "Bring you some water so you don't have to drink the church's wine. More food if you're hungry. Perhaps even a proper bed."

I leave her there on the floor, on a pile of dresses that will probably never see the light of day, making sure to lock the door after me.

The evening is darker than sin as I step out of the church and walk toward my cottage. The lone candle in the window would look inviting to anyone else but me. The fact is, I don't want to be with my thoughts. I want to be in the back room with her, even if I'm telling her things no one but Abe would know. But that's all the more reason I must be alone.

Suddenly, I sniff an unwelcome scent in the air.

I'm not alone after all.

"Father Aragon."

I turn to see one of the soldiers walking past the church and coming toward me, the same suspicious one I dealt with after Larimar's attack on the fishermen.

"What is it, son?" I ask as a caring priest would, pressing my palms together as if in prayer.

"You've been quite busy these nights," the soldier says, stopping a few feet away. "Always coming and going into the church."

How damn observant of him.

"God is active at all hours of the night," I tell him with my most patient smile. "I don't take time off from my mission."

The soldier's eyes are cold, and I wonder if mine look the same.

"You should be careful around here," he says, hidden meaning lacing his words. "At night. Us soldiers are few and far between. You're lucky I patrol here as often as I do."

"I don't fear anything except God's judgment," I say with reverence.

The soldier frowns and then gives me a sour smile. "Of course not. Well, just so you know. We don't want what happened to those fishermen to happen to you."

He then turns on his heel and walks away, disappearing past my cottage and into the darkness.

I don't want that to happen to me either.

Chapter Twelve

LARIMAR

I have a secret.

A secret I've been keeping from Priest.

A secret I plan to use at just the right time.

I first noticed it when he was strangling me.

When I felt my body going limp and the world going gray, I thought I was going to die. It did something in the very center of me, like a key fit into a lock and unleashed something that might save my life.

Something that would help me fight back.

I felt my teeth come in.

My jaw felt like it was cracking open, and I could feel the sharp teeth growing over my human ones in rows, like a shark's mouth.

I was prepared to bite his goddamned hand in half again.

But then, he let go. I don't think he noticed the change in me, and my teeth quickly retreated once the danger passed.

They weren't needed when he took his cock out and fucked between my breasts like a madman, like an unfettered animal, and came all over my face. I'm still finding it dried in my hair.

Now, however, now that he's tied me up and left me to my own devices, they might be needed. My hands are behind my back, and I wonder if they, too, might transform at some point, if there is something that will make them into my old claws. Is it anger? Is it self-preservation? Hunger?

I'm sure I'll find out either way.

So now that I have this secret, I must figure out how to use it.

And when.

"Will you show me how to pray?" I ask, willing my voice to sound innocent, but not too much, so as not to arouse suspicion.

Priest looks at me in surprise, lowering his glass of wine.

"You want to know how to pray?"

We're at his desk, me on the chair, him sitting on the edge of the table. It's been a few days since our last intimate interaction—our only kiss—and until now, he's been distant. Not cruel, but not kind either. I suppose I shouldn't expect much more than that from him. Perhaps I should be grateful, as he said.

Yesterday was mass. Through the walls, I listened to him talk again, preaching things I know he doesn't believe in—or at least, he doesn't believe in most of it. The rules, the guilt, the damnation. It seems to be that no matter what those poor people do, they are going to hell one way or another. I've been around humans enough to know that no one is *that* good at heart. Everyone is a sinner and will stay a sinner because that's the world we live in.

At least Syrens come by it honestly. We accept that we

aren't all light, but we aren't all shadow. We're those muddy shades in the middle, trying to do our best to stay alive. Life is too hard as it is to worry about what's going to happen to us after we leave it.

"I'm curious," I tell him, gesturing for the glass of wine. "After hearing your sermon yesterday, I wanted to know what it's like in there. What it's like to pray."

He rubs his lips together, and the memory of his mouth makes my own lips tingle.

That kiss scared him. Everything to do with me scares him, I can tell.

He hesitates before he offers the chalice, and I take it in my hands, tied together in front of me this time. How nice of him to give me some variety. He's also dressed me up in the general's wife's gown, a satiny green with a low bodice that makes my breasts look like they want to escape. I felt like a proper pet when he put all the layers on me, one by one. Any desire he may have felt while dressing me, he managed to keep hidden.

This morning, he brought in two of the pews from the church and pushed them together so they resemble a bed. I haven't slept on it yet, but so far, it seems the mound of clothes on the floor might be the more comfortable option.

I tilt the chalice back and swallow the rest of the contents in one gulp.

His dark brows rise appreciatively. "Alright. I can show you how to pray."

He gets to his feet and plucks the chalice from my hands, placing it on the table before pulling me up by my elbow. "Come on. Do you think you can hobble out there, or shall I carry you?"

"Why don't you see if I can learn how to walk?" I point out. I start tipping over, and he keeps me up by placing his warm palms on my shoulders. "I can't learn if you keep me hobbled. It's as if I still have a tail."

He stares at me for a moment and then nods. "Fair point. Promise you won't kick me?"

"I make no such promises."

He chuckles to himself and then bends down, breaking the rope apart with his bare hands as if it was just a strand of hair.

I feel like he did that on purpose, a reminder of his strength and what he could do to me.

How easy I am to break.

But I won't be broken without a fight.

He puts his hand at my elbow to steady me. Standing beside him like this, I'm also aware of how much bigger and taller he is too. Every inch of him is taut and hard and powerful, more beast than man, more animal than priest. It's strange that I've had his fingers inside me, that he's had his cock between my breasts, that we've both come in each other's presence, seen each other at our most raw and vulnerable, and yet it's in moments like this that I feel the difference in our statures.

He, the captor.

Me, the captive.

But when he asks, "Are you alright to walk? Here, lean on me and take it one step at a time," and his voice is gentle, his eyes full of concern, I wonder if the man inside him will ever win for good. If he can shuck away the monster one day, alongside this religion, free himself from both. If he can become the man he was once, the one with the name he no longer remembers.

I give him a reassuring smile. "I'll try."

I've had my feet bound this whole time, hobbling and hopping around the room when he's not here, working my muscles and testing my feet, making sure they're ready for the big escape. But now that I actually have to walk with one foot in front of the other, it's not as easy as I let myself believe.

I wobble, a lot, but Priest keeps his grip on me steady, leading me toward the door, toward the place where the salvation happens. My feet feel tight and thin, my toes continuously gripping the floor like they're claws. My calves are quick to ache, but I manage to put one foot in front of another until we're at the door.

He lets go of me long enough to unlock it, and I manage to stay upright.

Then, he opens the door and leads me through to a whole new world.

This place feels holy. The air is thick with reverence—there is no other way to explain it. Sometimes, back in Limonos, you would come across these sea caves where the sun would pierce the surface just so, shining light on the coral and the shimmering scales of the fish, and you could feel that it was a place of importance. Other times, there were caverns in the rock where the dead were buried, piles of Syren bones, and you could sense all the lives that came before you.

This church is like that. Perhaps not as natural, not as pure, but I can tell it's a place where people come to bring their hopes and dreams and fears and sorrows and lay them down, offer them up.

"What?" Priest asks me.

I've come to a stop, taking it all in.

"You don't feel it?" I whisper, looking up at the rafters. I suppose the place is simple—I've seen fancier in underwater kingdoms—but even in its simplicity, there is something palpable in the air.

"Feel what?" His gaze is curious as it rakes over me.

I shrug, feeling a little foolish. If a priest doesn't even know...

"I can tell it's a place of worship."

"Ah," he says slowly, running his fingers over his jaw. "I suppose you're right. I'm just so close to it that I've never noticed. Don't tell me you're about to become a woman of faith."

"I'm not a woman of anything," I say stiffly. "Just of free mind and free will."

"And yet the other day, you were judging the very people who come here to worship."

"I'm not saying I agree with what they are worshipping," I explain. "It's only that I can feel that they do. It's not about God. It's about desperation."

Silence stretches between us, and I worry I've offended him, even though I *want* to offend him.

"I see," he says carefully, rubbing his lips as he ponders my words. "You ought to be careful; your thoughts are bordering on blasphemous."

"And why would I care?"

"Because you're the one who just asked me how to pray." He takes my arm again and leads me over to the front of the church, a raised area in front of the aisle. There are a few steps leading up to it and then a long table lit with candles, draped with white lace. Behind that, a large silver cross is mounted on the wall, various other crosses and portraits of people on either side with windows made from colorful glass.

"Here," he says in a low voice, dropping down to his knees on the step and gesturing for me to do the same.

I pull up the hem of my skirt and attempt to kneel beside him, my movements awkward as I bend my knees in such a way, the green satin pooling around me like water. I watch everything he does—the way he places his hands together, palm-to-palm, fingers up, how he looks to the cross, the way he bows his head and rests the tips of his fingers on his forehead, closing his eyes.

"Our father, who art in heaven, hallowed be thy name," he says in a low, rich voice, a quieter version of the one I've heard booming during mass. "Thy kingdom come, thy will be done, on Earth as it is in heaven."

He then falls silent, and I can't help but hold my breath.

Finally, he opens his eyes and shoots me a shy glance. "You're supposed to repeat after me."

"Oh!" I exclaim softly. "My apologies. Can you repeat it?"

He shoots me a patient smile and then repeats the prayer over again, pausing at the end of each sentence for me to say it back.

"What happens after?" I ask.

"You can pray for specific things," he says, glancing up at the cross. "Or you can leave it as it is, as long as there is meaning in each word, as long as you are seeking to make this prayer a bridge between you and God. You don't just recite the words and not think about what they mean. That's pointless. Might as be elsewhere."

"So this is how you pray?"

He gives me a curious look. "Me in particular? No. It's just how most people pray."

"But I want to know how *you* pray."

His blue eyes study me carefully, and I know I have to rein it in. "Curious thing, aren't you? Wanting to know so much about the human world you despise."

"I never said I despised it!"

"I believe you said you killed men not because they were tasty but because they deserved it. In your words, *one less man is doing this world a favor.* Now, perhaps I'm reading into this, but that doesn't sound like you care all that much for mankind."

My eyes narrow. "You're a man—of course you wouldn't understand what I mean. I can think men are the most dangerous creatures of all and not want to condemn all of humanity for their crimes."

"Fair enough," he says, splaying his palms in a show of acceptance.

"So what do you ask for when you pray?" I ask.

His chin jerks inward. "You can't ask me that."

"Why not?"

His mouth opens and closes, trying to find the words. "It's personal."

"Is it like a wish? If you tell someone, it doesn't come true? We have that with the spinefish. Break off one of the spikes on their back and make a wish, but if you tell a soul, it will all be for naught."

He lets out a soft laugh. "No, not like that. It's just...it's between you and God."

"The very God you don't believe in?"

"I didn't say the man on the cross is listening to me," he says, nodding at the giant silver cross on the wall. "But someone is. They might not act on it, but they listen, and that's enough for me."

I wait a moment, strategizing my best approach. I feel like I'm back in the water again, in the murky depths, approaching my prey.

"So this God, this being, only listens to your prayers...and yet you feel you must uphold all your vows? For what?"

He gives me a steady look, his brows pulling together. In the flickering candlelight of the church, his handsome features seem sharper, more dangerous. He reaches into his shirt, and I see him grasp the beaded necklace around his neck like it might save him.

A thrill runs through my body.

Am I actually about to do this? Make my escape?

Will I make it out of this alive?

Or the better question is...will he?

Chapter Thirteen

LARIMAR

"I've told you," Priest says in a slow, measured voice, "my vows keep myself in line for me. For that humanity you pretend to care about."

I give him my most innocent smile and turn around so I'm facing down the aisle, the top step pressing into my lower back. "And how does fucking me mean the downfall of humanity?" I ask, reaching down with my bound hands to pull the hem of my dress until it's hiked at my waist. I spread my legs, making sure he has a good view of my bare cunt.

A rumble sounds from his chest, his brows lowered as he glowers at me.

"It's about control," he says thickly, and I can tell he's trying hard not to look between my legs.

"But making me come on your hand isn't about control? Or you coming between my breasts?"

"Christ, woman," he swears.

I nearly laugh. "Who is blasphemous now?" Then, I put my hands on myself. I should be ashamed at how wet I've gotten just from teasing him like this. "Fine then. If you won't give me what I want, I'll have to give it to myself."

129

His nostrils flare, the grip on his necklace making his knuckles white.

But he doesn't tell me to stop.

I move my fingers lower, the sound of my wetness incredibly loud in the silence of the church. It's hard to get purchase with the way my hands are bound together, but it's all part of the show.

I arch my back, my hair flowing behind me like a sheet. I moan, my mouth open. I feel his eyes on me, on my face, my chest, my open legs. They burn like fire under his gaze, making my skin feel hot and tight and exposed.

"You could help me," I whisper, staring up at the rafters. "You could help me in so many ways."

"You seem to be doing fine," he says in a raw, ragged voice.

I lift my head to see him staring at my cunt intently, like he's ravenous and desperate for a taste.

I spread my thighs even wider and watch him swallow the sight.

"You could loosen the rope," I say on a whimper. "Let me do to myself what you won't do to me."

He glances at me sharply, the line deepening between his brows. He assesses me for a moment, breathing heavily as he weighs his options. Tension crackles between us, stretching on seemingly forever before he reaches over and unties the rope binding my wrists, throwing it to the side.

Then, to my surprise and delight, he gets on the floor and moves between my legs. With a firm grasp on my thighs, his hard fingertips digging into my skin, he spreads them further, his mannerisms rough. His long black hair tickles my sensitive skin, adding to the sensation.

I gasp, and he stares up at me between my legs, silently asking if he should continue. The look in his eyes is starkly savage, that beast beneath the man coming through.

Yes. Eat me whole. Take what you want. Take it all.

A prickle of sweat forms at the back of my neck. I want to escape from his clutches, but at the same time, I want to be caught. I want to be his prey. I want him to feast on me and fuck me to the brink of death. I want to dance with that heaven he's always talking about.

"Devour me," I whisper to him. "Devour me until there is nothing left."

His jaw tenses, a low rumble escaping him, blue eyes blazing with hunger and need, and then he plunges his face downward.

I cry out softly, my hands reaching out to make fists in his hair. His beard razes my delicate skin, his lips both hard and soft as his mouth engulfs my folds, his tongue strong and moving deftly. One long lick, then another, making my world spin, making me want to beg for him deeper.

"Priest," I say through a groan, losing myself to the feel of his tongue. He fucks me with it, diving deep inside my cunt. It seems to be longer and thicker than humanly possible, filling me until I can't breathe.

He groans against me, and the vibrations cause my hips to buck up against his face. Neither of us is patient tonight. Smoke fills my veins, and I'm both floating and grappling for him, tugging on his hair as if to keep me here while, at the same time, I want to be set loose.

"Christ, you taste like my prayers," he says against me, his lips moving as he talks, his breath hot on my cunt, my eyes rolling back in my head. "I prayed for this, for you."

My heart catches high in my throat at his words.

He prayed for *me*?

Is he being honest, or is he telling me what I want to hear, trying to render me useless, at his mercy? Is he—

Ow.

He bit my damn clit!

I yelp, the sound echoing in the church despite my

tempered voice, and he sucks it into his mouth, moaning loudly now. I can feel the hot rush of blood, the pain quickly soothed by his soft, lapping tongue, and that heady, foggy bliss from his bite takes me over.

"I'm close," I manage to say, nearly choking on my words, my thighs squeezing the sides of his head. "I'm...I'm..."

It's too much. I'm wet with blood and desire, and his mouth is insatiable, frantic and messy, his lips and tongue swirling and sucking and licking, and every nerve inside me is pulled into a tight bunch. I'm chasing friction, chasing *something*. I fill with fire that has nowhere to go, and it builds and tightens and...

I come undone. In pieces. In ashes. Fragments scattered across this holy place.

I'm crying out his name, yanking his hair, my body bucking wildly until I think my hips might break his jaw. Heat explodes through me like a million lightning strikes, and I'm not sure where I am anymore. I'm not sure what I've become except this *being*, floating and soulful and free.

Then, in the back of my mind, I remember my plan.

There's really no point, no way I'll actually be able to escape.

But I have to try, at least once, and suffer the punishment for it.

"Priest," I whisper, pulling on his hair until I bring his head up toward mine. He braces himself on either side of me as he leans in, and I go to his ear, as if I'm going to whisper something, his hair falling over my face.

Instead of saying anything, I search the desperation inside me, that need to be wild and free, and I summon my teeth.

They lengthen in my mouth, my jaw sprouting in pain. My fingers do the same, the fingernails curving forward into hardened claws.

Priest stiffens as he notices, but it's too late. He's too

wrapped up in the taste of me on his lips to be as quick as he should be.

With a howl, I bite his ear with a savage snap, my teeth sinking into it and ripping the flesh right off.

He hollers, blood spurting, his hand going to protect himself, and I work as fast as I can, tearing down the side of his neck with my claws, ripping out muscle and sinew before I move out from under him. He tries to grab for me, but I slip out of his grasp, his hands too slick and bloody.

I don't have any time.

I start running down the aisle, heading for the main doors, spitting out parts of his neck and ear as I go, my feet stumbling as I try to run for the first time ever.

I'm almost at the doors when I feel him behind me, panting, growling like a rabid beast, ready to take me down.

I won't make it.

At least I tried.

He roars and tackles me from behind, and I twist in the air until he slams me down on my back, the wind knocked out of me.

His blood pours over me, dripping onto my face, and he grabs my hair, yanking it back before he goes for my neck. He bites me hard, though the pleasure is again quick to take over from the pain. He drinks from me, and I try to fight back, even though I know it's futile, even though I wanted him to catch me. My jaws snap, and my claws rake down his back, breaking through the fabric and leaving long, bloody gashes.

He cries out and brings his mouth off my neck, fumbling for my arms with one hand while he restrains me by the neck with the other.

"Was that your plan?" he yells as he briefly lets go of my throat to tear his necklace off and flip me over on my stomach, wrapping it around my wrists behind my back. "Was that your plan this whole time, to try and seduce me so you could escape? Say the things you thought I wanted to hear?"

I'm not even trying to bite him anymore. "It wasn't a good plan?"

"Do you want what you're asking for?" he roars, grabbing me by the back of my neck. "Would you even know how to handle what you're asking for?"

Before I can even try to answer, he pulls me straight off the floor by my neck, enough that I fear he might just snap it in two, like a hollow bone. My claws flail aimlessly, unable to catch the beaded necklace binding my wrists together, my teeth snapping but unable to get near him.

I wanted him to chase me, to pin me down, to throw me about and have his way with me—finally—but there's a chance he's so far gone with rage that he might actually kill me. Not just a tease of death, not just flirting with my demise —he might actually rip my head off, feast on my blood until I'm a dried husk, and be done with it. In moments, I might be dumped back into the sea to become food for the fish.

He takes me to the nearest pew and turns me around so the back of my legs hit it, my back arching as his grip tightens.

I stare at his eyes—wild, uncontrolled, like there's someone else behind them, someone who doesn't care if I live or die. The monster. I never wanted that part of him to come out.

I can only stare at him and wonder if this is it.

"Please," I manage to whisper against his choking grip.

Please let me live.

Please let me go.

Please take care of me.

Please fuck me.

Please...love me.

I would take any of them.

And then I see clarity come into his eyes, cold at first,

making their color glacial blue, like ice underwater. I see *him* emerge, the tortured human, the priest, even the blood-drinker.

With a deep, rumbling growl, he drags me down the pews, my bare feet barely touching the floor before he shoves me down so I'm kneeling on the bench.

"Is this what you want?" he cries out hoarsely, bringing his body behind me. He yanks up the hem of my dress until it's bunched around my waist, my bottom bare to him. I hear him fumbling with the fabric of his pants, and my heart starts to gallop in anticipation. I'm still wet from before, but now, it's bordering on being excessive.

"Is it?" he growls in my ear. "You like to play rough? You like to hurt and maim? Is that what you want in return?"

His breath is hot on my cheek, and I can hear the deep, rasping impatience in his voice, like he's angrier at himself for giving in. "Do you want my cock wedged inside you until you can't breathe? Is that enough for you? My seed dripping down your leg, my soul along with it? Is that it? Will that satisfy you?"

"Yes," I cry out softly, and I feel him pull his cock from his trousers, the energy of him radiating against the back of my thighs, the press of his solid, thick, intimidating length. It's velvet soft and hard at the same time—and hot, so very hot. I can feel it pulsing against me with every beat of his heart.

My cunt aches with need, sudden and wild, and I almost beg him again—he seems to like how I beg—but then his hand grips my bottom, fingers digging in hard as he shoves his cock inside my cunt in one, punctuating thrust.

"Priest!" I call out through a ragged exhale, his name carrying to the rafters.

"Is this what you wanted?" he rasps against my neck, his hips pumping against my rear, his pace quickening. "My vows torn to shreds to appease you and your appetite?"

I can't help but nod, a whimper escaping my lips.

It's exactly what I wanted.

"You think you're my salvation? You think you're my redemption?" he goes on, beard tickling my ears. "Do you even know what that would mean?"

I can't even form the words. I can't think. His hand goes to my throat, choking me, the other hand running down to my wrists, briefly fingering the beads around the necklace binding me together.

"I want you," he says breathlessly, grinding his cock in deeper. "Need you. Crave you like nothing else I've ever wanted. No absolution, no heaven, nothing. I must have you, just like this, cock deep in your cunt and praying to God that you'll never leave me, that I'll never be without *this*."

He reaches around my front, hand frantically moving the layers of my dress out of the way until he grabs my cunt, his grip possessive and hard. "This belongs to me, along with the rest of your body, your soul. Forever and ever more, we are bound."

With a fingertip on my clit, he creates rough, hard circles against where I'm slick and swollen. Whatever damage was done earlier from his bite has subsided, and I'm just as sensitive as I ever was. He reaches forward slightly, pinching it as if he were biting it again, and I gasp. It hurts, and yet I've never felt so desperate for the pain.

"I want you coming on my cock like the sea goddess you are," he says roughly. "I want it wet, so very fucking wet."

His fingers go back to work, swirling, pinching, pulling until my thighs start to shake, my neck arching back.

"Yes, yes," I hiss. "More."

"Jesus," he mumbles against me. "You're going to bring me to heaven when I don't deserve it. You're going to be drowning in my cum from the inside out."

He pulls back just a little, trying to catch his breath, and the whole church is fuzzy, like I'm somewhere else, in another world. Then his cock is driven in so hard and deep, there's no mercy, no mercy at all.

I cry out, the breath knocked out of me as I let go to the oncoming waves, to the pain that comes with the pleasure. My core feels like it's the sun, hot and spinning, the heat building until it obliterates me. I come hard and as loud as my voice will allow. My entire body pulses and quakes, the edge of the pew digging into my chest, hard enough to bruise.

"Oh, fuck me, here it comes," he pants. "Oh, God."

He ruts into me, pure animal, all beast, all man, and I hear his breath hitch, feel the rumbles of his groans, the hot spurt of his seed inside me. My body jerks and flails from the dying thrusts until it's boneless, until his pace slows and his hands are coasting down the back of my head, sliding through my hair in a gesture that's both absent and tender, like he's not really sure who I am or who he is.

"Larimar," he says, my name a whisper, an offering, something revered.

Then, he plants a kiss on my shoulder.

Sweet.

Soft.

"Priest," I whisper back.

He tenses with hesitation.

Then, he chuckles warmly.

"Sorry, I'm having trouble hearing you," he says. "My ear seems to be missing."

Chapter Fourteen

PRIEST

I never thought I would lose an ear. Frankly, I never thought I would lose any part of my body. When I was a monster, I was completely indestructible. I vaguely remember being attacked by people in self-defense, but I don't think they ever did any damage. Regardless, every part of me has always remained intact.

Until Larimar, my little fish, my sea goddess with an appetite for destruction, bit off my blasted ear, sliced open my neck, and left her marks down my back in bloody rows. I don't think I've ever experienced so much pain, but that agony was quickly replaced by the need for violence and the desire to fuck her.

It's fortunate for the both of us that my desire to fuck her won out.

In the days since I took her in the church, I've grappled with what has changed. My ear grew back, thankfully—turns out I'm more vain than a priest should be—and my wounds healed, but my relationship with Larimar has been altered. It's like I'm looking at her through a different lens. I've always desired her, wanted to possess her in an obsessive way. I yearned to keep her forever, whether that meant keeping her in the back room of this church or perhaps, one day, venturing out of this desolate, weather-beaten village and going else-where—maybe a pirate ship helmed by a crew of blood-drinkers, setting sail for seas uncharted with her by my side.

But those feelings came from a place of ownership, from wanting her to be mine. It's why I needed her to be bound to me in exchange for my magic. It might just be for show on her behalf, but I take it seriously. When I say I will travel to the ends of the earth to find her if she ever leaves me, I mean it.

However, after I'd been inside her, after I came until there was nothing left, after I gave myself over to temptation and sin, I realized what I'd been afraid of this whole time. I assumed that if I broke my vows, if I fucked her properly in the eyes of God, that I would be handing the reins over to the beast inside.

But that didn't happen.

I realized my true fear, what has always terrified me about my sea goddess, is how I felt about her. Not just as a possession or an obsession, something to own and keep and behold, but someone to protect, to cherish, with a part of her to covet.

Her heart.

But I wouldn't know what to do with anyone's heart. I am the last person who would keep it safe. If she gave me hers, I would only abuse it. I am not a good man, no matter my voca-tion, and I only know how to hurt the things I care about.

As for my heart? Well, I don't really have one. It was lost the day I was turned into a Vampyre. No, not lost. I didn't lose my heart that day.

I shredded it to pieces.

I liquefied it.

It dissolved the moment I killed my family.

Like it had never existed at all.

A man like that doesn't deserve to have a heart.

Despite Larimar reminding me of what I fear most, there was no chance I could stay away from her. Naturally, I couldn't anyway, since I had to check on her each day. I have the humble jobs of emptying her latrine bucket and bringing her food and water.

I kept the chain in her mouth and her hands bound. My body needed time to mend, and the last thing I wanted was to have her attack me and have to start healing over again. I shudder to think what other body part she might try and bite off. I know I gave her pleasure over and over again—and she knows what will happen to her if she tries to run—but I can't take my chances.

Sometimes I want to, though. Often. One more taste of that cunt, one more tight squeeze inside her. I want to feel the way she quakes on my cock when she's coming. I want to hear her breathless, greedy little noises as she finishes, the heaven only I can make her see.

And right now, she's standing in front of me with a carnal look on her sweet face. Such a juxtaposition—a devil and an angel in one, and she's naked, bound, and chained.

I hold a wet cloth in my hand, offering it to her from the washtub. I moved it here from my cottage, figuring it was a more dignified way to bathe than from a bucket.

"I figured since you don't have a tail anymore, you should probably bathe yourself."

I've loosened the chain just enough so she can speak, albeit muffled and slurred at times. "You'll have to untie me first," she says sweetly, showing me her wrists.

She only looks innocent. I know what those claws can do.

When I don't move for her, she rolls her eyes and climbs

into the tub, her long, wheat-blonde hair falling over her shoulder like an early Renaissance painting. "Fine," she says in a hard, muffled voice. "Then you'll be the one to bathe me."

I exhale heavily and nod. "Fine."

She sits down in the tub, the water barely covering her. It's freezing since I wasn't able to heat it up, but she doesn't seem to notice. I suppose that's another part of her Syren self that carried through since she used to swim in the waters offshore, rife with penguins and floating shelves of ice.

"Tell me something about yourself," I say as I rub a slice of olive oil soap across the washcloth and apply it to her shoulders. Her skin is so soft and smooth it slides right over her. "Tell me about where you were living before I found you."

"Living?" she says with a snort. "I was living everywhere."

"But you live in groups, in colonies, do you not?"

"I told you I was alone," she says as I bring the soapy cloth down over her back.

"But you came from a kingdom. Limonos, was it? You were in Acapulco. That's on the other side of the continent. Surely, you were with others from there to here. Why would you swim all this way alone?"

Her body goes still, and silence fills the room. "I was looking for someone."

This is news to me.

"Who?" I ask, the cloth pausing mid-spine.

"Someone who doesn't want to be found," she says quietly. "I'd rather not talk about it."

"Why not? I told you about my past."

"Not everything," she says as she glances up at me.

She's right—not everything. If I were to badger her anymore, she would make me confess my darkest sins.

I drop the subject. It's probably cruel to keep making her talk while she's gagged with a chain anyway.

I keep the cloth moving as I wash her everywhere, being

extra gentle over her breasts, between her legs. It's impossible not to excite her, not to provoke her sexual appetite. I make her come without even meaning to, and there are no prayers I can say that will keep my cock down, that will keep my mind from sinking into the mire of depravity.

By the time I'm done bathing her, I decide to revel in it.

I pick her up out of the bath, wet and naked, and lie her down on the pew.

"I'm going to feed from you," I tell her. "And you're going to let me take my fill."

Her eyes widen with anticipation. "Will you make it hurt?" she asks.

"I can try not to, but I won't make any promises."

"I'm asking you to." She gives me a wry smile. "Make it hurt."

Her plea makes my balls rise, my cock already viciously, painfully hard.

"Alright," I tell her, about to open the flap on my trousers.

"I have another request," she says quickly, and I stare at her to go on. "I want to see you naked."

I pause, my hand down my pants, fisting my cock. "Naked?"

"I've never seen a man completely nude," she says. "Not in a sexual way. Please. You're always clothed, and I'm always... not. It's only fair, isn't it?"

"If things were fair in your world, you wouldn't be my captive, would you?" I point out, but I decide to indulge her regardless. I take off my shirt, my pants, until I'm in the nude, the only thing left on my body the rosary around my neck. I know my body is strong, built to perfection. Being an immortal with preternatural strength means that everything is in peak physical condition, from my arms to my abdomen to my cock.

And from the way she bites her lips, the fresh smell of her arousal in the air, I know she more than likes what she sees.

My little fish is *hungry*.

I put my hands on her clavicles and shove her until she's lying back on the pew, and then I take her legs and raise them as straight as they will go, standing between them. Her cunt is completely bare and open to me, and I have the most sinful view of it.

I waste no time unleashing the heathen inside me.

I position my cock at her cunt, teasing for a few seconds with just the tip, barely pushing in until she starts squirming, rubbing her cunt, wet and slick, against me.

Then I give her what she wants, wedging my cock inside her as deep as it will go. It's a tight fit from this angle, but the more I jam it in, the more I feel her stretch around me. My eyes roll back in my head, my body trembling already.

"God," she cries out against the chain.

I pretend she's calling to me, that I'm her god.

I groan at the thought as my balls pull toward my body, tight as fists.

But what god would have a woman with her hands tied behind her back and a metal chain in her mouth? What god would hold such a woman captive so he could fuck her and feast on her?

I guess that makes me the Devil.

I push in to the hilt, my balls pressed against her ass and thighs, and stare down at the sight. She looks like she's being impaled, my cock thick inside her wet, pink skin.

"More, please," she whispers, her eyes locking with mine.

I grunt and start pumping harder, holding on to her legs for leverage, her calves on my shoulders, and soon, I'm rutting like an animal. I feel so incredibly strong like this, seeing her beneath me, her cunt sopping, her eyes glazed, her body mine for the taking. It almost feels wrong, like I shouldn't be relishing how much I'm overpowering her, and yet I am.

"More," she whispers again.

I grin at her, my voice ragged as I say, "I'm not done with you yet."

I pull out, my cock bobbing, shiny with her desire, as I flip her over on her stomach. She lets out a gleeful laugh that makes my heart skip a beat, but that's quickly overshadowed by the fervent need to come inside her.

But first, I want to feed.

And then, I want to give her something more.

I lean forward over her back and bite the side of her neck. My fangs pierce her skin, and her sweet blood flows into my mouth, trickling down her neck. I know I shouldn't feed from her so often, but I can't help myself. Her blood is as addictive as the rest of her.

"More," she groans.

"More what?" I ask against her neck, licking up the spilled blood. "Tell me, and I'll give it to you."

"More of you. I want to feel more of everything. I want to feel obliterated."

"Then your prayers shall be answered," I tell her.

I swallow her blood down and then straighten up. "Lift up your hips," I murmur to her, watching as her firm, full bottom rises in the air. "That's a good girl."

I lean down and bite her cheek, fangs sinking into the soft, pillowy skin.

She cries out, her body stiffening before she starts to relax into me.

Before she can move, I grasp her rear in my hands and spread her cheeks apart. Her tight little hole is clean, pink, and waiting for me, and I'm going to mess it all up. I lower my head, my nose pressing in first before my mouth, and she gasps as my tongue makes contact with her pretty puckered spot, tasting of the soap I washed her with.

"Oh my God," she cries out against the chain.

I keep probing, tasting, getting her hole as wet as possible for what I'm about to do. I pull back and bite her rear again, pulling the blood into my mouth before I spit on my hand.

I slide that hand over my throbbing cock, then between her cheeks, alternating until both are slippery.

"Bite down if you need to," I joke.

Then, I press the tip of my cock against her slick hole and slowly push in.

"Ahhh," she cries out softly.

"That's it, you can take me," I assure her. "I'll go slow."

"Priest," she groans, her body starting to squirm, as if to run.

I pause, placing my hand on her lower back. "You can tell me to stop."

She nods, swallowing audibly. "It's alright. I'm fine."

"You can take it," I tell her again.

"I can take it."

I grin to myself with a perverse sense of pride before I grab her hips and continue pushing myself inside her. Inch by inch it goes, and I spit a few times more to lubricate its path.

She moans loudly, and while she's not pushing her rear into me, she's not trying to run away either.

Slowly, I begin pumping, my cock glistening as I draw it out and then push it back in. She's so tight it makes it hard to see straight.

"More," she says. "I want to feel you everywhere."

My brows rise as I watch my length disappear inside her.

She says everywhere...

Still inside her, I reach over to one of the lit candles on the desk and blow it out. Smoke floats away from the wick as I pull the candle from the holder and turn it upside down, the smoldering end pressed against my palm, singeing it.

Brandishing it, I bring the candle down underneath her hips.

Her body tenses.

I run my fingers over the rim of her cunt, making sure she's still gushing before I thrust the candle inside her.

"Priest!" she calls out. The candle is nearly as thick as my cock, but she's so wet it slides right inside.

"That's it," I murmur, working both her asshole and her cunt. "See how well you take me? See how your body needs me, so ripe and greedy, ready to come any way that you can?"

She's panting now, moving her hips back against me, wanting more. I give it to her, the candle fucking her cunt deep, my cock shoved into her rear.

I've never seen such a sight.

"You like this, don't you?" I moan. "Being filled like this. Do you want to come, little fish?"

She nods, letting out a whimpering sound. She's so tense, trembling all over, so very close. All I do is slip my knuckle over her swollen clit, and she comes undone.

Her channel grips my cock, milking me until I'm violently hard, her breathless cries filling the air. Her head slumps forward as I start pumping into her with a wildness that surprises me.

"Fuck," I grunt. "Yes, yes."

This is it.

With a crude jerk of my hips, my orgasm is ripped from my core. I feel like someone has performed an exorcism on me, torn the devil out of my soul in a wave of hot cum. I fill her with it, and it keeps coming in torrents, hot and relentless.

I pump and thrust, her rear growing messier until I finally slip out. I watch as my cum drips out of her hole, running down over my cock, my balls, dripping onto the pew.

I don't think I've ever made such a mess before.

Without thinking, I swipe my fingers over my spent cum and shove it inside her cunt, pushing it inside with my fingers until she squirms, her body too sensitive. But I'm not trying to get her ready again. It's the sight of the gleaming white pearls on her pink flesh that does something to me, satisfies me like nothing else.

"Well," I say, taking a step back, my eyes coasting over the sight of her beautiful body.

She's going to need another bath.

Chapter Fifteen

LARIMAR

I never gave much thought to what mankind's version of heaven is like, but I'm fairly certain theirs doesn't involve a rusted chain in one's mouth. However, as I lie on top of the church pew, I feel as close to heaven as I'm going to get.

"Stay right there," Priest says to me in a low, rich voice, briefly placing his warm hand on the small of my back. The gesture is soft, but it sends a wash of shivers over my skin. Funny how he can defile me so thoroughly—bound, chained, with both a cock and a candle of all things—and yet a simple touch feels just as good.

Perhaps even more so.

I'm not going anywhere, I want to tell him, but of course, I can't speak clearly with the chain in my mouth.

I feel his presence move away from me, the sound of his trousers being pulled on, the sound of the lock being undone and the door opening. I turn my head to see him leave.

He doesn't lock the door behind him.

This is your chance, I tell myself. *Escape.*

But the relentless orgasms must have done something to my head.

They've made me weak.

Damn it. *I'm* supposed to be the one seducing him and rendering him helpless through sex, not the other way around.

How did he manage to turn the tables?

I exhale against the chain, my eyes on the door. I don't know where Priest has gone, but I can't imagine he will be gone for long. Does he know he didn't lock it?

I try to push past the postcoital haze and formulate a plan. I could get up and run. My legs work, and they aren't bound. I could run, albeit naked, outside and keep running until I find help. The villagers would help me, I'm certain of it.

But Priest would probably hunt me down as he did before, and frankly, I wouldn't mind if he subjected me to more angry sex.

Still, I have to remember why I gave up my fins to begin with.

I have to think about Maren.

I twist around and sit up carefully, trying to gather the courage.

It had been so easy to run the other day.

What happened to me?

Why do I feel compelled to stay this man's hostage?

Because you like it, a tiny voice inside me says. *Because you like being his captive. You like that he feeds on you and fucks you and makes you feel things you've never felt before.*

Because you are like him.

And you like *him.*

I swallow uneasily. No. I can't like him. I can't like any of this.

I've been driven by the obsession of finding my sister for the last eleven years, my one singular purpose. I've survived the loss of my father, the loss of my kingdom, the loss of my other sister. I've survived abuse at the hands of rogue Syrens, survived years of loneliness and despair as I've searched the oceans looking for Maren.

I can't give up now, even if I feel something for this man.

This monster.

This Vampyre.

But what if I'm never meant to find Maren?

What if I'm only meant to find *him*?

I hear footsteps outside the door, and I snap out of my thoughts, my heart racing.

Priest steps back into the room, shirtless but wearing his black trousers, carrying a bucket of water and a cloth.

He pauses for a moment, and hurt flits across his face as he looks me over before he continues walking.

"Were you planning on going somewhere?" he asks tepidly as he sets the bucket beside me.

I stare at him in response. I can't answer anyway.

He just nods. "Lie back down. Spread your legs."

My eyes widen. Again? We're doing this already?

"I'm cleaning you up," he adds quietly and gestures with a raise of his chin to do as he asks.

"You just bathed me."

"And I just made you filthy again," he says and motions again. "I wanted clean water for this."

I lie back on the pew, my hands bound beneath me, and stare up at the ceiling.

I hear the washcloth going in the water. It's deliciously cold and wet as he presses it against my inner knee and gently glides it up my thighs. He cleans me much like he did earlier, with delicate, methodical strokes.

He murmurs for me to flip over to my stomach, and I do so, parting my legs for him again. There is no shame with him, no inhibitions or humility, not when it comes to my body, but even so, I tense up a little as he parts the cheeks of my rear and gently dabs the washcloth there, that part of me a little sore from being used in such a foreign and savage manner.

"There," he says. After a few more minutes of tender care, he removes the cloth, and then...

SMACK.

I yelp against the chain, jerking from the impact of his palm against my bottom.

I glare at him over my shoulder, and he's grinning deviously at me, the kind of smile that soothes the sting. A smile that makes my heart stumble.

"Sorry," he says, not sounding sorry at all. "I couldn't help myself. I shall have to blame the monster."

Then, he reaches forward and grabs me by my shoulders, hauling me up to sit. "I'm going to untie you for a moment while I get this shift on you," he says, lifting the linen.

What's the point? I think as he reaches behind me and starts undoing the rope. *I'll only end up naked again.*

"Promise me you'll behave," he whispers against my ear, making my eyes roll back in my head. "Then maybe I'll undo the chain too."

I nod as he frees my hands. I wriggle my aching wrists, and he immediately grabs them, bringing them forward, a warning in his eyes.

Then, he lifts them up to his mouth, and with his gaze intently focused on mine like he's staring into my very soul, he places his lips on the soft underside of each one.

Goodness, I feel like I'm melting at his touch. It's as if he's trying to win me over with tenderness now.

And it's working.

I'll behave, I think. *I'll do anything you want if you keep looking at me like that.*

He smiles gently and then lifts my arms, slipping the shift over me and pulling it down over my head and chest.

"Good girl," he says appreciatively as he reaches behind me to undo the chain.

Then, he stops.

Sucks in his breath.

The energy in the room suddenly changes into something dark and cold.

I glance up to see him staring over my shoulder, and I follow his gaze to the door to see a man standing there.

I gasp against the chain, and Priest drops his hands.

"What is going on here?" the man says. He's dressed in authoritative clothing, which makes me think he might be a priest too, but then I see the sword sheathed at his side, a gun in his hand. I became very familiar with them after Asherah was taken.

Is this man a pirate? He seems too well-kept to be one. He even has one of those white curled wigs.

Priest doesn't say anything; he just puts himself between me and the other man.

"What are you doing to her?" the man says. "Step aside, Father Aragon."

"Please leave," Priest says in a hard, cold voice. "You are not allowed back here. This is consecrated ground."

The man snorts and brings out his gun, pointing it at Priest. "Consecrated ground. I know you are no priest, no holy man. I've always suspected as much—all these visits to the church in the middle of the night. Now, I see you're keeping a woman back here for yourself. Holy man indeed."

"She belongs to me," Priest practically growls.

"I'll let her decide who she belongs to," the soldier says as he smiles at me. "Don't worry, darling, I'll get you out here." He glares at Priest and shakes his pistol at him. "Step aside, Aragon."

Priest looks back down at me.

I suppose this is my chance.

This is all I was waiting for.

Someone to come and rescue me.

But then, to my utter surprise, Priest steps aside.

And my heart sinks with fear.

The man grins and walks over to me, keeping the gun trained on Priest as he approaches.

"You're beautiful, aren't you?" the man says as he leers at me. "I can see why he wanted to hide you back here." The soldier reaches out with his free hand and grabs my wrist, hard enough for me to cry out. "Don't worry, I'm here to help."

Priest makes a move for me, but the soldier pulls the trigger.

With a fiery blast, gun smoke fills the air, and I scream again as Priest is hit with a bullet to his chest. He goes down with a gasp, hitting the ground hard.

"Priest!" I try to scream against the chains, but the soldier hits me on the side of the head with his pistol, and everything explodes into sparks. I feel warm blood trickle down the side of my head, and I'm shoved down on the pew again, the soldier pushing up my shift.

He groans, pressing his hard-on against my rear as I thrash, trying to get out of the way, drowning in disgust.

"I doubt you've been properly fucked by a holy man," the man says, grabbing my wrists and yanking them behind my back, my shoulders dislocating again with debilitating pain. "He probably had to tie you up because he doesn't know what he's doing. Probably had to put this in your mouth so you wouldn't tell him how bad he was."

He hits me with the gun again, and I yelp, feeling my fight start to slip away. I try to get my claws to come out, but the way my shoulders are ripped from their sockets must be preventing me. "Or did he do it because you're a screamer? You know, I like it when they scream."

He grabs the chain at the back of my head and slams my

forehead down into the wood before he pulls my head back up again. I feel his other hand fumble in his trousers. "Let's see how much noise you make, darling."

I feel the chain start to come loose.

I feel my resolve start to slip away.

"I wouldn't remove that if I were you." Priest's voice rings out like a beacon behind me.

I open my eyes.

He's alive!

The chain comes undone and falls out of my mouth.

I feel the soldier twist around to look in Priest's direction, hear his confused gasp at seeing him alive.

"She bites," Priest adds.

And that's enough for me.

While the soldier is distracted by Priest's resurrection, my shark teeth emerge, and I find the strength to twist around to bite the soldier's hand. I chomp down on two fingers, severing them both at the knuckle.

The soldier screams in horror, blood spraying, and I spit the fingers out violently. If I'm going to eat any part of this man, it's going to be his heart, and he's going to watch me do it.

Meanwhile, Priest appears behind him, grabbing the man from behind, pulling off his wig and throwing it to the ground before wrapping strong fingers around each shoulder, holding the screaming soldier in place.

"Do you want to do the honors, little fish?" Priest asks me. His eyes have that strange red sheen to them, his fangs protruding as he talks.

I bare my teeth right back, matching his gruesome smile.

"Gladly," I tell him.

I move my shoulders so they roll forward and snap back into place, gritting my teeth through a scream. Then, I thrust my hand at the soldier, my nails turning into claws as I plunge my fingers into the man's chest, ripping through flesh and bone.

His scream echoes off the walls, and I see my reflection in his dark eyes. I look like a crazed monster.

Even more so when I rip his heart right out of his chest. I hold it in front of his face so he can watch as it gives its last beat. I want him to watch me eat it too, but I hesitate, wondering if that will be too much for Priest, if he'll think badly of me.

But when I glance at him standing behind the soldier, he just gives me an assured nod to proceed.

So, I open my mouth and stuff the man's heart inside, slicing through the tough muscle with a few snaps of my teeth, blood spilling over the sides of my lips.

I know the soldier sees me eat it, even if he's alive for just a mere second before he collapses, dead in Priest's arms.

That only makes me more ravenous as I swallow down his heart—it's the best thing I've tasted in a long time—and lock eyes with Priest. Something changes in his gaze, and he frowns. He knows that, right now, I could make a break for it. My teeth are sharp, my claws out; I can run for the door.

But I don't move. I just stand there, a bloodied corpse between us.

I'm not sure why it feels rather awkward, but it does, like we're both seeing each other in a new light, one perhaps only flattering to each other.

"You got shot," I point out, nodding at his chest while I wipe the blood from my mouth.

"I did. Wasn't the first time and won't be the last. It can't kill me."

"Then why did you step aside?" I ask. "I thought you were going to protect me."

"Larimar, I will protect you from everyone, including myself," he says gravely. "He wasn't going to make it out of this room alive regardless, but I wanted to see what you could do. I wanted to see how you'd take care of yourself. I wanted to see *your* monster."

"He was going to *rape* me," I say. "What if I couldn't have fought back?"

"I would have torn off his dick before he had the chance," he growls, his eyes burning into mine. "I didn't think he'd pull the trigger. Besides, you *did* take care of yourself. All of this? This is all you."

I suppose he's right. Even if Priest hadn't recovered, I managed to bite off the man's fingers. I tore out his heart and ate it. I might even be a little proud of myself.

"Since we have him, we shouldn't let him go to waste," Priest says, clearing his throat. "Did you want to help yourself to the rest of his organs while I drink his blood?"

"Do you think others will come?"

He shakes his head and steps back to place the soldier on the ground. "They would have been here already, but I'll be listening, just in case. I should have heard him coming before, but I was just...too preoccupied with you."

"With whether I would behave," I remind him. "I'd say I'm in the midst of misbehaving, wouldn't you?"

He gives me a crooked smile, fangs and all, that steals the breath from my lungs. "Then please, continue."

"Don't mind if I do," I say, getting to my knees beside the corpse. Priest does the same, snapping the dead man's neck to the side before biting and feasting. I dig my hand into the soldier's chest cavity and rip him down the middle, searching for his liver.

The two of us share a meal together, as lovers do.

Chapter Sixteen

Priest was on edge for a few days following our slaying of the soldier. Even though no others followed, he was paranoid that either the soldier had told others about his suspicions, or someone would have seen the soldier come by the church that fateful night.

But no one came to question him.

In fact, it has been nearly a week since it happened, and he says there hasn't been any word at all that the soldier even went missing. Priest thinks they desert their posts often enough that it isn't questioned. Being stationed in these parts isn't for the faint of heart, apparently.

Naturally, he made sure there was no evidence left of our feast. After Priest drained the soldier of his blood and I ate a few tasty, nutritious organs, he took the body outside and buried him. He said wolves would probably dig him out in a few days before the frost became permanent. When they were done with him, there would be nothing left.

"I won't be staying long. I have mass this morning," Priest says to me. He has just joined me in the back room, delivering my breakfast. This time, it seems to be bread, butter, and some sort of fish that doesn't smell quite right. I wrinkle my nose at it as he sets it on the desk where I've been sitting, dressed in just my shift, flipping through a bible. I've been trying to teach myself how to read to no avail.

"What?" he asks with a frown, noting my expression. "I finally got you fish like you asked. You don't approve?"

I pick up the end of it and lick it tentatively.

He groans as he watches me. "Please refrain from giving me lewd thoughts before my sermon."

I can't help but smile, even though the fish itself tastes like pure salt.

"I don't think humans know what good fish taste like," I remark, making a face.

Priest chuckles. "I think I do, *little fish*."

"But you're not quite human," I point out. "Besides, I don't taste like fish."

"No. You taste like a goddess of the sea," he says, his hands going to tug on the white cloth around his collar. "You taste like heaven on my tongue." Heat envelopes his gaze, turning it smoldering, and he suddenly swears. "Christ."

He comes around the desk and puts his hands on my hips, lifting me so I'm perched on the edge of it. I giggle, pushing my plate of breakfast away and running my fingers through his long, silky hair as he shoves up the hem of my shift and spreads my legs.

"Just a snack to get me through my preaching," he murmurs, ducking his head and assaulting me with his mouth until I gasp. "The taste of you will remind me what's worth sinning for," he rasps against my skin.

Heavens.

"As long as I'm on your mind," I tell him through a moan, my neck arching back. We've grown closer this last week, at least as close as a captor and captive can get. Every now and then, Priest will get this look in his eyes, like he's been reprimanded, and he'll put some distance between us. His gaze becomes glacial, and he smiles and talks less, treating me like something he tolerates—no longer cruel, but stiff and polite.

But it doesn't take long for him to thaw. Our bodies are quick to warm each other, constantly drawn into each other's grasp. I don't have to beg anymore for attention, don't have to ask to be touched. I'll still do it because he likes to hear it, but he's oh so quick to offer.

And I am enthralled with every minute of being in his company.

Especially when he's feasting on me. The sight of him between my thighs—dark hair, wide shoulders—only adds to the tightness in my chest.

I shouldn't want such a man, such a wolf in sheep's clothing, but I do.

I shouldn't want a man at all.

Fuck, how I do.

Priest moans against me, the vibrations making my bones feel like jelly. A pulse of thick arousal swells my clit, making my cunt spread, and his tongue penetrates me further, digging in and lapping up everything, hot and wet.

I will never get tired of the way he eats me, like he's abandoned every moral, every vow, every rope that kept him tethered. He feasts like he'll never taste anything again, his throat thick with ravenous grunts and rough cries of worship—not for his God, or the God of others, but for me. This priest is worshipping me with every suck, lick, and lap of his tongue.

I don't take long to come. I go off like a gunshot, writhing against the desk, squeezing his head between my legs, and he's merciless with his mouth until the bittersweet end. I'm left panting, feeling out of my body.

He straightens up and brushes the hair off my sweat-damp forehead, tucking it behind my ears with a tenderness that sobers me. His lips shine with my desire. I gesture to the mess, and he slowly brings out his tongue, licking his mouth clean.

"Can I trust you to behave if I leave you untied?" he asks, look at me more closely. Ever since we devoured the soldier, he hasn't put the chain back in my mouth, and he only remembers to bind my wrists when he feels like it— usually with his necklace, which he calls a rosary.

"You're still worried I might leave?" I ask, trying not to feel hurt. "Who else would give me such pleasure as you?"

He reaches up to his ear and grimaces as he touches it lightly. "I still don't think I can hear as well. Is it me, or did it grow back bigger?"

He has a point. Not that his ear looks any different.

"I'll be back," he says, reaching over and tapping his fingers on the bible. "If you're really interested, I can teach you how to read."

My heart flips in my chest. "Are you sure?"

He nods. "We can start this evening."

Then, he opens the door to the church and closes it behind him.

I hold my breath, wondering how much freedom he'll actually give me.

Then, I hear the lock turning.

Priest's sermon seemed to go longer than usual. Perhaps he felt guilty for what we did to the soldier, even though it was self-defense and the soldier deserved it. From what I heard through the walls, he spent an awful lot of time talking about guilt, more so than usual.

But when he finally ventured back to see me, he didn't

seem burdened by any of the words he had spoken. Instead, he seemed lighter than I'd ever seen him, as if a heavy weight had been lifted off his shoulders. He brought me some food and then came back again in the evening so our lessons could begin.

I have to admit, it was nice to see that side of him. I figured he would be a good teacher because of his deep, booming voice and engaging cadence when he's giving his sermons. I can't see how the villagers react, but I assume they hang on his every word. I know I do, even when I'm listening through the walls.

But when it comes to teaching me how to read, he's patient, compassionate, kind.

He seems to have limitless energy for it. He must have been trying to teach me for hours before it felt like my eyes were starting to cross.

"Alright, I'm afraid I'm going to need a break," I tell him. "My brain can only take so much."

He gives me a sheepish grin, and it somehow makes him look younger.

"Sorry," he says, closing the book. "I can get carried away."

"I've noticed. Where did you learn how to read? You must have had a good instructor."

He traces the gold letters stamped on the book's leather cover. "I learned in the monastery. I couldn't read when I was a human. I'd wanted to learn, but there was no use for it in my line of work."

"What about remembering spells?"

He shrugs. "They were all passed down verbally."

"Did your friend Abe teach you in the monastery?" I ask.

He looks at me in surprise, as if he didn't expect me to remember his name. "No. As methodical as he is, he doesn't have patience for those who aren't as bright as he," he says with a chuckle. "There were others who taught me there."

"Were they Vampyres too?"

"Most of them," he says. "A few humans."

"And they weren't worried they'd become your next meal?"

He lifts a shoulder. "If they were, they never told me."

"And so what did you learn on? I'm assuming the Bible."

"Yes. Some other books too. Ever heard of William Shakespeare? John Milton? Miguel de Cervantes?"

I give him a tepid smile. "You know I have not. I have only heard of Father Aragon, and that is it."

That brings another grin to his face. "Well, I know the Holy Book front and back, but perhaps my teachings are better spent on something a little more entertaining."

He gets to his feet, pushing his chair back and holding out his hand for me.

"Come with me," he says. "I have things to show you."

I stare at his hand for a moment, a fluttering in my heart. I'm almost scared, but it's a different kind of fear.

I swallow hard and put my hand in his as he grasps it with warm, strong, slender fingers. I can't help but narrow my focus on this moment—it's the first time he's treated me as more than a captive or a prisoner or even company, like someone he desires to be around.

He pulls me to my feet, and, as always when he's standing beside me, I feel so dainty and small next to his broad shoulders and height. As a Syren, being considered small or dainty was never a good thing—the bigger you were, the better the killer. The less likely that you would bend or break in an unforgiving sea world, the longer you would survive.

But somehow, as a woman, in his presence, I like the idea that he can toss me around, that I weigh nothing to him, that he can protect me against the dangers of this world, one that I know I'm not well-versed in.

"Where are we going?" I ask as we go to the door and he unlocks it with his key. "To pray?"

He smirks at me. "The way *we* pray is quite different from how others do it."

The question still stands as he leads me past the altar and down the aisle.

To the doors that lead outside.

I almost remind him that I'm not bound, but he knows that. It's why his grip on my hand is overly tight.

With his other hand, he pushes the heavy doors with ease, and they open with a loud creak.

I am met with the cold wind of a night sky, frigid, stark air that makes my nostrils flare, a breeze that blows back my hair. I inhale as if I've never breathed before, taking in everything that is bracing and clarifying. I stop where I am, the church doors closing behind me as I tilt my head back to look at the sky. There's a moon, a million stars, and, beyond them, a darkness like the deepest ink. It spreads and stretches into infinity, and at once, I'm overwhelmed by how beautiful it is, how small I feel.

"You're crying," Priest says in a low voice.

I reach up and touch under my eyes, feeling wetness.

I look at him in bewilderment. "We Syrens don't cry," I say, my throat and nose now feeling thick.

"You don't feel sorrow?" he asks curiously.

"We don't have tears underwater," I explain, wiping the tears away. "This is the first time I've ever cried."

"I see," he says quietly. He tilts his head back. "God can do that sometimes."

I blink at the stars. "What do you mean?"

"This is where I find God," he says. "Not in there." He nods at the church, then looks back to the sky. "There."

"In heaven?"

"In the universe, in nature," he says, gesturing around him.

My gaze follows, the moonlight illuminating the nearby cottage, the stunted, crooked trees that are perpetually wind-bent, the pebbled shore, the crashing waves of home.

"In you," he adds.

He says it so simply, I almost think I don't hear him right at first.

I look over at him, my brows raised.

"I find God in you," he repeats, his eyes shining like starlight.

If I ever had any resolve against this man's powers, I know I'm losing them all with those words. Here is the priest who finds his God in me.

Me.

Another tear rolls down my cheek, and I let out a strained laugh, swatting at it angrily. "Enough already."

Priest continues to stare at me, his gaze solemn. Then, he tugs at my hand. "Come on. Let me show you where I spend the days."

He leads me along a stone path lined with frosted grass. I marvel at everything as we walk, so thrilled and relieved to be out of the church. I feel closer to my true self now, the wildness of the landscape and the crashing waves, like it's unwinding my soul. Part of me wants to rip myself from his hands and run—not away from him or from anything, but just to feel my legs move in this clear, cold night.

Yet I'm curious to see where Priest sleeps. When he brings me into the cold, dark cottage, I guess I shouldn't have been expecting much. It isn't until he throws some logs on the fire and lights a few thick candles—candles I will never look at the same way again—that I see it has more personality than at first glance.

It's bare, with a bed in the corner, a desk and chair, thin windows, a small hearth for cooking and heat, two cushioned chairs beside it. There are a few boxes and chests where I assume his belongings are stored, as well as the washtub that he's moved back in here. But the walls are covered in crosses and paintings, giving life and flavor to the cottage that the back of the church never had.

"Take a seat," he says, sitting me down in one of the chairs. I sink into it—like sitting on a pillow. One would think the church pews would offer this same kind of comfort. "Would you like some tea?"

"Do you drink tea?" I ask him.

He gives me a wan smile and gives his head a shake.

"Then I'll forgo it," I say. I haven't had tea before, and I'm not about to start now. Besides, I'm not his guest, even though I feel like one at the moment.

He nods and then heads over to a shelf, plucking a few books off it before sitting down in the chair across from me. "Shall we start with *Don Quixote*?"

"You're going to teach me how to read now?"

"No," he says. "The lesson is over for the day. I'm going to read *to* you."

He studiously flips open the book and starts reading. He does so in the way he gives his sermons, and I am enraptured, hanging on each word about this man from La Mancha and his squire, even when I find myself getting tired, the room getting fuzzy. My eyes flutter closed for a moment.

Priest snaps the book shut and then comes over to me, reaching down to pick me up into his arms, bringing me over to his bed.

"I want you to sleep with me tonight," he says as he lowers me to the straw mattress. He isn't asking, but I don't want to say no anyway.

I just nod, rubbing my lips together in quiet anticipation.

Then, to my surprise, he takes my wrists in one hand, takes off his rosary with the other, and wraps it around my wrists. I expect him to attach them to the iron posts that line the bed, but he doesn't. I think he just likes the way it looks on me, bound by what he worships.

Though I know he's about to worship me.

He takes off his shirt, then his pants, and I absorb the sight of him, my gaze greedy and hungry. His cock is thick, hard as stone. I don't care if it's considered rude; I take my time to study the sight of him. I've slept with other Syrens before, males, females, the ones in between, but I'd never seen a human cock until I saw Priest's. I don't have much to compare it to, other than the soldier—I took a peek in his pants when Priest was preoccupied—but I know that this cock is magnificent: not as long as a male Syren's, but thick and wide and sculpted, with veins and hard ridges and velvety soft skin.

I'm already salivating. I want it in my mouth.

He gives me a lopsided smile as he prowls over me, his cock bobbing stiffly as he moves. I stare at the ridges of his abdomen as they flex, the sharp curve of his hips. I try to reach for his cock with my bound hand, desperate to feel its heavy weight in my palm, but he grabs my wrists and holds them above my head.

My blood is already simmering as he keeps my hands together and reaches down, steering his cock into my entrance. I'm wet and ready, legs splayed open, my blood simmering, the pulse of my heart rapid in my veins. I watch the ropey muscles of his forearms as he positions himself, teasing me with the glistening tip.

I gasp, jerking my hips upward, animalistic and instinctual, wanting all of him.

"Patience," he murmurs to me, his blue eyes heavy-lidded

as he continues this torturous dance, the head of his cock just kissing my cunt, a wet sound filling the room.

"I don't have patience," I tell him, trying to lift my hips again. "I want you inside me. If not there, then let my lips have you."

He growls and grabs my face, putting his thumb in my mouth.

"I know you would rather suck on my cock," he says with a groan. "But I'm only willing to lose the tip of my thumb to you." He gives me a lazy, lopsided grin and pushes the rest of his thumb into my mouth. I suck on it, watching his eyes flutter closed for a moment.

Then, he slams his hips forward against mine, his cock penetrating deep, and I'm breathless, gasping, all air pushed from my lungs, my heart hammering in my chest.

He grunts loudly, his lower teeth bared as if he's snarling, and he starts fucking me harder, enough that the bed moves, thrusting in and out as if he wants to impale me. Then, he suddenly slows down, pulling out halfway, running his mouth all over my body, his teeth grazing me, drawing blood.

My priest is a contradiction as he moves. His hands roam my body with desperation; they grip my hips, my stomach, my breasts, mean and bruising. His teeth are sharp, his bite hard. And yet, every now and then when he looks up to meet my eyes, there is softness there, something deep and wild but tender enough to undo the hooks around my heart.

Sometimes, the way he looks at me, intense and unblinking, like he's searing a path to my soul, is too much, and I have to look away, and right now is no exception. The vulnerability is unnerving, so I stare at where his cock disappears inside me, shiny with my desire.

We are joined, connected, even when he's being so rough that the pain briefly outshines the pleasure.

"Do you like what you see?" he rasps. "Do you like how I worship at your altar? You're mine. This cunt, this arse, this mouth. All of it is mine, Larimar. Every single inch I can penetrate is mine, and if I could penetrate your soul, then that would belong to me too."

But he *can* penetrate my soul.

I feel him there, loosening it until it has no choice but to belong to him. He's not just holding my body captive—he's holding my heart. And if he ever lets me go, I think my heart will be the last to leave.

"Look at me," he says through a rough groan. "Look at me, little fish."

I meet his eyes, and he holds them there with the pure intensity of his gaze.

"Tell me you're mine."

"I'm yours," I say, but the words are raw and whispered.

His lip curls, and he thrusts in harder, punishing me. "Tell me you're mine and mean it, damn it. Tell me, or I won't let you come."

Now he's being unfair.

"I'm yours," I tell him.

The funny thing is, I mean it. It's not because I said I would be bound to him—it's because I *want* to be bound to him. And when he's *that* deep inside me, I'm not sure how I can think otherwise.

"Fuck," he says gruffly. "Here I come, Goddess." His fingers reach down, giving my clit a few rough strokes. "And so will you."

He knows all that I need. His fingers give me bliss in seconds. I come hard, crying out as he keeps my hands pinned above my head, biting and sucking at my breasts, licking my mouth as I squeeze his cock until his orgasm is torn out of him.

"Yes," he begs into my open mouth. "Please. *God.*"

He comes with hard jerks of his hips, his hot seed spurting inside me, filling me up until I think there can't possibly be more.

And then, finally, he collapses, buries his face in my neck, his skin damp, the room smelling of our sex.

He's still inside me when he falls asleep.

Chapter Seventeen

PRIEST

I dream for the first time in a century.

There's not much of a narrative to it, just flashes of images. I see Larimar's shimmering tail underwater. The dead soldier clawing through his grave. Larimar nailed on a windmill, like the ones from *Don Quixote*. The moon over the water, impossibly large. Abe dressed as a knight, riding a horse made of bones. Larimar reaching into my chest and pulling out my heart before throwing it over her shoulder because it was still beating.

When I wake, I feel rested and alert, though, judging from the moon coming in through the window, I couldn't have been asleep for more than a couple of hours.

That same moon is illuminating Larimar, no longer crucified to a windmill, no longer discarding my heart. She is here beside me, hair spilling around her like liquid silver and gold. Her eyes are closed, her face a slate wiped clean. An angel of innocence, even when I know otherwise.

My heart makes itself known, beating wildly in my chest, as if it wants to punch its way through my ribs. All of this from just looking at her.

But I know what's really making my soul come alive like the soldier in my dream, crawling out of a grave.

It's because I fell asleep after fucking her.

I dreamed.

And she is still here.

She is bound only by that rosary. She could have left at any time during the night, and she didn't.

She's here.

She chose to stay with me.

I keep staring at her, taking in every inch of her face, her body, and something inside me begins to make room, like there's space now for something to live within me.

But it cannot be love.

I close my eyes to the sight of her, trying to grapple with the truth.

It can't be love.

I cannot love this woman, my captive, my pet, my Syren, my little fish. I cannot love her because I lost my heart centuries ago, and I know what happens to the ones I love.

My love stories never get a happy ending.

A cold sweat breaks out on my brow, and I slowly sit up. For the first time, I contemplate running. Leaving. I'll throw myself into that ocean and make myself drown. But I'll never drown; I'll never die. I am in love with this woman, and she will haunt me until the end of time. She will make a nest in my heart and stay there, caught behind the prison bars of my ribs. She is bound to me whether either of us likes it, and I will never be free of her, never be free from this feeling that's slowly taking over my existence.

I rub my hands over my face, trying to gain composure and calm my ratcheting pulse. There's something happening deep inside me, some strange sensation that comes from a dark place, that endless grave recently unearthed. It's not my heart, which feels as if it's balancing on a precipice, but something vile spreading in the marrow of my bones.

No. No, God, please don't let this happen now.

I have tried for so long to keep this monster at bay; this can't be happening now.

Fear jettisons through me, and I press the back of my hand against my mouth, feeling as if I might be sick. I glance down at Larimar sleeping soundly, and I know I can't be around her, not until I know I have things under control.

I quickly get out of bed and slip on my trousers, and then I step out into the night. The clouds have come in, and rain falls, cold and heavy, but I barely feel it.

I only make it halfway to the church when I feel it clawing up through me. I drop to my knees and vomit blood into the grass.

No. I must keep it buried. I must stay in control.

I must.

I've managed to hide that old beast deep down, no matter what was thrown my way. I used the rigid teachings of the book to keep me in line. I always thought that if I deviated from God's word in some way, that's when I would slip, and the monster would take advantage. I thought if I didn't kill, I would be saved. I thought if I didn't give into my lustful, depraved urges, I would be saved.

But, it turns out, none of that matters.

I killed that soldier, with or without Larimar's help, and the beast stayed asleep.

I fucked Larimar and defiled her in every single way possible. I became a slave to my deepest and darkest sexual desires.

And though the beast woke up, it didn't escape from its cage.

But now that I feel like my heart has gotten involved, now that real emotions are coming to light, *that* is what is bringing this monster inside me to life.

I knew keeping her here would be dangerous, not only for her, but for me.

And now I know why.

I spit and get up, stumbling the rest of the way to the church, barging in through the doors like a madman. I stagger down the aisle, leaving a trail of water in my wake, before collapsing on my knees at the altar. I already feel immense pain in my back, like my shoulder blades are splintering, and I arch my head toward the ceiling.

"Please!" I yell, my voice echoing off the rafters. "Help me! Save me, Lord. Save me from myself!"

I press my palms together in prayer, but my hands won't stop shaking. The darkness inside me builds, filling in all my cracks and crevices.

Light, I need light. Only light can cast out the darkness.

I stagger to my feet and grab the matches from the altar, lighting every candle, torch, and oil lamp I can find. I want this room blazing, I want it so bright that there is no place inside me for evil to hide.

When I finally come to the last lamp, the ever-burning chancel lamp on the altar's wall, I add more oil, making the flames dance dangerously high.

And in those flames, I see Larimar dancing.

Then, I smell her, hear her footsteps from outside the door moments before she steps inside.

"Priest?" she calls out.

I turn around to see her barefoot and walking down the aisle, dressed in only her white shift. The rain has soaked her through in the short walk over, her hair wet, her dress soaked and sticking to her. I can see her nipples clearly, the dark shadows of her cunt. Hot, liquid need thrums through me, stealing all that is good and moral until I am just a wicked man and feral beast.

"Get away from me," I growl, but I've already pulled my

cock out of my pants, making a tight fist. There is a deep itch inside me, painful and insidious, and I know she can make it go away.

She stops in the middle of the aisle and stares at me with her big violet eyes, which look nearly pink in this feverish light. With the flames blazing around her, casting flickering gold on her wet skin, she looks like angel escaping hell.

She needs to escape the hell I'm about to bring her.

"Larimar, please," I say, but my words do not match my actions.

My cock juts out from my hips, pulsing slightly with each wild beat of my heart.

"Why did you leave?" she asks, slowly coming toward me. "I woke up, and you were gone." She eyes the way I'm fisting my cock, pumping it. "Did I not give you enough pleasure?"

I let out a hoarse cry, wishing she wouldn't say such a thing.

"I need you to...go," I whisper.

"Why?" she asks, stopping at the foot of the steps. I'm up on the altar, looming over her like a deity, and I can't stop myself as I reach out with my free hand and place it on top of her head. I shove her down to her knees.

"Worship me," I tell her. "Suck me."

She blinks in surprise, probably because earlier, I had made her take my thumb in her mouth, telling her to stay clear of my dick. But I don't feel in control of my words anymore.

"I said do it," I snarl.

Apprehension falls on her face, but she reaches for me, wrapping her hands around my length. I want to hate myself for losing control, for letting the monster speak, but the sight of her on her knees, praying at the altar of my cock, is deliciously sinful.

I push inside her plush lips, and she starts sucking me, working me over with hot passes of her tongue, becoming more ravenous as she goes. There's a part of me that worries she might get too carried away, that the Syren part of her might come out, and I fear the beast will like that.

But then, when I feel my balls pull tight, my hands yanking roughly at her hair, enough to cause her to cry out in pain, I know I need my seed inside her.

I yank her head up by the roots, her teeth grazing my ridge as she goes, and then throw her backward onto the aisle.

She lands with a thump, a wheezing breath knocked out of her, and tries to get to her feet, but I move fast. I push her back down, and she yelps, pinning her hands back over her head. I notice she removed the rosary, and that does something to me, like the last bastion of grace and control I had was removed along with it. It's no longer there to remind me of salvation. The absence of it is a marker of my downfall.

"Priest," she says, her eyes a mix of fear and desire, but I care less about how she feels, and that's how I know the beast is winning.

"You should have listened to me," I rasp.

Then, I reach down and take a rough hold of her thighs, spreading them before I mount her, no hesitation except for the voice inside me that screams for her to run, to leave, to escape.

But that voice won't come out. Is this punishment for taking away hers, for making her words always be a whisper, for keeping that chain in her mouth for longer than I should have?

Is God smiting me right now for my past wrongs?

Or am I only doing it to myself?

I am doing it, a voice rattles from deep inside, one that sounds like Kaleid. That sounds like blood. That sounds like the Devil himself.

This is all for me. Fuck her, feast on her.

"No!" I cry out, and Larimar stares up at me with wide

eyes a second before I spear my cock inside her. I watch as her mouth opens in a silent cry, and I grunt, slamming my hips harder.

I bring my mouth to her throat, and I bite, timing it with a punishing thrust of my cock, drinking as much of her as I can. The monster wants me to fuck and wants me to feast, and if I give it that and just that, perhaps it will leave both of us alone.

But I know the wish is fruitless, like an unheard prayer.

I saw my dick in and out of her, viciously, violently, pinning her down so hard, I fear she might become one with the church floor.

"Priest," she says through a breathless gasp, running her hands down my back. I pull my head back, wanting her to soothe me, needing her to rein me in.

That was a mistake.

One look at her beautiful eyes, a stained-glass window to her exquisite soul, and I realize how in love with her I am.

"Larimar," I breathe, trying to hold my hips back, but it's like trying to bring in a runaway horse. "I have to tell you something while I still have a chance."

Her brows come together as she stares at me.

I cup her face with one hand, overcome with the urge to bare my soul. "I have lived so long, too long, without you. I don't know how I've survived any minute of it."

Her lips move, but no sound comes out, a softness washing over her features, like she's melting beneath me.

"That's why I am sorry it has to end this way," I say and drive my cock back inside her, rough movements that jostle her breasts beneath the shift. My skin feels like it's on fire, stretching and thickening, my cock lengthening.

"What?" she asks, but the monster won't let me explain.

It makes me reach down and flick and pinch at her clit until she's crying. The monster makes her come with pleasure and pain until she's a wet, quivering mess below me.

I bare my fangs at her, hissing.

She's still moaning, fighting through her climax, trying to stay sharp, knowing there's something terribly wrong, knowing there is danger.

Good night, Armand Alcaraz, the voice whispers to me, sinister and all-encompassing.

"Armand Alcaraz!" I manage to cry out to Larimar. "My name was Armand Alcaraz!"

I feel my bones breaking and stretching and shifting, some awful transformation taking hold, like hot swords are breaking through my back.

The pain envelops me from head to toe as I scream, and yet I still come, shooting my seed into her cunt, pumping and emptying until my mind is fully gone and only my smudge of a soul remains.

The last thing I see with my own eyes is the look of terror on Larimar's face as she stares up at me and two long shadows falling over her.

Wings sprouting from my back.

"Let us *prey*," the monster snarls at her.

Chapter Eighteen

LARIMAR

I can't say I didn't see it coming. I saw it happening as he was fucking me, little by little, tiny changes that I could sense were adding to something. I suspected the monster may have been coming out, but I didn't think he would lose total control. Priest has always been in control of himself, of me, of everything. I never thought it was possible for him to be anything but that.

But his eyes went completely black.

Then, his pupils turned red.

His skin began to darken, become thicker, leathery.

His cock began to hit against new places, swelling to fill me from the inside.

His fangs became longer, sharper than I've ever seen.

And then the dark wings sprouted from his back, large, wide, terrible wings with claws at the end, like the very illustrations of the Devil.

He became the monster.

"Let us *prey*."

And the monster is still inside me.

He puts his head back and roars, the dark leathery skin

spreading across his chest, wrapping over him. He raises his hands to the ceiling in a last-minute prayer of salvation or in a threat, and giant claws, far larger than mine, come shooting out of his hands.

You should have listened to me, his words ring through my head. He had told me to get away, to go and leave, but I thought he wanted time alone to talk to God.

I don't think God heard him.

While his back is arched and he's writhing with his transformation, I pull out from under him, glancing at his cock, which is far larger, longer, and harder than humanly possible, dark and covered in our cum.

He lets out a moan, and I take the opportunity to try to run.

But he grabs me by the legs, claws digging in, and tries to bring me to him.

I scream, but it dies in my throat, and then I'm ripping out of his grip, his claws slicing strips off the backs of my calves. The agony is acute, strangling me, and I collapse to the ground, knocking down a stand holding a burning candle.

The candle falls, the flames catching the edge of the altar cloth. I manage to get to my feet, pulling myself up by the rest of the cloth until it pools at my feet, my blood gushing, staining the white cloth red.

The monster tackles me from the side, and I'm slammed into the wall, my ribs breaking. A red oil lamp above us falls, and I manage to duck under his chest, rolling out of the way as the oil falls on the monster and the floor below.

My chest feels like it's caving in, but I can't give in to my injuries, can't give in to my pain. I have to put that aside, have to focus on staying alive. The flames from the altar cloth have now found the oil, and everything goes up in a whoosh of fire. The beast steps away from the fire before it has time to catch on him, but it's already licking up the walls, burning hot and fast, and the church starts filling with smoke.

I manage to get to my feet and run, but my legs scream with pain, and I'm stumbling on my knees in the middle of the aisle.

The monster lets out a roar, and I twist around to see him fly toward me. He's flying like a damned bat, giant wings flapping as he moves a few feet off the ground, but all it does is fan the flames, making the fire spread. It catches on the pews, burns the crosses, the tapestries, and by the time I push myself back up on my knees, the entire church is on fire.

He nearly catches me again, but then a burning rafter falls from above, landing on the monster's back. An inhuman cry is torn from his throat as the fire catches on his wings, and he falls on all fours, embers floating in the air toward me.

He starts crawling toward me, shaking off the burning rafter, and I know he's the Devil coming for me, straight out of hell.

Then, he looks up and past me, red pupils contracting, and I hear cries for help.

I turn around to see a group of people standing in the doorway of the church: two soldiers, two other men, and a woman.

"It's the Devil!" the woman yells while one of the soldiers runs toward me. I flinch, afraid of him, but he grabs me by my arms and hoists me to my feet.

"She's on fire!" he cries out.

I glance down at the hem of my shift, surprised to see flames there. Some of the oil from the lamp must have splashed onto me.

"She's bleeding," the woman says. "Her legs, her legs!"

The soldier picks me up in his arms and runs outside of the flaming church, followed by the woman, while the others stay inside. I hear screaming, and I don't know if it's from the monster or the men, but I feel myself starting to lose consciousness. The rain has stopped, and I stare up at the sky, watching as the moon comes out from a cloud.

"Put her in the ocean!" the woman yells.

It takes me a moment to register what she's saying.

"No," I cry out, trying to escape from the man's arms, but I'm too weak, and it's too late.

We're at the shore, and his boots are slipping on the rocks as he walks right into the water, the waves crashing beneath me.

He lowers me in, still holding on, and the woman is at my side too, trying to get my wet shift off, and then they stop.

Under the faint light of the moon, they stare at my legs in horror.

Saltwater washes over them, leaving shimmering scales in their place.

I scream, this time as loud as I once did, the spell broken.

I scream and I scream while the rest of me breaks.

Bones fuse, muscles stretch then tighten, ligaments wrapping around themselves until my legs are bound together as one, and the scales spread from my toes to my belly until it all becomes one tail and my fins unfurl.

The woman screams and gets to her feet.

"The Syren!" she yells. "She's a Syren."

The soldier lets go of me, stumbling backward until he falls on the beach, staring at me in horror.

A cry rips from my throat, loud, panicked, and I stare at my tail as I'm screaming, tears running down my face.

I am a Syren again.

Which means I have lost someone else I cared for.

Loved.

Priest is gone.

I look beyond the terrified faces of the villagers and behind them at the church as it starts to collapse, rafter after rafter falling, the whole thing going up in flames. More and more villagers are running toward it to help, and some are running toward me.

"We have a Syren!" the woman yells at them. "Come quick! Bring your weapons!"

I should probably eat her heart for that. I should probably eat his too. How quickly the fear leaves them when they have an army of people behind them.

"She's right!" someone yells as the mob gets closer.

I can't waste any time to see what happens next. Even with my teeth and my claws, I can't fight off all of them.

I take one last look at the burning church and everything that is dying with it, and then I turn over on the rocks, rolling back into the surf, letting it take me to deeper water. With a few quick flicks of my tail, I propel myself forward under the waves until I can see the deep.

Then, I dive.

Back to where I belong.

Interlude

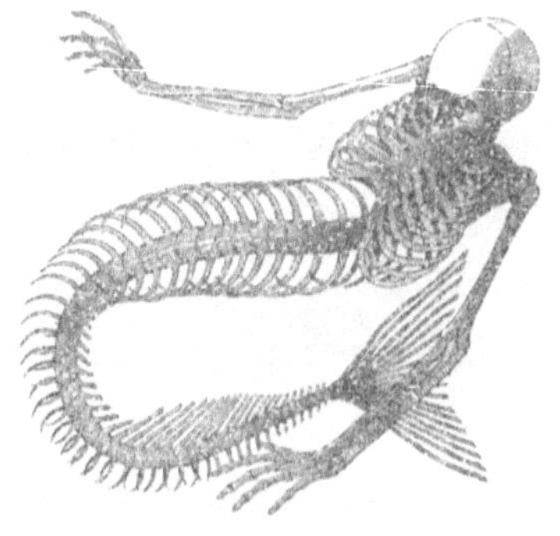

Chapter Nineteen

General Mendoza,

I am writing to inform you of the terrible news that the settlement of Nombre de Jesus in Chile has been destroyed. A fire broke out in the chapel, which resulted in the deaths of nearly all the villagers, as well as the sole clergy, Father Aragon. We are still unsure how the fire managed to kill everyone, as it was said to have happened at night and not during mass, but rumors have started in the nearby settlements, most of which are too preposterous to be true. That said, I feel it is my duty to inform you of what they are.

According to witnesses who came over from Primera Angostura, there was one villager left, a woman who had lost all her blood. She told the others that the Devil took over the church and sprouted wings. When the church collapsed, the Devil flew from the flames and picked up all the people with its claws, tossing them in the flames. Those who escaped, the Devil hunted down and bit, draining them of their blood.

She also said that the Syren who killed two men a few months earlier was found in the church with the Devil when the fire started. She looked like a human at first and had been on fire until she was placed in the sea—a trick, according to this woman. She said she saw the woman's legs transform into a tail right in front of her eyes. The Syren then swam away before they could capture her, and that is when the Devil flew out of the church, on fire, flying over the waves until it started to destroy everything and everyone in its path.

I do not know what you plan to do with these rumors. The only witness soon died shortly after. You know how these isolated settlements have a way of playing with people's minds. Several search parties from Primera Angostura and Ciudad del Rey Don Felipe have set out in the area on horseback and by boat to search for both this Syren and this flying monster. To my knowledge, they have found nothing.

The settlement is no more. Perhaps this is a

sign for us to put our resources elsewhere. If pirates want the Strait of Magellan, maybe it's best we let them have it.

With regards,

Halberdier of the Guard, Felipe

Chapter Twenty

Dear Doctor Van Helsing,

I am unsure if you remember me or not.
Even though I am told we blood-letters are able
to procure memories in our mind's eye, I'm
afraid the longer I live, the less space I have
inside my brain for everything and everyone I
encounter, and perhaps the same is true
for you.

But let me reintroduce myself. My name is
Eros Fausta. I worked with you at the
monastery, San Juan de la Pena. I helped
teach many of the reformed disciples how to
read and write, and I know you had formed a
deep friendship with one of them, the witch
Armand Alcaraz, whom you renamed Aragon.
I wasn't with the monastery for long—my

calling pulled me away elsewhere—but when I had returned much later, it was said that you and Aragon had left for a settlement at the bottom of the world.

I, too, ended up this way, for different reasons, on a ship that went through the Strait of Magellan. It was here, from the bow, that I glimpsed who I believed to be Father Aragon. Or rather, it had been the priest. He was half-monster, with a broken wing, standing on the shore and watching the ship pass. I could smell him, and I remembered his scent, which is what made me recognize him, for there were no real signs that it was the man I remembered.

I am in India at the moment, and I am unsure whether you are back at the monastery or if you perhaps were with Aragon down below. I don't know if you are alive, but I have a feeling you are. In the event that this is news to you, I wanted to let you know what I saw. There is a chance I was wrong—I was the only one who saw the monster—but I don't think I am. I wish I was. There seemed to be something wrapped around the creature's wrist—a rosary, perhaps.

Coincidentally or not, when we passed the settlement of Nombre de Jesus, there was nothing left of it. It had been burnt to a crisp, with only a few gravestones standing. A chilling sight, to say the least, and I've seen a lot.

I'm sorry if I am bearing bad news. I am even sorrier if Doctor Van Helsing is no more. I hope whoever receives this letter finds it to be helpful in some way.

Your old friend,
Eros Fausta

Chapter Twenty-One

To Captain Battista of the good ship
Nightwind,

I hope this letter finds you well, or finds
you at all. An albatross is a new delivery
system for me, but the Vampyre I have corre-
sponded with assures me it will find its way
to you in a timely manner.

I will be in the village of Valparaiso this
coming March with a dear friend of mine,
Aragon, who is also part of your Brethren. We
have heard you will be sailing through on your
way to the southern seas and would like to join
your crew. We both have experience fighting, and
while our morals might drive a human to church,
we are both of sound mind and constitution. I
have heard that you are heading to a Syren

colony off Roche Island, and Aragon has a bit of experience with Syrens himself. Perhaps he can be of some assistance on the journey.

Either way, we will be waiting for you. If you pass through, ask for Doctor Van Helsing, and they will fetch me.

Doctor Abraham Van Helsing

P.S. If you don't wish to have the Spanish attack you, do not fly the Jolly Roger. They are a prickly bunch.

Part Two

Chapter Twenty-Two

PRIEST

Five Years Later

"Nervous?" Abe asks me.

I frown, shooting him a quick glance before going back to watching the harbor. "Why should I be nervous?"

"First day in a new vocation has got to be rather nerve-racking."

"You act like being a pirate is a job."

"Isn't it?" he asks, but in my peripheral vision, I see him stroking his beard, something he does when he has a case of the nerves.

I can't blame either of us, though I think it's more anxiety that the ship won't show up at all.

We've been in the village of Valparaiso for six months, waiting for the *Nightwind* to come into harbor.

Six long, tedious months of waiting.

But to me, that was nothing.

I was alone for years in Tierra del Fuego, the wild lands across the Strait of Magellan. I only remember some of it, and I suppose that is a blessing. By the time Abe found me, I was a starving beast, having killed what settlers and natives I could find, then barely subsisting on guanacos and penguins, enough to keep me alive but not in good condition.

After that, he brought me up to Santiago for a few years, chained in a barn in an isolated farmhouse on the other side of the river. He operated under the guise of being a local doctor and would take trips into the city every now and then so as not to raise suspicions about him being there, but his true job was coaxing Father Aragon out and casting the monster back in.

It was dangerous work, but Abe assured me it was nothing like it had been when I'd first been turned. Perhaps the monster inside me had lost the thrill of depravity once it realized I lost Larimar. Or perhaps Father Aragon—Armand Alcaraz—knew how to fight back this time.

Either way, over a year ago, I put the beast away for good.

It's not gone—I can feel it in my blood, in my bones.

The darkness, the evil.

It's waiting to come out, biding its time for the right moment, whenever that may be.

But I no longer fear it like I once did. I survived my worst fear, clawed my way back to the light after I was drowned in shadows. I know that, no matter what happens, my psyche, my will, my constitution is strong enough to withstand the bad blood in my veins.

Perhaps one day, I'll make friends with the monster inside. Maybe we can coexist in the same body, two sides of the same coin, beast and man.

After all, I feel the beast is the driving force behind this next venture—becoming a pirate.

More specifically, to join the crew of the *Nightwind* under Captain Ramsay "Bones" Battista as they search for the colony of Syrens rumored to be by Roche Island. Since they are supposed Vampyres such as myself, Abe says they hope to capture a few from the colony so that the blood lasts them longer on their expeditions around the globe.

Of course, my true reason for joining their crew and becoming a pirate of the high seas is to look for Larimar. I have been dreaming about her for the last five years. Obsessing over her. Pining for her.

I have been hunting her in one way or another.

The one who stole my heart.

Who broke our bargain.

Who left me behind to die while she escaped into the sea and became a Syren once more, the true thing she always wanted. It was never me she cared about—she saw her opportunity for escape, and she took it.

I know it's unfair of me to feel that way, to resent her, to feel rejected and spurned, to feel as if she never upheld her part of the deal. I know it is unjustified, all this anger that's been simmering inside me. I know this.

But I can't help how I feel.

"Aragon," Abe says in a low voice. "You're doing it again."

I pause. My hand is at my ear. The ear she bit off. It grew back a little larger, I swear it did, and when I'm especially overcome with rage or grief or frustration, I tend to tug at my earlobe. Abe says it's one of my *tells*. In the past, he would tell me to rein in my emotions to keep the beast in check, but ever since the creature made his appearance in the church, the doctor is trying a new approach. He thinks that shoving emotions deep inside and hiding them behind a cold, unfeeling façade is what drove the beast to emerge. His new theory is that addressing the emotions will have better results in the long run.

I don't agree. I don't want to talk about my fucking feelings. I was happier when I was in control of how I felt, and how I controlled it was by ignoring it.

I sigh. "My apologies." I lower my hand, shoving it in my coat pocket.

"No, don't apologize," he says. "Tell me what ails your mind."

I groan, rolling my eyes, but I know he will only badger me until I tell him. "I'm just thinking about Larimar."

"Of course you are," he says matter-of-factly. "I'd venture to say that's all you've thought about for the last five years. What feelings have come up?"

What feelings haven't? Anger. Desire. I want to find her. I want to hurt her for leaving me. I want to hurt her for hurting me.

"I'm mad," I say. "I keep feeling slighted. Embarrassed, even."

"Hell hath no fury like a lover scorned," he chuckles.

"It's *woman* scorned," I correct him. "Shakespeare."

"No. It's actually the playwright William Congreve," he says. "And it's applicable to all genders."

"Regardless," I say, giving him a steely look, "that is how I feel."

"And you realize how unjustified these feelings are, yes? The monster took over your body. You tried to kill the woman you love. You ended up burning down the church. She fled into the night and disappeared into the sea because it was the only way she would survive against you and the villagers who turned on her. Then, you ended up setting the entire village on fire, burning most of the people alive, and drinking the blood of the ones you didn't. Yet somehow, *you* feel scorned that she left you..."

"I never said it was fair," I grumble. I don't need the events of that night brought back up, but they seem to come up every day. I scan the horizon again, anxiety prickling the back of my neck. "Are you certain the ship is supposed to arrive today?"

"That's what the boy from the next village said. He saw the ship with his own eyes."

"But how do you know it's the *Nightwind*?"

Abe looks at me, a twinkle in his eye. "The boy said it was moving under full sail and fast as lightning." He wets his finger and sticks it in the air. "Yet there's no wind."

"Just what I need, a damn magic ship," I mutter.

"Speaking of magic, I haven't told them much about you. They know you're a Vampyre, of course, and one of sound mind and constitution."

I let out a sour laugh.

"But I haven't mentioned you were a priest," he says. "Nor have I mentioned that you were, at one point, a witch. Or that you were turned. Best not to rock the boat, so to speak, before we're integrated with them. You know how Vampyres can be around witches, even former ones. And, well, they tend to thumb their noses at the monsters, think they're beneath them."

"Who can blame them?" I say under my breath.

"I did mention that you knew a thing about Syrens."

I balk. "What did you do that for?"

He shrugs with one shoulder. "I figured it would be extra incentive for them to make the stop and pick us up."

"Or it could be the reason we've been waiting here for six months," I point out, trying to control the rage bubbling up inside me. "They might not be coming here at all. You might have ruined everything."

He fixes a steady eye on me. "Or I may have made them curious. I assume they already know a thing or two about Syrens, since they hunt them. They'll likely want to know how you happen to know a thing or two as well. We always have much to learn from each other. I am sure they will see it that way too."

"They're pirates," I point out. "I don't think they care much for learning. All that matters to them is raping and pillaging."

Abe laughs. "Come now, even you know better than to believe rumors and legends. Besides, you slaughtered an entire village of innocent people, the very flock you were sworn to protect. I don't think you have a moral leg to stand on, Aragon."

He doesn't need to remind me. I reach for the rosary around my neck, the only thing I saved from my previous life. Somehow, even in the darkest parts of my insanity, I managed to go to my cottage and grab the rosary that had last bound Larimar's wrists together before I burned it and everything else to the ground.

That's why I can never fully blame the beast for what it did. There was a part of me in there the whole time. The beast wasn't sentimental—I was. I had the ability to push through every now and then, which meant, deep down, I was an animal too. Part of me thinks that I let the beast in and let it stay for as long as it did simply because I didn't want to confine myself to society's norms anymore, and certainly not the rigid teachings of the church. I want to be a lewd, hedonistic, primal being and not be bombarded by guilt for it.

As such, I am no longer a priest. My relationship with God, whoever that may be, hasn't changed much, but I can't, in good faith, be a man of...good faith. I can't be a willful hypocrite preaching from the pulpit. I slaughtered my own congregation. I am not fit to spout God's word.

You also nailed Larimar to the cross and drank her blood, I remind myself. Truth is, I was never fit for the job, but we all knew that.

"Ah, do you see what I see?" Abe says excitedly. He points

up the bay toward the port of Quintero, where a black ship appears jutting out from around the coastline. "That's the *Nightwind*."

"It's a ship..." I say, not entirely convinced. Our eyesight is better than a human's, but it has its limitations. But even as I say the words, I see how fast the ship is moving, despite how the seas are calm and the air is still.

And as it gets closer still, white sails full of magic wind, I begin to feel excited for the first time in a long time. There's a perverse sense of hope too, as if this will actually lead me to Larimar. I have no idea if she was with the colony before I found her or if she returned to them after—she was quite secretive about her whereabouts, which often made me wonder what she was hiding—but either way, this will do more than I did on my own. Even with wings, I could only do so much flying over the icebergs of the southern seas. Syrens don't need air, and there's no reason for them to come to the surface.

Which is also why I find the idea of Syren hunters intriguing. How exactly do they find them when the oceans are so large and deep?

I suppose I'm about to find out.

If they'll have me.

I look at Abe. He's grinning to himself with excitement, adjusting his hat anxiously. The poor sap has been through so much, pulled from his lofty work at the monastery to come down and babysit me once again. I'm sure some part of him wanted to leave me to my own devices—but being an immortal, the chances of me dying, even as a monster, were slim, and even if he didn't feel some sort of sentiment toward me as a friend, he does seem to have this strange urge to want to protect humanity from blood-suckers such as ourselves.

This will be good for him, I think, a chance to be away

from the demands of rehabilitating monsters. Maybe the pirates need their own moral compass on board.

But will it be good for me? That remains to be seen.

If I do end up finding Larimar, what will I do to her?

Will the monster make another appearance? Will he be worse to her than he was before? Will he kill her and then disappear, leaving me to deal with the consequences? Or perhaps he'll take over for good. I might be so despondent that I'll fully hand over control of my body, mind, and soul.

"They're going to ask me what I know about Syrens," I say to Abe as I pick up my satchel with my meager personal belongings, swinging it over my shoulder. "How much should I divulge about Larimar?"

"As much as you wish," he says as we start walking down from the ridge we've been standing on, heading to a winding footpath that leads to the beach. "What you tell them is up to you. On the one hand, if you're honest, they'll know that you didn't join their crew just to siphon their catch. On the other hand, if you're honest, they might think you're there to sabotage them."

"Why would I do that?"

"Well, you fell in love with a Syren. If they end up catching Larimar, are you telling me you wouldn't stop them from eating her?"

A hot coal of anger burns in my gut, and I clench my fists at the thought. "She's mine, Abe. No one else's."

"So you say. But if you tell them you were intimate with one of the Syrens they are hunting, there's a chance they might toss you overboard into the oceanic abyss. They would consider you too compromised."

I press my lips together in thought as we reach the shore. "They would be right."

"Then perhaps we don't tell them," Abe says.

"They'll want to know how I got my expertise..."

He sighs, staring out at the ocean as the ship gets closer and closer, sealing our fate. "Tell them the truth. It's easier that way. You saw what she did to the villagers. You captured her, you brought her to your house, you fed from her, and she managed to escape one day. No need to mention the part about giving her legs. They don't need to know about your magic yet."

"Or the fact that my house was a church."

"Perhaps it's best to tell them as little as possible. Vampyres are an ornery bunch, and I imagine pirates even more so. You'll fit right in."

It doesn't take long for the ship to come close. Soon, she's dropping anchor not far from shore, and a small rowboat is lowered to the water with a man aboard. The ship itself is impressive in both height and girth, and it hums with magical energy, giving it a life of its own, like a sentient being. I have to wonder how Vampyres happened to get their hands on enough magic to bespell a ship. Perhaps they might even have a witch on board. Vampyre witches are rare, but they aren't unheard of.

The rowboat gets closer, a Black man at the oars, who pulls in a few yards from shore.

"Ahoy there," the man says in English, casting a suspicious eye over us. "And who might you be?"

"Doctor Van Helsing and Aragon," Abe announces with a flourish of his hands, speaking the language fluently, just as I can.

"Aragon what?" the man asks. "Or does he only have one name?"

I raise my brows. It had always been Father Aragon, but now that I'm not a priest...

"Aragon Alcaraz," Abe says without hesitation, using the name I was born with. It doesn't sound terrible. "We've been waiting for your ship for six months. I sent your captain correspondence last year."

"Aye," the man says with a shrug. "Schedules are hard to keep in these parts. Well, I suppose you check out."

He starts rowing the rest of the way until the hull scrapes against the sand. Abe and I quickly walk to the boat, throwing our satchels over before climbing aboard. I wade in the water to my knees in order to push the tender out of the shallows.

Abe takes his seat on the wooden plank across from me and makes a disgruntled noise. The hem of his pants is wet.

You're not going to last a day, I think to myself.

I'd tell him so, but I don't want this man to kick Abe off for being unseaworthy, even though the man is shooting me a look that says, *And this man wants to be a pirate?*

"I'm Cruz, by the by," the man says, rowing us toward the ship.

"Pleasure to meet you," Abe says. "May I ask how many crew members you have? Are they all Brethren?"

"We have thirteen, including one human." Then he shakes his head. "Pardon me, *two* humans."

"Two humans?" Abe asks. "How is that possible? Oh, I see. You keep them as food. I was wondering how you would all feed while at sea. You can't possibly come across that many food sources in the middle of the ocean."

"It can be challenging," he says carefully. "But no, the humans on board are part of the crew. We make a point not to eat them." He sounds utterly serious, but he flashes a grin at us.

"What do they do?" I can't help but ask. "As crew. Do they know what you are?"

"Very much so," he says. "It's not an easy thing to hide. One of them, Sedge, is our cook. The other, Maren, she's the captain's wife."

"A woman on board," Abe says. "That's not bad luck?"

Cruz gives him a knowing smile. "Oh, not this lady. She's very much good luck."

"So what do you use as sustenance?" Abe asks. Always with the questions, and he's like a dog with a bone if he doesn't get his answers.

"We have our ways" is his simple reply.

"Hunting Syrens," I comment.

Cruz's gaze slides over to mine and holds it for a second. "Bones told me you know something about them. Or that's what your letter said. Is it true?"

I give him a cautious nod. "I do. I've hunted and caught one myself."

His eyes widen. "Pray tell."

"I'll wait until I talk to Captain Bones," I say. "Would hate to have to tell the same story twice."

Cruz absorbs that with a nod and keeps rowing until we're at the side of the ship. Up close, her energy hums even greater, the great height of her rising from the sea like a behemoth.

The *Nightwind*.

Heads poke over the railing and drop ropes down, which Cruz quickly attaches to either end of the skiff before it's hauled up out of the sea.

Then, our boat becomes level with the deck of the ship.

Standing there are a dozen grim-looking men with swords and pistols pointed our way.

The last thing I see is an oar heading toward my face.

Then, all the world goes black.

Chapter Twenty-Three

PRIEST

I don't know where I am.

But my head is slumped over, throbbing with a million, pain-filled stars.

Aragon, Abe whispers inside my head. *Aragon, wake up.*

Vampyres have always been able to communicate telepathically, but Abe and I haven't really felt the need to, since it's usually just the two of us alone.

Until now.

I groan and raise my head. It's dark, and everything is moving.

I blink hard and try to get my eyes to adjust, only to realize it's dark because it's somehow nighttime, with the sky full of stars and scattered clouds, and the world is moving not just because I was hit on the head with a blunt object, but because it *is* moving.

I'm on the deck of the ship, chained around one of the masts.

In front of me is a tall, swarthy-looking fellow, his dark hair tied back and a few days' stubble on his cheeks, dressed head to toe in gray. He has a sword in his hand, though it's down by his side, and he's staring at me with both curiosity and amusement.

"Father Aragon," the pirate says in a wry voice, and I jolt at the sound of my godly name. "Pleased to make your acquaintance. I'm Captain Battista. You may call me Bones or Ramsay —it doesn't really matter, since you won't be with us for very long. See, we don't welcome liars on board the *Nightwind*. It's not just me; you'd find out that I'm actually quite tolerant, but rather, the ship herself doesn't like dishonest crew. She gets rather...cranky."

As if on cue, the ship groans as it goes over a wave.

"Who are you calling a liar?" Abe says from behind me, chained to the other side of the mast. He's trying to sound annoyed, but I hear the pain in his voice. He must have been hit with the same oar.

Abe, I warn him. He has a bad habit of talking back and not reading social situations properly. Or not caring to.

"You, obviously, Doctor Van Helsing," Ramsay says, "if that is, in fact, your real name. Frankly, it sounds verily made up."

"It's Dutch," Abe says, spitting.

"Ah! That explains why it sounds like a turd in your teeth," he says.

I'd laugh at that if I wasn't so concerned with how he learned I was a priest.

"It is his name, and he is a doctor," I growl at him. "And I *was* a priest. I was Father Aragon."

"Oh, I know," Ramsay says to me, leaning on the sword, his hands casually draped over the hilt. "You might not think we can keep up with all the news and rumors that this world has to offer due to us being perpetually at sea, but we do visit many ports. We talk to many different souls—when we're not drinking from them—and we have other ways of getting information. I reckon I know a lot more than you think I do."

"Apparently," I say under my breath.

"So tell me, Father," he says, not impressed. "Why did you and the doctor lie about your past vocation? Were you ashamed of what you did in Nombre de Jesus?"

How in damnation did he know *that*?

Easy, Aragon, Abe's voice slides into my mind. *Let him speak first. Don't give away Larimar.*

"Wouldn't you be?" I ask, looking the captain dead in the eyes.

He studies me for a moment. "I suppose I would be. Then again, I'm not like *you*. I'm not a beast. It would surprise me to learn that a monster feels shame."

"As you can see, I'm not a monster," I say to him through gritted teeth. "*Presently*," I add.

"I just don't know," Ramsay says, straightening up. He looks down the length of the ship toward the helm, and I follow his gaze to see a beautiful woman standing near the wheel. "Maren, I'm afraid I'm going to need some of your feminine intuition with these two."

The woman picks up the hem of her teal gown and walks down the middle of the ship, the rest of the crew parting for her like Moses parted the Red Sea. She doesn't at all look like how I thought a pirate woman would look. Her dress looks clean and extravagant, her long, wavy black hair pooling around her shoulders, framing her ample breasts.

Ramsay moves out of the way as she steps in front of me and crouches down to my level, keeping just out of reach in the event that I try to grab or kick at her.

Her eyes are a piercing shade of blue, almost unnatural, and she stares at me so intently that I fear she's learned absolutely everything about me already, that there will be no lies safe from her.

I sniff as she continues to look at me. She smells clean, like a woman and the sea, reminding me of Larimar. There's something about her that makes my cock twitch, causes my heart to stumble. She doesn't really look like Larimar, aside from her breasts, and I suppose any woman will smell like the sea if she's been on it for too long. But still...

"I'm Maren," she says in a rich, hypnotic voice. I know that Cruz said she was human, but there's something about her that makes me wonder if that's completely true. "They say I'm a good judge of character, but I think they just want to pass the responsibility off on me."

"The responsibility of?"

"Whether you live or die," she says flatly, a curve to her lips.

"We're Vampyres," Abe protests.

"Yes, I'm aware," she says. "But you learn a lot when you've been at sea. It's an inhospitable place if you're unsure how to adapt. We've had members of our own Brethren who have jeopardized the entire crew. We've dealt with them accordingly, but we don't like to make those same mistakes twice."

"There are only three ways to kill us," I say, my voice thick.

"Yes. I know. Decapitation, fire, and being stabbed in the heart with a witch's blade," she says. "When we had a trouble-maker, we took off his head, then the rest of his body parts." She grins. "Slowly."

Hmmm. Perhaps that's why she reminds me of Larimar.

Then she sighs and, to my surprise, reaches out and touches my cheek, running a finger along it. Her nail feels especially sharp.

"I think you're a good man," she says, her eyes searching my face. "Handsome, for sure, but don't let my husband hear that."

"Maren," Ramsay says testily from behind her.

She grins. "He knows where he stands." Then her expression sobers, and I feel a little lost staring into her eyes. "But can we trust you? That is the question. You've been turned, but you were at one point a witch. Do you have a witch's blade you aim to use on us? Is that your purpose? To be a Vampyre slayer? Or perhaps there is no need when you can turn into a flying bat at will."

I swallow hard. "I can't turn at will."

"Well, that's even worse. If you can't control it, then we're all at risk. What if you decide to burn the ship down, with the rest of us on it, just as you did to your followers in the church?"

I don't have anything to say to that. All I have is my word, and honestly, I'm not even sure if it's all that trustworthy. It's the beast inside me that decides things in the end.

"Aragon is reformed," Abe says. "You will have to trust a doctor's opinion."

"Yes," she says tepidly, eyes flashing briefly over my shoulder. "We've heard all about your monastery."

"But how?" I ask. "How do you know about what happened at the village? About what I did?"

What else do you know?

"Word travels fast," she says. "As Ramsay explains, there are a lot of ports, and we have a lot of help in getting information."

Fuck, they are ridiculously vague for a bunch of pirates.

"It's magic, isn't it?" Abe says. "You use magic, the same that powers this ship when there is no wind."

Maren's face remains impassive, but I think Abe is right.

"A seeing crystal," I say to her slowly. "That's how. You have one."

What else did you see?

She exhales and straightens up. "I suppose you would find out sooner or later. Yes, we have one. We also have—"

"Maren," Ramsay says sharply. She's said too much, perhaps.

She nods at him with apprehension and looks back to me.

"I'm not the captain," she says. "I don't make all the decisions here, but I have as much stature and power as my husband and anyone else aboard this vessel." She sighs again and gathers her hair in her hands, placing it behind her shoulders. "I think we must defer to Nill," she says to Ramsay.

"Who is Nill?" Abe asks, his voice going high.

But I barely hear them.

My eyes are glued to Maren's neck.

On the three faint lines along either side.

Former gills.

Abe! I yell into his head. *She's a Syren. She was a Syren. Maren was a Syren!*

How do you know that? he asks.

The gills. On her neck.

It's then I notice Ramsay staring at me curiously, noticing where my attention is.

"Nill it is," Ramsay says, breaking into a slow grin before he waves at the rest of his crew. "Come on, boys. Let's make these two walk the bloody plank."

"The plank?" Maren says with a dry laugh. "I thought that was beneath us."

"Come on, luv. It's a little more entertaining than just chucking them overboard."

Several members of the crew come forward, untying the chains and manhandling us as they drag us toward the side of the ship.

This would be a fantastic time for you to let the beast out, Abe says in my head.

He's right, but in my panicked state, I can't seem to do anything except fight back, and that gets me a couple more whacks to the head and punches to the gut, along with the occasional bite from one Greek-looking fellow, who gives me a bloody grin. Normally, I can withstand a beating like it's nothing at all, but ever since I've been on this ship, I feel positively human in the way everything hurts.

I think there must be some magic here, weakening us, I say to Abe.

Yes, that must be the reason why I can't fight off ten men, he says mildly.

The crew jostles us over to the side of the ship, one of them removing the siding until there's a lone plank jutting out over the black, endless sea.

And in that sea floats a shark fin, ominously circling below.

"Aren't you supposed to discuss this with Nill?" I ask as several swords prick my back, urging me to move forward onto the board.

"You will be discussing it with Nill," Ramsay says, leaping up on the railing and leaning on one of the ropes from the mast. He points at the water with his sword. "That's him down there."

"A shark?" I exclaim.

"He'll be the judge," Maren says. "Trust me, he's good at it."

I try to twist around to face the crew. They're all enjoying this all too much.

"Bloody pirates," I growl.

They bare their fangs and hiss at me in return.

Normally, I would think I could easily take on a shark. I took on Larimar, and she was much more cunning and vicious. But with my hands bound and this weakening spell, I'm not sure I'll have much of a choice.

Perhaps we'll be alright, Abe says from behind me where he's being held on the deck, not bothering to put up a fight anymore. *A shark can't kill us.*

I give him an incredulous look. *It could bite off our heads.*

His face is immediately crestfallen. *Ah. Yes, I suppose it could.*

"Enough!" Ramsay bellows. "Let the judgment begin for the Holy Man. Walk the plank!"

I try to stand my ground, but half a dozen swords spear into my back.

I cry out and stumble forward, losing my footing.

I pitch over the side and fall toward the dark waves, moonlight reflecting on the crests.

The water hits me like a hammer, and I immediately sink until I start kicking. It's freezing cold, but to my relief, it doesn't bother me, which means whatever weakening spell they had on us up there doesn't work down here.

I dive under the waves and away from the sides of the ship, just in case. When I break the surface, I look around for the shark's fin, but to no avail. Abe's cry brings my attention to the ship as they push him along the plank. He handles it a lot more gracefully than I did, making it all the way to the end of the plank before one of the pirates shakes the other end, and he goes falling into the surf, sinking with a splash.

I quickly start kicking my legs over to him, moving my bound hands over like I'm pulling myself forward.

"Abe!" I yell, but he hasn't surfaced.

I dive under, opening my eyes to see him hovering in the darkness, looking at me.

What do we do? he asks. *Go to the surface? Start swimming? Which way? Where are we?*

I blink at him, the salt stinging my eyes, trying to figure out a plan of action. We can't drown, so we aren't in any danger there, but drifting in the ocean for eternity doesn't sound very enticing.

Then the shark comes up behind Abe like a ghost from

the darkness, a shadowy shape that would strike fear in the heart of any man, mortal or not.

Behind you! I yell.

Abe whirls around just in time to see the shark, his mouth opening in a watery scream, bubbles rising to the surface.

But the black-eyed fish pays him no attention and keeps gliding over toward me. Its mouth is open slightly, displaying rows of serrated teeth, and in an absurd instance of longing, I'm reminded of Larimar.

The shark comes right to me, and I'm getting ready to fend it off. If it bites off my hands, at least I'll be free of the chains.

It veers off to the side just before we collide, and I swirl around, watching it circle me, unable to take my eyes off it. It's a large, sleek, graceful, killing machine, and the way its empty eyes stare at me suggests an intelligence greater than I thought.

The shark continues to swim around me in lazy circles, expending as little energy as possible before it suddenly swims over to Abe with giant sweeps of its tail. It goes around him for a few revolutions and then suddenly takes off into the deep, disappearing from view.

Abe turns to look at me. *Do you think it's going to come back?*

I shake my head, staring into the inky black depths where the shark—Nill—disappeared. *I have no idea.*

Suddenly, there's a splash in the water from the direction of the ship, and two heavy ropes sink below the waves.

Perhaps this is a parlay, Abe muses.

The two of us swim as well as we can over to the ropes, grabbing them with our bound hands before kicking up to the surface.

Despite the fact that I can't drown, I still instinctively gasp for air. Then, I look up at the ship to find the crew peering over the sides at us.

"You passed the test," Ramsay yells at us with a big grin, the kind you want to punch right off his face. "Come aboard, mateys. Welcome to the Brethren of the Blood."

I give Abe a tired look, spitting out water as we start to climb the rope. "And you thought joining a band of pirates was a good idea."

Chapter Twenty-Four

PRIEST

"When was the last time you ate?" Ramsay asks us. It's been a couple of days since our trial by shark, and frankly, I'm still a little discombobulated by the turn of events. I have a hard time remembering the last time we fed. I have a hard time trying to remember what life was like before we boarded the *Nightwind*. It's as if everything that came before was just some hazy dream.

Or, in my case, a nightmare.

Though I still have Larimar at the forefront of my thoughts.

Her face is all I see when I close my eyes.

I try not to close my eyes.

"Five days ago," Abe fills in as we follow Ramsay and his brother, a grumpy-looking fellow named Thane, down the length of the ship. We just spent the day swabbing the decks and straightening the lines, same as the day before. Apparently, tomorrow will be more of the same. There's not a lot of variety on this ship, at least not for newcomers. I suppose I should be grateful we're not on latrine duty.

"Five days? Then you must be starving," Ramsay says.

"You've both been working hard enough, I reckon. Best you sample some of our goods."

Thane grumbles something under his breath.

"What was that, brother?" Ramsay asks, motioning with his hand behind his ear. "You have something you wish to share with your captain and new crewmates?"

Thane manages to glare at all three of us with one, swooping glance. "We should have picked up more bloodletters in Valparaiso," he says gruffly as we head down the stairs to the deck below. "We took on two more Vampyres; we should have picked up two more victims to make things even. Now, they're going to be feeding from our resources, and you, apparently, have no plans to make any stops going through the strait."

Ramsay gives his brother a tired look. "First of all, you know I don't like that term, *Vampyre*. We didn't give that to ourselves—the humans did. We're the Brethren of the Blood, and that is that, not some name handed out by the hand-wringing Christians in Eastern Europe. No offense, Father Aragon."

I raise my palm. "No offense taken. It's just Aragon now, not father."

I have told Ramsay this quite a few times since, but he either forgets or he likes to choose your name for you. I'm not sure what it is, but I know I have to pick my battles on this ship, or they will be picked for me.

"Of course," Ramsay says as we go down another set of stairs, past the deck where Abe and I have been sharing a small cabin with bunk beds. "But back to you, Thane, and your grumbles. We couldn't risk getting any more bloodletters while picking up these two. It would have been too dangerous, would have drawn attention to ourselves. We were lucky enough that our ship traveled past unscathed."

"Because you weren't flying your Jolly Roger," Abe says.

"That's the problem with you pirates: you always have to be telling the world exactly what you are."

Ramsay grins. "Don't you think that's the plan? Tell the world what it wants to see—pirates. Vicious marauders of the deep. Criminals of the high seas. Hide the truth—we're the monsters in every fairy tale."

"Poetic," Thane mutters. "Still doesn't make up for the fact that we have two extra mouths to feed."

"I could throw you overboard if that would help even the score," I say to Thane earnestly.

Ramsay bursts out laughing, and that gets me another dirty look from Thane.

"I would take you up on your offer, *Aragon*, but Thane is the best quartermaster we have."

"The only one you have," Thane points out.

"And he's needed to keep me in line," Ramsay goes on. Then, his expression darkens slightly. "Though lately, it seems we've switched roles."

Thane's golden eyes flash with something—regret or sorrow. More than that, I can feel the weight of history in them. I have no doubt this crew has seen and gone through their share of tragedy. None of us are immune.

I exchange a knowing glance with Abe, and we continue down the stairs until we're at the very bottom of the ship. Here, she creaks and groans with the sloshing sound of the waves beating the wooden sides. We've been lucky that the weather has been agreeable so far. We're offshore enough from Chile that we can't see the land, the ship itself having found an easier and faster course as we barrel toward the bottom of the world.

To where I had salvation for one, brief moment.

Salvation that came with violet eyes.

Until everything went up in flames.

Suddenly, we stop before a heavy door, and the smell of

human blood floods my senses, overpowering the scent of oil, brine, and salt that has permeated the ship for the last few days. I feel my fangs harden in my mouth, the hairs on my body standing on end, my pulse picking up speed.

Ramsay nods as he looks me over. "It's surprising, isn't it, that you haven't smelled them by now? I think the *Nightwind* does a good job of keeping it contained. Otherwise, we'd be reminded that we have them down here for the taking, and no crew could function with that."

"More of the ship's magic," I say, clearing the thirst from my throat.

He nods. "She provides when she needs to."

"So, you have humans in there?" Abe gestures to the door. Even the pupils in his eyes have gone red with hunger. "Ones you've kidnapped?"

"We call them bloodletters," Thane explains. "And yes, they've been kidnapped."

"They were given a choice," Ramsay says to him testily.

Thane stares at him for a moment and then shakes his head. "A choice. Yes, of course." He looks to us, his expression somehow even more tired than usual. "Back in the day, we would attack other ships or raid ports, and humans were the main cargo we were after—not just jewels and money and weapons, but the humans themselves. We kept them in the hold as prisoners and fed from them until they all died…a slow, gruesome death. But ever since *Maren* joined the crew, she wanted to change our tactics to one that's more humane and merciful."

"We give the humans a choice," Ramsay says, eyeing his brother with a hard, warning look, as if he doesn't want Maren mentioned again. "They become our sustenance or die. If you choose the former, you'll live and eventually be taken back to shore, albeit drained of a lot of your blood."

"And if you don't?" Abe asks.

"Well, you die, and we take you anyway," he says.

"But you can't possibly let these people out after you've been feeding on them," Abe says, the red starting to fade from his eyes and the insatiable curiosity of his doctor's mind taking over. "They'll tell everyone what happened."

"You seem to forget the power we possess naturally, Doctor," Ramsay says, tapping his temple. "We compel them to forget. At any rate, there's nothing a good old spell won't fix."

"Who on this ship knows how to use magic?" I ask, wanting an answer of some kind. Are there Vampyres who are also witches, who weren't turned like I was?

"I do," Ramsay says, his voice stern, his gaze telling me he won't divulge any more. In due time, I suppose.

Thane adds, "Even if the humans do remember what happened, no one will believe them."

"That's what they said about what happened in Eastern Europe," Abe points out. "But now we have the term Vampyre because there were one too many stories that legend turned into rumor."

Ramsay shrugs. "We're doing our best to be a little more moral. If it backfires, I have no problems sliding backward on the scale."

Thane lets out a wry snort. "Maren wouldn't let you."

"She lets me do what I need to," Ramsay says pointedly.

"Oh, but when the crew voices their displeasure..." Thane says.

"I take it not everyone is happy with your new system?" Abe asks.

"No," Thane says. "And we are supposed to be a democracy on this ship."

Ramsay just shakes his head. "Enough with this jibber-jabber. These men are starving, and I've been a most inhospitable host thus far."

To be fair to the captain, he has given us food, which was rather good, but not the sustenance we really need.

He takes out a skeleton key and opens the door to the hold with a loud creak.

The smell of the humans hits me like a fist to the face.

It's dark in here, but there is a lamp nailed to the wall, high off the ground, that gives off a low glow, casting the humans in deep shadow.

There are five of them, one woman and four men, all dressed in simple shifts, the white clothes splattered with blood. They are sitting on a pile of hay, chained to the wall by their hands, with enough slack to let them turn around, lie down, or reach for their latrine bucket. They all have empty plates beside them, where a few crumbs of bread linger, and there are jugs of water between each person.

Frankly, it looks like hell, and it smells like it too, even with their sweet blood scenting the air.

They all stare at me with dull expressions, their eyes glazed.

"Are they drugged?" I whisper to Ramsay.

He nods. "It's a combination of us feeding on them all the time and the rum we keep flowing through their veins. I swear, it gives their blood a little bit of a kick."

"Five people," Abe says, looking around the room with a discerning eye. "Five people for fifteen Vampyres?"

"This is why we need more," Thane grumbles.

"We take a little each day," Ramsay explains, walking over to a shelf and picking up a needle attached to a tube.

"You don't," Thane points out.

Ramsay shoots him an icy look.

"But you don't," Thane continues. He looks to us. "He has Maren."

"Ah," I say. I immediately think of Larimar. Those gills on Maren's neck must mean she's a Syren or still has Syren blood.

That explains why the captain gets special privileges from his wife. Her blood goes a long way.

For a sweet, terrible moment, I am plagued by memories of Larimar on the cross, naked and writhing as I drink her beautiful blood. I had her, had her in my hands, and I ruined it all.

"What's that?" Abe asks, gesturing to the needle, tube, and now a jug Ramsay has in his hands.

"It's how we get the blood," he says as he walks over to the woman. "There are very few of us who can handle feeding directly from them with our fangs. As you know, we tend to get a little...carried away. Some of us, like Thane here, can do it as long as there is another Brethren in the room to hold him back if he gets out of hand. Last thing we want is for greed and hunger to take over."

Ramsay then goes on to explain how the needle and tube create pressure, allowing the blood to trickle into the jug in a slow, controlled manner, something I know Abe is already well-versed in.

Abe seems quite impressed with it all, since this style of handling blood and sustenance appeals to him—he's always looking for the most streamlined way, avoiding all murder if possible. It's not that he particularly objects to murder—Abe has certainly never had any trouble killing humans for me— but he believes the only hopeful future for Vampyres, one where we can co-exist in secret beside humans, is to keep our dealings as quiet as possible.

Hence why he also doesn't seem too sold on the idea of letting these blood-drained humans go after they've provided for the crew, but we're new here and not about to tell Ramsay what to do. At least, I'm not. How he runs his ship is none of my business—I'm here for one reason only.

Ramsay makes quick work of preparing the humans, taking some blood from the woman, then the other men, until all five of them have filled a jug's worth. The humans don't even seem to know what's going on and have submitted to the process. At least they don't seem to be in any pain.

"Fascinating," Abe says as Ramsay hands him the jug. He tips it to his mouth, the blood pouring neatly straight down his throat. His pupils glow red, and Ramsay snatches the jug from him before he finishes the whole thing.

"My apologies," Abe says sheepishly, clearing his throat. "Seems I was hungrier than I thought."

Ramsay hands me the jug next, and I finish the rest of it. I'm no stranger to drinking blood from a cup, but it is the first time I've had various blood types mixed together. Can't say I enjoy it all that much—too messy for my palate—but I'm in no position to complain. It has certainly given me more energy, my senses sharpening, the gnawing in my gut subsiding.

With the jug empty, Ramsay puts everything back and tells the humans that someone will be by later to clean up and give them more food, and we lock up the hold behind us.

"I don't think you've really had a proper tour of the ship," Ramsay says to us. "We put you to work straightaway. Come."

Again, we follow him and Thane throughout the ship as he points out the various quarters. Aside from the hold where they keep the bloodletters, there's also a section for prisoners and one they dub the "chain room," where they keep unruly Vampyres. Then, there's the weapons room, stocked top to bottom with every gun, sword, and weapon you can think of, plus cannonballs and gunpowder. They point to a jail room at one end, though I don't go inside, and on the next level up, there's the gun deck, lined with cannons and closed ports, as well as some of the crew's quarters. On the next deck up is our cabin, closest to Thane's quarters, and Ramsay's. I have a feeling that we would normally be sleeping in the hammocks below like most of the crew, but perhaps we're treated a little better because of my past as Priest, and Abe because he's an esteemed doctor. Or maybe they just want to keep an eye on us.

Finally, we end at Ramsay's quarters at the very back of the ship. It's spacious, with lots of shining teak and draped tapestries, lined with bookshelves topped with figurines from various cultures around the world.

And an assortment of crystals. I look around for the seeing one, which should resemble a crystal sphere, but it's not in sight.

He's the witch, I think. Or something like it.

"Have a seat." He gestures to two velvet armchairs.

Abe and I sit down while Thane grabs a bottle of what looks to be whisky, skillfully carrying it and four glasses over to us. He pours us each a generous amount and then hands them to us.

"This whisky belonged to Francis Drake," he says. "The most infamous pirate of all."

"Privateer," Abe corrects him.

"If he's just a privateer, then I'm just a pirate," Ramsay says. "How about we cheers to us pirates, then?"

We clink our glasses together.

"*Salud*," I say in Spanish.

"*Salud*," the rest say.

The whisky goes well with the aftertaste of blood, smooth and nuanced. I try to take my time with it. Because of our metabolisms, we generally don't get too drunk, but it can happen from time to time, especially if you work on it.

"Now," Ramsay says as he leans back against his desk. His feet are crossed casually in front of him, his glass dangling from his fingers, but the look in his eyes is markedly serious. "How about the two of you tell me why you're *really* here?"

Chapter Twenty-Five

LARIMAR

Larimar!

The storm is coming.

I must see the storm.

I must see the sky.

Larimar! the voice says again, more urgently, laced with annoyance—a voice that makes my skin crawl.

I stare up at the surface, caught halfway between it and the Syren yelling at me from the fathoms below.

But I must see the sky.

I pump my tail to swim up, but claws reach out and hook into my fins, one of them tearing right through the delicate tissue. I growl and spin around to face my attacker.

Ullan leers up at me, holding my tail so I can't swim away, his mouth stretching into a macabre grin of jagged edges.

The hate I have for this Syren is palpable, and there's no doubt he feels the same way. He's the reason why I have so many scars among my fins and tail. He's what makes me regret joining the kingdom of Zellebos all those years ago.

Not that I purposely sought them out. After what happened with Priest, after I turned back into a Syren, I swam for my life. Even deep below the surface, I could see his giant, leathery form overhead, no doubt searching for me. I had to disappear so he could never find me.

Yet, part of me wanted him to. I wanted to know what he would have truly done with me. He transformed into the monster he always feared, but was that monster trying to kill me in the church? Or was it just trying to possess me in the only demented way it knew how?

In some ways, I think maybe I could have tempered the beast. I knew something about appealing to the monster inside. After all, I am one too.

But self-preservation is a powerful thing.

So, I swam. I swam through the depths of the dark seas, heading out into the open ocean. I was lost to myself, lost to the currents. My heart was shattered, and my lover was gone along with my legs, which meant the chances of trying to find Maren again were nonexistent.

I lost everything when that church went up in flames.

I don't know how long I drifted in the southern ocean, bumping listlessly against icebergs, being sized up by packs of leopard seals. I wasn't eating; I couldn't even stomach the taste of raw fish. It was as if being forced back into my Syren body was punishment after being on land.

I was half-dead when the Syrens of Zellebos found me. The queen, Sipha, brought me back to her kingdom, mended the wounds on my tail that still remained even after my legs transformed. She made me eat, even though I didn't want to, and protected me from the harm of the wild sea.

Everything was both fine and awful at first—fine because most of the Syrens of Zellebos tolerated me. They were suspicious of newcomers, and most of them were cold and unfeeling, but Sipha took a liking to me, so I was largely left alone. I had her protection.

It was also awful because I couldn't stop thinking about

Priest, couldn't stop remembering the way his hands felt, the way his cock worked inside me, the way he would look at me sometimes like I was a treasure to behold, something more heavenly than anything God promised. When he looked at me, I *felt* that in my bones, which is why I kept thinking about our last night together, trying to figure out what I did to turn him into such a rabid beast, into something that only wanted death and destruction.

Because it had to have been me. It's something I did that made him flip, though I can't for the life of me figure out what it was that night. He had untied me, took me outside to his cottage. I cried when I felt the cold night and saw the stars. He told me he found God in me. Later, he read a book called *Don Quixote* aloud until I fell asleep in his chair, curled up by the fire. I was human. I was whole.

He had been my captor in every sense of the word. He held my mind, body, and soul, but my heart was last to surrender.

He brought me to his bed, bound my hands in his rosary, and told me he wasn't sure how he lived so long without knowing me.

I looked into his eyes and saw something that wasn't there before.

I didn't want to think too much of it.

I was too afraid.

But what I thought I saw that night was my own feelings reflected back to me. I thought I saw his heart, open for once and completely mine.

And then I fell asleep in his arms, wrapped up in his strength and warmth, comforted by his steady breath and slow heartbeat, almost like a lullaby.

When I woke, he was gone.

I found him in the church.

And I immediately knew this was the end for us.

Our love lines had become hopelessly tangled, and his claws ripped them apart.

Larimar, Ullan sneers, *what do you think you're doing?*

He jerks me downward, and I cry out. I always try to give him nothing, since my reaction is what he wants. This Syren lives to torture me, and I've been fair game ever since Sipha died and the kingdom fractured.

Always going for the surface, he says, hands digging into my shoulders as he holds me in place. *It's like you're trying to escape what you are. You think the world up there is any better?*

I want to tell him I've been there, that I know it is.

Better the devil you know—isn't that the saying the humans use?

And I did know Priest. At least, I thought I did.

There's a storm, I say to Ullan, trying to keep my voice blank.

And that's interesting to you? Come on. Stay with the group. We're going for the shallows.

He lets go of me and swims off toward the shallower water near the banks of the island. I glance up at the surface. Though it's daytime, there is barely any light that filters down, all of it swept up in the big swells. The storms have always attracted me. I want to breach the surface and take in the wild and unforgiving sky that stretches above. It mirrors the stormy depths of the ocean in some ways, made more alluring by the fact that it's forever out of reach.

I follow Ullan to the shallows. I know if I don't, he'll physically make me, and I don't feel like having a fight at the moment. I never win.

Ullan took over as leader of the colony when Sipha died. She had been captured by a passing ship—at least, that's what Ullan said. He was supposedly with her when it happened. I always thought he killed her, one way or another. Perhaps he took out her heart, or perhaps there really was a ship hunting

Syrens, and he enabled her to get caught. He always wanted her out of the way, as well as so many of her followers, and he swiftly stepped into the role. He has no royal Syren blood, just the ability to use violence in every situation until he managed to appoint himself King.

Either way, I obviously don't trust him or those who carry out his orders, but some days, I know better than to push my luck. Other days, though, I push it anyway, just to feel something, just so I'm not forever swimming in the darkness, numb to the world. Those days, I want a fight. I almost like it when he maims me. It nearly reminds me of Priest, though it's not the same. There is no obsession or devotion in Ullan's eyes when he makes me bleed—there is only hatred.

Sometimes, I feel so blank and empty that pain is better than nothing at all.

I keep swimming toward the island. The shallows consist of dark rock with the occasional strand of sand that stands out like a bright patch against the void. Sometimes, we forage here for crab; other times, we brave the leopard seals and sea lions to try and capture some of the penguins on their daily feeding trips. If the other predators outnumber us, we usually move on. Depending on the time of year, the ice build-up can extend into the depths, though, at the moment, the ice is mainly contained to a flow on the other side of the island, giant chunks of it breaking off into the ocean, the water turning milky as the fresh water mixes with it.

But as the shallows come into view, I notice only a few Syrens, their bodies silhouettes against the bright blue strands of sand. None of them seem to be Ullan.

I swim toward them, and everything seems normal—there are two females and a male, all of them overturning rocks, looking for crab. My heart flutters in my veins, my gills feeling sticky. I'm anxious for reasons I can't figure out, possibly because every time I approach a group, I worry I'll be further ostracized. Once upon a time, I never took it personally when I was rejected by others—I was completely focused on finding Maren—but ever since Priest, I feel like every part of me has been worn thin.

As I get closer to the Syrens, though, I recognize them as being three of Sipha's closest confidants: Esmerelda, Vialana, and Meriw. They've always been kind to me, at least more so than the rest.

And yet, my anxiety hasn't retreated. I still feel as if there's something wrong, something I'm not seeing.

Larimar, Meriw greets me, his voice more curt than normal. *We've been waiting for you.*

I look at him in surprise. *Waiting for me?*

Yes, Esmerelda says, her tail twitching as she breaks apart a shell. *Ullan said you wanted us to meet you here to forage for urchins.*

I whip my head around, on high alert as I look for Ullan. He's still nowhere in sight. No one else in the colony is here either; it's just us four.

Sipha's greatest supporters.

It's a trap! I call out.

What do you mean? Vialana asks, sounding panicked but not panicked enough. *A trap set by who?*

Ullan, Meriw says. Then, his eyes widen as he looks over my shoulder. *Ship! Ship! Retreat!*

I turn to see a large vessel heading toward us, similar to the one that snatched up Asherah. With the narrow curve of the bay, we will have to swim under it to escape; otherwise, we'll beach ourselves.

There's a chance, of course, that the ship isn't here for us. Perhaps it's heading toward the shallows because it's about to drop anchor, the bay protection during the storm.

But I'm not about to find out.

I swim fast along the bottom, heading toward the deep so

I can pass underneath the ship undetected, when suddenly, Vialana screams.

I stop to see her tangled in a net while Meriw and Esmerelda swim away.

I can't just leave her there.

She's trying to rip the net with her claws, but to no avail. The net must be made of some kind of metal.

Larimar, she cries out frantically. *I can't get out.*

I reach her, my claws coming out, and I do my best to free her from the net, trying to saw through.

Go, she says. *Save yourself.*

Hold on, I tell her, trying to get her to focus on me. *I'm going to get one of the clams. Their shells can cut through anything we can't.*

But the moment I turn from her to dive downward, the water starts to become sliced into many squares.

It's a net rushing toward me, as if it had already been there.

A trap that had been set.

I yelp, and before I can swim out of the way, the net rushes up around me until I'm caught the same as Vialana.

And then, the net is hauled to the surface with me inside.

Chapter Twenty-Six

It's been a week since Abe and I walked the plank and had a trial decided by a shark. I'm still unsure how the shark decided anything, but I suppose if it bit our heads off, that would have meant we were guilty of something. Either way, we survived, welcomed into the crew as if nothing had happened, like we were old friends.

Well, I should say it's that way for Abe. Even though the doctor can be awkward and strange at times, he fits in well with this band of misfits and miscreants. All of them are equally odd in their own ways; I suppose that's why they're pirates and not living in the upper reaches of society as normal Vampyres do. High society loves those with money, and the immortals tend to have a lot of it. Still, it takes a lot to mold yourself to seem like an ordinary yet extraordinarily successful human and not the blood-drinking, murderous deviants we all are.

When it comes to me, however, I seem to have made good progress with everyone on the ship—everyone except for Maren. I don't possess a great deal of charm—I am far too grumpy for that—but what I have goes a long way when I'm dealing with a non-Vampyre. Yet, Maren seems immune. I don't run into her very often, which is quite strange when you're stuck on a ship together, but when I do cross her path, she treats me with distance and suspicion. It was her decision to make a shark the judge, but I'm not sure she agrees with the verdict.

I'm starting to wonder if perhaps she knows of my relationship with Larimar. I haven't said anything, and so far, no one has asked for any more information about the Syrens, nor has the objective of our journey been brought up.

Well, that's not quite true.

The other day, after we were treated to blood, Ramsay and Thane sat us down and questioned us about our true intentions. I let Abe do most of the talking. He convinced Ramsay that I need to be around my own kind for a change, that the isolation he thought would help cure me is what drove me to madness in the end.

I think they believed him. I expected them to badger me with the same questions, but they dropped the subject after that. What I really wanted was to ask about their journey to find the Syrens, but I didn't want to call attention to myself when they seemed satisfied with Abe's answer.

Strangely enough, our destination and mission haven't been brought up that often. Here and there, I'll hear a crew member talk about the island, and I assume they mean Roche Island. Some will talk about whether we'll find trouble in the Strait of Magellan, but nothing more than that.

It's fine with me. I can handle a strained yet cordial relationship with the lady of the ship. I've noticed that Ramsay is very protective of her; if I even stare at her for too long, he gets gruff with me, so I'm not about to try and win her over.

Besides, I know how to keep my place and when to bow my head. Now that we've been sailing for a bit, I'm getting rather used to being on the *Nightwind*. It reminds me of the comradery we had at the monastery, or at least in those later years when we had more humanity. After being stationed alone for so long, or with Abe's sole company, it has been nice to actually be around others, especially blood-drinkers. I know I'm different, and there's a bit of trepidation and curiosity from the others, but we're all birds of a feather.

Though I suppose I'm the only one who has ever had wings.

"Mew."

I startle and turn around to find an orange cat standing on the rack of pots and pans. I'm in the galley with the cook, Sedge, as he prepares tonight's meal. He's the other human here, other than Maren. A mute, but that's fine with me; I learned some basic sign language when I was at the monastery, taught by the monk Pedro Ponce de Leon to aid us when we had to live in silence.

Who is that? I sign to Sedge, moving my hands in a clumsy manner. I'm still rusty, and Sedge hasn't exactly learned the language I have, but the longer I'm with him, the more he's teaching me to adapt to the way he communicates. While I could talk to him, because he's not hard of hearing, I think he appreciates me signing.

Skip, Sedge says, spelling out the letters. *Ramsay's cat.*

The cat stares at me with piercing green eyes, its tail waving back and forth.

Skip mews again, tilting its head at me.

"Mew to you too," I say, tipping my imaginary hat.

Ships are great for cats, Sedge explains, his fingers moving so fast that it's hard to keep up. *They take care of the rodents.*

Do you have a lot of rodents? I try to ask, though my attempts are awkward.

Sedge nods gravely. *The blood.*

Ah. The blood.

I look back down at the food he's preparing, chopping up

fresh-caught tuna into steaks. No wonder it caught the cat's attention.

We eat well on the ship, even though we don't need to eat food. Sedge is a good cook, and he has to make meals for Maren and Thane's son, Lucas, who hasn't become a Vampyre yet and won't need blood until he's thirty-five, so Sedge often insists on cooking for all of us blood-drinkers, plus the humans in the hold.

Suddenly, the back of my neck prickles, and I breathe in a scent that reminds me of Larimar, making my heart skip a beat.

The cat mews, and I swear it raises its paw in greeting.

I turn around to see Maren standing in the doorway to the galley.

"Aragon," she says in a clipped voice with a tight smile. "Might I have a word with you in private?"

"Of course," I say. I nod at Sedge and walk with her out of the galley. From behind, I hear the cat drop to the ground and follow us.

"It's really good of you to use your sign language with Sedge," she says to me, her hands clasped at her front, but I don't believe the demure act.

"I learned it at the monastery. We had to live in silence for many years as part of our training. It's nice to be able to use it again."

"Mmmm," she hums as we walk down the stairs to the lower deck, her gold dress sweeping behind her. "I have to say, most of us were...apprehensive about having a man of the cloth on board. A Vampyre one, no less. But the fact that you haven't tried to tell any of us that we're bound for hell has been refreshing."

"As you know, I was a priest. I'm not anymore."

She glances at me over her shoulder. "Ah, yes. Why is that?"

I frown at her. "Because I'm not fit to be one. You know what I did to my congregation."

"I do," she says, facing forward again as we walk toward the back of the ship, both of us listing to the side as we do. We're a level above the hold, and the ship groans and creaks in its own eerie song punctuated by the slap of the waves. We are somewhere off the coast of Southern Chile, and the weather has taken a turn for the worse. Any day now, we're supposed to enter the strait, which should give us some relief.

"I find it peculiar that you were more concerned about me being a priest than about me being a turned Vampyre. A monster."

"I suppose a monster is something we all have to grapple with deep inside."

"But not you," I point out. "You're just a human."

She comes to a stop outside the closed door to the jail cell and quirks up her dark brow. "Even humans have the devil inside them." Then she opens the door and shows me into a room where a large, human-sized cage stands in the corner.

My mouth goes dry, and I'm on high alert. Is this a trap? No doubt I could fight her off, but if the rest of the crew joined with the intention of locking me in there, there's not much I could do.

"Don't worry," she says. "This is our jail. It's not for you."

I step inside the room and look at it from a distance. There are a few other items of interest in here—chains hanging from the wall and ceiling, a long, empty glass box with a lid.

She adds, "Well, I should say, it's not for you yet."

I frown at her. "Have I done something to offend you, my lady?"

"Possibly," she says. Then, she gathers her black hair and piles it on top of her head, showcasing her gills. "I know you've seen these. I know you know what they are. They said you have experience with Syrens, so you must know that I am one."

"A Syren with legs," I remark carefully. "How peculiar."

"Yes," she says, letting her hair back down. "It is very peculiar. I won't go into the logistics of it, but since you were a witch, or *are* a witch, I'm sure you can guess what happened."

Larimar's words ring in my ears.

I know a Syren who wanted legs instead of a tail. She wanted to be able to become a human, to walk and live on land. The sea witch was able to do that for her.

My mouth feels full of sand, and I try to swallow. "A witch gave you legs," I say hoarsely. "What kind of witch? How did that happen? When? Is that common?"

Her brows pull together. "It was a sea witch," she says warily. "Her name was Edonia, and as far as I know, it's not a common thing. I wanted legs so I could be on land."

"But why?"

She shrugs. "I was young and terribly stupid. I was angry at my father for ignoring me, for paying more attention to my older sisters. So I made a deal with her..." She waves a dismissive hand at me. "At any rate, it's a long story and, depending on how you behave, there are many days and nights ahead of us to tell it."

I'm trying to remember if Larimar ever said anything about her family or her sisters, but she never told me anything.

"What do you mean 'behave'?" I ask, thinking back to what she just said.

"I heard the rumors of a Syren being found in the waters by your village, and I heard your account of what happened."

"From who?"

"From Abe," she says with a coy smile. "You get that doctor some rum and he'll tell you everything."

Skip mews, and she reaches down to scoop the cat up into her arms.

"I know," she says to the cat. "But I have to make sure he's not a threat."

"Are you talking to the cat?"

"And the cat is talking back," she says frostily.

I ignore that. I suppose being on a ship for too long will do that to you. "What did Abe tell you?"

"That you hunted for the Syren, caught her, tortured her a little, fed from her, and then she escaped. How did she get away?"

I remain composed. "She was drying out. I put her in the surf to wet her tail, and that's the last thing I remember. She must have hit me with it."

"I'm glad she escaped," she says.

"I'm not."

She gives me a knowing smile. "And that's why I need to know if you'll behave. I can't have you capturing these Syrens and trying to torture or feast on them."

"No?"

"I'm a Syren, after all," she says. "Even now. With magic, I can get my tail back anytime I am submerged. I'm still a monster, same as you, and I must protect my own kind, even if we're feral beasts. You must have felt the same way about your kin at the monastery."

I blink, still perplexed by all of this. "But if you don't want any harm to come to the Syrens, why are you going after them? I heard this was a hunting expedition."

"It is," she says, a coldness coming over her eyes. "We're hunting one Syren in particular."

"Which one?"

"My sister," she says with a raise of her chin. "Her name is Larimar."

Chapter Twenty-Seven

PRIEST

"A ragon," Cruz says as he pops his head into the doorway of my cabin. "You told me to tell you when it's time. It's time."

I get out of bed, putting down my book. I have a rare talent for being able to read when the ship is heaving and hoeing and not get seasick. Abe has been on the top deck most of the last few days, his focus glued on the horizon and looking a cumbersome shade of green.

I follow Cruz up the stairs to the deck, my body immediately buffeted by strong winds and light rain and bitter cold that even I can feel seeping into my bones, the sun hidden behind clouds, making it dark as sin in the middle of the day.

I smell it before I see it: the familiar scent of a heartbreaking land.

Nombre de Jesus.

Cruz points to the shore to our left. Abe and Maren are standing at the bow, staring at it. Maren is dressed in a red gown that stands out amongst the endless gray, like a splotch of blood in the fog. I go to join them, wobbling as I go as the ship hits wave after wave.

"This is it," I say, taking my place beside Abe. "I didn't think we'd get here so soon."

"I remember the strait being calmer than this," Abe says, tucking his scarf around his neck, only for it to unravel again.

"Your memory is tainted," I tell him, though I'm sure mine is too. "The water was often wild here. We were just safe on shore, that's all."

"There really is nothing left," Maren comments. "You burned it all to the ground."

I know I should feel shame. The only remains of the settlement are a few charred structures. Even the church is completely gone, reduced to ash and blown away in the constant wind. Only a few graves from the cemetery remain, sticking out in the now-decimated surroundings, the last signs of humanity amongst the bent pines and canelo trees and the occasional guanaco.

I suppress a shiver. I can still taste the blood of that animal. I remember being a monster and starving, as if my insides were eating up my soul—at least, whatever was left of it.

But what I was really ravenous for was Larimar.

And being here now, all the feelings come flooding back.

Are you alright? Abe's voice slides into my mind, always concerned.

I swallow thickly and give the slightest nod. I don't want to talk about it, not in my mind, not ever, not anymore. It was one thing to try and grapple with my feelings, to come to terms with what happened on that fateful night and the years of degeneracy after. It's something else to be here again, sailing past the village where my entire life came crashing down for the second time, leaving my bleeding heart and fractured mind in my hands.

And now that I know we've plotted a course to find Larimar, everything has become more important and terrifying than ever.

I haven't told Abe what Maren told me a few weeks ago: that Larimar is her sister. I don't trust him not to flap his gums, especially now that I know he's susceptible to rum. I always knew he had a weakness, but I didn't think it was the god-awful grog they brewed on board.

No, I've kept it to myself.

I've stewed over the knowledge that seeing Larimar again isn't a fruitless task. My obsession with finding her these last few years has existed only in the darkness of my heart. I dreamed of what I would do to her if I found her, how I would make her hurt. I wanted to bite her, drink her blood, defile her. I wanted to keep her in chains again, nail her to the wall, make sure she couldn't leave. I wouldn't make that same mistake again. I'd deny her legs, make her keep her tail, and I would fuck that cunt anyway.

I wanted to make her bleed.

For me.

And for all time.

But some part of me knew that finding her would be impossible. I tried. For those years, I tried as the monster, but to no avail. Even when Abe found me and said he would help me get her back, I knew it wouldn't happen.

I truly didn't expect him to send a letter to Ramsay to ensure we could board the *Nightwind* and have a shot at it. Even when we did become part of this motley crew and set off sailing down the coast of Chile on the expedition to Roche Island, I thought the idea of locating Larimar was a fever dream.

Now, though, everything has changed.

Maren's sister is Larimar. She was the one Larimar talked about, the one the witch gave legs. I keep running it over and over again in my head, trying to dissect everything Larimar told me, to see if there was anything else she had said, but she kept her cards close to her chest.

She did say she was looking for someone—*someone who didn't want to be found.*

I have to assume it was her sister. Maren told me she disappeared and left her father and sisters behind in Limonos, never to see them again. She would later divulge that she ended up being found by a prince and married him, a mistake she wouldn't elaborate on. She was with the prince for ten years, traveling the world.

I wish Larimar was here now so I could ask her, so she could tell me what she went through, if she was searching for her sister this whole time.

But I know that if Larimar was here right now, she wouldn't be talking. She would be gagged with a chain. The only sounds coming out of her would be whimpers and cries of pain until she apologized for what she did to me.

Until she knew what it felt like to have your heart ripped from your chest.

You're doing it again, Abe says, and I realize I'm tugging on my ear.

Maren seems to notice, looks over at me and frowns, but she doesn't say anything. I had promised her I wouldn't touch any Syren, most especially her sister.

I aim to break that promise.

"There's a bad storm coming," Ramsay says, stepping onto the foredeck. He puts his arm around Maren and nods at the dark clouds on the horizon. "As soon as we hit the South Atlantic, we're going to get walloped."

Maren nods. "We'll be fine. The ship will take care of us."

"Aye," Ramsay says. "That she will."

"Maren!" the Greek Drakos yells from the crow's nest high up in the mainmast, waving his spyglass at us. "There's a shark ahead!"

"Nill!" Maren says, leaning over the edge of the bow.

"Careful, luv," Ramsay says, grabbing her shoulder firmly to hold her back. "You want to make sure it's Nill first before you dive in."

She grins at Ramsay in nervous anticipation. "I can take care of myself."

Then, she rips herself out of her husband's grasp and leaps overboard. Abe and I lean over the edge, watching as she swan dives perfectly into the water, though she's immediately swallowed by the gray waves.

Abe sucks in his breath. "She could hit the ship."

"She's a Syren. She'll be fine," Ramsay says, though he sounds a little nervous as well.

All three of us stare at the waves as they smack against the bow and beat against the hull, growing bigger as we approach the entrance to the Atlantic. Even with the excellent eyesight of Vampyres, it's still hard to see.

But then the bosun yells from the aft. "They're down here!"

Everyone scrambles to the side of the ship, where Cruz and Thane are already lowering the ropes to pull Maren back up.

Ramsay reaches over and picks her up the rest of the way while Thane, Ramsay's brother, yells at Lucas to get her a blanket. Before my eyes, I watch as Maren's teal-and-purple tail flaps underneath her dress then slowly changes into legs, no spell needed.

"Fascinating," Abe whispers.

Lucas runs over with the blanket, and Maren is quickly wrapped in it. Her teeth are chattering, her skin pale and blue. I suppose in the water, as a Syren, the temperature has no effect on her, but the moment she's back to being human again, it all comes crashing down.

She tries to talk, but her teeth chatter too hard, and someone hands her a mug of hot tea, which she cups in her hands while Ramsay holds her close, rubbing the blanket across her back.

"Take your time," he says.

Can this shark really talk to her? Abe asks in my head.

Apparently so, I tell him. Yesterday, they had sent the shark ahead of the ship to try and locate the Syren colony at Roche Island. They explained that while none of them can communicate with the shark, Maren can, as well as with other creatures of the sea, including whales, seals, and the Kraken. I'm not too convinced by that last one, since the Kraken is supposed to be an animal of old legend up in the North Sea, but Ramsay says the beast certainly exists, and that Maren can control it.

Regardless, she can talk to a bloody shark, so perhaps the beastie really does exist.

"She-she's in d-danger," Maren finally says, biting out her words. "There's a whole co-colony and-and another ship, an English ship. The-they've captured them. They've captured Larimar."

"Larimar!" Abe exclaims.

I keep my face immobile. He doesn't know that's the name of the Syren they're looking for.

Maren looks at him. "Y-yes. My sister. That's why we've g-got to rescue her." Then she looks to me and frowns. Despite her blue lips and her chattering teeth and the news that her sister has been captured, there's a look in her eyes that says she underestimated me, probably because Abe just proved I never told him about their relationship. That I can keep a secret.

But that look is short-lived.

Suddenly, determination comes across her brow, and she gets to her feet, shucking off her blanket. "I've got to swim ahead and get her."

"Maren, no," Ramsay says. "We'll get her together."

She shakes her head violently, her wet hair flying. "Nill said the storm is bad, enough to slow down even the *Nightwind*.

I'll be able to go under the waves. Nill will lead me there. I've got to go ahead—it's the only way I can try and save her before the ship leaves with her on board."

Did you know her sister is Larimar? Abe asks me. *Ah, but you have known and you didn't tell me. Frankly, I'm hurt.*

I don't have time to try and explain to Abe why I didn't tell him, because Maren suddenly starts running across the deck and leaps over the side, Ramsay screaming after her as she disappears.

A storm is coming.

And my Larimar is out there, captured by some other ship, by some other person who means to do her harm.

I wonder if now, of all times, my beast should be invited to return.

Chapter Twenty-Eight

LARIMAR

Chaos.

In seconds, my world descended into chaos.

The nets were drawn up to the deck of the ship, and I was dumped there in a heap. I don't remember much of it, except that I was kicked, poked, and prodded by various boots and weapons. I heard men laughing, calling me names. I didn't understand their language, the sounds harsh and guttural, but I knew when they were insulting me, spitting on me.

I must have snarled at them, swiped at them with my claws, tried to bite them, but they were prepared. It wasn't their first time hunting Syrens, and they knew what to do. They came at me with chains and a heavy object to the head.

The world was full of pain and stars before it went black, and when I came to, I was in this glass box, barely long enough to fit me, my tail curling up at the end. It's filled with murky salt water, my gills just getting enough in, though I don't think the water will sustain me for long. It's hard to say if they know much about Syrens and that we can breathe air if needed. I would rather breathe the air than be stuck inside this glass cage with filthy water.

Larimar.

I tilt my head to the side, wincing through the pain as I look over to see Vialana in the box beside me. We're in a ship's cabin, the water in our boxes sloshing as the ship slams into wave after wave.

You shouldn't have come for me, Vialana says, sorrow in her anguished eyes.

She's right. I shouldn't have. But I felt so powerless when I watched Asherah get taken by the pirates that I couldn't just let the same thing happen to another Syren.

Though I don't think these men are pirates. I had glimpses of them when Asherah was hauled up—they spoke another language, English, I think, and weren't dressed the same way these men are. These men remind me of that soldier back in Chile.

And I have a feeling they have the same thing planned for me.

My blood runs cold at the thought. I would rather take my own life than be subjected to the torturous, immoral whims of these men.

Ullan must have known, Vialana says. *But how?*

The thought of Ullan kicks rage into my heart, but all the fury in the world won't help me now.

Maybe he saw them in the area and led them into the bay, making sure we were there already, I say, pressing my hands up against the top of the glass, testing the strength. *Maybe he knows them somehow.*

But a Syren making friends with a human? she asks.

It happens, I tell her.

And sometimes, they fall in love with them.

Silence stretches between us. I wish I had known Vialana

better before this. She seems a lot sweeter than I thought. Perhaps I could have made more of an effort to get to know the Syrens instead of relying on Sipha.

But I'm tired of having so many regrets.

I'm so tired of everything.

My eyes close, and I drift off to sleep for a few minutes before I hear Vialana say, *What do you think they'll do to us?*

I don't know, I say. I remember what Priest said about exhibitions and museums and being kept in a glass box much like this one, people tapping on it, trying to taunt you, but I don't want to tell Vialana any of that. If a Syren's freedom is taken away, she loses all hope. She loses everything.

But you gained everything when you lost your freedom to Priest, I remind myself.

Suddenly, the door bursts open, three men staggering inside. They stink of alcohol, and I know that look in their eyes. Lusty and lawless.

They point at Vialana and shout at each other, their grins sloppy, leering. Disgust rolls through me, mixing with the rage until I feel as if I can't breathe.

I watch as they take off the glass lid, exposing Vialana beneath. She hisses and lunges for them. Her claws catch one of the men, nearly severing his arm, and blood sprays into the water, mixing with her already-red hair.

The man screams, stumbles back while holding his dangling arm, while the other men grab Vialana, quickly binding her wrists with wire. She thrashes in her box, the bloody water spilling everywhere, splashing over my own glass.

They haul her out, throwing her down on the floor. They yell at the man with the bleeding arm to wrap the rope around her tail, but by now, he's sitting down in the corner of the room, breathing slow and looking pale.

Another man comes into the room now. He doesn't even

pay attention to the injured man. No, he goes straight to the Syren and takes his penis out from his pants, long and foul-looking. He barks at the other men—one holds down Vialana from behind, holding her hair, and the other sits on her tail. While she's still screaming, trying desperately to escape, the newcomer straddles her and runs his finger down the front of her tail, trying to find her slit.

He cries out when he does, and Vialana screams again as his fingers penetrate her. When his penis does and he continues to rape her in front of me, her scream turns into her Syren's song.

It causes cracks to form in my glass box, fissures along the porthole windows. The men cry out from the sound, blood trickling from their ears, and yet they keep pinning her down, keep defiling her. I want to turn away—I can't bear to see the pain and humiliation on her face as she's violated so horribly, but I'm afraid to. I have to keep watch, have to stay vigilant, have to figure out how to fight back.

Her screaming continues, louder now, and the cracks in my glass box are spreading, deepening. One of the men punches her in the face to shut her up, which earns a repri-manding tone from the other, as if raping is fine but hitting isn't, and while they're distracted, I take in a deep breath of the dirty water. I gather all my strength, and with a scream of my own, I push at the glass until it shatters.

Water spills out in a rush, filling the room, and I flounder on the floor on top of the broken glass.

The men are yelling now as I try to push myself up to sit, the better to defend myself, when suddenly, more people burst into the room.

One man in particular, with a thick blond mustache, starts barking orders. From the way they jump and listen, I assume he's in charge. He points at me, and men come forward with chains, but I open my mouth and scream again, swiping my tail back and forth along the floor, taking them out. One man falls right beside me, and I act fast. I bite down on his nose, taking it clean off while my claws dig into his chest to find his heart. I manage to swallow down his nose, one of his eyes, and his cheek before shoving the heart into my mouth, trying to gather more strength.

There is chaos all around me, my scream mixed with Vialana's mixed with the men, but then someone has a chain around my mouth, the same way Priest did, strangling my scream in my throat. I try to bite through it, but the only thing I succeed in doing is chipping a tooth.

Then, someone else grabs my hands and tail, tying both of them together so I'm bent backward in an arc. I'm left there on the ground, watching as they attempt to do the same to Vialana, but she's not fighting back. In fact, she's completely still.

For a moment, I think that perhaps the man punched her too hard, but then I see the blood trickle away from her, and when one of the men steps back, I see the awful truth.

There's a heart in her hand.

Her own.

Vialana just ripped her own chest open and tore out her heart, killing herself instantly.

I freeze. Go numb. I know I said I would do the same thing if any of those men were about to touch me, but it's still such a shocking, horrible thing to witness. Defiled by these heathens and then destroyed by her own hand.

Even if I could find the courage to tear my own heart out, I'm shackled, unable to move.

The blond man turns red in the face as he yells more things I can't understand. They push Vialana's lifeless body into the corner, and then the man in charge turns to me, putting his hand to my face as he says something. He's not quite leering at me in that sexual way of the others, but his eyes aren't kind either. They spark with some sort of zealous fascination, and somehow, I think whatever he has planned with me is far worse than what happened to Vialana.

Then, he grins at me, and before I know what's happening, he hits me over the head.

I wake up underwater.

Moving fast.

And yet, I'm immobile.

I'm held in place, chains wrapped around me in three different places.

I look down to see the inky depths of the ocean below.

I look up and see nothing but the belly of the dark ship.

I've been chained to a piece of wood that sticks down at the bottom of the vessel, one that moves back and forth every now and then. When it does, the ship corrects course and moves in that direction.

Now what?

The last thing I remember was that blond man, perhaps the captain, hitting me, and now I'm here. Why would he do this?

Perhaps he thinks I need to be in water to survive, and both the glass boxes have been shattered. Maybe he thought tying me to the bottom of the ship was the best way to keep me captive until the ship gets to its final destination.

But where is that? Where are they taking me? What happens when I get hungry? Without being able to use my arms, I can't catch any fish while I'm tied down here. If they're going to be at sea for weeks before they reach port, I'll starve to death.

A better death than the one you would have had up there, I tell myself, my heart sinking at that last image of Vialana holding her own heart in her hand. At least here, I am safe and alive—for now. It's hard to say what could happen in the future. Maybe there will be a chance at escape when they swim down to loosen me—after all, they'll be in my world for once.

I try to keep that thought going.

I have to have hope.

There were times during these last few years where I thought all hope was lost. I believed that nothing mattered anymore, and I would do anything to escape my battered and bruised heart. I really thought death would be the perfect escape, a slow sink into oblivion.

But the moment that net fell, I felt the fight return, the fight for the spirit, the soul, the fight for life—not just survival, but a life worth living and thriving in.

I feel that fight start to creep in. Maybe it's a pointless cause, seeing as I'm strapped to the bottom of a ship as it heads somewhere to do something awful with me, but I won't let these men take me.

I won't let them break me.

I'm the only one allowed to break myself.

And I don't feel like falling apart anymore.

I don't know how many days pass. It's impossible to tell time with the dark ship blocking out the surface. The ship is constantly crashing into the waves above, which makes me think we're still in a storm. Every now and then, we'll pass by an iceberg, the bright blue ice shooting down into the depths, always so beautiful and eerie. Sometimes, whales or dolphins will pass, and I've reached out to them with a plea for help.

But there's nothing a whale or dolphin can do to help me. They can't undo the chains—one tried briefly but wasn't able to undo the lock with their nose—and they are naturally wary of people, especially people who would chain a Syren to their ship. Only the giant black-and-white dolphins with the tall dorsal fins would be able to damage the boat, but I haven't seen any of them.

At one point, I think I even see a shark, but I don't dare call out to it. I would be easy prey for one of them since I can't fight back. Besides, it might be a dream. Everything starts to fade into a dark haze, a half-awake, half-asleep nightmare. I'm now used to the water constantly streaming past my face and body, the occasional movements of the wood turning the ship. I want to keep the fight alive, but I feel myself weaken with each moment.

More time passes, drifts by with the ice.

Then, out of the darkness, I hear a familiar voice, one I never expected to hear again.

There is the ship, the voice says, low and deep and inhuman.

The voice of a shark.

Nill, I think to myself, opening my eyes to the dark seas. When we left Limonos, Maren's shark, Nill, stayed behind to wait for her. He was never my shark, but he was part of the family, and it hurt to leave him behind, even though he insisted.

But Limonos was in a whole other ocean, one where icebergs didn't exist, where the water was warm and full of bright coral and colorful fish. That's where Nill belonged, not here in the icy darkness of the southern seas.

The rudder, the voice says. *I see something attached to the rudder.*

I strain my eyes, trying to see through the murky water constantly churned up by the swells and currents. Someone is talking; I know I can hear them. Perhaps another shark?

This time, I am asking for food.

Hello! I yell. *Is anyone out there?*

Oh my Lord, I hear another voice say in awe.

But this time, the voice isn't just familiar.

It's the voice of my heart.

The missing piece of my soul I've been looking for most of my life.

Maren! I yell.

Larimar! I hear her reply.

It can't be. It can't. I keep staring into the sea, expecting to be hallucinating, hearing things. It can't be her or Nill—they both can't possibly be here. Nill is a stretch, but Maren is an impossibility. She traded her fins for legs! It's not possible for her to be a Syren again.

And yet, it was possible for me.

My heart clenches into a tight little fist, holding out all hope.

Maren, I'm here! I cry out.

And for the first time on my own, I pray. *Oh God, if you exist as Priest thinks you do, please, please, please.*

Let this be her.

There's silence for a moment, and then suddenly, out of the murky waters, two shapes appear, swimming toward me.

One is a shark.

One is a woman in a dress, tattered at the end with a tail sticking out, pumping up and down furiously as she propels herself forward.

Details appear slowly and then all at once.

The red of her dress, standing out like a bloodstain against the deep.

Then, flowing black hair.

A teal-and-purple tail.

Her bright blue eyes.

Her wide, heartbreaking smile.

She's so much older than I remember, not the girl I imagined in my head, but that doesn't make her any less beautiful or any less her.

Maren.

I know I told Priest Syrens don't cry underwater, but I feel the tears spill from my eyes anyway, carried off into the currents.

Larimar! she cries out. She swims right up to me and keeps pace with the ship, her hand on my cheek, marveling at my face while Nill circles around us, excitedly waving his tail back and forth. *I can't believe it's you. I can't believe we found you.*

You were looking for me? I ask in surprise. *I've been looking for you since the day you left. All this time, all those years, I've been looking for you.* I try to swallow the lump in my throat. *Asherah too.*

I know, she says, but before I can ask how she could, she gives her head a shake, her expression pained, though her smile is soft. *We have so much to talk about.*

But how did you find me?

She nods at Nill. *He helped.*

How did you find Nill? You were gone for so long; how do you even have a tail again?

Magic, she says with a knowing grin. *Come on, let's get you free.*

How? I ask as she starts swimming along the chains, running her hands over them, her red dress swirling around her. *Your claws can't break through. I don't think Nill's bite could do it either.*

I could try, Nill says. *But I think there is a better solution.*

He's on the other side of what he called the rudder, nosing a part of the chain. I can't twist my head back enough to look.

I can pick this lock, Maren says determinedly. *Nill, I need one of your teeth.*

Happy to provide.

I can't see it happen, but I hear Nill give a small noise of discomfort and then Maren apologizes to him, having pulled a tooth from his mouth.

Won't be much longer, Maren says as I hear the tooth scraping against metal.

Where did you learn to pick locks? I ask her. Would have been helpful to know when I was captured by Priest. Then again, if I had escaped the first chance I had, I would have never known what it was like to give myself over to someone like him. I never would have experienced those blissful highs.

Never would have experienced those terrible lows.

I've learned a lot over the years, she says. *But my husband taught me, amongst other things.*

I stiffen. *The prince? I heard you married a prince. That's why you made the deal with the witch.*

I did marry the prince, she says, her voice hard. *But I left him...in pieces.*

Oh.

I ended up married to a pirate instead.

A pirate? I exclaim.

Almost there, she says, her attention back to the lock.

But pirates killed Asherah.

Larimar, I know, she says. *As I said, we have a lot to talk about. The most important thing is getting you free and back to our ship.*

Ship! Are you kept in a glass box? That's what happened to

*me on this ship. I don't know what they are planning to do
with me.*

*I have a Syren tail in the water, but out of the water, I have
legs.*

How?

Magic, she says. *And speaking of magic...* I hear the lock
click. *You're free.*

The chains around me come loose and fall, rushing
quickly into the depths until I can't see them anymore.

I burst forward, swimming out of the way, and then watch
as the ship keeps going, leaving the three of us behind.

Suddenly, Maren's arms are around me in an embrace, and
she holds me tight as I hold her back with as much strength as
I can muster.

My sister.

I finally have my sister.

The hole in my heart I thought would never be filled is
now overflowing with love for her.

My sister, my family, my blood.

Come on, she says, grabbing my hand. *We'll be swimming
this way. About a day's journey, if not more, depending on how
the storm is blowing. The ship might be taking a beating.*

*Wait. You're taking me on the ship? I can't be with you the
way that I am,* I tell her, keeping pace. *You are human; you
have legs on land. I don't. I can't be part of your world, and you
can't be part of mine.*

I can, she says. *I will stay in the water with you as long as
you want, but don't underestimate me, dear sister. I have my
own ways of making things work.* She pauses. *There is someone
on the ship I would like to you meet. He's a witch. He'd be able to
give you legs. If you want, of course.*

My body tenses. I know there is absolutely no chance she's
talking about Priest, and yet my heart starts to thud wildly, like
it knows it's him.

A male witch? I ask. *And he's not the captain?*

Well, the captain does know magic, but it was taught to him with a very powerful magic book that we keep hidden. The man in question has innate magic within him. I know he was able to turn a Syren into a human once.

I stop swimming and stare at her.

What is this witch's name? I ask warily.

Aragon, she says, and it's like I've been punched in the heart. *Strangely enough, he used to be a priest.*

Chapter Twenty-Nine

PRIEST

"This storm will get worse before it gets better," Thane grumbles to me as we attempt to pull in a loose sail on the mizzenmast as it flaps out of control. The rope itself is scraping off all the skin on my hands, leaving the fibers bloody, but I barely feel it. There's too much happening at once for me to focus on just one thing.

"How can it get worse?" I ask, just as a giant wave crashes over the bow and takes out three crew members, throwing them down the deck and smashing them into the sides of the railings.

"When you're at sea long enough, you learn to listen to the ocean," Thane says. "My guess is the closer we get toward Roche Island, the worse the storm will get. Storms tend to use the wind and air currents from land to fuel themselves. Add in the fact that we're in the middle of Drake Passage, where the Atlantic mixes with the Pacific, and you've got a recipe for the world's roughest seas."

"You're talking like Abe now," I comment dryly. "From pirate to scientist."

I swear I hear him chuckle, though it could be the wind.

Might be the first time I've ever heard him laugh—not that I'm one to talk. That's probably why Thane and I find ourselves together often. We're both tall and stronger than most of the crew, which makes us handy on a ship like this, but I like that he doesn't ever feel the need to crack a smile, makes me feel like I can be as damn broody as I want to be. Sometimes, Abe gets a little annoyed with my relentless melancholy.

Sometimes, I get annoyed with his relentless optimism.

In addition, Thane has gone through the same sort of pain I have. He lost his wife, Samantha, who was also a member of the crew, during a battle with a Kraken a few years ago. He may not have murdered his own wife, but I still feel as if I can relate. I may not remember those decades clearly after her death, just as I can't even remember her name, but I can see on Thane's face that he is still grieving deeply.

And so am I.

Because there is new grief in my life that has made itself present every single day for the past five years.

And now, that sorrow I hastily tucked away inside is threatening to overwhelm me again. Everything hangs in the balance. This storm that bashes the *Nightwind*, battering the sides of the ship and throwing everyone around, is no match for the storm inside my heart, the one oscillates from the brightest hope to the darkest despair, no safe harbor in between.

Once we get through this storm, we'll either find Larimar or we won't. She'll either be in Maren's grasp, or she'll be lost to her forever. Lost to me forever, even more so than she already was, in the grip of some mortal, savage men planning to do who knows what to her.

Beyond this thunder and lightning, which is starting to feel like a message from God himself, lies everything I've ever wanted and never deserved. I've tried so hard to be a decent man after I turned, though perhaps I didn't try hard enough. Either way, I am prepared to burn the oceans to get her back, even if that means losing her to the flames in the process.

"Aragon," Thane warns me. "You need to let go."

I stare at him for a moment, wondering how he just heard my thoughts.

Then, I realize he's talking about the rope.

I open my hands, and the rope snaps out of my grip, the sail billowing out just enough to catch the wind.

Thane grabs the loose end, ties it up, and then pats me on the back.

"You're learning," he says. "But you have yet to learn how to stop drowning inside your head."

I grunt at that. Hypocrite.

I change the subject from my torment. "So, if the *Nightwind* is magic and the wind is always filling the sails, how come the rest of the weather doesn't obey?"

Thane shrugs. "You'd have to ask the ship that."

"You don't truly believe the ship is a sentient being," I snark.

He wipes the rain off his face with the back of his hand. "Well, I suppose I might, since I know both a talking cat and a talking shark, not to mention the Kraken and sea witches. Being a Vampyre should let you believe in a lot of things."

I shake my head as we move on to the next mast to help Lothar and Cruz with those sails. "Not me. I believe what I see."

He snorts. "And yet you were a man of God. Tell me, do you see God anywhere?" He waves his arms around just as another clap of thunder sounds, the rain lashing the ship even harder.

"I see signs of him," I say, almost too quietly to be heard above the storm. "But perhaps not enough for me to be a priest. Just a casual observer of the Lord."

Thane grumbles at that. "I can't figure you out, Aragon."

"Well, if you do end up figuring me out, please let me know," I tell him.

Because I don't know myself either.

"Ahoy!" Drakos shouts up from the crow's nest, his voice carried by the wind. "I see something!"

Thane and I step back around the sails and look up to see what direction Drakos is pointing in.

"Starboard," Thane says. Then, he turns around and cups his hands over his mouth and yells at Ramsay. "Turn to starboard!"

The boat starts tilting to the right, smashing over the waves that arc over the deck, drenching us to the bone.

"Avast!" Thane yells to Drakos. "What do you see?"

Drakos just shakes his head, trying to see through the spyglass before wiping the lens with his soaked shirt and trying again. "I reckon I saw a shark's fin!"

Everyone runs over to starboard, searching the waves for any sign of a shark or Syren. The swells are deep, the sky the dark, dusky bruise of a stormy twilight. Foam sprays everywhere, and the black clouds above pulse with flashes of lightning. I can't imagine what the humans down below in the hold must feel like—it's hard not to be seasick up here as it is.

"There!" Abe yells from the bow, pointing wildly.

We follow the direction of his finger just as lightning illuminates the waves, shining off a shark's fin that barrels down a swell.

My heart jumps into my throat, and I'm gripping the sides of the railing so hard, I might just break it in half.

Then, a dark head breaks the surface, an arm shooting out to wave at us.

"There she is!" Ramsay yells. "Hold on, luv, we're coming!"

"What about Larimar?" I cry out hoarsely, emotions betraying my voice.

Thane gives me a curious look for a moment before turning his attention back to the ocean.

Still, I only see Maren and the shark before Maren dives again, heading for the ship.

"Lifelines overboard!" Thane yells as everyone scrambles to let the ropes down. They enter the seas with a splash, though the waves eagerly throw them back against the sides of the ship with a thud.

But as much as my eyes scan the waves, searching for any sign of Larimar's blonde head, I can't make out much of anything. The lightning reflecting on the water likes to play tricks on you. I keep thinking I see her everywhere, but she never materializes.

Dread claws up my chest, making it hard to breathe.

What will Maren say?

That she couldn't find Larimar?

Couldn't rescue her?

That Larimar wouldn't follow?

That she already died?

That Nill was wrong?

I can't bear to not know. The seconds it takes for Maren to appear again are pure agony.

And then, Maren does, her face breaking through the surface and grabbing for the rope.

"Pull us up!" she yells.

"Us?" I can't help but shout, hope at the brink.

The men start pulling the ropes back, hauling Maren out of the water. Her red dress is little more than a few strands of clothing wrapped around her chest and torso, barely covering her bottom as her tail starts to transform into legs before my eyes, legs that wrap around the rope.

My gaze then goes to the waves below, to the shark fin

swimming beside the ship. It disappears, tail smacking the water as if Nill is diving down. I'm holding my breath, saying as many internal prayers as my soul can muster, not expecting an answer this time but asking for one just the same.

Then, I see a hand reach out from the surf.

Grab the rope.

And then, the rest of Larimar appears.

I feel I might have a heart attack on the spot.

She looks as beautiful as I remember but much thinner, and not agreeably so—dark half-moons sit under her eyes, gaunt hollows on her face. Her breasts are smaller too. My gut churns, wondering what happened to her.

Was it me?

Was this all because of me?

Then, she looks up and meets my eyes.

Looks directly at me.

And she doesn't look surprised to see me at all.

Her gaze is blank, but there's a fluttering in her jaw, as if she's grinding her teeth together.

I realize that, for all the scenarios I imagined, I didn't account for this one.

The one in which Larimar is alive.

The one in which she hates me.

Because how could she not?

She might have stayed my obsession.

But I was her desecrater.

She was my angel.

And I was nothing more than the Devil.

She gave me life.

And I left her to bleed.

All of that I see in just one look.

And then it's gone as she's hauled up the rest of the way and brought on deck with Maren, her focus everywhere else but me.

Ramsay is already at Maren's side, and everyone else has crowded around, tending to the two Syrens. It takes all my strength to stay back, to not rush over to Larimar, though I don't know what I'd do or what I'd say.

You don't seem that elated. Abe's voice slides into my head as he walks over to me.

Turns out, it's complicated, I mutter.

Remember to breathe, he says. *You're tugging at your ear.*

So I am.

I bring my hand down to my side, but my fingers dig into my palms instead as I make a fist.

What is the likelihood that your beast will make an appearance tonight? he says to me.

It won't.

You didn't really think this through, did you? he goes on, pointing out the obvious.

I glare at him. *Is this supposed to be helping me?*

The doctor gives me a kind smile. *I just want you to think things through now, while you can. Before you have a reaction.*

I already am *having a reaction.*

No, he says. *A reaction that could change our relationship with everyone on this ship. A reaction that could get us ostracized. A reaction that could put everyone's lives at risk. A reaction in which you end up breaking your own heart again.*

I want to snap at my friend, to tell him he knows nothing about heartbreak, but I don't.

Because he's right.

The last few weeks on the *Nightwind* have been some of the most enjoyable I've had in a long time, and I'm sure Abe has felt similar. Even with the hunt for Larimar in the back of my head, I was able to set it aside from time to time to focus on the journey, on the crew, on the camaraderie of being amongst like-minded creatures. The day-to-day tasks in keeping the *Nightwind* in tip-top shape have done wonders for my soul, more than preaching the gospel every Sunday ever did. As a priest, I was always struggling with my relationship with God, but here, I realized my relationship with men and Vampyres was the real challenge. It's one thing to think God has forsaken you because of the monster you became, but it's another when you think humanity has.

In the end, I was tired of being alone, of *feeling* alone. I think everyone gets that way eventually. The need for connection, no matter how hard we try to deny it, is more important than our need for salvation.

It's why the church and religion are so important to so many.

Why Larimar was so important to me.

She came into my life just as Abe left, showed me there was more than one way to truly connect with someone.

And now, she's here, and I have to be ready for her resentment and her rage.

I have to figure out how to put my own aside at the fact that she left me and broke her promise.

I have to find a way to control my temper and my own feelings before I destroy this second chance with her.

God, help me do it.

Or the Devil will step in.

I touch the rosary beads around my wrist and try to count back from ten.

The crowd parts, and Maren stumbles forward, holding on to Ramsay for support as the ship slams into another wave. She looks exhausted but triumphant, and when she spots me, she has a keen gleam in her eye.

"Aragon," Maren says to me before she steps out of the way, showcasing Larimar as Thane carries her. The volcanic fury inside me flares, wanting to erupt. She belongs in my arms, no one else's.

Easy, Abe says, just in time for me to hold myself back. *Easy, now.*

"This is my sister, Larimar," Maren says, eyeing me closely. "I request that you do your magic on her."

"My magic?" I repeat.

I can't keep staring at Larimar. She absolutely devastates me. Right here, as I stand, I see her, and I might as well be on my knees.

And she won't look at me.

That one glance as she was hauled up the side of the boat was all I got.

Instead, she rests her head on Thane's shoulder, staring at nothing.

Your reaction will determine our fate, Abe reminds me quickly.

"Yes, your magic," Maren goes on. "I know your powers are strong, Aragon, strong enough to turn a Syren's tail into legs."

By now, the crew has gathered around us, eyeing me with this new information, whispering to each other.

I turn my fury to Abe, my eyes burning into him.

"It wasn't me," Abe says out loud with a display of his hands. "I didn't tell her."

"He didn't," Maren explains. "Sometimes, our seeing stone tells us a lot about what happens in the future...and in the past. It's always nice if we can clarify what we see when we can."

"And your stone told you I worked my magic on the Syren I caught?" I ask carefully.

She nods. "There's a reason you were brought on board, Aragon. I knew you were a witch and a monster. I knew you had powers stronger than any of this crew could ever conjure. When the crystal let me glimpse what happened at Nombre de

Jesus, I knew we had to have you. Abe's correspondence with us was the sign we needed."

I swallow hard, running my fingers over my rosary beads, not caring if the action seems anxious to some. I am anxious. I am wild.

"I won't do it," I say.

Everyone gasps, and Maren looks like I slapped her.

Then, Larimar raises her head and looks at me.

She really looks at me.

Her gaze no longer holds a blank stare; instead, those beautiful violet eyes brim with pain and anger and shame.

"It's best you throw her right back in the ocean," I say, switching to Spanish so she can understand me, the words like razors in my throat. "Seems that's where she belongs, not in the world of men and monsters."

Not in the world of men and monsters like me.

"Priest," Larimar says reproachfully, hurt simmering in her voice.

She might have been told I was a priest, but it's the way she says it, with so much weight behind it, that makes Maren frown.

"Wait but a moment," Maren says, looking between the two of us. "Do you two know each other?"

"Seems your stone doesn't tell you everything," I say.

Chapter Thirty

LARIMAR

I could kill him.

If the man holding me would bring me just a little bit closer, I would launch myself at Priest with the last bit of energy I have, my claws extended and aimed right for his heart. But if I reached into his chest, I'd probably find the space between his ribs empty.

The man has no heart.

The man is a monster.

He never loved me. Of course he didn't. He never said he did.

He never had a heart to give.

There were many times during the swim with Maren and Nill that I thought about telling her, disclosing that I know this former Father Aragon and exactly how *well* I knew him.

But I couldn't bring myself to do it.

Because part of me was ashamed. That I was captured by a rabid Vampyre turned priest, and I fell in love with him. That he kept me prisoner and had his way with my body over and over again, and I loved every minute of it.

Even when Maren filled me in on her life after leaving

Limonos, all the horrors she went through with Prince Aerik, how her husband, Ramsay, the captain of the *Nightwind*, captured her and tortured her in a similar way, even though it seemed she would completely understand, I just couldn't tell her the truth.

Part of me hoped she was wrong about the name, that perhaps she had some other magic Vampyre priest pirate on board.

Part of me hoped she was right.

I thought I used the last of my strength to grab the rope as the crew hauled me aboard, aided by Nill's help, but it turns out the last of my strength converted into rage when I laid eyes on Priest.

My Priest.

My Aragon.

He hasn't changed a bit. The years have been so cruel to me; I've lost all my precious fat, my hair has thinned, and I know the shine in my eyes is gone. But he, he looks as dangerous as ever, just as handsome, just as wild. His long black hair, his beard, the piercing glacial blue of his eyes...even his clothes look the same, white shirt, black pants, though he now has a holster around his waist and a short sword.

And the rosary.

The rosary I left in the cottage.

It's now around his wrist.

He's here and he's human and he's whole.

Why did the monster have to come for me? Why did he have to change?

Larimar, Maren says to me sharply, bringing my attention back to the matter at hand. *Do you know this man?*

I swallow thickly and answer out loud, in Spanish, so *he* understands. "He is no man. He is a monster."

"You speak Spanish?" Maren asks me, even more incredulously.

"She does," Priest says, his voice low and measured, though I can see the anxious way he's touching his wrist, the sparks in his eyes. "So, until she learns English, I suggest we all speak her language. I assume most people on this ship speak Spanish as well?"

The men around us murmur. Must be nice to be immortal and have all the time in the world to learn as many languages as you want.

But what language we speak is the least of my concerns.

"What did you say to my sister before?" I say to Priest, goading him. "You said it in English."

"I asked him to give you legs," she says. "He refused," she adds bitterly.

I raise my chin. "Is that so? On what grounds?"

He doesn't answer, his jaw clenching.

A tall, lithe man with shaggy red hair steps forward from beside him and looks at the rest of the crew. "Perhaps it is for the best if we give Aragon and Larimar some time alone."

"I'm not going to be alone with him," I practically spit. "I have nothing to say to him."

"So sorry, but how is it that you know each other?" the man with his hair pulled back says, scratching at his facial hair. From the way he hovers protectively behind Maren, I'm going to assume this is her Vampyre husband.

"Why don't you tell them, Priest?" I sneer. "Why don't you tell them what you did?"

"They know what I did," he says quietly. "They just didn't know it was you."

"So they all knew you pulled me out of the ocean? That you kidnapped me, held me captive in the back room of your church where you would torture me and drain me of my precious blood?"

"Sounds familiar," the man remarks gruffly.

I turn my head to look at him. "Who are you?"

"Thane," he says. "Your brother-in-law. Pleasure to make your acquaintance, my lady."

I scowl at him. He's no different than any of these men. From the way they all stare at me, with that hunger in their eyes, these Vampyres are dying for a taste of me, just as Priest was.

I look back to Maren. "Did he then tell you that he lowered my defenses? Made me believe he cared about me?" I trail off, looking away, hating that I have an audience for this, that they have to see my shame. "Or perhaps he didn't even try. I fell for him anyway, soul, heart...*body*."

"Larimar," Priest says, his voice hoarse.

I ignore him, adjusting myself in Thane's grip. "And then one day, one day I thought I was his equal, and he let his monster come out. He tried to kill me. I only escaped by pure luck. I hit the ocean, and thanks to the way he bound his spell, the magic reversed, and I turned back into a Syren. I swam away while his church burned."

Maren rubs her lips together, thinking it over as she looks at Priest. "The stone wouldn't let me see who the Syren was. Had I known it was Larimar..."

"What?" Priest asks. "Would you have still brought me on board? Still let me join your crew?"

"Yes," she says, her eyes watering. "Yes, because I would have done anything to bring my sister back into my life. I need your magic, Aragon. I need you to let her have a proper life with me."

Priest's intense gaze slides over to mine. "And you, Larimar? Is this what you want? Or are these your sister's wishes?"

Everyone is looking at me, waiting for an answer.

But I'm afraid to speak the truth.

I'm afraid if I do, it won't happen.

Because this monster still has so much power over me, and I hate him for it.

I hate him for so much.

But mostly, I hate him because I loved him.

"Yes," I finally say, trying to sound strong and commanding, the opposite of how I feel. "I want you to give me legs again so I may join my sister on land, and I want to be able to turn into a Syren when I'm back in the ocean. Most of all, I want you to disappear afterwards. As soon as this storm clears, I want you on one of those small boats over there, and I want you set adrift."

"We can at least wait until we get to our next port," Ramsay suggests.

I shake my head. "No. I don't know how long that will be, and I don't want to be stuck on this ship any longer than I have to with that creature over there."

If Priest is hurt by my words, he doesn't show it.

Now, every head swivels toward him, waiting for his reaction.

He stares at me, and I can almost feel him probing into my mind, searching deep into the recesses of my heart and soul. What is he looking to find? I just told him—and everyone else —everything there is.

Then, he exhales deeply, his features softening a little. "I will give you what you desire," he says slowly, "but it comes with a catch."

"Of course it does," Maren mutters.

He keeps his focus on me. "I will do all that if you'll talk to me alone."

"And how can we trust you won't do anything to harm her?" Maren asks.

"You can't," he tells her. "But your trust isn't what I'm after. It's hers. And this decision isn't yours to make."

He's right. The decision is mine, and it weighs more than anything.

"You don't have to fear me, Larimar," he says, his gaze

steady. "Though you have every reason to. I will even be restrained in chains if that makes you feel better."

Frankly, that does make me feel better.

"You'll be restrained? Chained up?"

He nods gravely.

Oh, how the tables have turned. I almost smile at the idea of him being locked up for a change, with me being the one in control.

"And you'll grant me my wish first?" I certainly don't feel powerful as a Syren out of water, having to be carried everywhere.

"It might take a few days," he says. He looks at Ramsay. "Unless you have some provisions that might help speed this spell along? I work with physical matter; I can't conjure a spell from thin air."

Ramsay nods. "I can try and get you what you need. We have tonics, dried herbs, fresh ones that Sedge grows. Elixirs. You name it."

"A few days?" Maren says, brow heavy with disappointment. "What is she supposed to do before then? She's too malnourished to keep up swimming with the ship—in a storm, mind you—even with Nill's support keeping her afloat."

A pause stretches out between us.

"Do you have a bathtub?" I ask.

"The sun came out," Maren says as she steps inside, closing the door behind her. "The storm has come to an end."

"I could tell," I remark. "Most of the water has been staying inside the tub."

I've been in the copper bathtub in Ramsay and Maren's private lavatory for the last few days while Priest does what he needs to do to conduct his spell. The ship has been rolling and rocking with the storm, which in turn has made my bathwater slosh wildly, until I woke this morning to utter calm.

But though the end of the storm means smooth sailing for the ship, there's nothing calm about how any of us are feeling. Maren's voice may be bright, but there's an edge to her gaze, and I know from the way she gnaws at her lip that she's been just as anxious as I have about what's supposed to transpire.

"Have you talked to him today?" I ask her, meaning Priest.

She shakes her head. "No. He's been busy in his quarters." She pauses as she crouches beside the tub, putting her hand over mine as I rest it on the edge. "Is this really what you want, sister? Or am I forcing your hand?"

I give her a faint smile. "You know it's difficult to force me to do anything. This is what I want. Part of me feels like a traitor to all Syrens for doing this, but I'm not about to lose you again. I looked for you all those years so I could talk to you again, just like this. I made Priest give me legs in the hopes I would escape and then find you on land. I want to join you, you and this crew."

She grins. "The *Nightwind* would love to have you, but you shouldn't feel like a traitor. Just because you were born a certain way doesn't mean you have to love it. It doesn't mean you have to stay that way if you have the choice to change. The sea is filled with plenty of Syrens who would never do what we did, not in a million years."

"You said Syrens are a dying breed," I point out, and I can confirm that to be true from what I've seen.

She nods solemnly. "We are, but that doesn't change what we want, does it? I am choosing my own happiness. You need to choose yours. Besides, if Priest's magic works as before, you'll have the best of both worlds."

I make a noise of agreement, adjusting myself in the tub.

"Can I ask you something?" she asks after a moment.

Somehow, from her tone, I can tell it's going to be about Priest. "You may," I say warily.

"Did you really love him?"

I sigh and look away from her searching eyes. "I don't know."

"You do know, though. I can see it in you. I know what that looks like."

My head whips back around as I glare at her. "Well, I don't *still* love him," I say testily. "That's absurd. After what he did?"

"Love is a strange creature," she says. "It doesn't follow logic or reason. It just exists, and we can either make friends with it or become its enemy, but it doesn't stop what it is."

I clamp my mouth together, not about to say anything in retort, just as a knock sounds at the door.

"Come in," Maren calls.

"It's me," Ramsay says from the other side. "I have Aragon with me. He's ready to do the spell."

My pulse skips, and I sit up straight in the tub, adjusting my hair over my breasts in a strange display of modesty.

Maren looks to me for consent before she gets up and opens the door.

They join us, Priest wearing all black, a jar in one hand. Like in the church, it's filled with various items suspended in water.

He meets my eyes and gives me a faint nod.

I nod back, suddenly terrified. The sight of him scares my fragile heart, while the idea of the spell fills me with dread. What if it all goes wrong?

"I want them here for this," I quickly say.

"Of course," Priest says. "If only I can have you alone afterward."

A thrill runs through me, though it shouldn't, and I do my best to hide it. I exhale harshly through my nose. "Yes. That was part of the deal."

"Should she get out of the tub?" Maren asks. "Ramsay could hold her up."

"That won't be necessary," he says. "It's probably best for her to stay where she is."

He comes closer, his tall, large frame looming over me, his presence seeming to take up all the air and all the space in the room until all I can focus on is him.

The predator and the prey.

For a moment, I let the fear go, the bad kind of fear, and let the good kind in. I imagine that we're alone in the room together, that I'm naked in this tub before him and helpless at his feet. I ignore where my mind wants to go, how it keeps wanting to remember him as a flying beast who made me hurt, and instead, I think of the man who made me bleed. The one who drank from me, couldn't get his fill, who made pain and anticipation as sweet as a kiss.

"This might hurt," he says to me in a gruff voice as he reaches into the water.

Before I realize what he's doing, he plucks a scale off my tail.

"Ow!" I cry out, jerking out of his grasp.

The corner of his mouth lifts ever so slightly. Oh, he enjoyed causing that pain. Some things don't change.

"Bastard," I swear.

He raises a brow, and I know that look. He always gets it when I curse. I think it gets his blood running hot.

"Anything else you need?" Maren asks. "Fingernails and eyelashes, perhaps?"

Priest gives her a tepid glance. "Just some of her blood." He looks back to me. "Now, I can feed on you, or I draw blood some other way. It's up to you."

"I'm not letting your filthy mouth anywhere near me," I snarl at him, throwing out my arm. "Cut me with a knife if you have to."

He frowns and grumbles something to himself before he draws his sword from his sheath. Holding the open jar underneath my arm, he makes a deft cut with the sword's tip, right across my inner forearm. I suck in my breath and watch as a bit of blood trickles into the glass, certainly not at all like the first time he did it.

Then, he takes the glass and swirls the blood with the other contents before putting it under my lips. "You know what to do. You must drink it all."

I make a face. "It's vile."

"As am I," he says grimly. "And magic takes on its maker. Drink."

"Aren't you going to ask me what I'll give you in return?"

"Well, last time, you promised me your body and soul forever," he says, clearing his throat. "And look how that turned out."

"And you promised you would hunt me down, that the magic would ensure you'd find me, no matter how long it took."

He nods. "As it did."

"You also said I wouldn't want you to find me," I add.

"Are you arguing with that, little fish?" he asks idly.

I ignore the pang in my heart at the sound of my nickname and give my head a shake. "No."

But I'm lying.

And he knows it too.

"Then drink," he says.

I take the jar from his hands this time, try not to breathe out of my nose, then drink the contents back.

"*Caudam capio et tibi pedes dabo*," he begins to chant

while I focus on not vomiting. "*Vocem capio et servitutem tibi trado.*"

Somehow, I manage to swallow the disgusting liquid down while Priest continues chanting, and I'm just about to ask if that's all there is to it or if he's going to bite me like last time when he reaches forward, palming the side of my head and exposing my neck.

"Aragon, no!" Maren yells at him, like he's being reprimanded.

But Priest doesn't listen, and I have enough time to grip the sides of the tub, the empty jar falling into the water as I brace myself for his bite. It's as strong as I remember, his fangs sinking deep as he pulls back my blood into my mouth like he's ravenous.

I gasp from the pain, but pleasure soon takes over, and I find myself sinking into the tub, slipping into oblivion in a rushing stream of red.

"My Gods," I hear Ramsay whisper.

Then, I start to feel it.

Beyond Priest's feeding is another sensation, this one deep inside and strangely familiar. The feeling of bones being broken apart from the inside.

Suddenly, I'm screaming as the pain tears through my body, and Priest stops drinking from me. I glimpse at him standing back beside Ramsay and Maren, his mouth bloody, watching in awe as I begin to transform.

I pinch my eyes shut, my body writhing, water sloshing over the side of the tub, the world twisting and spinning in hot waves, like I'm being born again, bursting from the broken shell of my ribs.

I am not me anymore.

I am someone else.

I am everything else.

I am *magic.*

"You did it," Ramsay whispers. "Aragon, you did it."

"Larimar?" I hear Maren cry out, her hand at my cheek. "Are you alright?"

I lift my head and open my eyes to see my old body again.

Naked and in a bloody bathtub.

Two thighs, two calves, two feet, ten toes.

And the pink, hairless space between my legs that Priest knows so well.

I don't even bother covering up.

Let him look.

"It worked," I say, meeting his eyes. He's fighting to meet my gaze, though I have to say, Ramsay isn't doing a very good job of it either. When he catches me noticing, he quickly averts his eyes.

"I'll go get you some clothes," he says quietly before he leaves the room.

"Do you need anything?" Maren asks, grasping my hand. "Are you in pain?"

I shake my head. "I'm sore, but I'm not in any pain. But I do have a request for Priest."

He swallows hard. "What?" he asks thickly.

"You wanted a chance to talk with me alone? Then I get to choose when. And I want you locked up until then."

Chapter Thirty-One

LARIMAR

It's an eerily calm night and the moon is full, reflecting off the water so the whole ocean seems to glow. Every now and then, Nill's fin will break the surface, reminding us he's there.

Sometimes, I jump right into the ocean to test if the spell works. Each time, my legs turn back into a tail with only some discomfort, and I swim alongside Nill. Sometimes, Maren joins me, and we swim like we used to when we were children and didn't know any better, riding the waves at the bow of the ship, pretending the humans couldn't hurt us.

But tonight, the ocean isn't as inviting.

I've ignored Priest for too long.

According to him, I've already broken one bargain, and now, I'm breaking another.

He gave me legs on the condition that I would talk to him alone, and he's been in the jail cell for days, waiting for me to finally gather the courage to hear what he has to say. Though perhaps it's not courage I'm waiting for. Perhaps I'm waiting for armor to form around my heart.

But that will never happen. I'll never be able to protect

myself from him, even if he's chained up. I'll never not hurt at whatever he has to say. Our interactions always revolved around pain—why should that be any different now?

The sea might be calm, but inside, I am not. I never will be until I face him, face what we once had—or what I believed we had.

I glance back at the helm to where Thane stands with a man called Matisse. They nod at me but say nothing more. Everyone on this ship has been giving me great distance. I thought they would be leering at me, like the way those men on the other ship did. At the very least, I thought they would smell my blood and act like Vampyres, but either they all have manners, or Maren has scared them off, because they treat me like a lady, with respect, if not a little caution.

Truthfully, I feel like anything but a lady. I'm wearing Maren's fine gowns, but I feel like an impostor, like I'm only pretending to be human when inside, I'm a nervous, delusional wreck. I walk on two legs now, but they might as well be a tail.

I go to my chambers, strip out of the layers of clothing, and don my shift. I get into my bed, all the while trying not to think about him.

But I can *only* think about him.

In chains, waiting for me.

The imagery makes me throb.

I reach between my legs, touching myself, letting myself explore my new body for the first time again.

But I can't stop picturing Priest.

The way he touched me, like his hands did the worshipping and every prayer was on his tongue. He used my body as if it would lead him to heaven, and I used his as if he was leading me to hell. Sometimes, in the throes of our passion, we went to both places, both heathens and saints, lost and loving every minute of it.

I nearly bring myself to an orgasm, but I stop before I reach that peak.

I can pretend all I want that I don't still want him, but I'm tired of lying to myself.

I leave my chambers, padding barefoot down the stairs and down another until I'm where Priest is being held. It's quiet here, only the occasional creak of the wood and laughter far away in the crew's shared quarters, one last drink before they go to sleep.

I pause outside the door to the jail. I know he can hear me, smell me, knows I'm here. I'm giving him time to prepare his speech, the tiniest courtesy I can afford.

I hear the chains rattling.

My fingers curl around the handle, briefly turning into claws as I test myself, then back to normal as I open the door.

The jail cell is completely dark, and it takes a moment for my eyes to adjust.

I hear Priest's sharp inhale as he breathes me in.

I sniff the air myself. I was prepared for the cell to smell badly, but Vampyres themselves are extraordinarily clean, I've found.

I do smell him, though.

The scent of herbs and ocean and salt and pine and everything that makes my chest feel tight spin me back in time to Nombre de Jesus.

"Larimar," he whispers, rough, reverent. My skin washes with heat while an imaginary finger coasts down my spine.

I close the door behind me, casting everything in dark shadow. My eyesight is still as good as a Syren's, though I am unsure if it's as good as a Vampyre's.

"There is a lantern by the door," he says.

I fumble for it and find the matches, lighting it.

He comes into view, and I try not to gasp.

He's completely naked. Shackles around his wrists attach

to the ceiling with chains, shackles around his ankles are soldered to the wall. The chains are long enough for him to move about a little but not enough to explore the whole room. There's a bucket tucked away in the furthest corner that he can reach—I don't have to wonder what that is. There's another larger one filled with water with several bars of soap and washcloths piled next to it. Then, by the wall, sits an empty jar with red residue, which I assume is blood.

"Why are you naked?" I ask.

"Why not?" he replies. "Clothes are a hindrance if you can't wash them. Our sense of smell means we have to bathe frequently and often. No different than if you're here as a prisoner."

"You're not a prisoner," I tell him.

"I sure look like one."

He does. A very naked prisoner. My eyes coast up and down his body, relishing in the sight of him, not knowing if I'll see it again. It's his body that makes me think that if God or some kind of deity exists, he certainly favors some of his subjects. Priest would have been his prized creation from the very beginning, starting with his perfect face—the straight, noble nose above full lips and square jaw, the intense blue of his haunted eyes, his arched dark brows and long, shiny black hair that hangs to his collarbones. Then there's his body, the wide expanse of his shoulders, the rounded muscle that showcases all his power, the strong, ropey lines down his arms. His chest is firm and thick, with just a dusting of dark hair that peppers the line between his rigid abdomen to his flat stomach. His hips curve sharply down to muscular legs, and I know from experience that his rear is just as sculpted and taut. His sun-browned skin practically glows in the lantern light. If I am silver, then he is gold.

I know I shouldn't stare at him like this—I came here to hear what he had to say, not to ogle him.

But my cunt still pulses with need, my arousal picking up where I left off, and I have to admit, it feels good to be on the receiving end of this for once.

"You like what you see," he comments, his voice thicker now, throaty. He can smell my lust, and I can hear it in him, see it in him, even. His cock is no longer hanging heavily between his thighs—now, it's darkened with blood and standing at full attention, twitching with the movement of his breath, which is getting more labored by the minute. There's already arousal gathered on his tip, glistening in the flickering light.

"I do like what I see," I say, slowly walking over to him until I'm just out of reach. "I like being on this side of the game."

"Game?" he says, frowning. "None of this is a game, Larimar."

"You treated it like a game," I tell him, willing myself not to stare at his cock for a second longer. I keep focused on his eyes, although they are just as hypnotic. "You let me loose to see if I would run, and when I did, you tried to hunt me down."

"That wasn't me," he growls, moving for me, but the shackles pull on his wrists, keeping him in place.

"You say that," I say. "And I know. I saw the monster with my own eyes. But how do I know you didn't invite him in? How do I know you didn't enjoy the transformation?"

"Because the monster is a killer, and I am not!"

I stare at him for a moment. "Is that what happened to your family? You killed them?"

He swallows hard and gives a solemn nod, his eyes burning with shame, enough that it loosens a thread around my fractured heart. "I did. I killed them. I don't remember it all, but... I did."

I feel the weight of his confession, the air thickening with his regret. I suspected that's what happened to his wife and children, since he wouldn't talk about it, but it's still a lot to hear.

And yet, I'm not looking at him any differently. I don't think he's more of a monster. I just know now what drove him to this constant struggle for salvation, what has driven him to make up for the man he lost.

"But you are a killer," I say quietly. "It's your nature. You have to kill others to survive. We all do."

"You and I do," he says, straining against the chains. "The rest of the world seems to do just fine."

"Do they?" I ask, raising my brow. "We're the monsters but the humans aren't? You know that's not true. You heard what happened to me on that ship, what happened to my friend. Do you think they aren't part beast as well?"

He doesn't say anything to that. Finally, he sighs. "I killed my family. I've killed countless others since, hundreds. I suppose it doesn't really matter why I did it in the end."

"Were you going to kill me?" I ask, my voice dropping to a whisper, my heart high in my chest.

He stares at me, searching my face before he blinks. "I don't know."

"Oh," I say, looking down. I had really wanted to hear a definite no.

"But I didn't want to," he says. "And I wasn't in control. You have to believe me. If I was...I never would have hurt you." His gaze drops to my legs.

I turn around, looking at the backs of my calves. The reminder is there; the scarring where he sliced off my skin transferred to my Syren's tail and back to my human body, leaving ugly marks behind.

A reminder I'll always have.

"Larimar," he says.

I look back at him.

A muscle ticks at his jaw as he blinks at me, like he's trying not to say something. Emotions swirl in his eyes, tugging another thread loose.

"I'm sorry," he says in a low, rough voice. "I'm sorry for what I did, for all of it. From the moment I found you in the ocean, I'm sorry I ever subjected you to a heathen like myself, a sinner masquerading as a saint, a killer in sheep's clothing. I am a monster, little fish, in every meaning of the word, and I never should have brought you into my world. I should have been a safe harbor, but instead, I brought you the storm. My church was a sanctuary to everyone but you."

I want to tell him that it was only a nightmare at the end, that even when he tortured me, I found some perverse pleasure in it, a sick thrill at his possession, at how he desired and coveted me, so much so that he had to keep me by any means necessary. Perhaps a human wouldn't find such solace in his wanton and deranged desires, but my monster side only wanted more.

But I don't tell him that. No, I want him to suffer. I want him to grovel. I want him to know that even though I loved being his prisoner, loved being the object of his every thought and affection from sunup to sundown and all the dark hours in-between, he scarred me, both body and soul.

"I gave you my heart," I tell him, walking over to the bucket of water. "I fell in love with you, Priest. Fast and all at once, I was in love. And that night, I wanted to tell you. I woke up in the night to tell you. Ran into that church to tell you. Then I saw what my love turned you in to."

He shakes his head, his eyes welling with tears. Damnit, he shouldn't be breaking me all over again. "I am sorry," he whispers hoarsely. "Please. I didn't know."

"Would it have made a difference?" I ask, picking up a bar of oily soap that smells of lemons. "If I told you I loved you, would the monster have stayed away? Or would I have made it hungrier?"

He stares at me, a tear spilling over. I know what he's going to say: he doesn't know.

"It doesn't matter," I say, sighing heavily, though no matter how hard I exhale, I can't shake the weight of this, the weight of *us*. "What's done is done. I loved you. You tried to kill me. Story of our lives, is it not?"

"No," he says, shaking his head. "One chapter of our lives. The story isn't over. The story doesn't even need to have an end."

"Not for you," I tell him. "You'll be alive until the end of time. My story will end eventually, and our story will be done."

"Please," he whispers, trying to move against the chains, but they rattle as they hold him back.

"Please what?" I ask, hating how good it sounds to hear *him* beg for a change.

"Please...just *please*. Please don't go. Please don't give up on me. Please just..."

"Just what?"

His gaze is a loaded pistol. "Give me your heart again and I promise not to break it."

I nearly laugh. "Give you my heart? Priest, I don't love you. I might even hate you." I'm spitting out the words now, trying to hurt him.

"I can handle your hate," he says after a moment, adjusting his stance. It's enough for my gaze to drop down to his cock again. Of course; I think hate only arouses him further. "I might even crave your hate sometimes."

"And you still want my heart?"

"I want every part of you," he admits. "I *need* every part of you. You're mine, Larimar. No matter what you say or think or do, whether you cast me off in a boat, never to see me again, or if you put your heart behind a locked box for safekeeping. You're still mine. You'll always be mine. You have no say in the matter."

This sounds more like the Priest I knew, and I hate how much I love to hear it.

Hate how much my body answers his call.

"You treat me like I'm your possession," I say, putting the soap in the clean, cold water and crouching down to submerge a washcloth. "Like I'm something you own. Something you keep. Something you control." I straighten up, wringing the excess water from the cloth. "Yet, here you are, the one in chains. Seems like I'm the one keeping you at the moment."

"I guess our roles have reversed," he says darkly, desire blazing in his eyes.

I take a chance and step to the side of him, as far away from his hungry cock as possible. The heat of his body nearly overwhelms me, and I raise the washcloth. "You bathed me so many times," I tell him. "It's only fair I get to do the same."

A low noise rattles in his chest as I bring the wet cloth down over his chest, slowly running it down to his hips. He starts to jerk at the chains, but he doesn't try to move away from me.

"But when I bathed you, it wasn't torture," he says through a groan as I bring the cloth down over his thighs, down the taut muscles of his calves.

"How do you know?" I ask, straightening up to bring it down over his back.

His head arches back. "You enjoyed it?"

"Of course I did," I admit. "I would never tell you that, though. You'd probably have stopped if you found out I liked it."

"I would have made you come is what would have happened," he says.

I smirk at that, wetting the cloth again and doing the rest

of his back, enjoying the feel of his lean muscles beneath my hand. "Such a contradiction. No problems in sticking nails through my wrists, as if I was your personal Jesus, but you didn't dare give me pleasure without my permission."

"I'm sorry I happen to have *some* morals," he rasps, his back arching, his firm rear pushing against my hands.

I bite my lip, resisting the urge to bite his cheeks instead.

"Or was it just about humiliation?" I ask. "Was that your goal?"

"You don't wear humility well," he says.

"Do you? Can I humiliate you instead? Or will that only excite you?"

"Everything you do excites me," he says gruffly.

I wet the cloth again and come around the front, touching everywhere except his cock, which is practically begging for attention. "And if I don't let you come from that excitement, what then?" I tease.

He growls, practically snarling at me. He's so painfully aroused that it seems cruel to leave him like this.

So, I decide to torture him some more, in my own way.

I reach down and run the cloth over his cock from root to tip, feeling the heat in my hand, the heavy weight of it. He lets out a rough yelp, one choked with need.

"Just making sure you're clean enough for my mouth," I tell him.

He whimpers with frustration, and it makes me squeeze my legs together. I need to stay focused on denying him, not giving into my own needs.

I grab the oily soap, running it all over his body, leaving his cock and his rear for last. I wipe my palm over the fatty bar until my skin is slick, and then make a fist over his cock, give it two hard, firm shakes.

"God!" Priest cries out, bucking against my hand.

I quickly let go before he has a chance to come.

"Demon woman," he growls at me.

I can only grin, relishing in the power rolling through me. I love submitting to this man, but it does feel good to have him submit to me for once.

Then, I rub the washcloth over it and bend down. Without touching his cock, I run the tip of my tongue over the rigid underside before dipping into the slit at his tip, tasting the salt of the ocean.

Priest is swearing again, a string of curses that would make any pirate blush, and his whole body is strained, muscles bulging, veins standing out from his flushed skin.

"Had enough?" I say.

"Yes," he groans.

"Beg for me."

But he doesn't. Not for this.

"Very well."

I soak the cloth in the water and go around to his rear, wet between his cheeks with the cloth so that he's clean enough to eat from, though he already seemed sparkling clean before. Then I take the bar of soap and slide it up and down through the crack. His muscles tense, and he lets out a sharp hiss.

"Do you like that?"

"No," he says but somehow, I don't believe him.

"Are you telling me to stop?" I ask, concentrating the tip of the bar on his entrance, making it slick and slippery.

He swallows audibly, practically panting now. "No."

That's what I thought.

I rub my fingers along the bar and then slowly penetrate the ring of muscle.

"Oh God," he calls out, head going back. "Oh, fuck."

I smile to myself and start working my fingers inside, pumping them in and out like they're a cock. I watch as they disappear between the cheeks of his rear, watch as his muscles bunch, how he's standing on his toes, splayed and straining, his calves corded.

I don't think I'll ever be in such a position of power again.

I take it for all I've got.

I keep working him, and he's crying out, breathing hard, rough, inaudible sounds falling from his open mouth. I peer around him to see his cock bobbing with the movement, swollen and angry-looking, dying to be touched.

I know I'm torturing him now.

I won't let him come.

But then he surprises me.

He shouts out my name like a desperate prayer, and he comes anyway. He grunts as his cock jerks, and long ropes of his cum spurt out of the tip, arcing into the air and slashing across the wooden floor. I didn't think it was possible for a man to come without anything touching his cock, but Priest has always been full of surprises.

"Fuck," he groans, hanging his head, his entire body going limp in the chains. "What did you just do to me?"

I pick up the wet washcloth again and go back to cleaning him, his body jolting at my touch, still sensitive. "Believe you me, my intention was not to let you come."

"I know it was," he rasps. "There's a lot about me you don't know."

"Apparently," I comment, making sure all the soap is thoroughly washed away.

Then, I step back and stare into his eyes. I expect to see them heavy and sated, but instead, they are as wild as ever.

"Now that you've done the courtesy of defiling me," he says, "perhaps you'll let me out of these chains." He pauses. "So I can do the same to you."

Chapter Thirty-Two

PRIEST

Sugared lemons and salt water.

Larimar's scent still has the ability to undo me, even after all these years.

Though she definitely has other ways of undoing me as well.

I stare down at her, the intensity of my feelings rolling through me—love, hurt, lust. So much lust. My arms had been aching from being in chains for so long, but I don't feel any pain or discomfort anymore, not after what she just did to me.

She's staring up at me with fire in her eyes, though I can still see the pain there. She's furious at me, and I can't ever blame her for that. The last thing I expected was for her to do what she did. I know she didn't mean to make me come, that she was trying her own sinful brand of torture, but I didn't think she'd ever even touch me again.

But she did.

And that fire in her lavender eyes is also fueled by desire.

"What if I don't want you to defile me?" she says with a

raise of her chin. "What if I want to set you out in that boat so you can drift forever?"

"Then I shall give it to you," I tell her. "But is that what you really want?"

I'm taking a risk here. I'm prepared for her stubbornness to kick in, the hurt I caused her to be lodged too deep. The mere sight of the scars on her legs makes me feel ill; I can't imagine how they make her feel. She might really want me gone from her life forever, and I will have no choice but to obey.

I told her I would hunt her down and find her, that she was forever mine, that she belonged to me, body and soul. But even I have my limits. Even I have to find the courage to let her go if that's what she truly wants.

Frankly, it's what she deserves.

And I deserve to suffer for all my sins.

It doesn't mean she won't stop belonging to me, though. She always will.

"I want..." she begins and then trails off, looking away. Then she shakes her head and closes her eyes. "I don't know what I want, Priest," she says softly.

"You want to hate me," I say.

She swallows hard, nodding.

"Part of you does hate me," I add.

She stops nodding, pressing her lips together into a thin line.

"But part of you still loves me," I say. "I know you do. Otherwise, you wouldn't still be here."

Another risk. I didn't even know that Larimar was in love with me when all hell broke loose. I certainly don't know if she loves me still. But if there's a chance...

Her eyes open, her lashes wet. Seems we're both in the mood to make each other cry.

"Why would I give my heart to a man who never gave me his?" she says, her voice breaking.

I breathe in deeply. "It's not that I didn't want to," I tell her. "It's that I didn't have a chance. We both realized we loved each other at the worst possible time."

She swallows. "You love me?"

I want to tell her that of course I do. My love for her is intertwined with my obsession with her. She has a hold on me, lives in my veins.

But how is she supposed to know that? I've never given her any sign of how I feel, other than when I'm buried deep inside her, making her see stars. I've never told her how I've felt; I've only hurt her in every way possible.

I suppose hanging naked from chains is as good of a time as any.

"You've had your Syren claws hooked in my heart from the moment I first laid eyes on you," I tell her, hoping she can feel the gravity in my voice, the weight of my soul being laid bare. "I've never been able to escape. I don't want to escape. Even if you don't love me anymore, my heart will belong to you until my undying day."

I swallow down the lump in my throat. "I love you, Larimar. I worship you, I sin for you, and I would die for you, only you. So, if you want me gone from you forever, I can give you that. I will give you whatever you ask for. Ask, and you shall receive."

Her lower lip trembles, but she squares her shoulders, trying to hold herself together. Perhaps if these chains weren't holding me up, I would be on the floor.

"I want your heart," she says.

"You have my heart, little fish."

"I want your love."

"You have my love."

"I want..."

"You have every broken, wicked piece of me, Larimar, and you have my good pieces too. All the dark and all the light. You have all of them together, but it's only you who will make me whole."

She stares at me, her chin wobbling, and a single tear rolls down her cheek, which she quickly brushes away with her fingers.

"Now, will you undo me from these damned chains?" I growl.

She lets out a ragged laugh and looks around the room, spotting the key hanging from the wall. I exhale loudly, relief flooding through me as she walks over to me and reaches up with the key, releasing me from my shackle.

I pull my arm down, the blood rushing back into it, prickling like a thousand needles, but once she's released me from the other chain, I waste no time.

I grab her face, one hand at the back of her neck, ignoring the fact that I can't feel my fingers properly. "I love you," I whisper, my heart hammering in my chest.

Then, I kiss her.

Soft at first, while feeling comes back into my body, savoring the velvet of her lips, the taste of citrus on her tongue. A mouth I had dreamed about for so long, one I never thought I would kiss again.

Then, my grip at the back of her neck tightens, and as my body comes back to life, my hunger for her returns.

I kiss her deeply as the moment washes over me.

That she's here, now, with me, and that I'll never let her go.

My tongue dips deep, unyielding, starving, our mouths opening against each other as all the tension inside is unleashed. She whimpers, her hands trying to grab me where she can—my biceps, my chest, running her nails down my back.

There is urgency thrumming through my veins now, and I waste no time taking what I want.

I break away from our kiss, our mouths wet, our breathing heavy, our eyes wild as we stare at each other, overcome with lust, with love, with hate, and everything else in-between.

Then, I pick her up in my arms. My ankles are still shackled and chained, but I have enough room to turn around and push her up against the wall. I quickly shove the end of her shift up as she wraps her legs around me, and I position my cock at her cunt. I intended to tease her with it, to wait, but need burns through me like a forest fire, and I quickly spear my cock inside her until the air is pushed from her lungs. She's so wet and warm that my eyes roll back in my head.

She gasps, holding onto my shoulders, her fingers briefly turning into claws, sharp enough to pierce my skin. Of course, the pain only makes me more insatiable.

"Fuck," I groan as I start rutting into her. She's so tight, tighter than I remember, and I need this, I need this so much. I think I might die before I see this version of heaven again.

"Larimar," I whisper, my lips at her neck, biting lightly, biting hard, drawing blood. I drink and I fuck and I feel every-thing, everything. So many years, decades, centuries, so many prayers I thought would never be answered, all culminating in this moment, in the apex of not just desire, but love.

I love her.

She loves me.

And I need to come inside her like there's no tomorrow.

I grunt, picking up the pace, my hips slamming into her as I drive deeper and deeper, as if I'm trying to embed myself in her soul.

She's so wet too, her own cries so sinful, so raw, mixing with the slick sounds of our urgent coupling. The wooden planks behind her creak and groan, adding to the symphony.

I reach down, feeling the swollen knot of her clit, and she

lets out a ragged gasp as I start rubbing her in firm, quick circles.

"Such a good girl," I murmur, watching her face intently as her orgasm builds, seeing it in the pink flush on her fair cheeks, the dark swirl of her pupils, her shiny open mouth. I only break eye contact to stare down where my cock disappears inside of her, glistening with our desire. "Such a good girl with such a sweet cunt. Look at the way you take me, like you were made just for me."

Sometimes, I have to wonder if I did make her this way for me, so that we fit just right. Perhaps when I created the spell, I created the perfect woman, one who would be my final redemption.

But Larimar was perfect to begin with. Even if she stayed a Syren, I would have found God and all his devils inside her. I would have loved her with all of my dirty, wicked heart.

I would have found myself there.

Salvation.

"Can I make this better for you?" I whisper to her through a groan, my hips starting to move faster, harder, bruising her.

Her eyes widen in a look that says *how could this get any better*, but then I place my other hand at her throat and wrap my fingers around it.

"Trust me," I say to her, because I need her to trust me. I need her to believe that I would never want to hurt her. If she can submit to this, then she has nothing to fear.

She swallows hard, and I feel her throat bob against my palm.

I tighten my grip, slowly cutting off her air supply. Her gills won't work out of water. Her mouth opens, trying to breathe, the whites of her eyes showing around the violet.

"Trust me, little fish," I murmur, my cock still steadily thrusting in and out of her. "I won't do you harm. I just want you to submit."

I study her closely, looking for her consent.

It's there, in the barest nod.

I can't hide my smile as I squeeze her throat until she can't breathe.

Our eyes lock.

Good girl, I think.

Then, I circle my finger around her clit, wet and slippery and thick, giving her what she needs until she's coming.

Only then do I let her breathe again.

She gasps wildly for air, bucking against me as she comes, her cries bouncing off the wooden walls of the jail. Her cunt squeezes my cock so tight that I feel breathless too, and I fully let go.

With a couple of hard, final jabs, pushing myself as deep as I can go, I come with a strangled cry, cum spilling into her. My head goes back, my soul feeling like it's been torn out of me and put back together again. I feel flayed, exposed, barren, as if Larimar could look at my chest and see my ribs pulled back and my heart there, beating wildly and only for her.

Whether she sees it or not, her cunt milks me of every last drop until I collapse forward, my head resting against the wall, trying to catch my breath, trying to come back to Earth.

"Priest," Larimar whispers roughly, but that's all she says.

That's all she needs to say.

My name sounds like an answered prayer.

I take a moment before I pull out of her and lower her to the ground.

While she's panting, leaning back against the wall for support, I quickly bend down and grab the key from the floor to unlock the shackles at my feet. Then I glance at her legs, at my cum dripping down the insides of her thighs, mixing with her own.

I crawl over to her, the only time I'll ever crawl, and then I slide my tongue up her legs, savoring the taste of our unholy union. I run my mouth all the way up to her cunt and push the rest of it back inside with my tongue, causing her to give an involuntary squeeze, and I think she's getting aroused all over again.

I pull my mouth away, smiling softly to myself, then straighten up.

"In case you didn't notice, I'm not done with you yet."

Then I scoop her up in my arms, carry her across the room, and kick open the door, heading to my quarters completely in the buff. If Abe is there, he's getting kicked out, because I'm going to fuck the hell out of Larimar in my own bed.

And then, I'm finally, *finally* going to sleep.

Chapter Thirty-Three

For the second time ever, I fall asleep in Priest's arms.

But this time when I wake, he's not gone. I don't find him in a church, about to change our lives forever.

Instead, I find him right beside me, his strong, firm arm wrapped around my waist, holding on even in sleep.

And he *is* sleeping, his eyes closed, a look of total peace on his face as he breathes in and out steadily.

He is here and I am here, squeezed on his narrow bunk in his chambers, Abe having vacated the room earlier. Outside, gray light begins to filter through the salt-stained circle windows, and I know the sun will be up soon. The crew will be at work, and the ship will spring back to life after the night passes. Even just being kept in the tub for the last few days, I've been able to hear the day-to-day activities of the ship around me.

But for now, it feels like just the two of us in here, just the two of us in this world.

My feelings for Priest are at times complicated, but they are unchanged.

I love him. I loved him then and I love him now, and I don't believe it was his magic that brought us together again, that brought him right to me and me to him. I believe it was simpler than that. I believe it was fate. Fate brought me to him, him to Maren, and both of them to me.

I can't say I don't carry fear in my heart, but it's a different kind of fear now. Perhaps the beast that lives inside him will always lurk there, just out of reach. Maybe I'll see only a glimpse of it every now and then, in the piercing red pupil of Priest when he's overcome with bloodlust, or in the rough handling of our fucking. Maybe when he pushes me toward death, like he did last night when he choked me, that's when I'm actually looking at the monster inside him.

But last night was a test. I submitted to him. I trusted him. I figured if he's going to try and kill me, he should get it over with.

Yet, I didn't die. Priest took great care to make sure I was alright, that I was only experiencing the finest pleasure. And when we were done, he took his time to make sure I was satisfied and safe, enough so that I fell asleep in his arms.

So for now, my fear of that monster reappearing, those nightmares of the church that sting of his ultimate betrayal, will have to go ignored. I'll face them when they rear their ugly heads, and hopefully, I won't have to face them alone. Priest will stare down his demons by my side.

My main fear is that if Priest and I are forever bound to each other...how long does forever last?

He will live forever. He will carry my heart with him for the infinite stretches of time and whatever lies beyond it, but I will only be here for three hundred years, maybe less now that I'm human. Perhaps I'll only have a hundred years with him before I die, before I get old and gray and sick and perish.

Or maybe fate will dole out a bitter hand and give me even less time than that. I might be a savage, able to fight back and take a good beating, harder to kill than your average human. Syrens are strong in so many ways, and I know that strength is still inside me. But if I'm shot? If I'm stabbed? If I'm set on fire? If I'm poisoned or somehow become susceptible to some human disease, or if I fall into the ocean in front of the wrong group of sharks, then I die.

And Priest will go on.

Though the chapter of our lives in Chile had come to a close, a new one is just starting. Our story is continuing.

But it will have to come to an end eventually, and that will happen when I die.

I don't want to die.

I am under this man's spell, and I intend to be for all time. I don't want to watch his face as he watches me pass on, having to live on through life without me. He already lost his wife, and though it was by his hand, I can see what that loss did to him. If I go, will he submit to the monster and exist in agony? What will it be like to watch everyone around me never age while I do? What happens if we have children? Will they an immortal like him, or will he have to eventually watch them die as well?

He stirs a little, his breathing stopping and starting.

"Priest?" I whisper.

He lets out a low moan and pulls me closer to him, nuzzling his nose through my hair and along the back of my neck while he presses his cock against me, already hard and hot.

"You're up early," he murmurs.

"I thought you didn't sleep."

"Only after you tire me out," he says. He adjusts himself and brushes my hair back behind my ears, delicately nibbling the shell. My body immediately responds to him, ravenous, like he's uncovering hunger previously living dormant.

But I don't want to submit just yet. I can't, or I'll lose both my nerve and my focus.

"Priest, I want to ask you something. Something important."

He goes still. "Alright."

I take a deep breath, but his arms hold me tight.

"I've been thinking about this...perhaps not for too long, but I don't think it's something one needs to dwell on."

Silence swirls around us as he waits for me to go on, his breath bated.

"You're an immortal," I say. "And I'm not. And I don't think it's fair that an immortal and mortal can fall in love."

He clears his throat after a moment. "Nothing is ever fair. We both know this well."

"But...what if there was a way around it?"

He stiffens beside me and moves so that his hand is on my arm and he's peering down at me, the black curtain of his long hair tickling my skin. "What way is that?"

"Turn me into a Vampyre."

He blinks at me and then gives me the most incredulous, sour grin. "You know that's impossible."

"Impossible?" I sit up, nearly hitting my head on the bottom of the bunk. "It's not. You're here. You're proof of it, living proof that you can be transformed."

The blue in his eyes turn to ice as his gaze hardens. "I was—"

"A monster. I know. We know."

He glares at me and lets out a huffy growl.

"But you were a human before. A witch, perhaps, but a human. You were mortal. You were transformed, and you became the monster. But I'm not human. I am a monster too. My body has been able to handle being both human and Syren at the same time, so I should be able to handle being a Vampyre too."

"No," he says, shaking his head vehemently. "Absolutely not."

"But what if I beg you?"

"Larimar," he says sharply, grabbing me by the chin and holding me there as he spears me with his angry gaze. "I will not make you into a creature as foul and vile as the one I am."

"But will you make me into a Vampyre? If there was a chance I could drink blood and live forever by your side? Would you grant me that?"

"There is no chance of that happening without losing your soul in the process."

"How can you be so sure?"

"You can talk to Abe about it if you don't believe me. He's seen it firsthand. It's been his calling, his entire life. When he left me behind in Chile, he went back to save and rehabilitate more of us. He knows how futile and dangerous your request is."

"Fine," I say tersely. "I will talk to the doctor about it."

His eyes narrow. "Larimar."

"Or is it that you don't want me by your side forever? Just for a hundred years so you can move on to someone else."

I expected to rankle him a little, wanting a reaction, but I wasn't prepared for the one I got.

Abject despair lining his face.

His shoulders falling, his hand trembling slightly as it moves along my jaw to cup my cheek.

"The fact that you won't be by my side until the end of time is the heaviest cross to bear. It's one I don't even let myself think about, because if I did, I don't think I could survive. I would be turned back into a madman. The idea that, one day, I will have to lose you is...my version of eternal damnation."

His voice is raw, fractured, and I think I see the edges of a crack forming around him too, like his whole being is on the verge of coming apart in front of me. The selfish side of me—my own monster—wants to push that crack until it breaks, to have him fall to pieces the way he made me shatter.

But the human side keeps me above such moral lows.

Because I love him.

And even though there's a pettiness inside me that still wants him to suffer for what he did to me, I love him too much to do that.

"Then let me," I whisper to him, reaching out and trailing my fingers along the prickly hair of his beard. "Let me live with you and love you across time."

He closes his eyes and moves his face to the side, pressing his lips into my palm. "Larimar. My sea goddess. My little fish. You're mine for eternity, stretching across life and death. Love doesn't die, not like mortals do. It is eternal in itself."

I run my thumb over his soft lips. "I'm going to talk to Abe," I whisper.

His eyes fly open, flashing like a thunderstorm. "I will not allow it."

"You can't stop me from doing anything," I say sweetly, smiling something wicked now. "One word to Ramsay and Maren, and you'll be back in chains."

"You wouldn't dare," he seethes.

"I would if you tried to stop me," I warn him. Then, I give him my coyest smile. "Besides, you liked being in those chains. You liked exactly what I did to you. I think there's proof of how much you liked it staining the floor."

He growls at me.

I growl right back.

Monster to monster.

Chapter Thirty-Four

A week goes by in a blink, like no time has passed at all. Life at sea has become both comforting and monotonous, the same day in and day out, the weather holding steady, aside from the occasional heavy swells that roll through.

In that week, I have tried to further convince Priest to turn me into a Vampyre.

He flat out refuses to even have the conversation.

I can't blame him at all.

And yet, I keep trying—partially because every time I do, he uses sex to shut me up. I'm not sure he realizes how he's trained me, but neither of us are complaining in the end.

Tonight, however, I have decided to seek out Abe. Priest doesn't know my plan, and I waited for the right time so that I had the privacy to do so. At the moment, Priest is playing a card game with Ramsay and Thane, and I'm waiting for the chance to leave and say I'm going to talk with Maren.

But Maren told me she is taking a nap during their game, as she often does, stealing a bit of quiet. I do plan on talking to her about my plan, because it could involve her as well—if it's at all possible, would she want to become a Vampyre too? Join Ramsay for eternity? I would assume so, because the two of them are awfully in love, but she has changed a lot over the years. Her quest for adventure has quieted a little, perhaps because she's living it every day.

Yet, I could see her as a Vampyre, sucking the blood out of humans like a creature of the night. It would suit her. I think it would suit all Syrens.

I wait until the drinks are flowing and Priest starts to win a few rounds of the game, which assures me he won't suddenly quit, before I excuse myself and disappear down the ship. I find Abe exactly where I thought he would be: on deck, up in the crow's nest. He's taken quite a liking to observing the sea from that height, probably studying us all scurrying below him like ants.

"Abe!" I yell up the mast. "Do you have a moment?"

I see his red mop peer over the side. "Want me to come down?"

"I'll come up!"

I've never climbed the mast before, but I figure it can't be hard. One hand over the over.

But halfway up, I have to pause, my muscles shaking. I'm still gaining strength again, this body is still new, and I've actually never climbed anything before. I have to take a few deep breaths before I continue up, calming my shaking nerves and muscles.

Finally, I reach Abe on the tiny wooden platform, my heart hammering in my chest. I bet the Vampyres don't expend this much effort. Everything they do is effortless.

"Afraid of heights?" Abe asks me as I lean back against the mast, away from the railing.

"No different than staring down into the abyss of the ocean," I say.

"Even though swimming and falling to your death are completely different?"

I give him a dirty look. "I'll try not to think about the difference."

He stares at me with amusement. "What can I do for you, Larimar? I assume this is about Aragon?"

"Can you turn me into a Vampyre?" I ask, not caring if I'm blunt.

He doesn't look surprised at the question. "You're asking if *I* can?"

"Priest. You. Anyone on this ship."

"You want to become one of us? Because I think you're already an honorary member of the Brethren."

"I want to live forever," I tell him. "I don't want to lose Priest. I want to be by his side for all eternity."

He scratches at the dark auburn hair on his chin and looks off into the sunset. "Yes, I suppose love does that to people."

"Can you do it?"

"You've discussed it with Priest?"

I pinch my lips shut and nod.

"And I assume he's against the idea."

"He says I would become a monster. Would I become one?"

"Well, you can see why he might think that. That's what happened to him."

"And in your experience, is that what always happens?"

He stares at me for a moment, seemingly deep in thought.

"You know, Larimar, you surprise me." He pauses for a moment. "Your constitution is quite astounding," he says, putting his hands in his pockets. "Your willingness to embrace everything. Your devotion to your sister, to the ones you love. You live life to experience it, and you don't let anything hold you back. You are a ferocious, brave little soul, and I can see why Aragon has fallen in love with you so."

I have to admit, I get a little choked up hearing him say such things. "I don't think anyone has ever observed me like that."

"That's my job," he says with a chuckle. "It's what I do. It's what I'm good at. But don't discount Aragon. He sees you too, all of you. That's why he loves you, and the last thing he wants is to jeopardize that. He's not worried about you running amok on the ship and hurting anyone—he's worried you'll lose all that makes you beautiful. Your soul."

Heat creeps up on my cheeks. "It would be nice for him to tell me that."

He laughs. "It's easy for me to tell you because I'm a casual observer. I don't have anything at stake. My heart isn't on the line. It's hard for Aragon because of the way he is, the ways he has broken and put himself back together. It makes everything that much...harder. But you know he feels that way, you can see it. We all can. And actions speak louder than any of the words I have just spoken."

I think that over for a moment, staring at the horizon as the sun begins to dip down, the blues of the sky deepening, reminding me of Priest's eyes, the way they darken with lust.

"One time, a monster at the monastery escaped," Abe recalls. "We were all so worried. It had happened before, with disastrous consequences, and we thought it would be the same, a trail of blood and body parts left in their wake. But while there was blood...we found something surprising."

"What?"

"We found the monster. He had bitten a human, turned *them* into a monster. The beast inside said he had wanted the company. The strange thing was that he didn't create another monster. He just created a Vampyre. Sure, the man was a little feral, I suppose. Had a voracious appetite, but he didn't physically transform, and he was in control of himself. He knew who he had been and who he still was. We never did find out if he turned out to be immortal, as one day he left with the monster who turned him in tow, off to live happily together."

I stare at him. "Why didn't you tell me this earlier? Why didn't you tell Priest?"

"Because neither of you mentioned wanting to turn you into a Vampyre."

"What about Maren?"

"She doesn't know."

I reach out and grab him by the collar, my claws coming out and digging into his skin. "You need to tell him," I growl. "You need to tell Priest what he can do. You need to get him to turn me into a Vampyre, turn Maren into one too so she can live forever with Ramsay."

His chin jerks inward as he tries to stare down at my claws holding him. "Do keep in mind that I only have this anecdotal evidence to support my theory. It happened once. I never saw another monster turn a human after that. Monsters usually killed them. It's never a wise decision to base things on one previous outcome."

"But now this is a risk worth taking," I tell him. "Priest has to see that."

"Then you will have to tell him," he says calmly. "And I will be the one to back up your claim."

"Well, we're doing it tonight then," I tell him as I start to climb down the mast.

"Just realize what immortality means, Larimar," Abe calls after me. "It means you still live after the world has burned to the ground."

"I'll live on a scorched Earth if it means having Priest by my side."

I hear him sigh, and then follow down the mast.

I march straight down to the galley where Priest and the pirates have gathered, grabbing a knife from Sedge's counter as I go.

I have to think fast, act fast. Vampyres move like a blur; they'll stop me if they have any idea what I'm about to do.

And if I give it any more thought, I'll lose my nerve.

I have to take the chance.

I have to be the one to do this.

I have to force Priest's hand.

Above all, I must have faith. Faith in an unknown god, faith in fate, faith that my own strength will save me and see me through, that I'll come out of this no more of a monster than I already was.

I march through the room, Priest, Ramsay and Thane all turning to see me approach.

Priest notices the knife in my hand, and his eyes widen, mouth dropping open.

He probably thinks I'm here to kill him.

I take a deep breath, lift the knife, and bring it to my chest, down toward my heart in a sharp, stabbing motion.

Just as Abe yells from behind me to stop.

But he didn't need to.

Because Priest is faster than I thought he would be.

In the time the knife tip presses into the skin of my chest, Priest has gone from sitting at the table holding a bunch of cards to holding the blade of the knife itself, the cards still falling in the air, a delayed reaction to his speed.

"Don't," he growls at me, gripping the blade so it's cutting into his own palm, its blood trickling down onto my chest. "Don't."

"Larimar," Abe chides me from behind. "I didn't say for you to kill yourself. Good heavens."

"I wasn't trying to kill myself," I practically whine. I let go of the knife's handle, and Priest brings it away from me. "I was just trying to make Priest choose me."

"Choose you?" Priest asks as Ramsay takes the knife from his bloody hand.

"To be yours forever. To become a Vampyre."

"Larimar," he snaps at me. "We've been over this."

"And Abe knows something you don't."

"For my part, I don't know what the devil is going on," Ramsay says. "Larimar wants to become a Vampyre? Surely, you jest. You know what would happen to you."

"Explain, Abe," I say.

I expect Abe to let out a despondent sigh, but instead, he tells the others what he told me in the crow's nest. All the while, Priest is silent, his expression guarded as he takes all the information in. Finally, at the end, he quietly says to Abe, "Why didn't you tell me this before?"

"You never asked," he says. "I didn't think this would come up."

"So..." Ramsay begins, "that means Aragon could turn Maren into a Vampyre too."

"You're not seriously considering this," Priest says to him, his eyes flashing.

Ramsay shrugs. "I love my wife. I want her for all of my days. Why wouldn't I want her to become a Vampyre? Why wouldn't I bring her immortality if I could?"

"Ramsay," Priest says, warning him.

"What? I never considered it because, as we all know, she would be destroyed in the process. But if what the doctor says is true..."

"And it is true," Abe points out. "But I must reiterate that it was hardly a controlled study. It happened once. It might not happen again."

"Is that a risk you want to take?" Priest asks the captain.

"Everything is a risk," Thane mumbles, speaking up. "Even immortality isn't a guarantee. We have to take chances, or we die anyway."

Silence falls over us. We all know he's talking about Sam.

"You can do what you wish with Larimar," Ramsay says to Priest. "But my wish, my request, is that you grant us a lifetime together. I want you to turn Maren into a Vampyre."

Priest shakes his head. "The responsibility if something goes wrong..."

"Is mine to bare," Ramsay says determinedly. "And Maren's too. This will be her choice in the end."

"What's my choice?"

We swivel around to see Maren standing at the entrance of the galley. She slowly walks down the aisle, taking note of our expressions. "What's going on?"

Ramsay walks over to her with an impassioned look, gripping her face in his hands. "If you could live forever, just like me, as a Vampyre, would you do it?"

"But of course," she says quickly. "We've talked about that. But that's never been an option." She glances over at Priest. "Because of what I'd become."

"What if it didn't have to be that way?" I say to her. Ramsay drops his hands from her face as she squares off toward me. "What if Priest had the ability to turn you into a Vampyre and only a Vampyre?"

"Because he's a witch?"

"That might help," Abe notes.

"Because I'm already a beast," Priest says bitterly. "Because I was turned. According to the doctor, it's a gift of sorts."

"And I still think the fact that we're already monsters,

Syrens, means we're used to staying in control," I tell her. "We were never human to begin with."

Maren walks over to Priest, and I can see the hope building in her eyes with every step. "You could turn me into an immortal? A blood-drinker? You would do that for me?"

Now Priest seems to be pushed into a corner. "I never said I would."

Her eyes spark with determination. "But would you? I'm asking you, Aragon."

He doesn't say anything for a moment, and I don't know what he's thinking.

"It's a risk."

"I like risks," she says with a slow grin. "Taking risks has gotten me the life I wanted."

"Do I have to beg you?" Ramsay says. "Get down on my knees and take your wee cock from your pants?"

At that, Priest bristles, giving him the most offended look while Abe and I burst out laughing.

"I'd do anything for my lady," Ramsay adds, putting his arm around Maren's waist and holding her to him.

Priest looks around the room. So far, he's the odd man out.

There's a battle inside him, a need to stay pious, a need to avoid guilt.

Then, he closes his eyes and runs his hands over his face.

"Fine," he concedes.

Maren and Ramsay let out happy sighs.

"But you won't be happy when she becomes a monster," he grumbles.

"I'll take her in any way, shape, or form," Ramsay says with a smile.

"Alright, so," Abe says, clapping his hands together, "I reckon we should get started." He pauses. "How should we get started?"

"Well, I have to kill her," Priest says.

"This is macabre," Thane mutters under his breath.

"And then bring her back to life," Priest adds.

"Hmmm," Abe says. "Kill her or bring her to the brink of death? That's a fine distinction to make."

Priest looks at me. "And you're just okay with me doing this to your sister?"

I nod. "If it's what she wants, yes."

"And then you can turn Larimar," Ramsay says to him.

If it's a success, is what Ramsay doesn't add, but he doesn't need to. We all know what hangs in the balance.

"Where's that knife?" Abe asks. "We need it again."

Everything after that happens rather fast.

Maren is made to sit down in a chair. There's a quick discussion of how she should die. At first, Ramsay insists that he'll stab her in the heart, but then he changes his mind, and Priest says he'll do it. Then, Abe suggests that a stabbing in the heart might result in instant death, let alone trauma to Maren, so the best way is to sever an artery so that she bleeds out fast. That gives enough time for her to slowly die but not quite pass over.

Of course, while all of this is going on, I'm wrestling with the fact that this was all my idea, and if anything goes wrong, it will be my fault. I wanted to become a Vampyre, but I didn't want to bring Maren into it this way. I wanted to discuss it with her privately first, to see if it would work on me. I wanted to be the sacrifice, not her.

But that's not the way it turned out.

And now, I'm so damn scared that maybe this isn't the best idea. Maybe there needs to be another instance of this working other than the one that Abe provided. Maybe all these hopes about Syren blood taming the monster are just reaching for something.

"I should go first," I blurt out as Abe holds the knife, set to make a cut along her neck with surgical precision.

Maren gives her head the barest shake, mindful of the blade below it. "If it wasn't for me, you wouldn't have fallen for an immortal anyway. And if it wasn't for you bringing Aragon into our lives, I wouldn't have the chance to be with my love forever."

She turns her gaze to Ramsay and gives him the most adoring look.

He returns it back, ten-fold.

And then Abe slices open her neck.

She cries out, her hands automatically going to her neck to stop the bleeding.

I rush forward on pure instinct, trying to save her, but Thane has his arms around me, holding me back. "Let your lover do his work," he says in my ear. "Let him save her."

And so, I watch.

I watch as the blood flows from Maren's neck and she grows paler, Ramsay holding onto her hand and coaxing her, as if in a reverse birth.

Then, Abe nods at Priest to step forward, just as the light in my sister's eyes begins to dim, and a dark, shadowy fear enters my heart.

Priest takes the knife from Abe and slices open his wrist.

More blood pours.

He holds his wrist up to Maren's mouth while Ramsay pries her lips open.

"Drink," her husband whispers in her ear. "Drink, luv, please."

And Maren has just enough life in her to swallow.

Thane lets go of me, but I'm holding onto him now for comfort, and we both stand there, watching and waiting and...

Maren's eyes close.

She stops swallowing.

Crimson trickles from the corner of her mouth.

And then...

She gasps, a god awful, death rattle of a gasp.

Her eyes fly open, and for a second, they're red, a glowing crimson, and then they return to blue as she sits straight up.

Her hand flies out to grab Ramsay, and then she leaps up straight out of the chair and jumps on him, knocking him to the floor.

She goes for his jugular, and I catch a glimpse of fangs as I laugh.

They did it.

It worked.

"Jumping Joseph!" Abe yells. "She's a Vampyre!"

"May I be damned, it worked," Thane says in quiet awe. "I'm going to have a sister-in-law for the rest of my life."

"She'll be busy trying to get her fill from him," Abe says. "I reckon that she'll need human blood after awhile, but Ramsay's will be enough to sustain her for now." He looks at me. "But you, Larimar, you'll be able to feed off Priest, just as he's able to feed off you. He was human once, and he will always carry that part with him."

"I never said I would do the same to Larimar," Priest says gruffly, stubborn as ever.

But when I walk over to him and put my hand over the blood that flows from his wrist, now down to a trickle, the expression on his stoic face softens.

And he gives in.

"Don't make me beg to be part of your life," I tell him.

He manages the faintest smile. "But you know I like it when you beg."

Abe brings the knife over, holding it out like an offering. "I am ready to do the honors again."

"The honors are all mine," Priest says, taking the knife

from him. "She is mine to hurt and mine alone. She is mine to turn. She is mine. Forever."

He sits me down on the chair. I keep looking at Maren, at what a feral creature she's become as she sucks at Ramsay's neck, but he does seem to be enjoying it, and every now and then she unhooks her fangs to give him a passionate, bloody kiss, grinning at him like a young girl in love. Suffice it to say, she's no more of a monster than she was before.

"Are you sure you want me to do this?" Priest asks, but he no longer looks unsure of himself. Instead, he seems eager.

Excited.

Eternity waits at the edge of his knife.

"Yes," I tell him.

He presses the blade against my neck.

"Wait, wait!" I cry out, carefully. "Kiss me first."

He grins at me and leans in for a long, deep passionate kiss, the kind that makes my toes curl.

"I love you," he whispers against my mouth. "Always and to the end, whatever end that may be."

"I love you," I say back, giving him another quick kiss on his lips, the side of his mouth, his chin. "Always and to the end, whatever end that may be."

We stare into the other's eyes for a moment, lost to each other, hearts tangled, murmuring everything we need to know.

And then he swipes the blade across my neck.

Chapter Thirty-Five

PRIEST

"That was quite the risk you took," Abe says reproachfully, but when I glance at him, he looks more impressed than anything.

I try to shrug, as if it was nothing, as if I didn't feel like God himself with the future of humanity in the balance. If I had slipped, if I had turned Larimar into a monster, then I would have become the Devil instead, unleashing more of his minions in the world.

But I didn't.

"I only tried to find a solution to what she wanted," I tell him. "To what we both wanted."

We're sitting on top of a stack of crates in the middle of the ship, repairing fishing nets for Sedge. Even though Larimar and Maren are blood-drinkers now, they still like to eat both human food *and* Syren food, and fish are a happy medium. Sometimes, the sisters will jump off the ship together and find the fish themselves, but we've been sailing at a fast clip today, and if we can drag these nets behind us, we might catch enough so that Sedge can cook up a feast.

"Yes, but what solutions are as simple as granting one

immortality," he says. "You couldn't have known that it would work."

"I didn't," I tell him. "But you did."

"I merely had a hypothesis," he says with a sniff. "The risk was still yours to carry."

I sigh. Figures that even though Larimar talked to Abe privately about her wishes, he still pretends he wasn't involved at all, as if he wasn't the one who used the knife on Maren. But the doctor likes to get his sticky little fingers in everything.

I decide to run with it. "I figured that they're monsters too. They know how to control that side of themselves that humans don't. That I never could. The perfect candidate for turning one into a Vampyre that can keep its sanity."

"Speaking of," he says, lowering his voice. "You're going to have to test the beast eventually."

I stiffen at that. For some time, Abe has had the notion of trying to let the monster out on purpose, but we both know it doesn't seem to work that way. Heightened emotions are what brought the beast out in front of Larimar that time, but that was beyond my control. At any rate, I think I've learned how to control the way I feel about her. I don't let it scare me anymore.

I'm no longer running away from the fact that I'm in love with her.

When it comes to love, she's the predator and I'm the prey, and this time, I've willingly let myself be caught.

Sometimes, it's good to submit.

To an extent, in any regard. I certainly submitted in those chains the other week, but that was a onetime thing. She's the one in chains going forward.

"Too risky," I tell him.

"What's risky is the fact that you can't control it, and it might resurface when you least expect it. If you could bring the monster out, perhaps in a controlled environment, then you'll always have it under your power. You'll have nothing to fear." He pauses. "And neither will she."

The doctor is right about that. Even with Larimar being a Vampyre, even with her Syren ability to fight back, I can tell she's still worried about a reappearance from the beast. I traumatized her back at that church. I hurt her, tried to kill her. That's a hard thing to get over, no matter how changed I may seem, no matter how powerful she might feel.

"At the very least, she's immortal now," he goes on, picking up on what I'm thinking, "so even if things did go sideways, chances are she'd be alright. Besides, you have the Brethren of the Blood here to keep you in line."

I try to concentrate on the net. "I'll think about it."

"Well, you best be thinking about it before we hit Cape Colony and the Dutch East Indies," he says. "Once we go into port, we all have to be on our best behavior."

"And I do say it's not a moment too soon," I comment with a sigh. The humans in the hold are dying. There is no chance they will make it to land and survive if they're let go. They will die on this ship, despite Maren's best intentions. They'll probably die soon—Ramsay suggested we shoot them and put them out of their misery. Says it's the humane way of dealing with livestock, and I suppose he's right about that.

But with the humans gone, that means us blood-drinkers will run out of food. There's a chance we might be able to find another ship, but Maren has her qualms about us killing everyone we come across. It's easy for her to say since she can survive off food if things get tough. Same goes for Larimar. Neither of them seem to need blood the same way that we do, though that doesn't mean they don't crave it the same.

But we can't keep this cycle forever. We'll need to feed from humans eventually.

We go back to working on the nets, falling into comfortable silence. At least we can keep pulling in fish, and though it won't nourish everyone, it at least tempers the hunger for now.

It's been a couple of hours now, the sun high in the sky, a bright blue cloudless day in the South Atlantic, where fair weather is hard to come by, when Maren starts running down the deck. She and Larimar have been at the bow this whole time, talking or gossiping or trading Vampyre growing pains. They both have a near-death experience they can share.

"Ramsay!" she yells, and I notice Larimar is running after her. "Turn the ship to port!"

"Why?"

She runs on up to the helm while Larimar comes over to me, a feverish glint in her eyes. I've seen that look before. She had that glow before she ripped the heart out of that soldier and ate it.

While Maren yells at Ramsay about something to do with Nill and a ship, Larimar says to me, "We found them."

"Found who?" I frown.

"*Them*," she says, that look in her eyes intensifying so that the violet is turning bright pink. "The bastards who captured me and raped my friend."

My jaw clenches. "How do you know it's their ship?"

Larimar filled me in on what happened to her when she was captured by the other ship, on how she was trapped by a male Syren who made her life a living hell, along with another of her kind, how she was taken aboard and kept in a glass box and had to watch as her friend was brutally raped, so much so that she reached into her own heart and tore it out, the only way of escape she knew. The same bloody humans who then chained Larimar to the rudder—a torture known as keel-hauling to my fellow pirates—and left her there to die...or meet a much worse fate in port.

"Nill saw it," she says. "He went off in search of any ship that could be used for, well, sustenance. He recognized the name and the flag. The *Gelderland*. We can catch them, Priest. We can catch them and kill them all."

I can't help but match her vengeful grin. "To port!" I yell back at Ramsay.

But he's already barking orders and turning the wheel, and everyone else starts running around and adjusting the sails, yelling, "Aye, aye, Captain!"

"Well, this certainly would help our depleted stock," Abe says.

"Yes, but this time, we aren't listening to Maren," I tell him. "We're taking all of them on board, torturing them to our hearts' content, and drinking our fill. I personally will rip the fucking heads off any of the men who even looked at you," I growl to Larimar. "Piss down their bloody throats."

"Not if I get to them first," she says with a raise of her chin.

My God, I could kiss her right now.

So I reach out and grab her face, and I do just that.

"Wonderful how murder makes the both of you turn into lovebirds," Abe comments dryly. "I suppose I should go and give you both some privacy, see if someone else needs my help."

He leaves, but I barely notice.

I kiss her deeply, hungrily, feeling both the physical need for her and the craving I have for her soul. If I could throw her down on the deck and ravage her in front of everyone, I would, but she's still a lady, even if she's a monster too.

She pulls away, her face flushed and breathing hard, and in this strong sunlight that hurts my eyes, she's the most beautiful creature in this entire world.

And she is my entire world.

"We can kill them all together," she says. "You drink their blood, I'll eat their hearts, and maybe we can fuck on top of their bodies."

I lean down and groan into her neck, my cock growing painfully hard. "If you're not careful, I won't last that long."

She reaches down and rubs her hand over the rigid lines, pressing in until it pulls a gasp from my lips, and I rock into her hand.

"Aragon!" Thane yells. "Larimar! We need you both to focus!"

I glare at him over my shoulder from where he's manning the sails with Cruz. "And I need you to look away from time to time and pretend we're not here."

But as much as I want to fuck Larimar right here, right now, there is chaos swirling around us in all directions. The entire crew is buzzing like an electrical storm, excited for a fight, their hunger for fresh blood driving them.

I straighten up and give her hand a squeeze.

I won't let any harm come to her. I know that battles will sometimes take the life of the immortals, such as what happened to Thane's wife, so I'm going to be extra cautious. Of course, I will let her feast and drink, but I'll be the one to kill each and every one of those men.

All I can say is thank the Lord that I listened to her pleas and turned her into a Vampyre. Had I not, the chances of her getting hurt or killed would be much higher.

Yes, a voice whispers inside me, a voice I hadn't heard in a very long time.

Suddenly, I go still, afraid to move.

"What is it?" Larimar asks.

I don't want to scare her. Not now. Not now. I can't scare her; I can't lose her.

Panic begins to claw through me.

This can't be happening again.

"I'm fine," I manage to say, though the words are a whisper.

Abe! I yell in my head. *The beast is talking!*

I'll be right there, he says, and he races over to my side in seconds flat.

"What is happening?" Larimar asks, looking between the both of us, her voice rising.

Abe glances at her. "Nothing, dear. Just a bit of doctor-patient confidentiality. Would you mind giving us a moment? You understand."

I nod at her to go on, and she does, reluctantly walking along the deck toward the helm while she keeps throwing concerned glances at me over her shoulder.

What happened? Abe asks, putting his hand on my shoulder. *Look at me. What happened?*

I meet his eyes. *I heard the voice. Of* it.

What did it say?

It said yes.

To what?

I was thinking about how grateful I was to listen to Larimar. Now that she's immortal, I don't have to worry so much about her getting hurt or killed during a battle.

A good point, he says with a nod. *And it said yes to that?*

I nod.

Nothing else?

No.

He frowns, the cogs behind his eyes turning. *Can you talk to it? Ask it something.*

What?

Make a bargain with it. Choose something that would benefit you. Find out how you can be the one in control. This might be your shot, Aragon.

What if by talking to it, I'm only inviting it in?

Then invite it in. This is what we have been talking about. This is the controlled environment.

Shouldn't I be in chains first?

Don't you think that would start things on the wrong foot, going on the defensive like that?

I frown at him. *Are you on the monster's side or mine?*

He gives me a small, knowing smile. *I knew the monster before I knew you. You are one and the same. The fact that it said yes, agreeing with you when you said that it was good that Larimar is immortal now, means that it wants to be on your side. It knows it can't really harm her now.*

That's not exactly true. The beast could bite off her head or tear out her heart. But I don't even want to think about it, lest I give it any ideas.

Talk to it, Abe coaxes.

I look around. Everyone is paying attention to the sea as the *Nightwind* sails on in hot pursuit of the Dutch ship. The only one looking at us is Larimar.

Alright, I say and close my eyes. Abe keeps his hand on my shoulder to steady me, and while I'm grateful for it, I also feel quite silly, standing here in the middle of the ship like this while everyone else is running around.

Are you listening? I ask the beast, searching for the dark spaces deep inside, the places I've been too afraid to go, where I know my demons live.

No answer.

And then a faint reply, so faint I barely hear it.

I am always listening.

I try to gather my courage. *What do you want from me?*

It wasn't the question I wanted to ask. I wasn't even supposed to ask a question; I was supposed to tell it the terms of our bargain.

I want you to make peace with your dark side, the beast says. *I want you to make peace with me.*

You are my dark side?

Armand Cruz, he says, my old name making me shiver. *I am you.*

But you came when Kaleid…you came from Kaleid, when he killed me, turned me. He gave you to me.

He did not. I came to your rescue. You would have died had I not appeared. Your dark side kept you alive. I kept you alive.

He turned me into an immortal.

But that's not how immortals are made. Had I not stepped in and made you go to the dark place, you would have never survived in the world.

You made me kill my family! I yell inside my head, fists clenching at my sides. Abe's grip on my shoulder grows strong.

We all do things we do not mean, it eventually says. *But sometimes we do things we do, things we could never entertain, that we would never admit to ourselves.*

I never wanted to kill my family. I seethe.

Never? Oh, there were times you thought about it. When the kids were loud and your wife showed no interest in you. When you resented having to work all day, every day except the Lord's day.

You are wrong.

I am right because I am you. Within each human is a great capacity for evil. There is a shadow that forms within us since birth. You—we—were well versed in these shadows. We used them in our witchcraft. You called into the darkness so often, Armand, is it any wonder that it called back? They called you Armand the dark, do you remember? Do you remember all the magic and the spells you did that brought harm to others?

I never harmed…

But I remember now.

I remember being a child and killing a snake with a sword, chopping it up into pieces while it was alive, not because I was curious but because I was so angry that my father had died so young, and I wanted to take it out on something. The rage that came over me, it was like I was possessed by the Devil itself, back when I thought I was young and innocent. I sliced and sliced and sliced until I became someone else entirely, and I lived with that guilt every waking day because how could I, a child, do such a horrible thing?

I remember the seething jealousy I had over my neighbor, the way his wife looked at me in the way that my own wife never did, enough so that I stole her away one night for a mutual tryst. When she became pregnant not long after, she came to me, and I had to pretend I had no idea what she was talking about, had to pretend that I'd never talked to her a day in her life.

I remember sabotaging the blacksmith in the neighboring town, putting a spell on him that caused him to lose all feeling in his hands so that I could take over his clients. I did so, reaping the benefits, and I never gave him his feeling back.

I remember feeling the white-hot rage seeping through when my children disobeyed me and reminded me they were another mouth to feed.

I never wanted to kill them, I whisper inside.

You didn't, the beast says. *But your dark side did. The one that lives deep within, the one you never wanted to face because if you did, you'd be looking at your own face. You'd be looking at me.*

I shake my head. *No.*

Yes, it hisses. *And the sooner you make peace with it, the better off you will be. There is a difference between having these thoughts and desires and acting on them. The more you push them away, the stronger the pull is. The harder you try to be good, the more I'll try and rein you in. We are victims to our broken souls and unnourished hearts. We want so much, we covet, and we deny it. We live our lives pretending to be better than that, but we aren't. The rage that made me lives in every single being, monster and human alike. And every now and then, if you're too afraid to face what you truly are, it will be unleashed.*

But there are good people, I say. *There are good people in the world. I've seen them. Selfless people who will do anything for another.*

There are people who are better than you, morally, spiritually so. There are people who are braver than you, too. But even the best people harbor the darkest secrets sometimes. Every face you look at is fighting a battle they aren't always aware of. And most of them are losing.

Silence.

I feel leveled out by what the beast has just told me.

I never wanted...I...

But now, everything feels like a lie.

I am a bad person, I can't help but think. *I always was.*

We're all bad, the monster says. *But we're all good, too. Perhaps the best approach is a bit of balance.*

I swallow hard.

Are you okay in there? Abe asks, his voice jarring against the raspy whispers of the beast. At least this means he can't hear our conversation. I would hate for him to know how awful I truly was before I turned.

He knows, the beast says. *Abe knows. I'm the one who has been talking to him when you weren't available. He's a true friend, you know. Sees all the ugliness inside you and still stays by your side, because he's no better either. He's just made peace with his darkness, the same way you'll need to make peace with yours if you want us to coexist.* It pauses. *If you want me to agree to your bargain.*

The bargain.

What was I going to offer him?

What did I want in exchange?

You wanted to make friends, the beast says. *You wanted to use me when you could and stay in control. Right now, you're thinking, deep down, that you want to spread your wings and fly to that ship and take down every single person on it, punish them for their sins, punish them for what they did to Larimar.*

But I don't want to punish Larimar.

Then I stop.

Or do I?

Ah, the beast says. *There is the progress. You do want to punish her.*

I swallow hard and nod. *I do. I want to punish her for breaking her promise to me and for leaving me, even though I understand why she did, even though it's not fair for me to feel this way.*

But feelings aren't fair. And that is something that comes with being human too. However, now that you know you want to punish her, are you afraid that you're going to?

I think about that for a moment, searching inside my soul. *No,* I say honestly. *I don't want to hurt her, not unless she asks me to. I want to protect her with all I have. I want to carry out her revenge for her.*

And so you may, it says. *For you are ready.*

Then, a dark, buzzing feeling starts forming inside me, and my eyes fly open. The sunshine is no longer so bright; instead, the sky has been dimmed. Abe is staring at me with an urgent expression, more excitement than concern.

"What happened?" he whispers.

I shake my head and look around at my surroundings. There's a ship far in the distance, and I realize that everyone has been shouting and talking impatiently, but I hadn't heard any of it. Larimar is at the bow now, Maren by her side, and she looks over her shoulder to meet my eyes, raising her brow in question.

"That's the Dutch ship," I say.

"It is," Abe says. "A lot of time has passed while you've been in your head."

"No one has said anything?" I search the faces of the crew.

"Oh, everyone has been giving you strange looks, but no stranger than normal." He stares at me deeply. "Tell me what the beast said."

"The beast said I'm ready."

Abe breaks into a toothy grin. "Most excellent. So, pray tell, what are you going to do about it?"

I roll back my shoulders, feeling a familiar tinge deep in the muscles. Something moves under my skin, like my muscles and bones are coming awake.

Darkness spreads within me like spilled ink over paper.

It seeps into my marrow.

I submit to the shadows.

I become the beast.

I put my head back and scream as the pain rushes through my broken body. The world grows dimmer still, all sound now a hush in the background. I know people are running over to me to see if I need help; I know some are staying back because they know.

I let the beast take over.

Just a little.

Just enough for my body to change and for my blood to boil and for the darkness inside me to intertwine with the light.

No fighting anymore.

I look down at Abe and unfurl my wings. I'm taller now, and I cast him completely in shadow.

"Well, hello, old friend," Abe says with a genuine smile and a tip of the hat.

"Hello again," I say, as myself, as the monster. "I have something I need to do."

I start flapping my wings, blowing back Abe's hair, attempting flight.

"Don't kill everyone, Aragon," Abe chides me. "It seems

it's been a while since this crew has seen battle. Let them have a little fun. Let Larimar have her revenge. And for God's sake, remember we need to keep some alive for blood."

I grin at him. It must be the ugliest grin in the world.

Then, I turn around and look at Larimar, who is holding on to Maren in pure fright, Ramsay standing protectively in front of them, ready to fight me by any means necessary.

I nod at them and then start pumping my wings until I'm taking flight, soaring over the side of the boat and down over the water, gathering up extra air from the waves before I shoot straight up into the sky.

The beast lets me laugh.

No, I let myself laugh.

I'm going to avenge the woman I love.

And I'm going to love every minute of it.

Chapter Thirty-Six

"Blast my eyes!" Ramsay swears in wonderment as Priest soars overhead.

My Priest, who is now the monster once more.

My Priest, who has spread his wings again, a terrible creature that has taken to the skies.

For a moment there, I thought I might die.

I had forgotten I was immortal. I've only been immortal for so long, it's natural to think death is coming for you when it's staring you in the face.

And his monster had been staring at me in the face.

But unlike the time in the church, I saw Priest in that creature's eyes.

I saw a man still in control, a man with a soul.

A Vampyre with wings.

He flew off toward the Dutch vessel, leaving the *Nightwind* and its crew in awe.

And I already know what Priest is going to do.

He's going to hunt down every man on that ship.

He's going to make them bleed.

As scared as I am of that creature, I don't want to miss the massacre either.

"So, that's the monster," Maren remarks as she stands next to me.

I nod. "Yes. That's the one."

She lets out a dry laugh. "He's a lot more terrifying than I imagined." Then, she reaches out and puts her hand on my shoulder, as if remembering what happened to me. "Are you alright?"

I give her a reassuring smile. "I think so. I certainly didn't expect to see the beast again or so soon. But I feel better about it than I thought I would. Perhaps because he didn't come straight for me, trying to kill me."

"Or perhaps because you know deep inside, you are nearly impossible to kill," she points out softly. "I don't know about you, but being immortal really does have you looking at life differently."

She's right about that. Ever since Priest cut my throat and let me bleed out before bringing me back to life as a Vampyre, life has looked different. It's not just that I see more; colors are more vibrant, I can see things in more detail, I can see things that are very far away. It's not just that my sense of smell, hearing, taste, and even touch have been heightened—having sex with Priest is almost too intense at times with all these new sensations.

No, it's something deeper than that, more than just my newfound strength and powers. It's knowing that you have eternity on your side. It changes you, makes you braver, less afraid of whatever life may throw at you.

Although, I must admit, I'm not fearless when it comes to matters of the heart. Being an immortal doesn't shield you from all the usual human worries. Vampyre hearts still break as easily as any other.

And while I may carry the fear of heartbreak with me, that

doesn't stop me. I'm going to love Priest with all that I have, until the end of time.

And that means learning to love the monster too.

"Maren, luv," Ramsay says, coming over to her. "In the event that this battle gets out of hand, would you be able to call the Kraken to take down their ship? Might be good also to leave no evidence of what we're about to do."

She nods. "I will, but let me get my fill first. I can't let you boys always have all the fun."

He grins at her and then runs off, grabbing a rope from the mast and climbing up it.

"Lads!" Thane yells, his broadsword in the air. He glances at me and Maren and gives us a curt nod. "And ladies. Here we be! This is it! Are we ready to board and show these bastards no quarter?"

"Aye!" the crew yells, grabbing their weapons and getting into their battle positions. A few of them are down below on the gun deck, arming the cannons.

Maren and I look over the bow as the other ship gets closer and closer, the *Nightwind* coming in at full speed.

"You might want to stay out of the way for now," Cruz says to us, brandishing a sword before climbing up on the railing of the bow, holding on to a rope for balance. "Cannon fire can decapitate you."

"This isn't my first battle, Cruz," Maren says frostily. "And besides, they'd already have fired on us if they could. I dare say Aragon has already taken care of them."

We all look back to the vessel as we start closing in on it, see the blood splatters on the wood that Priest left behind. The occasional man runs down the deck and then seems to hide. One looks at our ship, screams, and then jumps overboard.

White-hot, simmering rage starts to build inside me.

"Cowards," I growl. Then I yell at the rest of the crew. "You find one alive, you save him for me!"

"Aye!" they yell back, just as eager for me to have my revenge.

"Steady, steady as she goes!" Thane yells back to the bosun at the helm.

Some of the sails are taken in quickly, and the ship starts to turn at an angle so that we're coming in on the side.

Cruz runs down the rail and jumps over the closing gap between the ships, while Ramsay yells, "Come on boys, let's feast!" and swings over on a rope. The rest of the crew on deck waits until the sides of the ships are flush against each other before throwing over grappling hooks to secure them, our cannons shoved into their ports. Seems they didn't even have the time to arm their own.

Priest, I can't help but think. *Please save one for me.*

"It's time," Maren says, grabbing my hand as the Brethren climb over on the Dutch ship. "Let's find the men who captured you."

We jump across the water and onto the other vessel, our movements effortless now that we're Vampyres, and start running amok along with everyone else. The crew of the Brethren always struck me as being so civilized compared to what I'd heard about pirates—especially when it comes to personal cleanliness—but now I see their savage side. They're running everywhere with their weapons drawn, pulling out the cowardly humans from their hiding places, stabbing them thoroughly before biting them and drinking their blood.

"I thought they were supposed to keep some alive?" I say to Maren as we make our way down the stairs to where the majority of screams seem to be coming from.

She makes a tsking sound of disappointment. "They're supposed to, but sometimes the bloodlust gets the best of them. Now that I'm a Vampyre, well, I can't say I blame them."

Then she spots a man cowering in the corner behind a barrel and lunges for him. My sister grabs him by the throat, her Syren claws coming out and slicing through his skin. Then, with red eyes and a monstrous roar, she bites the man's neck and begins feeding.

"Don't forget to eat the heart," I tell her as I keep going.

I've only fed from Priest, and that was right after he brought me back to life with an insatiable appetite for blood—one that has since waned, perhaps because I knew our supplies were low—and while I do feel the hungry urge to drink blood, my vengeance is on the forefront of my mind, clouding all other thoughts.

I hear another scream and a deep, menacing growl, and I know where I can find the beast.

I run right to a room at the end, where the door is half-open, claw marks having shredded through the wood.

I take in a deep breath, steadying my nerves because I know it won't just be Priest on the other side but the monster too, and then I step inside.

The delightful smell of blood fills my nose, and I'm back in the room I was first captured in.

The beast stands in the corner, so tall that he has to stoop over, his wings unfurled and taking up the whole breadth of the room.

In his hands is Ullan.

Ullan.

The beast holds the Syren by his shoulders, giant dark claws digging straight into his skin. There's a glass box filled with water on the floor that Ullan has been dragged out of, only his tail still submerged. There's a chain around Ullan's mouth to prevent him from biting and screaming.

Seems the Dutch crew went back for more Syrens after

they lost Vialana. I have to wonder when they discovered me missing from the bottom of the ship.

Larimar? Ullan says in shock, staring at my dress, wondering how I can possibly be walking.

I glance up at the beast. He really should be hideous, those fathomless eyes, the snarling teeth, the dark leathery skin. And yet I still see Priest somehow. I see the man I love in there.

The beast stares back at me and nods, letting out a low growl.

He's been waiting for me to finish the job.

I feel a flutter of warmth in my heart, as if Priest had just performed the most romantic gesture. I suppose it wasn't easy keeping Ullan alive when all he wanted to do was—what was the saying? Rip off his head and piss down it?

I bring my attention back to the traitorous Syren.

Did the Dutch turn on you? I ask Ullan. *Did you make a little bargain with them to take me? Take Vialana and the rest? Did they betray you in the end when they went back to get more? Or did you set us up, hoping we would be captured?*

Ullan blinks at me, his gills opening and closing, trying to figure out how to breathe properly.

Tell me the truth, Ullan, I say, slowly walking toward him. *Tell me the truth so that I may put my curiosity to rest, and perhaps I'll let you live.*

The beast lets out a low, rattling sound, his claws digging in, drawing more blood. The sight of Ullan's blood makes my own veins thrum. I want my revenge, but maybe Syren blood will go a long way for the rest of the crew.

Tell me the truth and I'll make sure you're taken alive, I add, trying not to smile.

There was no bargain, Ullan finally says, his voice high and panicked. And weak. *I saw the ship, knew what they were there for, and I signaled to them to come into the bay. They thought they were hunting me; they didn't know you were down there.*

I nod. Strangely enough, now that I hear what happened, the truth makes no difference to me. *I see.*

You can't trust humans, Ullan says, wild-eyed.

Now, I grin. "No, you can't," I say aloud, even though I know he doesn't understand me. "But we're not human anyway."

I look to the beast again, finally feeling relaxed enough in his monstrous presence. "What should we do, Priest?" I ask, hoping I'm reaching him. "Keep the Syren alive so we can all feed off him for years to come? Or let me take out his heart and have him watch me eat it?"

I don't expect the beast to talk back, but it does.

"I am of two minds," the monster says, his voice terribly low and chilling and utterly inhuman. "Priest would want you to keep Ullan and torture him for eternity. I would rather eat the Syren's head. I suppose you could have the heart."

"Generous offer," I say. "I thought you were saving him for me."

"Priest is saving the Syren for you so that you may have your revenge. What I want is to eat its brains."

I try not to curl my lip at that. Ullan is looking between the two of us, trying to figure out what we're discussing. Probably a good thing he has no idea.

"Alright," I say. "For the sake of the Brethren, we will take Ullan on board. I suppose keeping him half-alive in the hold for a couple of hundred years while we slowly take his blood might be the best revenge I can get."

The beast nods. "I also have some humans I've saved for you," he rasps. "One happens to be the captain. They're in his quarters. Don't worry, I removed their legs so they can't escape."

"That was very thoughtful of you," I tell the beast.

I swear I see the monster grin.

I pick up the ends of my gown, like a lady, and leave the room while the beast drags Ullan along, the tail thrashing around like a dying fish. Outside, there is still chaos in the ship, filled with the occasional scream, the air smelling of blood.

I run into Ramsay and Thane, who show me the way to the captain's quarters.

The beast wasn't lying when he said he removed the men's legs. There are three humans lumped together in the middle of the cabin, all of them bleeding out. Their legs are nowhere to be found, which must mean the beast ate them. I have to wonder what that means for Priest when he comes back to his Vampyre form again, but I suppose we'll figure that out when it happens.

There are also bite marks in all of them, to which Ramsay and Thane look a little sheepish, although there is one human who is untouched.

The captain with his bushy blond mustache stares up at me with dazed eyes as Ramsay goes over and hoists him up to the sitting position.

I smile at him. "So, we meet again, Captain," I say to the man as I saunter over to him. "I bet you didn't think you'd see me alive. I bet you didn't think I'd have legs either. And I bet you didn't think I'd be the last thing you'd ever see." I frown at him mockingly. "That's an awful lot of thinking that you didn't do."

I stop in front of him and crouch down to his level, reach out with my Syren claws, and let one trail down the side of his powdered face, drawing a thin line of blood.

"So, allow me to let you stop thinking about what's going to happen next," I go on. "I'm going to tell you what's going to happen. I'm going to bite you and drain you of whatever blood you have left. Then, just before you die, I'm going to reach into your chest, pull out your heart, and eat it in front of you. Then, I'll do the same to whatever crew members are left."

I pause, taking my finger away from his face and licking the blood off the tip of my claw. It dances on my tongue like fire, the hunger striking me deep. "Finally, at the end of all that, the Kraken will come and take down your ship so that no one will ever know the truth of what happened to you, no evidence that you ever even saw Syrens. It will be like you never existed."

I glance up at Ramsay, who is still holding the captain up.

"Any last words?" Ramsay says to the captain.

But I don't even give the captain a chance to reply.

I lean in and sink my teeth into his neck, giving him a savage bite, the first pure human I've ever had a chance to feed on.

The blood flows into my mouth, and I feel everything inside me come alive, like being reborn all over again. Priest's blood was lovely, but I was in such a strange, ravenous state after I turned that I wasn't able to take my time and appreciate it.

There was also a part of me that didn't want to hurt Priest or take too much blood from him.

But now, I have permission to be my fully wild, feral, violent self.

So I feast and I feast on the captain's blood.

Then, as he starts to die, I make Ramsay hold his eyes open so he can see me tear out his heart and eat it in front of him.

And then I leave the captain as a dried husk, and the rest of us go through the remainder of the ship, searching for any survivors that the beast may have left behind.

By the time we're done and back on the *Nightwind*, twilight has fallen, and every crew member has blood and a look of satisfaction on their face. We have six humans still alive to put into the hold, and Ullan has been transferred to the jail cell, along with the glass box, to be kept for as long as he'll stay alive.

I'm standing at the railing as the *Nightwind* has started pulling away from the other ship, while Maren is swimming in the moonlit waters below, waiting for the Kraken. And I've been waiting for my own beast to make an appearance. After he flew with Ullan onto our ship, he disappeared somewhere. Abe assured me that he probably wanted to be alone to transform back into Priest.

But I'm starting to fear he won't transform back into human form at all.

What if he decides to stay the monster forever?

"Little fish."

I smile to myself in relief and then turn around to see Priest walking down the ship toward me. He looks as beautiful as ever and every bit the pirate priest, with his white open shirt showcasing the rosary around his neck.

"I was afraid I wouldn't see you like this again," I say to him.

He grins at me and takes my hands in his. "Would you still love me if I stayed as the beast?"

Even though he says this lightly, I don't take it so.

I squeeze his hands, staring deep into his familiar blue eyes.

"I would still love you in any shape or form."

The gravity of my words hangs in the air between us. His face softens for a moment and then, "But would you *love* me if I stayed the beast?"

I bite back a smile. "Are you saying would I fuck you in beast form?"

I don't need to point out that I already did once, though that wasn't really on the best terms and doesn't really count.

"That's exactly what I'm saying," he says.

I shrug, acting coy. "Perhaps. We have eternity, after all. Plenty of time to try something new."

He laughs at that, a rare but joyous sound that makes my heart skip several beats, and then he grabs my face in his hand, puts his arm around my waist, and pulls me to him, kissing me hard.

Kissing me like I'm his.

And I kiss him back like he's mine.

Because he is.

Forever now.

"There it is!" I hear Abe shout from the crow's nest.

Priest and I break apart and look over to see Maren swimming back to the *Nightwind*, Nill by her side, and the great tentacles of the Kraken reaching up out of the water. They wrap around the sides of the Dutch vessel and start to pull the ship right in two.

I lean my head against Priest's shoulder, my hunger sated, my heart happy, and we watch as the ship disappears beneath the waves, leaving only sparkling starlight behind.

THE END

A Ship of Bones and Teeth

PROLOGUE

There was no moon on the night I decided to sell my soul. The waters were as dark as octopus ink and, for the first time in a long time, I was afraid. It's as if I finally realized not only what I was about to do, but what I had already done.

A month ago I had left my family behind without a second thought. With just my shark, Nill, as my sole companion, I turned my back on my sisters, on my father, on his kingdom, and swam toward another future. I was always reckless and impulsive, wanting more than the ordinary life in the depths of Limonos, but I'd never done something so rash and dangerous before. I'd never left home.

It's not that I hadn't hinted at it. How many times I'd drifted through the towering green stalks of the kelp forest with Asherah, talking about how all I wanted was to get away, or swam through the coral gardens with Larimar, wishing that my life was more than what my father set out for me. But my sisters never listened to me—I was the youngest and easily dismissed. A princess in name only, never to be queen, never to have any power of her own.

And so one day, I left. I started swimming south along the coast, leaving the sea and the kingdom behind, heading toward waters even warmer, deeper, and darker. Nill swam with me, my loyal protector since I was born, never questioning what I was doing.

Eventually I grew tired and sent Nill to the surface to see if it was safe to take a look. When he assured me it was, I rose up and broke through the swells.

A whole new world awaited me. Instead of the dry and rocky landscape that surrounded Limonos, here everything was lush and green, with parrots flying from the trees, squawking as they went. The sky wasn't as brilliant a blue as it was at home but there was drama and danger in the big dark clouds that rolled in over the surrounding mountain peaks thick with vegetation.

And on the beach was the most beautiful man I had ever seen.

Of course, I had seen men before. Before my mother disappeared, she would often bring them down to the depths of Limonos and offer their organs to us. Asherah, the first born, would get the heart, Larimar would get the liver, and I would usually get a kidney. I had always wanted a man's heart, but my mother said it was something I had to earn. I never got a chance to ask her how I could earn it, since my mother was hauled out of the water by sailors one night, never to be seen again.

As a Syren our first instinct is to lure men to their death. We seduced them, drowned them, and ate them, their body providing us with enough power and nutrients to last us months. They are a rare but much-wanted delicacy. But I had never hunted for a man before, and even though my first instinct upon seeing this particular man should have been to seduce him in order to destroy him, all I wanted was just to seduce him. I was only sixteen at the time, barely an adult, and the sight of him did something to my insides. He made me feel things I had never dreamed about feeling before. I was hungry in a different, more compelling way.

I was such a damn fool.

In seconds I had fallen for him, swallowed up by lust, and this man became my obsession. I spent my days hidden behind the rocks in the shallows, spying on him while Nill circled the waters behind me. The human was traveling with a troupe of people who catered to his every whim. At night he slept in a tent on the beach, the white canvas like a ship's sails, a parade of women disappearing inside, their raucous moans making my body ache with need and envy. During the day he lounged on the sand entertaining guests, gorging themselves on fine food. I found myself wanting to try everything they were eating, but had to settle for clams and crabs and sea cucumbers that lived in the shallow waters around me.

I didn't understand English at the time, but I eventually realized they addressed him as "Prince Aerik."

What I did understand was that I needed him to be mine. Something I could finally call my own. All my life I had felt so fractured and lonely, my father kind but firm and distant, my sisters the light of his life after mother disappeared. But me, I was left with Nill and that was that. No one ever glanced my way or wondered how I was. I was just the third sister taking up too much space in the sea. Even the other Syrens in the kingdom ignored me. Though I was no one within my own family, I was also too different and regal for those outside of it to befriend me.

And so I thought, foolishly, that if I could get this human, this Prince Aerik, to become mine, then I wouldn't have to be alone. But he lived on land and would never survive more than a few minutes below the surface of the sea. He would never be a part of my world.

That's when I knew I would have to become part of his.

As a child, I was warned about the sea witches, beings that possessed magic that let them shapeshift at will, enabling them to live both above the water and below it. Though Syrens were the ones humans feared, us Syrens feared the sea witches. They had the ability to grant us wishes, yet none of their gifts came without a price.

But I was young and headstrong and imprudent. I wanted adventure, I wanted to see what life was like above the sea, I wanted to become something more than I was. I wanted *love*.

And so I set about calling forth a sea witch. My sisters had told me that they liked shiny things as offerings and that they would respond to my Syren call. I spent the evening darting about, finding things that caught my eye like brightly colored coral in saturated hues of red, orange, and yellow, tiny purple starfish, rare glowing azure seaweed and pearls I coaxed from the reluctant mouths of oysters.

Once I had gathered these shiny pieces of the sea, I swam down to a canyon with walls of rock and coral rising up around me, a place with fantastic acoustics. Then I began to sing.

As far as I knew there was no specific song that conjured the sea witches, it was just our voices in general that might draw them to us. All Syrens had enchanting and beautiful singing voices and mine was no exception. I just didn't like to sing since it made me the center of attention (unless either of my sisters were singing, then no one would even hear me).

But there I sang. I sang for the sea witch, I sang about wanting to make a bargain, about wanting a life on land, to win a man's heart, and after what seemed like forever, Nill started doing protective circles around me, signifying that a sea witch was coming.

The first thing to appear were the tentacles. They were giant, slithering ropes with suction ends and puckered purple skin. They didn't belong to the sea witch, but instead to one of the Kraken, the giant sea monsters that the witches controlled.

The rest of the Kraken was hidden in the murky blue depths of the ocean, though I could faintly make out small glowing yellow eyes.

Then Edonia came forward, walking toward me on two legs along the seafloor, completely nude.

She was stunning. I had heard sea witches were ugly hags, but this wasn't the case at all. She was soft and pale, with long flowing white hair that moved around her head like sea snakes. She looked human more than anything and I was immediately jealous of her.

"Sweetheart," she said to me, her voice melodic but low. "Tell me what ails you?"

I was so dumbfounded by her that I couldn't speak.

"You have made a call for assistance from a sea witch, have you not?"

I nodded and she approached. Nill started to come in between us but before I could tell him to stay back, a tentacle whipped toward him, grabbing him. Nill cried out, a sharp sound that very few creatures could hear, and the Kraken wrapped itself around his middle, squeezing him tight.

"No, stop!" I cried out. "Don't hurt him!"

Edonia smirked at me and suddenly all her beauty seemed to vanish. She may have been pretty, but she was cold and ruthless and I immediately knew I couldn't trust her. "A precautionary measure. Depending on how this goes, I'll have him set free. Otherwise..."

I understood the threat. I had called her forth for a favor and now she was the one in control.

"Tell me what you want, sweetheart," she said, sounding

bored. "So that we make this deal in haste. I don't have all night."

For a moment I had forgotten even why I had called her, what possessed me to do such a reckless thing as conjuring a sea witch. But then I remembered. The longing inside me, that need to belong to someone and someplace, it was too visceral to ignore.

"I saw a man on the shore," I said as her watchful red eyes narrowed. "His name is Prince Aerik. I want to become a human and I want him to fall in love with me. Can you help?"

She chuckled mirthlessly. "Oh, honey. Yes, I can. But nothing I do comes without a price."

I looked around at the shiny pieces of the sea I had gathered just as the Kraken's tentacle came out and swept them all away. All that effort for naught.

"You think that will do?" Edonia laughed. "So naïve you are. Tell me, how old are you?"

"Sixteen," I managed to say.

"Sixteen. So very young. And you think you know what love is at such an age?"

I didn't say anything to that.

She studied me for a moment. "But I can see that perhaps it is love that you lack at home that really ails you. A sense of discontent. Of not belonging. Yes?"

I nodded. I looked over at Nill to make sure that the Kraken wasn't hurting him but suddenly Edonia was at me, her sharp fingernails at my chin and forcing me to meet her eyes.

"I'll tell you what," she said. I found myself lost in the swirling red of her eyes, like coral in a whirlpool. "I will grant you what you wish for, so as long as I take something of yours in return."

The fact that she could grant my wish had my heart

leaping with joy and possibility, so much so that I didn't think any price would be too high to pay.

"What do you want?"

"Your voice," she said simply.

"My voice?"

"It's beautiful," she said with an air of contempt. "We all know that Syrens have the ability to lure men into the sea with their song. I would like the chance to do the same. The Kraken are wonderful pets, but they lack the finesse. They know how to kill and maim and destroy, but they don't know how to lure."

"But you're a witch. Surely you can do that to men already."

"Not all men are created equal," she said sharply. "Some men are resistant to a witch's charms. Your voice wouldn't just be a thing to hear. I will need your tongue."

"My tongue!" I cried out.

"A mermaid's tongue is a missing ingredient for my book of magic."

"Take my tail then if you're to give me legs," I protested.

"Oh, I will be taking that too. Now listen here, my sweet, because you only get one chance to decide. With my spell, I will give you legs. I will take away your gills and your claws and your fangs and your strength and make you a beautiful woman. And you will find your prince and make him your own, should you wish. But you won't be able to become a Syren again. You won't be able to live under the sea. You will be a human through and through. You won't live three hundred years, you will live maybe sixty, if you're lucky." She paused and dug her nail deeper into my skin. "Are you still interested?"

I should have said no. Why didn't I say no?

But instead, I said, "And that's not enough price to pay?"

Her eyes went cold. "You want to become a human and

experience that world? You want the love of the prince or whomever you choose? Then you must know that the human world isn't equal to the Syren's world below. No, it's worth *more*. The human world is a world where you will control your own destiny. To be the person that you, and only you, decide to become. As a human, you can do what you wish, be who you want. You'll be a woman, and a woman has all the power up above. The world will be yours for the taking. Everything you desire, you will find the means to have."

She knew all the right things to say. She was lying through her pointed teeth.

"All I ask in exchange is your tongue," she adds with a shrug, removing her fingers from my chin. "If you're lucky, it won't make much difference to you at all. Humans are adaptable."

When she put it that way, it didn't seem such a large price to pay.

"But I'll never see my father and sisters again," I lamented.

"You swam away from them, did you not? You already left for a reason. You already made your decision before this night. Besides, there's nothing to stop you from taking a boat to your old kingdom one day. Perhaps they'll pay you a visit. The world is your oyster, and you are the pearl, my sweet."

Maybe it wouldn't have to be the end. Maybe I really could take a boat until it was above Limonos and if I dove below, even if just for a minute, maybe I could see them and tell them I was okay.

"Okay," I said to her. "I will do it. But first I want you to let Nill go."

Edonia looked at the Kraken and smirked. The Kraken squeezed so hard that Nill's black eyes started to bulge and I screamed.

Then one of Nill's many teeth popped out, spiraling to the ocean floor.

"Release him," Edonia said begrudgingly to the Kraken.

The tentacle loosened and Nill swam away quickly, heading in the direction of Limonos. I had no doubt that he was going to tell my father what I did.

Edonia walked over to the fallen tooth and picked it up, then came back to me and placed it in my palm.

"There. You can have a reminder of who you used to be. Whenever you regret your life above, you can remember that the only friend you ever had was a damned shark."

"Wait. Why would I regret my life above?" I said, starting to panic.

But Edonia didn't say anything. Instead she grinned, a most malicious smile that still haunts me in my dreams, and grabbed a knife that seemed to be conjured out of nothing.

The tentacle that had been holding Nill shot out and wrapped itself around me, the end holding my mouth open.

I screamed.

Then Edonia took my tongue in her fingers, swiped the sharp blade across it until my head exploded with pain and the water filled with my blood.

The screaming stopped.

Acknowledgments

First off, I have to thank my editors and proofreaders, Laura, Alexa and Sandy. Because of their literally tireless commitment, this book was able to be completed and they all too my shenanigans in stride with delay after delay after delay. This book belongs to them! But please note, they did not edit this acknowledgement section, so any mistakes are my own (nor are they making me say this :D)

Second, I noticed a couple of months ago that authors are always talking about their team. I thought to myself, "who has a team? I've been doing this since 2011, I don't have a team." Because to me a team is a group of people who move together to help you. I always thought I was supported by many different moving parts.

However, on this book I really did feel like I had a team. From my editors, to my cover designer Hang (who I've been working with for TEN years now) who created not one but two different covers (one for arcs), to all the artists I've commissioned for this book who produced such lovely work and were so great to communicate with (I'm looking at you especially, Alicia!), my sharp-eyed beta reader Betul who helped me change course at the last minute, AND of course, the invaluable Lauren B Cox who makes everything happen and is there for me when I text her late at night with another Menty B. Whether they all know it or not, they really are my team and I am honored to have them!

So, I always start my acknowledgements by talking about how hard this book was to write (occasionally I talk about how easy it is). And yes, this book was hard. It took time to feel my groove because I know people wanted another ASOBAT, but Priest and Larimar are not Ramsay and Maren. I knew right away that this was going to be a dark, quieter and sexier book and that I had to let it be. I knew that it wasn't ASOBAT part two, and it took time to accept that (and accept that it might disappoint some people who wanted more of the same).

So there was a lot of working this out in my head and on the page, and at the same time, I was dealing with other deadlines in my life, neurodivergent burnout, depression, family issues AND getting a new puppy. Many different factors conspired to make this book a challenge to actually get down the words.

BUT...I pushed through somehow. Couldn't have done it without the team above, but also Scott and Perry Palomino (our new puppy...and if you haven't read EIT, yes that's a girl's name). Scott especially went above and beyond with taking care of this rambunctious scamp and I will always and forever be grateful to him. He has saved me so many times over and I really hope this book is successful enough so that I may buy him a big present. He deserves that and so much more.

Scott, I love you until my undying day. This book is for you!

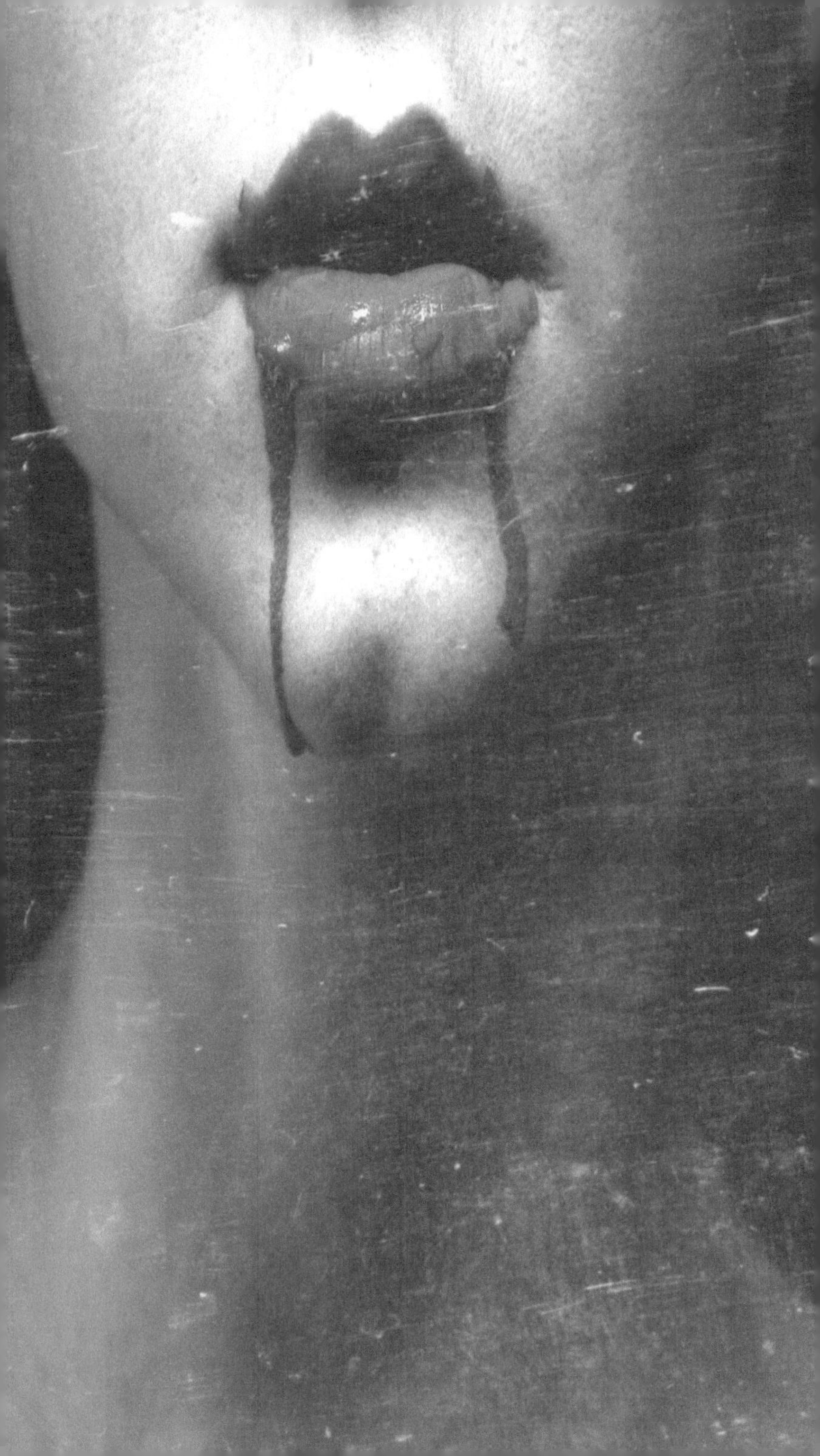

About the Author

Karina Halle is a screenwriter, a former music & travel journalist, and the New York Times, Wall Street Journal, and USA Today bestselling author of River of Shadows, The Royals Next Door, and Black Sunshine, as well as 80 other wild and romantic reads, ranging from light & sexy rom coms to horror/paranormal romance and dark fantasy. Needless to say, whatever genre you're into, she has probably written a romance for it.

When she's not traveling, she, her husband, and their newly adopted puppy—Perry—split their time between a possibly haunted, 120-year-old house in Victoria, BC, their sailboat the Norfinn, and their condo in Los Angeles. For more information, visit www.authorkarinahalle.com

Find her on Facebook, Instagram, Pinterest, BookBub, Amazon, and Tik Tok.

Also by Karina Halle

And With Madness Comes the Light (EIT #6.5)

Come Alive (EIT #7)

Ashes to Ashes (EIT #8)

Dust to Dust (EIT #9)

Ghosted (EIT #9.5)

Came Back Haunted (EIT #10)

The Devil's Metal (The Devil's Duology #1)

The Devil's Reprise (The Devil's Duology #2)

Veiled (Ada Palomino #1)

Song For the Dead (Ada Palomino #2)

CONTEMPORARY ROMANCE

Love, in English/Love, in Spanish

Where Sea Meets Sky

Racing the Sun

The Pact

The Offer

The Play

Winter Wishes

The Lie

The Debt

Smut

Heat Wave

Before I Ever Met You

After All

Rocked Up

Wild Card

Maverick

Hot Shot

Bad at Love

The Swedish Prince

The Wild Heir

A Nordic King

The Royal Rogue

Nothing Personal

My Life in Shambles

The Royal Rogue

The Forbidden Man

The One That Got Away

Lovewrecked

One Hot Italian Summer

All the Love in the World (Anthology)

The Royals Next Door

The Royals Upstairs

ROMANTIC SUSPENSE

Sins and Needles (The Artists Trilogy #1)

On Every Street (An Artists Trilogy Novella #0.5)

Shooting Scars (The Artists Trilogy #2)

Bold Tricks (The Artists Trilogy #3)

Dirty Angels (Dirty Angels #1)

Dirty Deeds (Dirty Angels #2)

Dirty Promises (Dirty Angels #3)

Black Hearts (Sins Duet #1)

Dirty Souls (Sins Duet #2)

Discretion (Dumonts #1)

Disarm (Dumonts #2)

Disavow (Dumonts #3)